HIS CONFESSION

The Black Door Trilogy, Book One

By S. Valentine

HIS CONFESSION

Limitless Publishing, LLC
Kailua, HI 96734
www.limitlesspublishing.com

Formatting: Limitless Publishing

ISBN-13: 978-1-68058-487-5
ISBN-10: 1-68058-487-1

Dedications

Mom, I want to say a massive thank you for being amazing and supportive, and always listening to me going on and on about my books. And Stefan, thank you for believing that I could achieve my dreams.

Authors Note:

Please note that safe sex is practised by all persons throughout this novel, unless otherwise stated.

Chapter One

Gabi

Present Day

Gabi stared at the door, pensive. It was an ordinary black oak door. The gold handle gleamed under the lights of the club and a red glow emanated from the bottom, alluring her to enter. Gabi wasn't sure whether she found it inviting, or frightening. The door was all that stood in her way, shielding her from the perilous and almost alien world beyond its wooden panel. Gabi knew if she entered, she would defy all boundaries she had ever set for herself. But if she turned and walked the other way, the sleepless nights would continue, curiosities of the unknown would drive her crazy, and worst of all, she would lose him.

She watched as Darion blew out smoke from his cigar, making it swirl around him, obscuring her view for a split second. He leaned back on the velvet sofa, taking in the surroundings of his lavish club, his green eyes glittering in triumph.

"Beyond that door is everything anyone could ever want to be *fully* satisfied. The club is great for voyeurs, fetishists, and exhibitionists," he informed her, blowing more smoke. "Whether they're married, in a relationship, single, of any sexual preference, they can come here, socialise, and meet adventurous, like-minded people."

He passed her the cigar. Gabi hurriedly took a long drag. As the smoke escaped her red glossed lips, she noticed a salacious longing on Darion's face. Feeling a blush warm her cheeks, she turned her head from his intense scrutiny.

"Some people like to watch, some like to be watched, some like to engage in roleplay or fantasies. If they like the look of somebody, they can have them."

Gabi remained silent. She swallowed the lump that formed in her throat. As she suspected, not only did Darion own a gentleman's club, but a swingers' club too. More importantly, he wanted her to experience it all. She had never felt so astounded in all her life. What was she doing in a club where people swapped partners like one big meat market? It sounded dirty, seedy—a place where they indulged in filthy fantasies. Why did *these* types of people get married, or continue relationships, if they weren't fully satisfied by them?

She couldn't comprehend how people could share an intimate moment, such as lovemaking, in front of an audience, how they could get intimate with strangers, people they knew *nothing* about. She stubbed the cigar in the ashtray, and drained the last of her white wine.

As Gabi took in the people around her, she noticed that they weren't the stereotypical old, bored, married couples. They didn't look seedy. There were attractive people of all ages. Beautiful men and women were laughing, dancing, and flirting. It looked like a normal club, except that it was far from it.

Darion leant forward and slowly poured himself some whisky. As he took a large swig, the ice cubes rattled in the glass. When it was empty, he settled it gently on the table and turned his attention to her. She drew in a breath when his hand stroked softly up her bare thigh. Her heart pounded rapidly, and she was unable to ignore the needy ache that persisted between her legs. She hated the fact that such a slight touch turned her on *so* much. The way that he looked at her made her feel like the most desirable woman in the world.

"We've got mirrored walls, hot tubs, swings, whips, toys. *Anything* you want, we've got. You just wait until you see the club in action." He winked, and his mouth curved into a slow, inscrutable smile. Gabi could tell that he had given this talk many times.

He continued to explain what was lurking behind the door as his fingers vanished up her skirt, causing her stomach to tighten in anticipation. Gabi watched him talking. His words were tinny and vacant-sounding as her arousal took over her concentration, making her forget for a moment where she was. As if reading her mind, he stopped talking, his expression darkening as his eyes became wild with need.

His gaze fell on her swollen lips for a moment, where it lingered, and she knew he was about to kiss her. Slowly leaning toward her until their foreheads were touching, he slipped his tongue into her mouth, caressing hers with gentle strokes. She felt flushed, plagued by excitement. His hands seized her face as he deepened the kiss, hungrily, possessively, devouring her mouth with urgency. Their lips crashed together until Gabi eventually pulled back for air.

"I can't wait to fuck you," he said, his voice a hot whisper, his expression every bit sinister.

Gabi's mind had been opened to a lifestyle she had previously been unfamiliar with. She was a different woman now. Her confidence had gone through the roof; Darion knew it too. He liked to show her off, he liked that other men eyed her lustfully, wanting what he had. But how could he be willing to give her to them so freely?

Coming to her senses, she hastily pushed down her skirt. Her mind was now spinning with confusion, fear spreading through her gut. She couldn't deny that the playrooms sounded tempting, and a tiny bit of her *was* curious. But if she participated, would it intensify the passion, or destroy their relationship?

Darion straightened, and she noticed that his wickedly possessed expression had suddenly turned serious. "There's something more I need to tell you, Gabi." He paused before adding, "I haven't been entirely truthful about myself."

Darion slowly climbed to his feet and held out

his hand. Gabi stared at it hesitantly. Whatever it was, she knew it couldn't be good. She cast a nervous glance at the playrooms one final time. She had two options. Flee the scene, and leave Darion, the man she loved, forever. Or walk through that door, and turn her back on life as she knew it.

Chapter Two

Five Months Earlier

Gabi pressed her foot down on the accelerator of her Mercedes convertible. Her heart pounded in her chest, the ache intensifying. With shaky fingers she wound down the window and inhaled a deep breath of air. It didn't relieve the knots that were tangled in her stomach, the sickening feeling when you just *knew* something wasn't right. Loosening her grip on the steering wheel, she sank into the seat.

The repetitive sound of the wipers scraping against the glass filled her ears. The rain was lashing down fast and had been for the past hour. Thick snow covered the dark streets. The only dim lighting came from the overhead street lamps, but they were far and few between. Undeterred by the unpredictable British weather, Gabi's mind was clouded with questions that needed answering.

It was time to find out why her fiancé, Lawrence, had matches to a gentleman's club in his pocket. Not only that, but they were from a club situated in

Westhaven, a town about an hour away. She felt awful for having snooped through his belongings, but she'd been looking for clues, anything to explain the recent change in his behaviour—the drunken late-night returns, the secret phone calls, their pathetic excuse for a sex life, and his distant, snappy moods, which were apparently a result of being inundated with work.

Confront him, her sensible side had said. *Yeah, right. If he was guilty of seeing someone else, perhaps even a dancer, as if he'd confess.* So her suspicious side had won. She'd jotted down the address to find out for herself.

Gabi peered through the windscreen. The high-rise buildings of the city had faded into the distance, along with the shimmering lights and hustle and bustle of the busy streets. All she saw now were shops, offices, bars, a church, and other enterprises all crammed together, evident of it being a small town.

After five more minutes of driving, the satellite navigation indicated that Gabi had reached her destination. She slowly veered down a side street, and was relieved when she found a space to park. When she switched off the engine, she remained rooted to the seat for a moment, mentally building up courage with a pep talk. *I can do this.* She breathed deeply, taking a moment to calm her frenetic heartbeat. Giving the overhead mirror a final glance, she ran a hand through her long, blonde locks and smoothed down her black, knee-length dress.

Gabi couldn't believe what she was about to do.

But she wouldn't be able to rest until she knew for certain that there was nothing deplorable about Lawrence's visit to the club. She thought he detested those sort of places.

Exiting the vehicle, she trod carefully in her nude Jimmy Choo stilettos as she made her way past several closed shops and followed the sound of music. After meandering down back streets, she took a final left turn. The music was now louder and clearer. She stood beneath flashing lights, her silhouette on the pavement before her. Gabi lifted her gaze to take in a club. It was an average, square, brick building. There were blacked-out windows upstairs except for one, which let out a red glow. Several lights flickered from the large overhead sign, which read *'The Black Door.'* Another fluorescent light depicted the outline of a nude woman dancing.

Gabi's heart skipped a beat when a man sitting near the door startled her with a cough. She caught her breath as she took in his appearance. He was in his mid-forties, with long, dark, slightly greying hair. His brow was pierced, and tattoos covered his arms. She felt her cheeks warm slightly as he slowly scanned her body. He grinned admiringly.

"Stop perving, Len."

Gabi swivelled around to see a pretty redhead, dolled up to the nines. She appeared to look about the same age as Gabi, twenty-seven. Her eyes danced with merriment and a knowledge beyond Gabi's years, a sure sign she'd experienced and seen a lot more of the world than Gabi had.

"Hello to you too, Lex," Len said drily.

8

"Darion here yet?"

"No. He should be here around ten. You need him?"

"Nah. Hey," she acknowledged Gabi. "Are you going in?"

"Er...yes," Gabi said, gathering her wits. "Yes, I am."

Gabi stepped into a fog of cigarette smoke. Rock 'n' roll music blared from gigantic speakers. The club was surprisingly bigger than it looked from the outside. Her vision had to adjust to the dimly lit room, which had gentle illumination coming from ceiling spotlights and a main chandelier. She ran her fingertips along one of the many red circular sofas that occupied the room. The expensive velvet was soft on her skin. There were matching red curtains, which offered privacy in booths to her left and right.

As she moved toward the bar, her heels clacked against the black marble floor. For a second, she was transfixed by the stage before her, where half-naked women were seductively gyrating. One dancer was hanging upside down on a pole, her thighs clamped around it. Several men were watching intently, and others were playing cards, talking, and drinking. Even though it was fairly busy, Gabi noticed only a handful of women.

"What can I get ya?" Lexi asked, peeling off her jacket to reveal a tight red corset, her voluptuous breasts spilling over the top. Her frilly matching underwear and thigh-high boots completed her racy look.

Gabi gracefully slid onto a stool at the bar. "I'll have a white wine, please."

Lexi studied the overhead shelf before her, and called out to a scantily dressed brunette, "Hey, Marnie! We outta wine?"

"Should be some out back."

"One minute," she told Gabi, flashing a friendly smile.

Seconds later, she returned with a box, dumping it at her feet. Tearing it open, she took out a bottle. Just the sight of it made Gabi lick her dry lips, eager to pour the alcohol down her throat and rid herself of the lump that had lodged itself there. Hopefully, it would also calm her racing heart. When Lexi poured a glass, Gabi took it hurriedly and downed it in one go, barely getting a whiff of the vinegary scent.

"Tough day at the office?" Lexi asked.

"Thanks. And yeah. I mean, no."

"Trouble in paradise?" She began loading the shelf with the bottles.

Gabi nodded.

"Men, huh? Can't live with 'em, can't live without 'em. I'm Lexi."

"Gabi," she responded, her hands falling into her lap. An uncomfortable silence loomed in the air. Gabi cleared her throat and went in for the kill before she lost her nerve. "Can I ask you something, Lexi?"

"Sure." She shoved the now empty box under a counter.

"I can't believe I have to do this, and it's completely humiliating, but I need to know."

"What is it?" Lexi folded her arms across her chest, a concerned expression etched on her face.

Gabi rummaged through her Louis Vuitton handbag and retrieved her iPhone. "I know you probably don't remember every single customer that walks in here, but do you recognise this man at all?" She held up her mobile, which had an image of Lawrence on its screen. "He's my fiancé," she added quickly. "I think he's cheating on me."

Lexi peered closer to the screen.

Gabi waited with bated breath for her to answer. She studied Lexi intently for any telltale signs: a flicker of recognition, a flash of guilt, a nervous twitch—but there was nothing.

"Never seen him in my life. Marnie?"

"Yeah?"

"You ever seen this man in here before?"

Marnie's curious gaze flitted over Gabi. "Are you with the police or something?"

"No. I'm trying to find out whether my fiancé is cheating on me."

"Oh." Marnie stared at the screen long and hard. She shook her head. "We get so many men in and out, it would be almost impossible to recall," she responded before dashing off to serve customers who were now lining the bar.

"What made you think to come here?" Lexi asked.

"I found the matches from this club in his pocket."

"These?" She picked up a black strip of matches, the club's name printed in gold, swirly writing.

Gabi nodded.

"Honey, he could have picked them up from anywhere. Sometimes we hand them out for advertising. I wouldn't worry about it."

"Maybe," Gabi said, although she wasn't sure she was convinced of Lawrence's innocence. She put her mobile away and rubbed her aching temples. She was exhausted. "Can I get a lemonade, please?"

"Sure. No more wine?"

"I wish, but I'm driving."

"Shame. You look like you could use a strong drink."

Lexi handed her a glass with ice and a small bottled lemonade. "Anyway, I've gotta go dance. I hope you sort everything out with your fiancé."

"Thanks."

Gabi took a sip of her drink and scanned the club again. She'd expected the gentleman's club to be trashy and unpleasant, but it was actually tastefully decorated, luxurious even, with a relaxed vibe, and the dancers were stunning. The crowd grew as several people poured through the entrance, finding tables as close to the stage as possible.

"Marnie."

Gabi turned her attention toward the sound of a male voice.

"I need you on the pole. Gina can take over here."

"Sure, boss," Marnie responded cheerfully, running a hand through her silky locks. She leant over the bar, her lips meeting his.

Gabi saw a grin creep over the man's face whilst they were kissing. He slowly pulled away, giving Marnie a wink before she made her way toward the stage. Gabi's gaze followed Marnie as she slowly swayed past tables, her body looking sensational in the small tight skirt and crop top that she was wearing. The crowd clapped as she climbed up the steps, her huge platforms not appearing to affect her confident, sexy stride. The spotlight followed her every move. When she spun around, her hair flew out behind her beautifully.

After a few twists on the pole, Marnie faced the audience, seductively running her hands down her body. She gyrated her hips, removing her top at a leisurely pace. Wolf whistles filled the air. Her bra was next to come off, revealing perfectly rounded false breasts.

Gabi turned to look at the man who Marnie had kissed. He was focused on the dancer, smiling proudly. He must have sensed Gabi watching him, as his gaze met hers. Coyly, Gabi quickly turned her attention back to the stage.

Marnie was now bending over, teasing the audience. Several notes were thrown at her feet. Gabi swallowed and moistened her dry lips with her tongue. The girl looked unbelievably sexy, the way her body moved, her perfect rhythm matching the beat of the music. She seduced the crowd with her wide, come-to-bed eyes.

"You okay?" Another girl strolled over to take her order, presumably Gina. She had long, blonde waves that cascaded down her back, her slightly curvaceous body concealed in a silver dress that left little to the imagination.

"I'm good." Gabi straightened.

"Can't tempt you into a private dance, can I?" Her brows arched.

Gabi shook her head. "Maybe some other time,"

she replied, not wanting to offend her.

Gina made her way back over to the boss. They appeared to be flirting, until he told her it was her turn on the stage. She stuck her tongue out at him, her silver piercing flashing under the club lights. As she wrapped her arms around his neck, she said, "I'm not meant to be on until midnight. Desperate to see me naked?" Gabi couldn't help but overhear their conversation.

She stole a glance at the man again. He examined Gina's body as he let out a dirty-sounding laugh. She leant in and kissed him passionately. *What's with that man?* Gabi tilted her head, trying to get a better view. The corner of the bar, where he was, didn't have the best lighting. As Gina proceeded to walk away, he smacked her lightly on the bum.

"Len, remember, when she gets here, treat her like the queen. She's one of our top clients." The boss was now talking to the doorman who had appeared. "Champagne, the full fucking works. Then leave her to it. She likes privacy."

"Sure thing."

The boss then rose to his feet, stepping into the light and providing Gabi with a much clearer view. Her lips parted as she did a double take. He was *gorgeous*. He stood tall, dominating the area, exuding an air of confidence. His brown hair, worn back behind his ears, hung down the nape of his neck, the sort of hairstyle that could be worn loose, free of product, effortlessly sexy, or smoothed back for the sophisticated look, which was how it was styled now. His chiselled jaw was covered with light stubble beneath full, enticing lips, and above them were green eyes that glittered playfully under the ultra-violet lights. He wore black jeans and a matching shirt, the sleeves rolled up casually. He looked like he'd walked straight off an Emporio Armani advert.

Lennie must have said something amusing as he grinned cheekily, showing off straight white teeth. Could he be any more perfect? "I knew I could count on you, Len." He patted the man on the shoulder before he strolled off.

The boss took out a silver box from his pocket, retrieved a cigar, and popped it in his mouth, lighting it. He took a long drag, slowly blowing out the smoke. He stood there for a moment, before sitting down on the stool next to Gabi. "Pour me a whisky, darlin'," he told Marnie, who had returned.

She followed his command and passed him a glass half full of liquor. He drank it in one go, set the glass on the bar, and ordered the same again. With another drag on his cigar, he sent smoke through the air in Gabi's direction.

She moved her head slightly and looked at him. God, he really *was* sexy. She raked her fingers through her hair, ensuring it was tidy.

"You from around here?" he asked, his brow slightly furrowed, as if he were trying to figure out whether he had seen her before.

Gabi shook her head.

His gaze fell on her lips for a second, his pupils dilating dangerously, like those of a predator focused on its prey. He dragged his lingering stare back to hers.

"Well, if you want another drink, you tell the girls it's free of charge." He swigged back the whisky he was passed, and stood up. "I'm Darion Milano."

Darion. Such an unusual name, but a nice one.

"Gabriella Woods," she said, introducing herself.

"You not interested in a job here, Gabi?" Even though they had only just met, the shortening of her name rolling off his tongue seemed to fit, creating a somewhat intimate bond between them.

"Doing what?" she asked too quickly.

"Stripping." He raised an eyebrow, and stubbed out his cigar.

The way he stood towering over her powerfully and slightly intimidatingly made her intake a small breath of air. His broad shoulders were set, and his firm chest was mere centimetres away, within her reach. She could just imagine the feel of her palm flat against his chest, in contact with his soft skin, which she suspected he had beneath his shirt, and hard muscles that would no doubt meet a perfect V shape of his pelvis. His naked form invaded her mind, making her core tighten with longing.

What the fuck? She crossed her legs, clamping her thighs shut as excited tingles shot through her body from the vivid mental image that both shocked and thrilled her. She'd never fantasised about another man before.

As he remained looking down at her, darkness clouded his eyes, his intense scrutiny undressing her, just like she had done with him. Feeling embarrassed and exposed, she folded her arms across her chest defensively, although she was flattered by his flirting. Her heart was racing wildly; desire pumped through her body like a drug. As much as she wanted to look away, she was unable to tear her gaze away from him. She had never felt so drawn to a man in her life. As a blush darkened her cheeks, Gabi eventually averted her gaze, immediately coming to her senses. She was engaged. To Lawrence.

"I don't think so," she managed to croak out, having almost forgotten that she hadn't responded to his offer.

"You can earn a hell of a lot of money doing it." When Gabi failed to respond, he continued, "Well, it was a pleasure meeting you, darlin'." He gave her a ghost of a wink and vanished into the crowd.

Gabi found herself wondering where he was going. There was nothing wrong with wanting a bit of company.

Was there?

Chapter Three

Fifteen minutes had passed; Gabi assumed Darion wouldn't be returning. *Why do you even care?* she scolded herself. The sole reason she was at the club, in search of answers when it came to Lawrence, had seemed to vanish from her mind. Her gaze flitted around the room, searching for Darion, and then she saw him. He was deep in conversation with a couple. He shook hands with the man, and landed a kiss on the woman's cheek before leading them outside.

Darion reappeared a few minutes later, to which he ordered another whisky at the bar. His hand accidentally brushed past Gabi's bare thigh as he pulled out a stool. She tensed, feeling goosebumps race over her body. She hadn't felt another man's hand on her in seven years. Darion's mouth curled upwards, his pupils raw, almost glowing, and she wondered whether it *had* been an accident. Feeling her face flame, she focused on her drink.

"So…what brings you to a place like this?" he asked, sitting down.

"I, um, just popped in for a drink on my way through Westhaven," she lied.

He lit a cigarette and offered her one.

She shook her head. "No, thanks. I don't smoke."

"Good for you. I kept planning on giving up, but I thought fuck it, we should stick to what gives us pleasure in life. We only get one chance, ya know, why limit ourselves?"

Gabi held in a laugh, finding his way of thinking somewhat amusing.

"I'm tired." He stretched his arms above his head, causing his shirt to ride up, revealing the washboard stomach she'd guessed he had. "I've been partying for five days straight." Catching her surprised expression, his brow rose. "I take it you don't party much."

The chance would be a fine thing. "Yeah, but not for days on end."

She had been so occupied with studying in her teenage years that she missed out on most of the wild parties. She hadn't gone out dancing, drinking, and experimenting like most girls had when they were her age. She had been so dedicated to passing her exams.

"You're missing out big time," he informed her.

"Well, I was more occupied with things that were higher priority than partying."

"I bet I could teach you a thing or two." He nodded vehemently, grinning cheekily. "But I won't." His expression turned serious, reassuring her.

He won't? Why not? Was he married? She

hadn't seen a ring. She toyed with the rim of her glass. She had never met anyone like him before. He seemed so cool and laid back. He was the complete opposite of Lawrence. She couldn't help but find him intriguing.

"But that don't mean we can't have a little fun." He raised his brows suggestively. "You fancy a shot of the strongest drink we have? Absinthe. Eighty percent."

Eighty percent! The highest she had ever drunk was fourteen percent, her usual red or white wine.

"I really should be getting back. Besides, I can't drink. I'm driving." Her fingers tightened around her handbag as she stood up to leave.

"Why don't you take a taxi home, and collect your car tomorrow?"

"I'm not sure." Gabi mulled over the idea in her head. It sounded tempting. What was the point in rushing back to an empty house, to climb into bed alone, and be unable to sleep, worrying about Lawrence and what time he'd come home, if at all?

"Have a little fun. You look like you need it." His lips curved upwards.

Why does everyone keep saying that? Did she have *miserable* tattooed on her head or something? As if he wasn't going to take no for an answer, Darion walked behind the bar and placed two shot glasses before her. He filled them with black liquid. Gabi bit her lip worriedly as he handed one to her. It smelt ridiculously strong. When was the last time she had actually let her hair down? She couldn't remember. Perhaps one shot wouldn't hurt.

She clinked her glass with his, and tossed it back

quickly. She grimaced. It instantly ripped through her throat, tearing at her chest, burning inside like flames. Her stomach churned, and she felt as if she would vomit. She coughed then took a slow breath, holding it in.

"Good?"

"It's harsh."

"You want another?"

"No way," she shrieked.

She didn't know how he did it, but he managed to persuade her into having another shot. The second was worse than the first, although she didn't get how that could be possible. Before she knew it, they were seated on a sofa in the corner of the club, the table laden with a variety of drinks.

An hour passed, and Gabi found herself laughing harder than she had in a long time. It made a change, having someone actually listen to what she had to say. Not only that, but Darion seemed interested. She didn't know whether it was him, or the alcohol, but she felt completely at ease, like she'd known him for years.

He began telling her about all sorts of life experiences, some funny, some embarrassing, and some terrifying. He really had led a colourful life. She had disclosed that she had an older brother, and learnt that he had a sister, five years younger than his thirty-one years. Whilst she had been brought up in London's posh Mayfair before relocating out of the city and meeting Lawrence in her college days, Darion had lived in the rougher parts. Westhaven had been his home since the age of eighteen.

"So, did anything else make you want to own a

gentleman's club, besides the obvious?" she asked, topping up her glass of wine, knowing that she probably shouldn't be drinking more.

"Not really."

She prevented herself from chastising him. Typical man.

"It was my dad's fault." He leant back casually on the sofa, his arm draped across the top. "He liked a drink, or twenty. So when my mom was at work, he took me to all these bars and strip clubs. He knew the bosses, so they let me in, but I had to sit in a corner quietly with a soft drink." His drunken, slightly unfocused eyes lit up at the memory. "I was in complete awe. It was like every kid's fantasy come true. The women were something else." He beamed. "Since then, I always wanted my own club." He swigged back a shot of Sambuca. "And to make something of myself, I suppose."

For some reason, she wanted to ask about his relationship with Marnie and Gina, but stopped herself. She didn't even know why she was curious.

Speak of the devil.

"Darion," Gina interrupted them. "Call for you." She nodded to the back of the bar.

"Is it important, or can it wait?"

She put a hand on her hip. "I wouldn't have called you otherwise."

Darion reluctantly and shakily climbed to his feet. He stood over Gabi, stumbling, and then, unable to balance himself, he fell onto her. Gabi was pinned against the sofa, unable to move under his weight. Her heartbeat instantly quickened. He lifted his head, his face only inches away from hers.

She could smell the cigars and alcohol on his warm breath. She felt a hard bulge against her pelvis. Heat swept over her body, and a tingling sensation persisted between her legs, as she became aroused.

Darion's mouth curled wickedly, as if he knew the immense effect he was having on her. He studied her mouth. Gabi hated herself for feeling a desperate desire to kiss him. Darion moved his body slightly, his erection sending an excited shiver down her spine.

Ignoring her throbbing groin and the overwhelming urgency to pull him into her and kiss him fiercely, she inhaled a deep breath and attempted to sit up. He stroked a blonde strand away from her face. "I'll be right back," he said softly, and scrambled to his feet.

Gabi sat up and readjusted her dress, feeling awkward. She decided she'd had enough for the night; guilt consumed her. She grabbed her bag and pulled her coat on. Before she left the club, she self-consciously double checked that no one had noticed her and Darion's little collision. The club was a blur of lively people too fixated on their erotic surroundings to care about anything or anyone else.

Once outside, the cold, fresh air instantly hit her face, feeling sharp in her lungs. Taking out her mobile, she opened the Internet browser and searched for a local taxi number. As she clicked the call button and held the mobile against her ear, she was unable to refrain from shivering. She could see her breath forming in the air.

Failing to get an answer, she tried another number, willing someone to pick up. No answer.

Ending the call, she scanned the streets, wondering whether she should go search for a taxi, but she didn't know which direction to head, or whether she'd slip on her beautiful, but impractical heels. Or whether she'd make it at all, given the state she was in.

"Hey, Gabi, where you going?" Lexi appeared, slinging her bag over her shoulder, indicating she'd finished her shift.

"Home." Gabi stifled a yawn. "Do you know where I can get a taxi? I'm not getting an answer on the phone."

"Yeah, but it's 6 a.m." She jerked her chin upwards. "The taxis are usually outside Sky Bar now, which is just closing. They'll be going back and forth for a while."

Gabi shoved her mobile into her bag.

"You're welcome to crash at mine."

Gabi didn't know how much longer she could take the bitter air seeping through her coat, and she needed sleep. Pronto.

"Don't worry. I won't kill you in the middle of the night." She giggled.

"Are you sure you don't mind?"

"Not if you promise to make me a coffee in the morning." She winked.

It took them all of five minutes' walking until they were at Lexi's small one bedroom apartment. She pulled out the sofa bed, handed Gabi some pyjamas, and disappeared into her room.

Relief mingled with blissful pleasure swept over Gabi when she finally got out of her dress, and into the warm pyjamas. As she lay under the covers,

Darion's sparkling eyes, dangerous smile, the smell of his strong cologne, and the firmness of his body came rushing back to her.

Darion was like a magnet, drawing her to him. She knew that she had to see him again. Maybe it wasn't Lawrence that couldn't be trusted after all. Maybe it was her.

***

Darion

Darion put the phone down in satisfaction. Another member to add to the club's ever-growing list, and a rich, well-known client at that. He walked unsteadily over to the mirror, running a hand through his hair. His eyes were bloodshot. He was completely drunk. He pulled the tin of cigars out of his pocket, popped one into his mouth, lit it, and headed back toward Gabi.

As soon as he had seen her, he had to do a double take; she was naturally stunning. He liked the way she laughed a little nervously, that her wide smile was genuine, and her twinkling eyes were friendly. It was rare that women like her came into the club.

He found Gina in the corridor. He noticed her perfect, bouncing breasts before he looked up at her face. She was smoking a cigarette where it was quieter, like she always did. He watched her plump lips suck on the cigarette and slowly blow the smoke out. He felt himself grow hard. He didn't know whether Gina was seducing him on purpose, since she'd noticed him, but then again she oozed sex. Everything about her spelt sex. That's why he had hired her, no audition needed. Looks really could get you so far.

"Hey, baby." She gave him a lopsided grin. "Everything okay?"

He nodded. "Everything's great, babe."

"Going back to your little honey?" she said, sneering.

"You jealous?" he asked outright. Gina always had to be the centre of attention.

"Should I be?" She straightened, obviously testing the water. Gina hated competition. He knew she wanted more from him. Then again, he also knew that she was bisexual and confused. Maybe she just wanted to be loved. But he couldn't offer her love. No way. He offered love to no one.

"Gina," he soothed, cupping her face with his hands, careful not to burn her with the cigar. "You know it's never gonna happen with us, right?" He'd told her many times.

"I know." She shrugged. "If you need some company later…" She paused for a moment before continuing. "You know where I am."

His lips met hers. She was reluctant to respond at first. He gripped her ass, pulling her closer to him, and within seconds she was all over him. He enjoyed sleeping with Gina; besides his ex-wife, Eva, she was one of the naughtiest women he had slept with. She was exciting, fun, experimental, and would do pretty much anything he suggested. He loved that about her.

He pulled away, eager to get back to Gabi. "I'm

gonna get a drink."

He stepped back into the noisy bar and ordered another whisky. He knew he'd had too many, but he couldn't stop himself. He downed it quickly, and walked to the corner where they had been sitting, where he had fallen on top of Gabi and instantly gotten aroused. He knew that she felt it too. Her mouth had dropped like she hadn't known where to put herself. She was in for a big surprise.

He stopped dead in his tracks when he noticed that the seats were empty. Surely she hadn't bailed on him? He rarely experienced women leaving him. He raised his eyebrows in surprise, then shrugged. He had really wanted to get her back to his office. He sighed. There was no way he would be able to sleep that night without some action. He had worked himself up, got all hot and bothered.

He sauntered back to the corridor where Gina was stubbing her cigarette into the metal bin. He nodded his head toward his office, indicating for her to follow. He was sure he saw a small smile teasing her lips. He heard the clacking sound of her heels as she followed him. At least he could always count on her.

Darion allowed her to enter the room first, examining her from head to toe in delight. He slammed the door behind him. She licked her lips, a smug expression forming on her face. He yanked his shirt over his head and made his way toward her. After a few moments of passionate kissing and tearing at one another's clothes, they were both naked, and everything on his desk was scattered to the floor. They spent hours exploring one another's bodies, as if they were new to each other. They liked to take it slow, sensual at first. And then they would ravage one another brutally—rough, hard, sweaty sex.

But for the first time in his life, Darion closed his eyes and thought of someone else.

Gabriella Woods.

After he and Gina reached a satisfying climax, an exhausted Darion lay on the leather couch, panting. Gina joined him, pulling a cover over their naked bodies. He allowed her to rest her head on his chest, her arms draped around him. After an hour of staring at the ceiling, listening to Gina's gentle snores, he closed his now heavy lids.

There were a few things about Darion Milano not everyone knew.

One was that he hated sleeping alone.

Chapter Four

Gabi

"Gabi, I was literally in the middle of important paperwork, and you've interrupted me," Lawrence snapped. "If I didn't answer the first two times, surely you'd assume I was busy and not call a third time?"

"I'm sorry," Gabi mumbled, sinking further into the couch. "I just wanted to see how work was going."

"Busy, as usual." He sighed heavily. "What did you get up to last night?"

"Not much, watched a bit of TV, and had an early night." She felt bad for not being truthful, but she didn't want him to know that she'd been in a strip club, snooping around, doubting his fidelity.

"Well, I've got to go. I've got a lot going on, Gabi," he said drily, as if what she was saying disinterested him. "I'll be working all weekend, so I'll see you Sunday night."

"Okay, bye."

Pompous prick. Annoyed, she shoved her mobile into her bag. Before she started to dwell on the way that Lawrence sometimes spoke to her, she surveyed the room instead. The whole living room could have fit into the bathroom of her five-bedroom house. And unlike hers, it wasn't adorned with expensive furnishings, which were colour coordinated with everything in its perfect place. She noticed a rack spewing out DVDs, shoes strewn across the floor, several photographs in mismatched frames. Regardless of the untidiness, it felt like a proper home. Not like hers, a show home. It was comfortable. As she was about to stand up and look at the photographs, Lexi appeared, startling her.

"Hey," she greeted Gabi warmly, pulling her hair into a messy topknot.

"Morning." Gabi turned to face her.

"I wasn't eavesdropping or anything, but these walls are paper-thin, so I caught the gist of your conversation. Your fiancé sounds like a tosser." She lit a cigarette. "No offence." She flopped onto an armchair.

"He can be," Gabi agreed with a giggle.

"What's his problem?"

"He was working, and I interrupted him." Gabi pulled her knees up to her chest, hugging them.

"So what?"

"He's just a little uptight about work at the moment. Deadlines. Possible redundancies. He works away most weekends. I should be more understanding really, but I just get all these crazy ideas that he's cheating." She studied the floor. "I get so lonely sometimes." She felt the burn of oncoming tears. "Anyway." She rose to her feet, her cheeks pink with embarrassment. "I suppose I better head back. Thanks for letting me stay. I appreciate it."

Lexi stood up, pushing her fringe out of her face. "Wait a minute, is he working away all weekend?"

Gabi nodded.

"Then why are you rushing back? Stay here a little longer."

"I wouldn't want to impose, I…"

"Impose?" Lexi cut her off. "You're not imposing. Come on." She headed into the kitchen. "Besides, you promised you'd make me a coffee, remember?"

Gabi got the impression that maybe Lexi was just as lonely as she was, and enjoyed the company. In the kitchen, they took a seat at the breakfast bar, drinking coffee and talking like old friends. Gabi was *really* taking to Lexi. Other than Mallory and Suzie, she didn't have many friends. Ever since she had gotten with Lawrence, her social life had plummeted.

"So, you're a barmaid as well as a dancer?"

"Yeah." She grinned. "We dancers like a bit of variety."

Gabi sipped her drink. "How did you get into dancing?"

"I had uni debts a few years back, and my friend was making a lot of money, so I thought I'd give it a go. I've been doing it ever since. Amazing money."

"It must have its disadvantages."

"Well yeah, you have to deal with drunks, losers,

31

stalkers." She drained the last of her drink. "But security is pretty tight at The Black Door." She shrugged. "It's a job, you know. Besides, it's boosted my confidence so much."

"That's great."

"I get such an adrenaline rush, it's like I'm a star up there or something." She laughed. "When you're dancing, you're so focused on not fucking it up that the nerves you get from being watched kinda vanish. Performing feels *really* good."

"You, Gina, and Marnie look amazing."

"Well, Gina's usually off her face," she bitched. "Whatever she can get her hands on, she'll take. She's so insecure when she's sober. She's like a different person."

"That's a shame."

"She's had bad experiences though, been stripping about ten years, seen it all. One guy followed her for weeks, scared the shit out of her. She's been attacked, treated like some whore by so many men. Just because you dance nude, they think they're entitled to touch you." She shook her head in disgust. "But Gina feels much safer, now that she works for Darion."

Gabi stiffened at the mention of his name.

"So, do you have anything planned for later?"

"Not that I can think of."

"You fancy coming back to the club, make a night of it? It'll be fun." Lexi walked to the sink, and rinsed her cup under the tap.

"It's not a good idea…"

"You were upset a moment ago, and you said that you get lonely. Perhaps you should start thinking of yourself for once."

Gabi was silent.

"C'mon. It'll cheer you up."

"Did anyone ever tell you you're a bad influence?" There was a hint of amusement in her voice.

"All the time." Lexi beamed.

Gabi bit her lip. Finally, she sighed, giving in. "Okay. But I'm not drinking. I've got to drive home tomorrow."

"Whatever you say, Gabi."

She felt butterflies in her stomach at just the thought of being back at The Black Door. What would Lawrence think? The rebellious side of her was excited, and didn't care.

***

When midnight came, Gabi was sitting at the bar of the club, a glass of sparkling water in hand. She felt refreshed after taking a long shower at Lexi's, and she'd found herself applying more make-up than she usually would have. The smoky grey shadow accentuated her brown eyes, and the pearly gloss made her lips shimmer. Her hair hung perfectly straight down her back, like it almost always did.

She gave a dancing Lexi a quick wave, and turned her attention to the bar. Gina was wiping the surfaces and arranging glasses on the shelves. Gabi got the impression something was up; Gina seemed quieter than yesterday, barely making eye contact when serving customers. Gabi guessed she was sober because she was acting so different.

"Are you okay?" she asked.

Gina nodded. She pulled a bottle from the shelf, popped the lid off, and then drank the contents until it was empty. "You try getting up there sober as a judge."

"Oh, I wasn't judging you."

When she felt someone else's presence, Gabi looked up. It was Darion. Although she had half suspected he'd make an appearance, she hadn't thought it'd be so soon. Oblivious to anyone around him, he poured a drink and sat at the corner of the bar. Gabi's heart began racing frantically. She took a deep breath, trying to stop the nerves that had overcome her.

"Hey, boss." Gina headed toward him.

He greeted her by pulling her in for a kiss. Gina grabbed a handful of his hair as he hooked his arms tightly around her waist. They kissed passionately, like nobody else was in the room, before they pulled apart, giggling.

Gabi, feeling uncomfortable, found an empty table and sat down to watch Lexi dance. She took in her friend's flawless body, the way that she held her shoulders back, head high, a dazzling smile on her face. Gabi was unsure she'd ever have that much confidence again. It wasn't that she was unattractive, far from it, but not hearing any compliments or praise for a long time had made her a shell of her former self. On the outside, she portrayed someone who was content with herself, with her designer clothes, perfect make-up, well-kept hair and nails, but realistically it was all just a mask she was hiding behind.

Gabi wasn't surprised when Lexi was motioned to a booth to give a private dance. Who wouldn't want to see everything she had to offer up close and personal? She felt a little alone and out of place when Lexi joined the bald man and drew the curtain after them. Marnie then proceeded to take the stage, garnering looks of admiration with every sofa she passed.

Gabi lifted her drink to her lips and took several gulps. Shifting in her chair until she was comfortable, she decided she'd appreciate the music and make the most of her night. Who knew when she'd get to go out again? Feeling an unexplainable envy twist her heart for a man she barely knew, Gabi found herself glancing over her shoulder at Darion. He laughed hysterically as he joked and flirted with the bar staff.

"Is this seat taken?" a man slurred, breaking her focus.

She shook her head, thinking he wanted to take the chair. She was taken aback when he sat down.

"You look bored." He hiccupped, staring at her cleavage.

"I'm okay."

"You sure? I could entertain you."

"No, thanks." She interlaced her fingers, silently wishing he'd go away.

"You think you're better than me, you snotty little bitch?"

Gabi opened her mouth to speak, but it was no use trying to reason with a drunk. Unexpectedly, he yanked the top of her dress down, exposing her bra.

"If I want someone like you, I can have them." His voice took on a vicious tone, specks of spit landing on her face.

"Get off me," she shrieked. Gabi attempted to push him off, but since he was stronger than her, he pulled her legs apart, running his hands up her dress. Terrified, Gabi slapped him. She instantly regretted it when she saw the anger flash in his eyes. He clenched his fist, and his knuckles met her cheek. Her vision went blurry for a split second. She blinked several times. She had never been hit with such force before. Well, except one time with Lawrence, but she tried to block that out.

Before she knew it, Darion had raced over. He forcefully yanked the man from his chair by the collar of his jacket. The offender's knees buckled, which sent him crashing to the floor with a thud. Darion's hand was curled into a tight ball, his jaw twitching with rage.

Before he could land a blow to the man's stomach, Gabi found herself pulling him away from the scene. She didn't know if she was worried or if she was trying to protect him. Lennie caught sight of the commotion, and rushed over.

"I'll get him out, boss."

"Fuck you," the man drawled, rising to his feet. He grabbed his drink and tossed the remainder over Darion and Lennie.

"What the fuck?" Darion growled, rage and disbelief showing on his face. He looked like he wanted to kill the offender there and then.

Lennie quickly dragged the man away as he screamed and swore, his glass smashing to the floor.

"Don't you ever fucking come back to this club, you hear me?" Darion's yell was cold, his glare murderous. When it was safe to do so, Gabi released the tight grip she had on his arm.

He stood for a second, his chest rising and falling with deep, heavy breaths. His white t-shirt was covered in spots of alcohol. He scanned the crowd, noticing the customers staring. "What?" he shouted. "It's nothing you ain't seen before." They looked away, continuing what they were doing. Darion turned his attention to Gabi. "Come to my office. You're bleeding."

"I'm fine."

Darion interlaced his fingers with hers, and she had to practically sprint to keep up with his quick strides. Her palm grew clammy in his, the closeness making her stomach flip. She hated the fact that she was shy around him when she wasn't intoxicated.

When she entered his plush office, she took in as much of it as she could before Darion ordered her to sit on the counter. It was modern, everything either black or red in colour. A black leather sofa occupied one side, and a large oak desk and leather chair stood before a window, which overlooked the street. A circular mini-bar and fridge took up another corner, the shelves stocked with a selection of fine and expensive spirits. One wall was decorated with silver framed photographs, which Gabi was unable to make out from a distance. Overall, just like the club, the room screamed elegant and expensive. Darion had obviously done very well for himself.

He stood before her and jerked her face sideways, tending to her cheek with an antiseptic wipe. The attacker's signet ring had caught her skin, causing a small cut.

"Thanks for helping me out."

"No problem." He threw the wipe in the bin and gently stroked her face. "If he'd have tried that somewhere deserted, and you were alone with him, I don't think he would have stopped," he said. "I've seen his type many times."

Gabi remained silent, admiring Darion's features. With both hands, he brushed her hair back from her face.

"You be careful, darlin'."

She nodded, pleased that he had come to her rescue. She wasn't used to feeling protected. Darion seemed like a real man's man, not afraid to get his hands dirty. Lawrence was the type to avoid fights, get the police involved, and hide in the crowd.

"Here, drink this." He passed her a bottled water from the fridge.

Gabi drained half of it, not realising how thirsty she actually was. As she screwed the lid back on, she was unable to refrain from watching as Darion pulled his damp t-shirt over his head, revealing his strong shoulders, firm body, and muscular back. Gabi's stomach somersaulted, desire surging through her bloodstream. He was every bit as hot as she'd envisioned he'd be. She was insanely attracted to him. There was something about Darion. Something dangerous. Mysterious. Intriguing.

He approached the sink at a leisurely pace, washed his hands, and splashed water on his face. When he returned to stand in front of Gabi, she watched the water droplets trickle down his face. He took a towel and slowly dabbed at the wetness. He remained standing over her, silent, his gaze lingering on hers. Darion's face was expressionless, making it difficult for her to tell what he was thinking. He glanced down at her engagement ring, and his brow lifted a little, as if noticing it for the first time. A flicker of disappointment passed over his face. He looked so strong, tough on the outside, but Gabi sensed there was much more to Darion. "Right, all finished."

He didn't move as she stood up to leave, her body slightly brushing past his. As they made contact, they looked at each other, locked in the moment, slaves to the attraction that existed between them. His expression was dark and needy, and he took a deep breath as if trying to pull himself together.

Gabi grabbed her bag. "Bye," she mumbled, scurrying out of the office awkwardly.

Out in the corridor, she leant against the wall, catching her breath. She hung her head in defeat. She hated what her hormones were doing to her. *Get a grip, Gabi.* Regaining her composure, she stole one last glance at the door to Darion's office before heading to find Lexi.

***

Darion

Deciding to focus on paperwork, Darion collapsed on his leather chair. Perhaps that would get rid of the throbbing bulge in his trousers. He adjusted himself quickly, then propped his feet on the table, grabbing a folder. He didn't trust himself around Gabi. He had seen the ring on her finger. He didn't want to make the first move, nor did he want to ruin a relationship.

If she wanted him, she knew where he was.

Chapter Five

Gabi

It was 7 a.m. when Gabi and Lexi stumbled out of the club. Last night, they had sat drinking and talking for hours, and before they knew it, the club was closing. Not quite finished with the concoction of drinks on their table, they'd stayed put. Gabi hadn't seen Darion for the rest of the night.

She felt irresponsible for getting too drunk to drive home, and for going back on her word, but she'd been having so much fun that she hadn't wanted the night to end.

She tightened the cord on her coat and wrapped her arms around herself. The snow hadn't cleared, and the air was still bitterly cold. She wanted nothing more than the comfort of her own bed, shower, and luxuries.

"Hey, Lex."

"Hey, boss."

Gabi snapped to full attention. Darion was standing outside the club, leant against the wall, a

41

cigarette hanging nonchalantly from his lips. In the light of day, the stubble shadowing his jaw was more noticeable. His eyes were also greener than she'd thought, especially when the sunlight glinted in them. He slowly walked over, blowing smoke as he did so. An excited shiver ran up her spine.

"Gabi." He nodded her way.

"Hey."

"Didn't you go home last night?" Lexi took the half-smoked cigarette from his outstretched hand and took a puff.

"No. I caught up on paperwork, fell asleep in the office."

"You missed a good night."

"I'm sure there will be plenty more." He shoved his hands in his jean pockets.

"So, Gabi." Lexi faced her, tossing the cigarette butt to the ground. "Will you be okay getting a taxi from here? I gotta head to my sister's, babysitting duties."

"I'll be fine."

"Don't be a stranger." Lexi pecked her lightly on the cheek. "Come and see me soon."

She nodded.

"Darion, wait with her until she gets a ride," she instructed. "We don't want a repeat performance of last night." She gave them both a little wave, and made her way up the street.

An awkward silence hung in the air.

"You look cold," Darion said a moment later. He stood in front of her, rubbing his hands up and down her arms in an attempt to warm her up. There was that undeniable charm again, emanating from him. He was probably so used to flirting that he didn't even know the effect he had on women.

"Where's the taxi rank around here?" Gabi stumbled slightly.

"There's one a few streets away. But I can take you home."

She looked at him. She was trying to get away from him, not be stuck with him on a long ride. "Thanks for the offer, but a taxi will be fine."

"I insist," he said firmly. "Let me get my jacket." He tore his gaze from her, and made his way into the club.

Whilst Gabi waited, she checked her mobile. She had no texts or missed calls from Lawrence. She was disappointed, but also relieved. She was disappointed because she was obviously never on Lawrence's mind, but relieved because she didn't have to make excuses for her whereabouts. She shoved the iPhone in her bag and Darion was soon beside her, pulling on a black jacket. When he rested his warm hand on the small of her back, uncertainty settled in her gut. She was overwhelmed with lust and longing, no matter how much she tried to fight it. He led her down the street, and when he removed his hand, she found herself envying the women that got to hold it, feel it, have it all over their bodies, taking them to pleasured heights Gabi knew she'd never known. She could bet money that nothing about Darion was ordinary.

As Darion examined an impressive looking motorbike for a second, the words *Yamaha R1* emblazoned on the black body, Gabi felt a thrill of excitement. She had never been on a bike before.

"I won't be taking you on that. I don't wanna risk it in the snow," he said. "The last thing we want is to get stranded together, right?" He grinned cheekily.

Gabi stopped herself from making a flirtatious remark back.

A few yards down, after passing an Audi, which she assumed was also his, he led her to a black matte Jeep. With its huge wheels and tinted back widows, Gabi found herself admiring the automobile. The man had good taste. She climbed onto the passenger seat, getting a whiff of the vanilla air-freshener. The Jeep was immaculate. Everything inside was gleaming. She pulled her seatbelt on.

Darion climbed in, slamming the door shut. He started the engine, the stereo coming on automatically. Some rock band blared from the speakers, similar music to what the club had played. He strapped his seatbelt across his body, and turned to look at her, his face serious.

"Look, you don't have to feel uncomfortable around me," he began, "I don't bite." Then he flashed her a devilish grin, as if saying, *unless you want me to*, a gleam in his eye.

"I'm not uncomfortable." *Nervous, more like.*

She knew that once she collected her car from Westhaven, she wouldn't be seeing Darion again. She felt sadness rise up inside her, and mixed emotions whirled around in her head.

Darion's grip was tight on the steering wheel, his jaw slightly twitching. She wondered whether he was having the same thoughts, then dismissed it. He didn't know her. Besides, didn't he already have two girlfriends? She couldn't talk though, as she wasn't single herself.

He sped down the roads that were clear of snow, causing her to grasp hold of the door handle. She stole a quick glance at him and noticed that he was already looking her way. He turned his attention back to the road.

"So what's your address?" he asked, his face again unreadable. She provided him with the location details, and he nodded. "I've been that way before."

"Really?"

"Yeah, we get people in the club from all sorts of areas."

Gabi twirled a strand of hair around her finger, unsure of what to respond with. "So you like rock 'n' roll?" She died inside of humiliation. What a *poor* subject starter.

"I love it." His face lit up.

Maybe the subject wasn't so bad after all.

"I love all music, particularly rock, metal, and jazz. In fact, this is one of my favourites."

He turned the volume higher on the stereo. He began nodding his head slowly to the beats of "Physical" by Nine Inch Nails. She had heard it play in the club; Lexi had danced to it. The sound of the guitar and the softly sung vocals created a sexy feel-good atmosphere in the car. Gabi let out a little laugh as she listened to the lyrics Darion sang. The song was definitely *him*.

He placed a cigarette in his mouth. Struggling to get the lighter to work, he took both hands off the steering wheel, fiddling with it. Gabi leant over to take hold of the wheel, steering the car to the right slightly. He managed to light it, taking a long puff, and nodded to thank her.

"I wish I could have taken you on my bike," he shouted above the music. "You would have loved it."

She felt a little disappointed, wishing she could experience riding on the motorbike with him.

"There's a live band at the club every few months." He turned the music down. "You and your friends should come one night."

"Maybe." Darion needed to be reminded that she was engaged. "I'll bring my fiancé along."

To her surprise, he said nothing.

Droplets of rain landed on the windscreen. The sky was becoming dull and grey. The mood seemed to suddenly change in the car. Gabi remained looking out of her window, concentrating on the lyrics of the song that was now playing. A woman's beautiful voice was accompanied by a piano. It sounded sad. She looked down at the stereo, and she saw the song was "Bring Me To Life" by Evanescence. She took a deep breath, wondering why she was going home to Lawrence and to a life she often questioned, *is this all there is?*

An hour later, they were on her road. The car passed immaculate, decent-sized gardens, which led to fancy painted doors of modern big houses. It was the sort of place where it was perfect to raise children, and the neighbours were friendly, and looked out for one another.

The streets were still covered in a blanket of

snow, through which Darion accelerated gently, although the Jeep didn't appear to struggle much. He pulled onto a grass verge, pulled the handbrake up, and killed the engine. Gabi had just unbuckled her belt when she noticed he'd climbed out to hold the door open for her, like a true gent. Charming, as well as handsome. He really was the whole package.

Well, here I am, home sweet home.

"Can I offer you some money for the ride?" She rummaged in her handbag. "For the petrol cost?"

"Don't worry about it."

"Thanks. I really appreciate it." She paused. "Can I invite you in for a coffee?" The invitation was purely out of politeness. She hoped he'd decline, not wanting any complications.

"No, I'd better get back to the club, got an event to organise this weekend."

She nodded. She stood waiting for him to get back into his Jeep, but he didn't. He touched her chin, tilting her face near his, and gently pressed his lips against her cheek, lingering for longer than he needed to. His soft, warm lips left her heart racing. They stood staring at one another for a moment, in silence.

"See ya, Gabi," he finally said.

I really really really want to kiss him. She hated herself for being so attracted to him. "Bye," she replied sensibly. Story of her life.

With that, Darion climbed back into the Jeep and drove off, vanishing down the road. The sound of the engine got quieter as the Jeep moved further away, getting smaller until it was out of sight. Gabi realised that she had stood and watched him leave.

Turning on her heel, she made her way toward her house, fumbling in her bag for her keys. It had been an unusual couple of nights. She was glad that Lawrence wasn't yet home. As Gabi always parked her car in the garage, he'd have no clue that it was in Westhaven.

Once inside the warmth of the lounge, she collapsed on the sofa, exhausted, both mentally and physically. She took out her mobile and glanced at the screensaver of Lawrence. He was a good looking man with his ash blonde hair, piercing blue eyes, and an average build, although there was nothing distinguishing or particularly interesting about him.

When she had first met him, an older man eight years her senior, she thought he was good for her. He was hard working, ambitious, and sensible. And even when the arguments began, and the relationship grew boring and difficult, she stuck it out, telling herself that chemistry and excitement weren't important for a relationship to succeed. Now she wasn't so sure.

She wriggled her body until she was lying down. She wondered what Darion had planned for the day. Irritated, she rolled onto her side. *Forget about Darion. You're engaged.* Digging into her handbag, she pulled out a manuscript, which she was editing for work, and began reading it. If anything would take her mind off of him, that sure would.

How wrong she was.

Chapter Six

Gabi lay in bed, staring up at the ceiling. She'd been tossing and turning for a good hour. She looked at her neatly ironed work suit, which was hanging near the window, next to Lawrence's. Their shoes were lined neatly on the floor underneath. Their bags were on the chair with everything in them that they needed for tomorrow. It was always the same routine, preparing themselves for the next working day. The film *Groundhog Day* certainly came to mind, living the same day over and over. This wasn't living; it was existing. She wriggled onto her side, accidentally nudging Lawrence, who had again returned home late.

"You awake, Gabi?"

"Yes, I can't sleep."

He turned to face her, giving her a lopsided grin. Oh. She was getting his good mood this time. He kissed her gently on her forehead, and pulled her closer to him for a cuddle. After a few minutes, he slid his hand under her gown. Gabi froze. He opened her gown and began kissing her neck. The

49

smell of alcohol filled her nostrils.

She closed her eyelids tightly. Something was wrong. On the rare occasions when they did have sex, she could usually still enjoy it once they got going, but she wasn't enjoying his hands all over her body. Oblivious to her discomfort, his mouth met her breast. Gabi shifted slightly away. Not getting the hint, his breathing grew heavier as he kissed her other breast. Darion's face appeared in her head. She shot into a seated position.

"I can't sleep because I have a headache." She pulled the gown around herself, fastening the cord, praying that Lawrence hadn't seen the bewildered look on her face. "You go to sleep."

"Okay." He shrugged, and tossed over so that his back was facing her.

Gabi lay back down in darkness, staring at the wall before her for what felt like an eternity. When her eyelids became heavy, and exhaustion kicked in, she eventually drifted into a deep sleep.

***

Gabi woke to the sound of the alarm piercing through her ears. Groaning inwardly, she reached out lazily and pressed the off button. She slowly peeled her eyes open, welcoming in the bright sunlight. Stretching her limbs, she yawned before reluctantly dragging herself out of bed.

She trudged to the bathroom, which she always used first, as it took her a while to get ready. She switched on the tap, allowing the steam of the shower to warm up the room before she slipped her clothes off and climbed in. Careful to not get her hair wet, she luxuriated in the hot water that cascaded down her body. It was heavenly.

When it was Lawrence's turn in the bathroom, she perfected her make-up, and ran a brush through her locks until they hung silkily down her back. She dressed in a grey pencil skirt, a crisp, white shirt, and Saint Laurent platforms. She looked as glamorous as she possibly could for work.

It didn't take long for Lawrence to change into a smart grey suit, and so together they descended the stairs for coffee and toast. Lawrence took up residence on his usual stool at the kitchen table, and began leafing through the morning's newspaper, whilst Gabi began reading the manuscript again. Music was playing from the radio in the background. They always made sure that they had at least half an hour free in the morning to just relax.

"It's Tom's birthday today." Lawrence stopped reading for a moment. "The whole office is going out for a few drinks after work, so I'll probably be back about half ten."

"Sure." It wasn't like she had a say in the matter anyway. "Lawrence?"

"Yes?"

"I need to ask you something, but I don't want you to get mad."

"Go ahead."

"Are you having, or have you had, an affair?"

His eyes widened, whether in disbelief or worry, Gabi couldn't quite tell. Clearing his throat, he said, "Don't be ridiculous. Why would you think that?"

His condescending tone irked her.

"I found matches in your pocket, from a gentleman's club."

"Tom gave them to me. You know he's into that sort of thing."

She hadn't known that. "You haven't visited a club with him, have you?"

"Are you serious right now? You know I hate those grubby joints. Give me some credit." He took a swig of his drink. "What's brought all this on?"

She shrugged. "You seem cold and distant lately, Lawrence. And you always take phone calls in private."

"Gabi, the calls all are work related. I'm stressed at the moment. The company's having some problems right now. That's all there is to it." He looked her squarely in the eye. "I wouldn't lie to you."

She decided to drop the matter before he lost his temper. The last thing she wanted was a full-blown argument to ruin her day. She guessed she'd never know for sure. All she could do was trust him.

He slowly stood and glanced at his watch before pulling his jacket on. He groaned as he peered out the window, where light raindrops hit the glass pane.

Gabi perked up when she realised her all-time favourite song was playing. She turned the volume higher, and swayed her hips to the music whilst she cleared the plates from the table, dumping them into the sink. She grabbed Lawrence's hands, pulling him toward her for a playful dance, to lighten the mood. He hastily pulled away.

"Come on, Gabi, don't be silly. Have a good day at work." With that, he left. No kiss goodbye. Nothing.

Gabi froze for a moment, her heart sinking. An ache tightened her throat as Lawrence's rejection became unsettling. Perhaps her friend Mallory had been right for all those years; maybe she and Lawrence weren't suited. Determined not to get upset, she focused on cleaning the kitchen. When everything was spotless, she switched the radio off.

She was applying another coat of lipstick when the sound of Mallory's car horn reverberated in her ears. Hurriedly grabbing her bag, Gabi hooked it over her shoulder. As Mallory worked in the same office, they took it in turns to drive, and fortunately for Gabi, that day was Mallory's turn.

She set the house alarm and locked all the doors, then she entered the warmth of Mallory's sports car. Mallory was combing her blonde shoulder-length hair in the rearview mirror, whilst puffing on a cigarette.

"How's it going, sweetie?"

"Good. You?" Gabi strapped the seatbelt across her body.

"I'm great."

"I don't suppose you want to do me a huge favour later?"

"What is it?"

"Take me to Westhaven to pick up my car?"

"Why is your car in Westhaven?" Mallory's forehead wrinkled in confusion.

"The last couple of nights…" Gabi sighed. "I don't even know where to begin."

"What happened?"

"To cut a long story short, I found matches in Lawrence's pocket, from some club, got some idea that he was cheating on me."

"What?" Her mouth dropped. "Well, is he cheating on you?"

Gabi shrugged a shoulder. "I confronted him, and he swore he'd never do that to me."

"Shit. I hope not, Gab." The tyres screeched on the ground as Mallory set off. "So, what happened at the club?"

"I found no clues. But, I ended up staying there and partying with a girl called Lexi."

Mallory smiled. "About time you let your hair down. How did you get home?"

"I got a ride." Gabi knew she could always tell Mallory things in confidence.

"And who gave you this ride?" She raised a brow, then turned her head back to concentrate on the road.

"Some guy."

"Some guy?" Mallory was looking at her again. "Hmmm, why have you got the cat-that-got-the-cream look?"

Gabi studied her pink nails, noticing she had chipped one. "The owner of the club, Darion. He offered."

"Sounds eventful, probably the most fun you've had with a man in ages." Mallory chuckled. Although she could tolerate Lawrence in small doses, Mallory had witnessed Gabi's fun personality take a backseat, especially when Gabi's fiancé was around. "Well, when we collect your car, we could have a drink in this club too, if you like?"

"I'm not sure that's a good idea, Mal."

"Why are you avoiding going in? Did you kiss this guy?"

"No, I did not," Gabi exclaimed.

"But you fancy him, right?"

Gabi shook her head, trying to keep a straight face.

"Don't lie to me, Gabi. Is he hot?"

"I wouldn't know, Mal. I don't look at other men."

"Bullshit! It's natural to notice a hot guy."

Gabi burst out laughing, her crimson cheeks giving her away. "Okay, he's not bad."

"Well, I'll see for myself later." Mallory smirked. "And we *are* going in for one drink. Just a Coke, or something."

Gabi hesitated. It was no use arguing with Mallory; she was pushy and always got her own way. Perhaps it would be polite to say thanks to Darion again for the ride home, maybe buy him a drink, although it was his club, he could help himself.

When Gabi was finally on the fourth floor of Miller & Co. Publishers, she retreated to her office, closing the door behind her. She needed to be in silence to concentrate and finish the manuscript. She put her reading glasses on, slipped off her heels, and made herself comfortable. The woman in the story sounded wild and adventurous, not sticking to any rules. Gabi wished she was more of a risk taker. She kept reading, and before she knew it, several hours had passed. Mallory disturbed her when she brought a coffee.

"How's it going, sweet cheeks?" she asked, tapping the door shut with her foot.

"I've got four more chapters, and then I'm done." She looked up.

"I edited like, one chapter of mine, I can't get into it today." She placed the cup on the desk before lighting a cigarette and sitting down, resting her feet on the table.

"You know you're not supposed to smoke in here." Gabi smiled, reminding her friend like she had done for years.

"Yeah, yeah, crank the window open, would you?"

Gabi pushed the window open, allowing a breeze to enter the room. "So, how's Steve?"

"Great, as ever."

Steve was Mallory's perfect match. They always spent quality time together; whether it was partying, eating out, exploring, travelling, even watching a movie indoors, they had a good time. Gabi sometimes felt envious and wished that her relationship was more like theirs.

"Are you looking forward to seeing Darion later?" Mallory teased. "Perhaps you two will get it on."

"No, he has a girlfriend." She shuffled the manuscript, creating a neat pile. "Not just one either."

Mallory almost spat out her coffee. "You're joking?"

"Well, he kissed two of his bar staff."

"Maybe he's got an open relationship thing

going on, or maybe he just appreciates meaningless flings."

"It's not my concern," Gabi said.

"Yeah, right." Mallory regarded her suspiciously.

"Mallory, stop it. I'm engaged to Lawrence."

"I know, I know." She threw the cigarette out of the window. "I just can't wait for the day when you pack that old man in."

"He's not that old."

"Well, he acts it."

Gabi ignored her friend's cruel comment.

"I worry about you an awful lot."

Gabi felt her chest tighten at the way Mallory was looking at her, with sympathy. She hated it. It made her want to wallow in self-pity, and second-guess every little aspect about her life, and not just relationship-wise.

"What do you mean?" she asked.

"You need to get the old Gabi back. Don't let Lawrence kill your fucking soul," she erupted, shaking her head vehemently. "You need more confidence, for starters." She huffed. "Perhaps you should go to assertive classes, or something. Make new friends, get new hobbies."

Gabi mulled over the idea in her head. She'd been so focused on keeping Lawrence happy over the years that she had completely neglected her own happiness, the things that made her who she was.

"What was it you told me you used to love…dancing! Join a new class." She folded her arms across her chest.

Gabi had done performing arts in her college

days. Music and dancing made her feel alive.

"Maybe." She shrugged.

"No 'maybe.' Do it."

Mallory stood up and made her way to the door. "I'll see you later." She blew a kiss. "And you'd better get those nails fixed." She closed the door behind her gently.

She examined her nails, and decided that she would email her boss, Phil, and ask for the afternoon off. She worked so hard, and hadn't had time off in a while. Phil was easy going; Gabi couldn't see him having a problem with it. Plus, he was pretty close to her parents, one of the reasons she was lucky enough to have her own office. He replied minutes later, advising her it was fine. She was pleased. She had several hours to get her nails done, maybe even a facial and a pedicure. Picking up the phone, she called her regular nearby salon and made an appointment.

"Where are you going?" Mallory asked at the elevators.

"I've booked the afternoon off, I do need my nails fixing, and maybe a pedicure or something."

"Okay, I'll see you back here at five. Have fun."

Three hours later, Gabi stepped out of the salon feeling rejuvenated, like a new woman. Her hair had been washed, dried, and curled, and now hung glamorously down her back. Her coral polished nails shimmered in the daylight. Back in the office everybody complimented her, stating that they preferred that particular hairstyle.

"Wow, I love it, Gabi." Mallory stroked a ringlet. "Trying to impress a certain someone?" She winked.

"No," Gabi responded defensively, her voice coming out a little higher pitched than usual.

"I'm teasing. Come on, let's go get your car."

Mallory was eager to get to the club. Gabi, on the other hand, was a bundle of nerves.

Chapter Seven

They had had no problem finding the club with Mallory's sat-nav. Gabi was relieved, as she knew that she definitely wouldn't have remembered the journey by heart. The sky was beginning to get dark, and the snow showed no signs of disappearing.

Gabi wasn't overly enthusiastic about their plans to have a drink at the club. Overwhelmed with anxiety, she opened the window a little, to allow fresh air to fill her lungs. She needed to stop getting so worked up over Darion. But there was something about him that made her slightly bashful and excited at the same time.

Once outside The Black Door, Mallory stopped in her tracks. "Gabi, you did not tell me it was a strip club." An amused expression crossed her face as she pushed open the front door. "So, it's upstairs?"

Gabi looked at the upstairs door; she hadn't noticed it before. She wondered what was inside, considering music was coming from there. Did

Darion also own it? "No. It's through here."

Mallory shoved Gabi to the bar excitedly. "We haven't been out in so long," she screeched, grinning. "We seriously need to go out more, Gab."

"I agree."

"I know Lawrence hates you spending time with me, but screw him." She giggled. "Do we not always have fun?"

"We do. And Lawrence doesn't hate you at all."

"Sweetie, stop protecting him. The feeling's mutual, I'm not offended."

Gabi remained silent.

She and Mallory pulled out stools at the bar and ordered a Coke each. Gabi saw no sign of Lexi, or Darion. The club was quieter than usual, as it was still early, and the atmosphere was chilled. The music was at a volume where Gabi didn't have to shout to be heard. Without the dancers entertaining on stage, or hanging from the poles, it resembled a normal bar. Gabi felt herself relax.

"Fancy a shot?" Gina appeared from the stockroom.

"No, thanks. I'm here to pick up my car."

"I love your hair." Gina fingered a tendril before sauntering off.

"So do I."

Hearing the husky, familiar voice sent a delicious shiver down Gabi's spine. Trying to keep her lips a straight line, when all she wanted to do was grin, proved difficult. She twisted around, feigning nonchalance. Darion Milano. He was wearing black jeans and a matching t-shirt that clung to his impressive biceps. His hair was slightly dishevelled, like he'd just rolled out of bed, and he hadn't yet shaved the light stubble that shadowed his jaw. He looked sexy, rough and rugged, and definitely still appealing.

Mallory turned around to look at him. Her expression was one of delight.

"I'm here to collect my car. We thought we'd pop in here first."

"Right." He nodded.

"Erm, this is my friend, Mallory," she added, realising she'd forgotten her manners. "Mal, this is Darion."

"Hey." He winked.

"Nice place you got here."

"Oh, you haven't seen it all."

All? He must have owned the upstairs too. Curiosity swept over Gabi.

Darion shouted to Gina to get his white t-shirt, black blazer, and hair gel from the back room. She obeyed and handed him some neatly folded clothes, along with the gel. He pulled his t-shirt over his head, revealing his naked torso. And as he turned, they caught sight of his muscular shoulder blades, which led to a trim waist. Mallory's mouth hung open as she nudged Gabi. Now dressed in the white t-shirt and blazer, Darion scooped some gel into his hands, rubbed them together, and smoothed back his hair. Gabi couldn't help but notice the transformation. He looked handsome. Smart.

"Meeting a client," he informed them.

"Darion, you can't, you're drunk," Gina sternly told him.

"Relax, darlin'." He pulled her toward him and

kissed her forehead. Gabi felt a stab of jealousy. Even Mallory's smile had vanished. Darion told Gina he'd see her later. He backed away slowly, and set off for the door. He only managed a few strides before customers began approaching him, shaking his hand, satisfied and appreciative grins on their faces. When Darion finally managed to pull away, Gabi turned her attention back to Mallory.

"Well, that was brief." Mallory crossed her arms over her chest.

Gabi shrugged. Darion was a popular man.

"You were right though, he's some serious hot stuff, what I would *do* to him." She burst into laughter. "If I was single, of course," she added.

Gathering up their drinks, they ambled toward the sofas in the centre of the room. The two of them made themselves comfortable, and they focused on the dancers that were now occupying the stage. When fifteen minutes passed, Gabi made her way to the bathroom. She stared at her reflection in the mirror before adding red gloss to her lips. As she walked out, she noticed Darion standing in the gentleman's bathroom, talking on his mobile.

"Mr. Taylor, you will be *more* than impressed. Come down, check out the club, bring your wife…definitely. Okay…see you soon."

He ended the call, sliding the mobile into his pocket. Gabi watched as he turned on the tap, and splashed water on his face. She was about to leave when he turned around and noticed her.

"Gabi," he called out. "Can I speak to you for a second?"

"Um…sure."

When he showed no sign of leaving the bathroom, she entered. He snaked his arm around her shoulders, his weight resting on her body. He rubbed his nose along her cheekbone gently, and leant into her ear to whisper, "Would you say you're open-minded? Or set in your ways?"

She thought for a moment. She definitely wasn't set in her ways; she could sometimes be persuaded to try many things. She wouldn't hesitate at trying pretty much anything once, as long as it was within reason. Her lips formed into a pout. "I'd say I'm pretty open-minded."

He nodded contently, as if she had chosen the correct answer.

"Why do you ask?"

"No reason." His arm dropped to her waist, but he pulled her into him, guiding her back to the bar. She could feel the heat of his body, smell the sweetness of his cologne. When he tightened his grip, bringing her even closer, she badly wanted to wrap her arms around him and bury her face in his firm chest, to be as close to him as possible. To feel protected. Wanted. Desired. All the things she lacked from Lawrence.

Darion surprised her by leaning down into her neck, his breath tickling her skin. "I asked because there are a lot of things I'd just *love* to do with you, Gabi."

She looked at him. Even though he knew she had a fiancé, he wasn't backing down. He was making it clear that he was available. He was trouble.

Mallory saw them and waved them over excitedly. She was sitting with Lexi in one of the private booths. Gabi tore herself away from Darion and joined them.

"Hey, you came back soon." Lexi grinned. "I just met your friend here. She's cool."

Gabi perched on the sofa. "I came to collect my car. And to thank both you and Darion again."

"Don't worry about it." Lexi waved dismissively.

"How were you gonna thank me?" Darion asked, and she was unsure of whether he was teasing or being dead serious. His face was devoid of emotion.

Gabi lifted her drink and drained the contents to excuse her silence.

After they had talked for a while, Darion suggested they play a game of blackjack for money. The game quickly became intense and competitive. Within minutes, Mallory and Lexi had lost. It was just Gabi and Darion left. He eyed his cards, and then looked up at her, clearly trying to read her expression. Gabi gave nothing away.

She watched as he slowly placed a card down on the middle of the table. Gabi looked at her cards. She refrained from smiling; she had been dealt a good hand. She placed three cards down, and then knocked on the table to indicate that she had one card left. Darion grinned, placing four cards down, and knocked the table himself, holding one card up, his gaze fixed on her.

Damn. She picked up another card. He also picked up another card. She checked her two cards, and felt smug again—they matched. She knocked the table again. Darion took in a slow breath, staring at his cards, and then slowly put one down. Gabi placed her two cards on top of his. She had won.

"Fuck. You won." He threw his head back and laughed.

She giggled, happily scooping the notes into her handbag.

"Another game?" he asked.

"No, Daz." Lexi fixed him with a stern look. "You always get carried away, and you know it."

Darion's lips opened, and then closed, as if deciding it was best to remain quiet.

"Here comes my best customer." Lexi tilted her head, observing the crowd. "See you later, Gabi. Nice to meet you, Mallory."

"Likewise."

Lexi sauntered off to meet a gentleman at the bar.

"Come on, let's dance." Mallory grabbed hold of Gabi's hand, yanking her to her feet.

Gabi allowed Mallory to twirl her around. They danced in their little corner, talking and laughing away, treating the occasion as a girl's night out, which *was* long overdue. Gabi's sides began to ache from Mallory's endless jokes, and when she caught her breath, she made her way to the bathroom again. Once inside, she sat on the toilet lid, and allowed her head to fall in her hands. She closed her eyes, unable to refrain from chuckling to herself. What was she doing back at the club?

Maybe it was partly due to Lawrence messaging her, stating that he'd be late home again. The thought of sitting before the television, shovelling down a ready-made meal, hadn't seemed appetizing. He always had somewhere else to be, other than home. She had a feeling that their relationship would never improve. Sooner or later, Gabi knew she'd get sick and tired of trying.

Feeling someone's presence, she looked up to see Darion standing over her, a ghost of a smile on his lips.

"Your friend was looking for you." He crouched down and took her small hands in his, the caressing of his fingers making her throat go dry and her heart hammer against her chest. Trust Mallory to send Darion looking for her. She knew her plan.

"I'm tired," she mumbled, her eyelids beginning to feel heavy.

"Me too, beautiful." He grazed her neck gently with his lips. "Me too."

Gabi groaned inwardly, the vixen inside her telling her to forget Lawrence and the crap he brought to the table, and kiss Darion. Just one little kiss. A feel of his soft lips. Just to see if it ignited something within. Just to see if there really was a connection between them. She willed herself to be strong, but it was a battle she was losing fast.

As Darion cupped her face in his hands, he turned her willpower to dust. She wanted his full lips on hers, wanted to taste his tongue, to see if he was a good kisser. Her heart drummed frantically against her chest. She fancied Darion so much. Although she knew she'd be coy at first, she knew he could be the one to make her feel alive and daring.

"I'd better go home." She snapped out of her thoughts, and stood up.

Darion's expression looked panicky as he also

rose to his feet. "Will I see you again?"

"I can't," she said softly.

"Gabi." He pressed his body against hers, backing her up against the cubicle wall. His lips met her neck, where he planted several gentle kisses. Gabi allowed her eyes to close, as his touch ignited a spark in the pit of her stomach, just as she'd hoped it would. "Before you go back to your ordinary life, to your fiancé," he said in between kisses, "and never walk in this place again," he continued, his hand stroking her back, caressing her ass, and pulling her closer into his rock hard erection, "fuck me." His voice was ferocious. His gaze swept greedily over her body, his hunger and lust visible.

Gabi's mouth dropped open at his abruptness. *Who the fuck do you think you are?* was the response that rose to her lips, but she didn't say the words aloud. She was flabbergasted; she doubted they'd be nothing more than a splutter.

"I know that if I have you now…" he whispered roughly, his lips mere centimetres away from hers, "I know that you'll come back."

Gabi stepped aside, outraged at his arrogance. "What makes you so sure?" she asked sharply.

Darion's mouth curled upwards as he leant in to create a bond of intimacy. Keeping his voice low, he said, "It never fails."

With that, he reluctantly disentangled himself from her and exited the room. Gabi confronted the mirror before her. She realised that her hands were shaking ever so slightly. From anger, or excitement? She wasn't sure. She smoothed her hair down, fiddled with her shirt, and headed for the club. She was relieved to find that Mallory was ready to go. Gabi knew that if she was asleep when Lawrence returned, then she wouldn't have to make up any lies of where she'd been.

Before getting into her Mercedes, Gabi thanked Mallory for the ride. Her friend responded that it was no problem, and that she'd had a good time. Gabi had passed her number to Lexi, promising to keep in touch, although the likeliness that she would was slim. On the drive back, she replayed Darion's soft warm lips on her neck and his hands over her body. *Shit!* Why had she gotten herself into this mess?

Chapter Eight

It was a Saturday afternoon, and Lawrence and Gabi were at some horse-racing show, which Gabi didn't particularly care about, with his work colleagues. They sat at a table on a balcony viewing the race. Although Lawrence was making a bit of an effort to spend time with her, she was bored to tears. She adjusted the stupid oversized hat on her head, and turned to her fiancé.

"Oh, it's just ridiculous, the children of today." One of the older women was still droning on.

Gabi yawned. Lawrence agreed with her, ranting about today's society, but Gabi didn't bother to listen to the negativity. She scanned through images in her mobile to busy herself.

"Come on, Trudy," Lawrence shouted to one of the horses. "Gabi, can I get you a drink? Some more food?" He motioned a waitress over.

"I'll have a glass of red wine, please."

His brows pinched together in confusion.

"In fact, make it a large one," she added.

"Fine." Lawrence repeated the order to the

waitress. "And a lemonade for me." He turned to Gabi. "What's wrong with you?"

"Nothing, I just fancy a drink. It's not just you who gets to have all the fun, Lawrence." She manufactured a grin, and pecked him on the mouth, which he edged away from. Public displays of affection were definitely not his thing. She *hated* that. She was an affectionate person, and sometimes all she ever wanted was to hold hands, cuddle, and rest her legs over his. Lawrence cared too much about what others thought.

Gabi was pleased that the afternoon passed quickly. Lawrence hadn't won a thing, which he never did. In the car on the way home, "Physical" by Nine Inch Nails boomed through the stereo. Gabi remembered hearing it in Darion's car. She felt butterflies in her stomach.

"Leave it on," she quickly said when Lawrence leant over to switch it off.

He looked at her, said nothing, and focused on the road. Gabi watched her fiancé for a few seconds. Maybe she could really work on the relationship. Maybe she could try to spice and liven things up. The relationship wasn't a total failure. They had some things in common, shared some views, and when Lawrence wasn't stressed from work she enjoyed his company. Plus, she still loved him. Didn't she?

Taking a small breath, she decided to just go for it. She ran her hand up his leg, stroking it slowly. He let out a laugh. Whether it was due to discomfort, she didn't know. She continued up his leg, until she met the bulge in his trousers. She massaged it softly.

"Stop the car," she said in a low, sultry voice. "I want you now."

"What?" he shrieked. "Now? Are you crazy?"

"Let's have a little fun."

"Gabi, I'm not pulling over and having…" He sighed heavily. "Somebody could see us."

"Not if we park somewhere secluded."

He slammed on the brakes near a grass verge, pulled the handbrake up in anger, and turned to look at her, switching the engine off. "What is with you lately?"

She looked dumbfounded.

"You're acting differently, you're dressing provocatively, drinking in the house after work."

She looked down at her knee length cream dress. It was hardly *provocative*. It showed a little cleavage, but what was the crime in that? Plus, she worked so hard, wasn't she entitled to a drink? And he was a fine one to talk.

"Lawrence, I'm twenty-seven, not seventy. You should relax more," she said through gritted teeth.

"You shut your mouth, Gabi," he warned menacingly, his fist clenched.

She didn't flinch this time. "What are you going to do, Lawrence?" She looked him squarely in the eye. "Hit me again?"

"What's your problem, Gabi?"

"I'm not happy," she told him honestly, turning to look out of the window. She felt a painful lump form in her throat, and hot tears started to build on her lower lids. "I'm bored. And I feel neglected. You're never around." Her voice shook with emotion. Tears that had been threatening her for months forced their way free. Her chest began to shake as uncontrollable sobs took over. She buried her face in her hands, feeling needy and pathetic.

"I'm sorry, Gabi, I'll try harder to make you happy." Lawrence leant over and wrapped his arms around her as he apologised profusely.

When she had eventually calmed down, he continued driving. They lapsed into silence. It took them all of fifteen minutes until they were home. Once inside the house, Lawrence surprised her by picking her up and carrying her to the sofa, kissing her hungrily. She responded, falling backwards.

They tore at one another's clothes until they were both naked. His teeth tugged at her neck, whilst his hands pulled at her hair roughly. She clawed at his back, before parting his lips with her tongue. When he was inside her, she let out a fake cry of ecstasy. No matter how hard she tried to enjoy it, she wasn't turned on anymore. She felt like crying inside. She hated herself for feeling the way she did. When they had finished, and she had faked an orgasm, they quickly dressed.

"I do love you, Gabi," he told her. Hearing him say that made her feel warm inside. But was love enough? "I'm sorry for the way I treat you sometimes."

Gabi climbed to her feet and squeezed his hand. "I'm going to have a bath."

"Sure."

She vanished to the bathroom, where she had a long soak in the tub. Afterwards, when she was dressed in her silk nightie, she crawled under the freshly washed bed covers and opened a book to read. She was four chapters in when Lawrence lay down beside her. Grabbing the remote, he switched the television on to watch a crime programme. Deep down, Gabi knew nothing would change. Sure, they could force moments of excitement, but the passion, the connection, was definitely missing. And as for trying harder at making the relationship work, yeah, right, she'd heard that a hundred times before. She focused on her book and shut the world out.

***

Darion

Darion dropped his keys onto the table and kicked his boots off. Next, he stripped off his clothes, so that he was only in his boxer shorts, and collapsed onto the sofa. It had been a long day at the club, attending to the books and sifting through new membership applications. Although he was exhausted, he didn't fancy a night of tossing and turning.

He felt for the TV remote under the cushions, switched the TV on, and lay down. He flipped through the channels. Nothing was on that he fancied. He switched it off.

Staring up at the ceiling, his foot tapped anxiously on a cushion. He hated silence. He should have stayed at the club. At least there he had the sound of chatter, laughter, and music beyond the door. Not to mention the girls always popping in and out of his office to check on him.

He ran his hands up and down his face, sighing heavily. Glancing at the wall clock, he noticed that it was still quite early. He was bored, restless.

He chewed his lip, deep in thought. He needed company. He leant over and rummaged through his jeans pocket for his mobile. Darion knew, if left alone, he'd think of Eva and drive himself crazy, drinking himself into oblivion, or gambling online. He scanned his contact list: Carrie, Diana, Ellie, Evelyn, Gina, and Halle. There were so many available girls. There was only one who matched his drive and completely got him. He touched the call button on the screen and held the phone to his ear. She answered instantly.

"Hey, baby," he said softly.

"Hey, you."

"You busy?"

"Not particularly."

"You wanna come around?"

"I'll be there in fifteen."

Darion let the mobile drop to the floor. When fifteen minutes passed, he dragged himself off the sofa to answer the door. She stood before him in a long, black mac coat. He moved aside so that she could enter. He knew that he shouldn't disrupt her when she was at work, but he needed her. She shrugged off the mac and placed it neatly on the back of the armchair. She wore high, transparent platforms, her legs were never ending, and her curvy behind, and full, round breasts were covered by black lace material. He shut and locked the door.

"Gina." He walked over to her.

"Darion." She chuckled dirtily, as if she knew

what was coming.

He began kissing her hard, backing her against the wall. He let out a moan as she unzipped his trousers and released his throbbing cock. She giggled in between kisses and slowly slid to her knees. Her wide blue eyes stared up at him as he filled her mouth. Gina loved foreplay before having sex. Who was he to refuse?

Falling onto the nearest armchair, he allowed the pleasure to take over him—mind, body, and soul, Eva nothing but a distant memory.

For one night, anyway.

Chapter Nine

Gabi

The next two weeks passed in a blur. Soon it was another ordinary Monday morning. Gabi was in the office standing by the printer, watching the pages pour out, in a complete daze. Mallory startled Gabi by creeping behind her and digging her fingers into her sides.

"Got you a doughnut." She shook a paper bag. "Now, take five minutes out, will you? You've been working nonstop."

Gabi followed Mallory into the office, shutting the door behind her. Mallory slouched in a chair, smiling. "You're looking great today, may I say." She glanced down at Gabi's red Jimmy Choo stilettos, which matched her shirt.

"Thanks."

"So, what did you do this weekend? Anything exciting?"

"My life, exciting?" She laughed, diving into the paper bag and taking out the doughnut.

"Well, guess where me and Steve went?"

"Where?"

"A strip club." Mallory laughed wickedly. "After we'd been to a restaurant, we ended up walking past one. I could tell he wanted to go in. So we did. It was wild, Gab. We had a private dance."

"Ooh," she teased playfully. "Sounds fun."

"We had an awesome night after that." Mallory winked. "Trust me, like *so* much hotter than usual."

"Well, at least someone has a decent sex life." She giggled. "I tried to seduce Lawrence in the car the other week, and he looked at me like I had three heads."

"Oh, Gabi." Mallory groaned. "You and Lawrence are so mismatched. How long have I been telling you this? You're flogging a dead horse." She shook her head, the distaste apparent on her face. "I think you need to call that relationship a day, seriously."

Gabi looked up, her forehead creasing with confusion. "I can't. Even though it's not exciting, and it's stressful at times, I care about him. Plus, we're meant to be married next year." She bit her nail nervously. "If I left him, I'd feel so lonely."

"Lonely, not missing him. There's your answer. Don't stay with somebody because you're afraid of being lonely." She studied Gabi suspiciously. "Care about him." She screwed up her face. "Do you still love him?"

Gabi sighed in frustration. "I honestly don't know."

"Have you heard anything from Darion?"

His name made her sit up with interest. "No,

why?"

"He was more your type. Definitely exciting. You need a man to bring you out of your shell, really take charge, and I don't mean in a fatherly way," Mallory said, making a dig at Lawrence.

"Don't go there, Mal. Besides, he has two girlfriends, remember? And probably many more."

"No, they're not his girlfriends." She grinned mischievously. "I was talking to that redhead girl that night."

"Lexi?"

"Yeah, Lexi." Mallory propped her feet on Gabi's desk. "She said she's slept with him in the past, so has Gina, and half the other dancers, but they're not his girlfriends. Apparently he's been married before, and hasn't trusted women in years since the divorce."

"Really?" Gabi's brows rose.

"His wife cheated on him."

"Oh."

"He likes you. I could tell by the way he looked at you. It was different from how he looked at them."

"Whatever, Mal." She laughed incredulously. "He just wants another notch on his bedpost. In so many words, he told me, before I go back to my mundane life, to fuck him, and that if I did, he was certain I'd come back."

Mallory grinned with glee. "What a sexy bastard." She giggled.

Gabi's mouth dropped open. "Look, I better get some work done. I'll see you tomorrow, okay?"

Mallory stood up. "Remember what I said about

Darion. You know what I'm saying is the truth, you like him." She pulled the door open. "You're just too afraid to take the risk."

When the door shut after Mallory, Gabi sighed heavily and slumped in her chair, in no mood to continue working. She knew that Mallory only had her best interests at heart. She'd try anything, if it meant getting Gabi away from 'soul-destroying Lawrence,' as she often called him.

Massaging the side of her aching neck, her thoughts began to wander. Did she love Lawrence? She was a muddled mess, she knew that much. Sometimes, when someone shows you so much of their bad side, it's difficult to remember the good parts, why you loved them in the first place. Not being able to recall the last time she had really laughed with Lawrence made sadness rise up inside her. Had he damaged the relationship beyond repair? Had he tarnished the way that she now saw him?

Gabi pushed herself off the chair and plodded toward the window. Black clouds were gathering ominously overhead, and it was beginning to snow. Great, just what she needed.

When five o'clock made a painfully slow appearance, Gabi left work. Mallory was staying in town to have a drink with some colleagues and didn't need a ride home. In the car park, which was situated across the road from Miller & Co. Publishers, Gabi made polite chitchat with work staff, and finally said her goodbyes.

In the warmth of her car, she turned the radio on and let it play at a low volume. Her phone bleeped.

It was probably Mallory apologising. When she stopped at the traffic lights, she checked her mobile. Her call log stated that she had a missed call from a number she didn't recognise. Her brow furrowed in confusion. She pressed the number and speaker icon, and let the mobile rest in her lap. She sat patiently, listening to the ringing sounds, wondering who it could be. It was probably work-related—a client wanting an update on their manuscript. Eventually, she received an answer.

"Hello," she began. "This is Gabriella Woods. I had a missed call from you."

Silence.

"Hello?" She heard a blowing sound, as if someone were smoking. She tensed, instantly knowing who it was, a pleasant warmness spreading through her entire body.

"Can I see you?"

"Who's this?"

"You know who this is."

Gabi was slightly annoyed, but also secretly pleased that he had contacted her. "How did you get my number?"

"Lexi."

"You know I'm not available, Darion."

"I'll delete your number then?"

Panic struck her. "What do you want from me?"

"I don't know." He hesitated. "I want you, Gabi."

She inhaled a deep breath. "You don't even know me."

"I wanna get to know you. I can't stop thinking about you. It's driving me fucking insane." He paused. "Come and meet me."

She appreciated his honesty. Never in a million years would she confess she was the same. "I can't, Darion."

"Gabi, meet me at the club at midnight. If you don't, I'll take the hint, and I'll delete your number."

Gabi hung up. *Fuck!* What was she supposed to do? She turned up the volume on the radio. She groaned inwardly, and her head flopped back, hitting the headrest. Maybe it was time she took control of her own life and her happiness, to stop kidding herself when she thought things would improve with Lawrence. Maybe they were both better apart. Surely they deserved something more, something better.

She was bored, lonely, and unhappy. Lawrence must have had his own reasons for staying out late, drinking and whatnot. Perhaps he was also unfulfilled and bored to tears. Gabi decided there and then that she had to take a risk. Maybe meeting Darion had been a sign that the grass really was greener without Lawrence, regardless of whether Darion stayed in the picture.

***

Darion

Darion leant back in the leather chair and lifted his feet up to rest on his desk, not caring that his paperwork was getting creased. His mind raced. He didn't know why he had just called Gabi. Was he sexually frustrated? He booted the side of the desk, annoyed with himself. He had several women on speed-dial that he could've rung for a quickie. Had he grown bored of them? The sex had grown predictable; he knew their every move, and the order in which they did them. They weren't stimulating him enough, mentally or physically.

He needed a challenge. Something new, exciting, and fresh. Surely Gabi wouldn't be able to satisfy him how Gina or Eva had, though. They were tough competition. They were wild. Bondage, outdoor sex, role playing, dressing up, toys, threesomes, they had done it all. Gabi seemed *vanilla*. Then again, it had been said that it was the quiet ones that you had to watch out for. Plus, he had a habit of bringing out the naughtiness in the women he bedded.

As much as his women enjoyed casual sex, half of them got attached. He didn't get it. They knew the score, he always stated the rules. He hated rejecting them when they wanted more. But they should have known better. Why did every woman think she was the one to tame the bad boy?

But Gabi, she had a fiancé. Why was he even contemplating a fling, or whatever he was after, with her? He didn't want to break up a relationship. His ex-wife had devastated him, turned his world upside down. No way could he cause another man the same pain.

If only he could stop thinking about her. He thought that if he left her to make the first move, then maybe he'd feel less guilty about starting something with her. Yet it had been two weeks, and he'd heard nothing. Now he wanted her even more. He didn't know whether it was because he couldn't have her, or whether it was the chase that he liked.

He ground his teeth. She was probably just like all the rest. She had to be if she would willingly cheat on her fiancé. Well, he would see later. Even so, for some reason, it didn't put him off her. He was attracted to Gabi on more than just a physical level—there was something about her. He hated that she made him feel vulnerable, bringing out insecurities that he tried to bury deep, made him want things that he'd avoided for so long.

The bottle of whisky before him looked extremely tempting. He drank more than usual since he'd caught his former wife, Eva, cheating on him. He shook his head, trying to erase the thoughts. He didn't want to start replaying everything in his mind again. He already couldn't sleep alone; his thoughts kept him awake. He allowed his one night stands to stay the night and cuddle. Not that he particularly wanted to cuddle them; he didn't feel a close connection. Yet that comforting contact allowed him to drift to sleep and not think about Eva.

He heard the grumble of his stomach and realised that he hadn't eaten anything all day. He stood up and stretched. He'd have to pick up a sandwich from the corner shop. He grabbed his wallet and made his way out of the club.

A part of him wanted Gabi to meet him later, to see if she fancied him in return. Another part of him wanted her to do what was best for her and stay away. He *knew* he'd hurt her. He always unintentionally hurt them.

Chapter Ten

Gabi

In the hallway, Gabi hung up her coat and handbag, and slipped off her shoes. She found Lawrence in the lounge reading the paper, with the television on. He put down his reading when he saw her and offered to run her a bath. She shook her head.

"No, thanks." She sat down. "We need to talk."

His face fell.

"I'm not happy, Lawrence," she told him bluntly. "I haven't been for a while now."

"What are you saying?" His low voice had a chilling bite to it. His face was a mixture of rage and panic. "I thought we agreed I'd try harder to make you happy?"

Gabi cowered, sinking slightly in her chair as she caught sight of his clenched fists. Lawrence had promised never to hit her again. With his murderous expression, and veins throbbing near his temples, he looked ready to explode, and Gabi wasn't so sure he

85

would hold true to his promise.

"Things never change." She straightened, feigning bravery. "I can't do this anymore," she said sternly, her glare unfaltering.

Lawrence's silence disturbed her, made her nervous.

"Did you hear me, Lawrence?" she repeated, rising to her feet, towering over him. "It's over."

She took a step back as he slowly stood up too. She observed him, looking for any signs that he was about to lose his temper. Instead, he dropped to his knees, his arms wrapping around her legs tightly.

"I can change," he pleaded.

Gabi looked down at him in astonishment. She felt tears welling up, so she drew in a deep breath. She couldn't let him guilt-trip her. She had to do what was best for them both.

"Please don't make this any more difficult for me." She shook her head. "I don't feel satisfied in what we have."

"Gabi, don't do this," he raised his voice, standing up.

"I'm not happy," she screamed back. "Listen to me, Lawrence!" Rage overtook her, and she felt heat flood her face.

He grabbed hold of her hands. "I know I messed this up. I neglected you; put work first, controlled you. I'm sorry. Forgive me. I'll do anything to make you happy."

"It's too late. I don't have faith in this relationship. I care for you, but I'm tired of all this."

"What is it that you want, Gabi?"

She shrugged.

"I'll wait for you, please." His voice shook with emotion. "Go and do what you have to do. I'll wait for you."

Stunned, her mouth fell. She had never had Lawrence down as the begging type. "That wouldn't be fair on you."

"I don't care, Gabi, I'm not prepared to throw all these years away. I want to marry you, for Christ's sake." He stroked her cheek. "Gabi, you will never find someone who loves you as much as I do."

Would she?

"I'm going out for a bit. I need to clear my head," she said.

"Okay, I'll wait up for you?"

"Don't. I'm not sure what time I'll be back from Mallory's."

She ascended the stairs, her eyes spilling tears. She had tried to end it, it definitely hadn't been easy. If she wasn't happy, or fulfilled, how could he be? Gabi had to stick to her word. There was no going back.

She changed into a v-neck tight black dress, which exposed her cleavage. She sprayed on some perfume, applied lipstick, and ruffled her hair. Scanning her selection of heels, she decided to go for her black Louboutins, which had soles as red as her lips.

Gabi felt her heart hammering against her chest as she left the house. As nerve-wracking as it was, she needed to face Darion and find out exactly what he was after. She needed to face her demons once and for all, and get rid of the confused thoughts whirling round her head.

Gabi knew that she'd need a stiff drink to calm herself down once she got to the club, so she decided to take a taxi. En route to The Black Door, she had a strong urge to tell the driver to turn around. Maybe she should stay in her comfort zone with Lawrence, work harder at what they did have. *Don't bottle it.* She had to do it. She wanted a change in her life, and only she could change it. Was Darion the answer, though? Or was he an escape route?

Time to do this. When she stood outside the club, she took a deep breath. She checked her watch. It was 11.50 p.m. She couldn't believe that he'd given her an ultimatum. "Delete your number," he'd said. For some reason, she couldn't bear it. The thought of never seeing or hearing from him again bothered her. Perhaps she just needed to get it out of her system, see what he was all about.

She strode into the club and found Darion at the bar, flirting with Gina. How surprising. He sat up immediately when he saw her. She could tell by his expression that he hadn't expected her to come. Maybe he wasn't so cocky after all; maybe it was just a front. Gabi was glad he appeared sober. Teamed with grey jeans, he was wearing a white t-shirt again, which revealed his firm chest, washboard stomach, and strong arms.

"Can we go somewhere private?" She stood over him.

"Sure."

He led her behind the bar, and toward his office. As her heels clicked against the tiled floor, she felt a little shaky, fearing her legs would give way.

Inhaling deeply, she straightened her posture, gathering courage. When she was finally standing in his office, she took in her surroundings. Gabi noticed the screen on his computer. It was his email inbox. It stated there were fifty-six unread emails. There was also a lot of unopened mail on his desk, one piece in particular was from a solicitor. Was he in some kind of trouble?

Turning her head, she took in the pictures that adorned one wall: Darion fishing, swimming with dolphins, skiing, skydiving, and a huge picture of him standing in the bar in the centre of about twenty beautiful women. On closer inspection, she realised it didn't look like the club. She could make out a cage, and some type of leather swing. She wondered where it was. There were other photographs of him with stunning women at parties, and at clubs. It sure looked like he led a happy, carefree life.

"Take a seat." He pointed to the chair on the opposite side of the desk.

Gabi did as she was told. "Why did you want me to come here, Darion?"

"You know why, Gabi." He poured himself a drink. "You want one?" His stare swept over her admiringly and slowly.

She loved the way he looked at her; it made her swell with confidence. "Do you have wine?"

"I have everything, Gabi."

The telephone rang, echoing through the office. Darion snatched up the receiver. It sounded as if it were a new client of some sort. Maybe somebody wanted to hire the club for a private party. Gabi couldn't help but eavesdrop. Darion clicked on his computer, and confirmed that he'd received something of some sort. He was promising to show the caller around the place. When he ended the call, he stood up swiftly.

"I'm sorry, Gabi. I've gotta go." He grabbed the grey blazer from the back of his chair. "We'll have to do this later."

She was surprised, and she knew it showed. "*You* made me come here," she said, her voice sharp, annoyance consuming her.

"Gabi, wait in the bar, have as many drinks as you want, I'll be back in an hour or two." He placed his hand on her arm, his fingers slowly caressing it, his gaze devouring her hungrily. She watched as he swallowed, as if contemplating doing something. Kissing her, perhaps?

"If you're not back in an hour, I'm gone." Gabi brushed him off. There was no way that she was waiting two hours for him; she was pissed at agreeing to one hour. "You rang me, remember?"

"An hour," he said confidently. "See you soon."

Back at the bar, Gabi downed shot after shot. She felt completely miserable and confused. Lexi and Gina were occupying the poles, and Marnie was serving the customers. She focused on the stage. All attention was on Lexi and Gina. Gabi wondered what it would be like on stage, to be the centre of attention, with every single person in the room lusting after you. She also wasn't a stranger to the pole, as she had taken classes in the past for fitness purposes.

"They look good, don't they?" Marnie asked.

Gabi nodded. "They look fantastic. I bet it feels

unreal up there."

"It does. Why don't you get up there? The customers would love a new face."

She laughed. Marnie was serious. "No way."

"Honey, I feel nervous every single time, but alcohol is the best cure. Give it a go. Let loose. Be wild." Her eyes twinkled mischievously.

Gabi shook her head with a soft laugh. She didn't have the confidence to sing karaoke, let alone dance teasingly to a room full of horny men.

As she watched Marnie collect empty glasses, she sighed heavily. She always played it safe, sticking to the rules. She wished she could be unpredictable, spontaneous. Gabi didn't want to be the straight laced girl any more, the one who never took risks, never trying anything shocking or new yet desperately wanting to. She wanted to be the kind of girl she had read about. Gabi had always thought she'd settle down and meet someone who would bring the hidden daring side out of her. That person definitely wasn't Lawrence.

She remembered one Valentine's night; she'd lit candles in the room, and dressed in sexy underwear, stockings, and heels. She had bought a sexy DVD for her and Lawrence to watch, and some toys for couples. She had wanted to spice up their sex life. He hadn't been interested; everything had gone untouched. All of it was still sitting in the box. If she remembered correctly, she was pretty certain he had fallen asleep. That was the last time that she had tried anything new with Lawrence. And sex had been the same ever since: missionary position, wham bam, roll over. She felt bitter. She could have

been the caring, fun, faithful girlfriend. If Lawrence
had just opened up, or fulfilled her needs, she
wouldn't be in the club again. She hastily wiped
away a tear that trickled down her cheek. She was
upset that she hadn't realised sooner that Lawrence
wasn't the one. So much wasted time.

Ordering another glass of wine, Gabi was
pleased when Lexi returned. The dancer took a few
minutes out, sat with her, and talked about life in
general. She excitedly showed Gabi images of her
nieces from her iPhone. Marnie then strolled over,
and leaning her elbows on the bar, proceeded to
bitch about one regular that couldn't keep his hands
to himself.

"He's a right old perve." She screwed her face
up as if she was sucking on a sour lemon.

"Which client?" Lexi asked.

She shrugged. "You know, I can't remember his
name…he's about seventy. Always wears a tux."

"Bill?" Gina approached. "Mr. Filthy Mouth and
Wandering Hands?"

"Yep."

The girls bust out laughing.

"He's harmless, though." Lexi retrieved her
cigarettes and offered them around. Marnie and
Gina took one each without a moment's hesitation.

Gabi listened to them gossiping for a good five
minutes. They were all slightly merry from alcohol,
and laughing continuously. Gabi felt relaxed, like
she'd known the girls for a long time. She really
had made some new, unexpected friends.

Gabi didn't realise that it had been an hour and a
half since she'd seen Darion. She would have been

out of the club in a shot, had she checked the time. She wasn't about to sit around twiddling her thumbs, waiting on another man. Hell no. Been there, done that, worn the t-shirt. It hadn't been a good fit.

"We better get back to work." Lexi rose to her feet. "Darion will be over, and you know what he'll say."

"I don't pay you to sit around bitching," Marnie mimicked, chuckling.

"Besides, we wouldn't want Wendy dancing for too long. She might pull a muscle." Gina flicked her long hair back and stared daggers at the black-haired beauty on stage.

"Meow," Marnie teased.

"She's just jealous," Lexi whispered to Gabi.

"I heard that," Gina snapped. "I'm not jealous. Ain't nobody got the moves like me."

Gabi was unable to stop the wide smile that spread across her face. She watched as Marnie returned to take drink orders, whilst Gina took to the stage and Lexi prowled the club, greeting and flirting with the customers in hopes they'd request a dance.

Gabi stretched her arms out and held in a yawn, deciding it was time. She needed to find Darion and face the strong attraction between them. Whether they would give in to all their temptations, or clear the air and resist it, she had no idea.

Chapter Eleven

Gabi wove through the busy crowd, pushing through people until she saw him. Darion was standing at the far end of the club, watching her. She bit her lip and made her way slowly toward him, their gazes not leaving one anothers'. "Black Hole" by Muse was playing, creating a sexy feel in the room.

Gabi could see the slow rising of his chest as he remained rooted where he stood. Gabi fiddled with her nails anxiously. Her emotions were running wild. He seemed so close, yet so far away. She wanted him. She couldn't control it.

Although she'd only had a few partners in her life, and usually made them wait at least a month before getting intimate with them, she didn't have the patience when it came to Darion. A part of her told her to slow down, to wait, to make him work for it, to make him wine and dine her first. But the daredevil side of her told her to just go for it, not to overanalyse everything in life. Gabi sure as hell didn't want to ruin the moment that was for sure.

Maybe she should grab the bull by the horns for once, and let her body overrule her mind.

All she knew in that moment was that she desperately wanted to kiss him. Gabi hoped and prayed that he was feeling the same. Her hands shook, her heart thundered.

When she was before him, she noticed that he was breathing heavily. His jaw was tense, his face etched with raw, hungry passion. He admired her body through the flimsy material of her dress, and slipped his hand underneath the hem, stroking her thigh gently. Gabi felt the adrenaline rush through her veins, her skin tingling. He kissed her cheek, then her neck, with slow, soft kisses. She tilted her head, allowing him more access. His kissing grew harder, faster, his heavy panting hot on her neck. His hand ran higher up her thigh. It was wrong, so *wrong.* Forbidden.

Placing a flat palm on her stomach, he backed her toward a private dancing booth. Gabi stumbled on her heels, falling onto the sofa. As he slowly pulled the curtain shut, Gabi tried to ignore the dizzying rush of emotions and the blush that flamed her cheeks. He towered over her, and she had never felt so intimidated, or excited in her life. She looked up at him warily. He nudged her legs apart with his, and stood between them. Darion cocked his head to one side and gave her a tempting, salacious grin that unnerved her, his eyes flashing dangerously. As he pulled off his top, dropping it to the floor, Gabi released the breath she'd forgotten she'd been holding. She took in his sculptured body: large biceps, tight abs, and a smooth chest, which rose up and down with each ragged breath. Gabi's stomach tightened hard with desire as he leant closer.

"If you want me to back off," he said, his voice low and husky, "I will."

Did she want him to? Did she *really* want to walk out the club and never see him again? Did she want to return to her old life? Gabi felt the fear. She couldn't. She couldn't handle not seeing Darion again. She had waited so long to feel his touch. She wanted him every time she saw him, and yet she barely knew him. It was a dangerous game.

"Tell me."

She answered him by snaking her fingers around the back of his neck, and pulling him onto her. Her tongue parted his lips, darting inside to massage his. Lips and tongues crashing together, she kissed him with so much passion and hunger that she felt heat rise inside her, her body tingling and aching for him. She buried her fingers in his hair. They kissed until neither of them had any breath left, all their pent-up sexual tension erupting fiercely.

He pulled back, licking his lips, a naughty gleam appearing in his eyes. He let out a low, evil chuckle, which thrilled and frightened her simultaneously. He ordered Gabi to remove her dress.

"Here?" Her mouth dropped.

"Here."

"Darion…" She swallowed, focusing on the curtain apprehensively. Surely Darion didn't want to get intimate in the busy room, with just a thin piece of material hiding them from the crowd. He didn't appear fazed in the slightest.

"No one can see us, Gabi," his smooth voice

assured her. "No one will disturb us."

"But, what if they—"

"Sshhh." He placed a finger over his lips. "Besides, it's all part of the excitement."

She chewed the inside of her cheek for a moment, thinking it over. She was equally flabbergasted and tempted. As Darion set a knee on the sofa, leaning over her, he placed tender kisses on her neck. Whilst her mind made her protest, her body betrayed her by straining toward his. The alcohol she'd consumed boosted her confidence, spurring her on. Darion's kisses got firmer, and she found herself moaning involuntarily, falling further back into the sofa. Gabi knew she was no longer able to put up a fight. She was delirious with lust.

"Take your dress off," he repeated.

She hesitated a moment before pulling it over her head. When she was only in her underwear, she waited for his next move, the suspense almost unbearable. His tongue and lips traced down her neck again, his stubble grazing her skin. She wriggled. Darion's hands slid down her shoulders, where he gingerly slipped down her bra straps. Gabi breathed sharply when he unhooked it and tore it from her body.

He studied her breasts, and a low, satisfied moan escaped his lips. He knelt back and peeled off her underwear, dragging it slowly down her legs. As he admired her naked body for a moment, Gabi self-consciously tried to close her legs, but he forced them apart.

"Oh, Gabi..." he murmured appreciatively. "You don't know what you've let yourself in

97

for…darlin'."

He picked up half a bottle of alcohol someone had left, and poured it over her chest, her stomach, and between her legs. She gasped at the cold sensation. As he placed the bottle back on the table, Gabi felt the tension coil in her stomach. His mouth met her breast, his tongue lapping up the alcohol, circling her nipple, bringing it to a hard peak. She let out a moan. He continued to suck her breasts equally, before clamping his teeth around a nipple, and gently tugging, causing her to arch her back in pleasure.

"You like that?"

His tongue flicked over it again repeatedly, before biting roughly. His fingers pinched her other nipple sharply. *Ahhhhh.* Her head fell back, and she closed her lids, savouring the sensation of her hardened nipples being teased. As he licked, kissed, and sucked, she placed her fingers over her pulsing clit, massaging it tenderly, longing for him to release his rock-hard cock and enter her. Darion's tongue travelled down her body, licking her stomach, lapping up more alcohol. She arched her body further backwards, begging for him to go lower. He looked up at her, an animalistic hunger covering his face.

His tongue circled between her legs slowly, teasing her. She fisted his hair, pulling on it. His tongue movements became faster, desperate. A low cry escaped her throat. Darion definitely knew what he was doing. His skilful fingers assisted his tongue, making her body jerk from side to side, unable to take the intense pleasure, yet she begged him not to stop. His tongue licked her, then stopped, licked her, then stopped. The teasing was torturous.

Her head whipped to the side when she heard talking and laughing of people seated just outside the curtain. Excitement collided with fear. Adrenaline pumped through her blood.

She yanked his head between her legs, urging him to continue. She felt his smile on her hot skin. He continued to lick, nibble, and suck between her legs. The muscles in his broad shoulders clenched with each of his thrusts, turning her on. She ran her fingers along his shoulder blades, squeezing them, and digging her nails in as he met her sensitive spot.

She panted, her heart going wild. She lay there, rocking her hips against his face, completely aroused. Darion was feasting on her. He took her swollen and sensitive clit between his lips and sucked. She bit her hand, trying to keep her uncontrollable moans in, hoping that she wouldn't be heard. With his thumbs, he parted her, and drove his tongue in deep, and back out for several minutes, the vicious flicks of it making her quiver.

Oh my god. She gripped the sides of the sofa, panting. With each jab of his tongue, she felt delicious vibrations rush through her body, which made her thighs tremble.

Gabi quickly looked down. Darion watched her as his tongue worked inside her. She could feel her cheeks growing red, but she couldn't remove her focus from him. His fingers slid in, opening her, filling her. He pounded away, pushing deeper, harder, and faster. The smacking sound of his fingers against her wetness filled her ears. She felt her pelvis burning with each thrust, and she raised her hips so she could feel more of him. Her breathing grew heavier, the tingling sensation making her inner muscles tighten and grip his fingers.

"Gabi," he growled. "You taste so good…"

"Don't stop," she pleaded, feeling the pressure start to build as he pushed in a fourth finger. The curve of his fingers massaged her swollen G-spot as he slid in and out in a hurried rhythm. She rocked against his hand, bouncing her hips up and down, an agonised cry of ecstasy escaping her lips. *Fuuuuck!*

As he hammered into her endlessly, raw lust on his face, Gabi knew she was close. Her head thrashed from side to side as his mouth and fingers urged her toward climax. She flexed her hips, rocking toward the orgasm that was only seconds away. With a few final thrusts and strokes of his tongue, she surrendered. She took a deep breath, and another, and another, her insides tightening and quivering, and she groaned loudly. Hard spasms of pleasure rippled through her. Her whole body was shaking, her heart thundering. She was too choked with lust to speak.

After a few moments, she felt her body start to relax, her breathing and the thumping of her heart begin to slow. Darion sat up, looking smug, his pupils glittering with triumph. He slowly wiped his mouth with the back of his hand. Gabi shoved her hand in her hair, unable to believe how different Darion was from anyone she had ever met.

Darion joined her on the sofa by lying on top of her and resting his weight on his elbows. She could feel the button of his trousers on her clit, and wanted him inside her. He kissed her softly.

Her hands travelled down his bare back before they grabbed his firm ass, pulling his body into hers impatiently. She opened her legs invitingly, brushing herself against his thick erection, sending a divine shiver up her spine. He shook his head slowly, a devilish smile crossing his face. Gabi knew he was making her wait.

As Darion rested his head on her chest, she lay staring at the ceiling, gathering her thoughts. Guilt hit her like a sharp slap in the face as she pictured Lawrence. She never wanted to hurt him intentionally, but she couldn't keep away from Darion. If she wasn't daydreaming about him, she was picturing him as the character in every manuscript she read, and when it was erotica it was too much for her to handle. She knew that he'd exceed every book she ever read. He was unbelievably tempting. He only had to rest that smouldering green-eyed gaze on her, and she was no longer in control of her own emotions.

Coming to her senses, she sat up and pulled her bra on hastily. She stepped into her underwear, avoiding eye contact. A hot shower, where she could scrub herself clean, entered her mind. She was disgusted with herself, for how much she'd enjoyed it. For how much she wanted it again.

"Gabi." He grabbed her tightly, pulling her toward him. "If it's too soon, I'll give you time."

They began kissing again, their hands all over one another, exploring eagerly. Gabi pulled back, not wanting to get aroused again. Her head was all over the place. She slipped on her dress, and headed to the bathroom.

Standing before the mirror, she took in her reflection. She tied her hair up, letting a couple of curls hang loosely by her ears. *Time to go home and sleep next to Lawrence after what you've done.* Tears trickled down her cheeks, but she wiped them away.

Darion offered to take her home, which she accepted. They sat in silence as he drove carefully in the snow. The only sound came from the windscreen wipers, which were pushing away the falling snowflakes. She looked at Darion's serious expression, his clenched jaw, and his fingers that were drumming on the steering wheel. He was deep in thought again. She hated it. She wanted to know what he was thinking. Not knowing only added to her confusion.

"I don't want this to be it," he said softly.

She was quiet.

"But I don't think you should see me again." She watched as he swallowed. His eyes appeared sad, not matching his spiteful words.

She had an inkling as to why he was pushing her away. She felt pity for him, remembering what Mallory had told her. His former wife had cheated on him, so he couldn't trust women, couldn't get too close to them. Gabi wondered how he'd be able to trust her, knowing that she had betrayed her own fiancé.

"Why are you saying this?" Now she really felt dirty. Used.

"Look, I know you're not happy in your

relationship." He glanced at her. "I know you're seeking attention, love elsewhere. I can't give you that. It will end in tears with me, Gabi. You should keep away."

"Well, maybe I should find out for myself."

He switched the stereo on to block out further conversation. They both went silent again. Gabi wished he hadn't meant it. How could she not see him again after what had happened at the club? She was more attracted to him now than ever. Was she looking for love? Or was she just looking for a bit of fun, an escape?

Gabi sighed heavily as Lawrence appeared in her mind again. She began thinking of excuses to tell him. She couldn't hurt him this way and risk him finding out where she'd been. She'd have to say that she and Mallory had shared a bottle of wine, and she had planned to stop the night, but changed her mind. She'd have to lie and pretend that she had gotten a taxi home.

She quickly sent him a text explaining the situation. She received a text back instantly. Lawrence advised he was happy that she was coming home, he hadn't been able to sleep, and would see her soon. The guilty feelings flooded in.

She caught Darion glancing at her mobile, his eyes narrowing, his lips a thin line of jealousy. He grabbed hold of her hand and squeezed it tightly. When they were parked a few doors down from her house, he leant over and kissed her passionately. She felt herself growing hot and bothered. She scolded herself for getting so worked up over a kiss. The low grunting sounds that came from him indicated that she had the same effect on him.

"Stop, my neighbours might see," she said, panicked as his hand crept up her dress.

He grinned. "Even better."

She pushed him playfully.

"You looked so fucking sexy tonight," he drawled before putting a cigarette into his mouth and lighting it.

"What will we do?" she asked.

He blew out the smoke. "It all depends on you. Can you take a risk of getting hurt?"

"So, you'll definitely hurt me?" she snapped.

"I don't think I can give you what you want." He paused. "And I don't know if you can give me what I want."

"What's that, then?" She tucked a strand of hair behind her ear.

"Everything."

"Be more specific." Her mood shifted to irritation.

"Let's just say me and your fiancé are worlds apart. If you were to be with me, Gabi, you will not be the same person you are now. It might be a bad thing. I don't even know if I can be in a relationship." He shrugged. "I don't think I'm ready." He puffed hard on his cigarette. "Look, forget I said anything. Just stay away, okay?" He'd changed his mind, his jaw was tense again, his fists clenched.

"I'm not asking for a serious relationship now, we barely know one another." It was true. "I want to get to know you, that's all. See what happens."

"You're willing to take the risk of getting hurt?"

"It's too late now." She already liked him. She couldn't go back.

He lifted her head up by her chin and looked at her. His lips settled on hers again. A wave of lust washed through her loins. She had to force herself to pull away from him. She couldn't deny the strong chemistry between them. Maybe he was worth the risk of getting hurt.

"I'll see you soon?" She had made up her mind.

He half smiled, then licked his lips. "Don't say I didn't warn you."

Gabi stepped out into the dark night and walked toward her house. She felt like a naughty teenager sneaking home. She sighed as the happy expression slipped from her face. What was she getting herself into? If Darion only wanted a fling, would she be hurting afterwards? Maybe he'd get to know her better and fall for her? They could end up serious, couldn't they?

She remembered his words—he wanted 'everything.' *You will not be the same person you are now*. It was just the beginning. Regardless of what he wanted with her, she couldn't fight her curiosity. Gabi couldn't wait to see what he had in store for her, couldn't wait to unleash the vixen inside. She had begun an affair. She didn't even know who she was anymore; she already wasn't the same person.

One thing was for certain, though—when it came to Darion Milano, she was excited.

Chapter Twelve

Gabi couldn't stop the blush that warmed her cheeks when she received a sex-text from Darion. He detailed explicitly what he wanted to do to her. He was trying to persuade her to meet him.

"What's so amusing?" Lawrence walked in, the morning's newspaper clutched under his arm, a cup of coffee in hand.

She looked up. "Oh, just Mallory being her usual funny self."

"I'd hardly call her funny," he scoffed, sitting down.

Gabi placed her mobile in the pocket of her jeans and slipped on a pair of rubber gloves. She began scrubbing at the cutlery in the hot, soapy water. The radio was playing, which lifted her mood even higher than it already was. She couldn't stop replaying in her mind the image of her and Darion kissing, in the club, on the sofa. She was glad that her back was facing Lawrence; she knew her dreamy expression couldn't be missed.

She was certain that she had fancied Lawrence at

the start of their relationship, but had never felt this chemistry with anyone before. Just the thought of Darion turned her on, and the sight of him made her want to jump on him, wrap her arms around him, and kiss him passionately. She took a deep breath, trying to stop the butterflies from going crazy in her stomach.

Gabi had never thought that she would be in a situation in which she'd be betraying her fiancé. She had tried to explain again to Lawrence that it wasn't working, and maybe they should have a break, take some time apart. He had declined, stating he couldn't bear to be away from her. He had clung onto her like a small child, until he had fallen to sleep.

She had cried silently to herself. Lawrence had said that he would wait for her, whatever it took. Did that mean he was giving her permission to go out and find herself? See other people?

"So, honey, do you want to come fishing with me? The snow's stopped, and the sun's out a little." Lawrence closed the paper he had been reading and folded it in half.

Fishing. She couldn't think of anything more boring. She silently groaned to herself. No wonder she was feeling old. "Um, no thanks. I might have a bath, do a bit of reading."

"Come out. Bring your reading with you." He walked toward her, wrapping his arms around her waist. "Or I could take you shopping, or a restaurant, treat you." He was trying to make an effort. Guilt pierced her heart.

"No, I'm not up to it." He was obviously trying

to play happy families by ignoring everything that she had told him last night. She had to be consistent with her decision and not string him along. She couldn't let him think there was any hope.

"I think I might go and enroll for dance class," she told him, having made up her mind that she did need a new hobby. Something that she could feel passionate about.

Lawrence laughed, as if the idea were ludicrous. "Gabi, come on, you're not fifteen anymore."

There it was again—the negative remarks that wore down her confidence. Her shoulders sagged as she felt herself deflate. Maybe it was a stupid idea.

Lawrence grabbed his coat. "I'll see you later?"

She nodded. "Have a good time."

When the front door closed behind him, she focused on the cleaning. She allowed music to play in the background to perk her up a little. An hour later, when she had completed the washing and wiping of kitchen surfaces, she made her way to the bathroom. She was soon lying in hot water, bubbles surrounding her. The sweet smell of Jo Malone oils, and the scent from the candles she had lit, filled her nostrils. Gabi allowed every muscle in her body to relax, sinking her head in the water and swirling her hair around. The sound of her mobile bleeping caused her to sit upright. She wiped the soap from her face and quickly dried her hands on the nearby towel. Opening her text messages, she saw that it was from Darion. He asked if it was safe to call her. She responded that it was.

"Hey," he said softly when she answered on the first ring.

"Hi." She grinned.

"What you doing?"

"I'm in the bath."

"Nice." He paused. "How about we video chat?" His soft, sexy voice was enough to persuade her.

"Okay."

She could now see him on the screen of her phone, sitting in his office. His brows shot up as he saw that she really was in the bath. A slow, lazy grin surfaced on his face.

"God, Gabi," he moaned in agonised ecstasy. "You have to let me see."

She let out a laugh, but felt her confidence swell. "Impatient, are we? Can't you wait until the weekend?" she teased.

"No, I definitely can't."

She lowered the camera and allowed him to view her smooth, naked, wet body. She heard him suck in a deep breath.

"You're amazing. Play with yourself, baby," he said in a low, husky tone. "Please."

"No." She giggled coyly.

"C'mon, Gabi, I've seen it all before."

He had a point. She bit her lip, unsure.

"Gabi, you *never* have to feel shy around me. Remember that."

She positioned the mobile over her body, holding it steadily with one hand. Her other hand slid down her stomach slowly. She paused for a second, looking at the screen. Darion's tongue was tracing along his bottom lip.

Settling her hand between her legs, she stroked her sensitive clit repeatedly, letting out a soft moan.

As she rubbed her fingers round in circles, a needy ache shook through her body.

Darion groaned. Gabi watched as he positioned the camera over his crotch, his hand vanishing under his boxers, the trousers above which were unbuttoned. She could see that he had gripped his hard cock firmly, the fast movements visible through the material. Gabi sighed in pleasure. The feel of her fingers, and the sight of him touching himself, aroused her.

"You're so fucking sexy, darlin'," he growled. "That's it, keep playing…"

"I wish it was you touching me," she said breathlessly.

He pursed his lips, swallowing. "I wish it was me."

As she pressed and rubbed against her palm, her inner muscles squeezed as wave after wave of pleasure shot through her. Her thighs began to tremble slightly.

"I'm close," she panted, feeling the pressure start to build.

"Don't come." He let out a frustrated growl. "I wanna make you come. I'll be there soon."

"What?" Her mouth dropped open. "You can't. What if Lawrence comes back early?"

"It's a risk I'm willing to take." She saw the seriousness of his expression as the mobile was turned back on his face. "I'll be there soon."

Before she could explain that it wasn't a good idea, the screen went black as he ended the call. Gabi attempted to call him back, but she received his voicemail. Dropping her mobile to the carpeted floor, she sighed. She wanted to see him, of course she did. Before she made herself think of all the reasons why it was wrong, she resumed to washing her hair.

She massaged shampoo in, rinsed it out, and followed it with conditioner. She couldn't believe how attractive Darion made her feel. Just by seeing her, he couldn't stay away from her. She hoped and prayed that he would *always* look at her that way, for however long their fling lasted.

Dipping her head under the water a final time, she then climbed out of the bath. She dried and wrapped the silk red robe around herself, and made her way into the bedroom. There was no point in dressing, she was sure the robe would soon be off. She did however apply a little make-up, and did a quick blast with the hair-dryer.

Half an hour passed, and she was lying on her bed, waiting for him. She had had to switch on the television in an attempt to ignore her nervous feelings. She tried her hardest to concentrate, but it was difficult knowing he would be in her house soon, *their* house.

The doorbell startled her. She raced down the stairs excitedly and opened it to find Mallory. Her heart sank, and her face fell. Nonetheless, she invited her friend in. Usually she didn't mind Mallory's or Suzie's unexpected visits. Thankfully, Mallory hadn't noticed her disappointment. She led her into the kitchen to prepare coffee.

"I was passing through and thought I'd pop in." Mallory pulled a designer box out of a bag. "You like my new boots?" She held up a black, fringed boot with red soles—Louboutin.

"They're beautiful." Gabi took it from her, examining it. "I have to borrow these some time."

"No probs." Mallory beamed. "Not before me, though. Steve's taking me out Saturday night."

"Oh, anywhere special?"

She nodded. "Spa hotel…pool, jacuzzi, room service, and a bit of something else." She laughed.

"That should be nice." Gabi poured the hot water into a cup and stirred it quickly. Darion would be there soon, and she had no idea what to do. She handed the coffee to Mallory.

"So what's new with you?"

Gabi sat down and hung her head in her hands. "I tried to break up with Lawrence."

"What?" Her mouth fell open in genuine shock. She clearly never thought she would see the day. "And?"

"He won't accept it. I don't know what to do."

"Do you really want out of this?" The atmosphere grew tense, and Mallory shifted in her seat. "Was it my comments and jokes? I'm so sorry, Gabi, I didn't mean to—"

"It's not you," Gabi said, cutting her friend off. "You know it hasn't been great for a while, I've been kidding myself."

"Well, what will you do?"

Gabi shrugged. "What can I do?"

Mallory reached across the table to squeeze her hand. "You just do whatever makes you happy. I'm here for you, whatever your decision."

"Thanks, Mal. I appreciate it." She gulped back her coffee unsure of what else to say.

The doorbell rang half an hour later. She racked her brain, trying to think of excuses. Could she turn him away after he had driven so far? She stood up, her legs shaky.

"That must be the man about the wardrobes," she lied quickly. "Lawrence wants them changing. He's coming to measure up, and talk through designs. Would you mind excusing me for five minutes, Mal?"

"Absolutely not. You take your time."

Gabi closed the kitchen door behind her. She felt awful for lying to her friend, but what she was doing was unacceptable, and wrong. She knew Mallory was easygoing, but this was taking it too far. She couldn't expect her friend to understand an affair.

She pulled the door open. There he was, leaning against the door frame, a huge smile spread across his face. He was wearing casual navy jeans and a long-sleeved black top. He looked as sexy as ever. His chin-length hair was smoothed back, his eyes sparkling in the sunlight. As much as she wanted to throw her arms around his neck and kiss him until she was breathless, she ushered him in, advising him to be quiet.

"I have company," she whispered.

She led him up the stairs and into her bedroom. As soon as she pushed the door shut, he pulled her around to face him, and began kissing her hard, passionately, like he hadn't seen her in months. She responded. It had only been a day, yet she had missed him. He removed her gown in an instant.

"Gabi…" He had that weak, vulnerable look

again, a slight sadness in his usually seductive eyes. "Are you sure you wanna do this?" His voice shook.

"Yes." She attacked his clothes, taking each one off, throwing them to the floor, all while kissing him.

He stood before her, naked. Gabi sat on the bed and took in his full physique for the first time. She had to clamp her lips together to hold in the impressed laugh that was threatening to break free. His flat abs, his broad shoulders, his muscles in all their glory, made her stomach do somersaults. And then she glanced down at his cock and had to fight the urge to let out a gasp. It was long, thick, and erect. Gabi took in a quick breath, anticipation spreading through her. Darkness had now taken over his face, as it held that same predatory stare. Possessed. Hungry. He knelt over her, bringing his mouth down on hers, opening her lips to allow his tongue to slip in and explore greedily.

"Gabi!" Mallory's voice shot up the stairs. "Can I use the bathroom?"

She pulled back, breathless. "Erm, yeah," she shouted back.

"Great. I need to touch up my make-up, and sort out this hair of mine."

She froze when she heard Mallory's footsteps creak the stairs. She hoped she wouldn't pop by the bedroom. Darion looked up at her, waiting for instructions.

"Yes, I'd like solid oak doors for the wardrobe," she said, loud enough for her friend to hear.

Darion raised a brow questioningly.

Gabi shook her head, as if to dismiss it.

"Would you like those doors mirrored, ma'am?" Darion teased. "So you can watch me fuck you in them?" His breath was low and hot on her neck.

She giggled.

She heard the bathroom door close. He began kissing her firmly again. What was with Darion and almost getting caught? He lowered his head to her chest, and took her breast in his mouth, sucking her hard nipple frantically, cupping the other one with his hand. Gabi moaned softly. She threw her head back, enjoying the sensation.

He began biting her nipple gently, and then he lowered the soft bites down her body. She squirmed at his every touch. He massaged between her legs, making her wet. She gasped as he parted her, and slowly traced a finger up and down her opening. She heard him shuffle down the bed, and tensed when she felt the wet tip of his tongue flicking her clit.

"Darion," she hissed, squirming in protest.

"Sssshh…" he silenced her.

She grabbed a pillow, burying her face in it, not trusting herself to keep silent. He cupped her bottom mercilessly to adjust her angle. His tongue teased her clit, flicking over it repeatedly with fast, firm strokes. Gabi's breathing became heavy, and she shivered at the warm rush of his breath. The wetness of his tongue on her skin sent her senses reeling. He opened her further, and plunged in with the tip, jabbing at her, satisfied grunts escaping his lips. She wriggled and moaned incoherently into the pillow, as he sucked and licked ferociously. She fisted the bed sheets, grinded her hips, rubbing her pelvis against his sharp stubble, in desperate need to be filled. *I want you now, Darion Milano!* His tantalising flicks drove her crazy. He pulled back for a second, and bit into her thigh, causing her to yelp loudly. She prayed Mallory didn't hear. He quietly chuckled.

"Don't you dare think about coming," he said hoarsely, rolling her onto her front in one quick movement.

His lips met her waist, soft tender kisses travelling up her spine. When his weight was on top of her, and his mouth was nuzzling the back of her neck, without warning, he thrust himself into her. She buried her head deep into the cushion to muffle her moans. *Fuck!* His thickness filled her snugly.

The bathroom door opened, and Gabi stilled again. She hoped that Darion would stop, but he continued to thrust in and out, fast and hard, not caring if they got caught. His fingers grabbed her hair roughly. She gripped onto the edge of the mattress, her body rocking into it.

"Gabi?"

"Yes?" Her voice came out a low moan.

"I'm going to head off. I'll catch you soon, okay?"

"Okay," she managed to respond.

"Bye, sweetie."

She heard Mallory's footsteps head down the stairs. As soon as the front door closed, Darion slammed into her with excessive force, causing her to scream out in pleasure. He picked up his pace, hitting into her faster and faster. She was relieved that she no longer had to be quiet; it was proving to be an impossible task. Darion sat up, and gripping her by the waist, he lifted her behind higher in the air so he could have deeper access. Before long, she told him she was going to climax. She couldn't take anymore.

"Not yet," he told her, withdrawing. He flipped her onto her back.

His hungry gaze burned into her, his chest moving up and down from his heavy panting. He slowly licked his lips before he stood up, towering over her. She looked at him, waiting for his next movement, writhing in frustration, desperate to feel him inside her again. She hated that he was leaving her hanging. He pulled her up by the hand.

When she was on her feet, he picked her up, backed her against the bedroom door, and entered her again. She was impressed by how strong he was, his bulging arms supporting her weight. She wrapped her legs tighter around his waist, her arms around his neck. He continued to pleasure her, bouncing her up and down. He groaned appreciatively at every single thrust. Each time she dropped onto his hard length, she threw her head back in ecstasy.

"Darion…" she cried out breathlessly. "You feel so good." She took his tongue in her mouth, and grabbed a fistful of his hair.

"Gabriella Woods," he panted, "you haven't seen anything yet, trust me."

Gabi brought her head up to look at him. She shyly wanted to look away, but didn't. She couldn't believe how much Darion pleasured her, how good he felt, how compatible they seemed to be. Her lips trembled with the noises that escaped. He continued to thrust faster, eager to bring her to an orgasm, simultaneously cupping her breasts, kneading her tender nipples. When he brought his tongue down to flicker over them, she bit her lip to contain her moans. Gabi had waited so long for this, and she knew he felt the same.

"Mmm…" He took a breast into his mouth, sucking it gently. "You're fucking beautiful, Gabi. Do you know that?"

She gripped onto his shoulders to rock her hips onto him even faster, to feel him as deeply as possible. The length of him elicited a sharp pain, but mixed with pleasure, it felt delicious. Her face flushed with lust. Gabi felt herself tighten around him, the tension building in her body. By the anguished expression on Darion's face, she knew that he was close too.

They kept their stares locked until they climaxed loudly, their bodies shuddering forcefully, the release as good as they'd imagined. Gabi clung to him tighter, her tense body becoming limp. Darion didn't move or withdraw for a few seconds. He leant against her, her body pressed firmly against the door. He was out of breath, as was she. The feel of his naked skin against hers made her burn with desire. She could see his perfectly shaped ass in the mirror behind him, his strong thighs, and long lean legs. He really was the whole package.

She sucked in a deep breath and wiped her forehead with the back of her hand. Her body was drenched in sweat. She could smell him all over her. She loved it. She kissed him on the lips, making him respond with soft moans in between each kiss. She wanted him again. With his hands on her waist, he lifted her up into the air so that she was looking down at him. The adrenaline pumped through her veins. He slowly lowered her until she was back on her feet, and pulled her into him so he could plant a kiss on her forehead.

When she had dressed in the gown and him, still naked, they lay on the bed together, side by side. She felt herself relax as he stroked her hair. She rested her head on his chest, closing her lids. She could hear the beating of his heart. She felt like she could lay in his arms forever.

"I wish I could wake up next to you," she murmured dreamily, her never-ending smile making her cheeks ache.

"Well, that's not gonna happen, is it?" She couldn't make out if it was jealousy, sadness, or fear that made him sit up. "I better go."

"Not yet," she pleaded.

"I need to go. Your fiancé will be back soon. I don't wanna get you into any trouble." He was on his feet, getting dressed. "Come to the club soon, okay?"

She nodded. "I will."

When he was dressed, he stood, staring at her intently. His finger stroked his bottom lip as he appeared deep in thought. She wished she could read his mind.

"What is it?"

"Nothing." He blinked, as though she had interrupted what was in his head. "You take care, Gabi."

She led him down the stairs to the front door. He turned to face her. Both his hands cupped her chin as he tilted her head up to kiss him, her tongue massaged his. Gabi didn't want Darion to go, but knew he had to. She felt his erection pressing against her leg, and wanted him then and there, in the hallway. Darion disentangled himself from her.

"See ya, Gabi."

She waved and watched him climb into his car. He looked back through the windscreen and blew her a kiss. She closed the door, and went back to her bedroom, a grin forming as she felt all giddy. She quickly removed the rumpled sheets, pulled clean sheets from the drawer, and changed the bed. The smell of him lingered in the room. She breathed it in. Stealing a glance at the door, she couldn't believe that they had just had sex against it. She erased the thoughts, trying not to reminisce about the fact that she had just cheated on Lawrence.

After she had a shower, she lay in bed, with a reality show playing on TV. She was unable to concentrate on it, feeling ashamed, guilty, and emotional again. She needed to pull herself together, and quick.

Twenty minutes passed before she heard Lawrence's key in the door. She climbed under the covers and pretended to be asleep. She couldn't face him or make small talk after what had happened. Her eyes were tightly shut when she heard him walk into the bedroom. He paused for a moment before pulling the covers up, and properly tucking her in, ensuring that she was warm. When the door closed after him, she focused on the white wall for what seemed like an eternity.

Darion had been right. Once he'd had her, he knew she'd come back.

Chapter Thirteen

Darion

Darion's fingers tightened on the steering wheel as he pressed his foot further down on the accelerator. He inhaled the cold air seeping through the window, and tilted his head back, keeping his stare fixed on the road. Surely he didn't *like* her, did he? He slapped the dashboard in frustration. He had *hated* women for years, judged them all the same. He couldn't trust women. Shouldn't. Not after Eva. He had done absolutely everything for her, supported her, cared for her, and gave her everything she wanted. After her betrayal, he had slept with as many women as possible, nothing but no-strings-attached sex, no emotions involved on his part, no heartbreak. It suited him just fine.

Forget Gabi. He couldn't trust her; here she was, cheating on her fiancé. Was it different with her, though? Did her fiancé treat her badly? He didn't know her circumstances, or what her relationship was like. For some reason, he sensed there was more to it.

He rubbed his hand up and down his face, distressed. Darion hated himself for being so attracted to her. If he didn't ever discuss his feelings with her, kept her at arm's length, never let himself get attached, then surely he'd be okay. He could handle that.

But fucking hell, he hated himself for playing part in ruining a relationship. Then again, *he* was single. *She* was ruining it. But then again, it had been him who had instigated it. He had rung her. He had chased her and seduced her until she caved in. He had gotten what he wanted.

He felt sick. He was no better than the man that had been sleeping with his ex-wife behind *his* back. Gabi's fiancé would be hurt in all of this, just as he had been. Could he really stay away from her, though? He wasn't sure whether he wanted to continue seeing her to have as much fun as he possibly could, or whether he was seeking something more, which was something he had had no intention of doing.

He decided to take it one day at a time.

***

Gabi

Gabi was relieved that she had two weeks' annual leave from work. Normally she'd find a room in the house to redecorate, completely change the colour scheme and furniture until she was satisfied for another year or so. She decided against it this time. She wasn't planning on being in the house forever. The sooner she and Lawrence were over, and the sooner he accepted it, the better. She knew she would have to make some tough decisions. She wasn't afraid of renting an apartment, and she wasn't afraid of living alone. But what if leaving Lawrence turned out to be the worst decision she had ever made?

She took a sip of her tea, and then lay on the couch, staring absentmindedly at the television before her. She didn't know what to do with her two weeks off. Mallory and her other friends were working throughout the day, and she had already watched so much daytime television she was sick of it. She was tempted to call Darion, see if she could spend some time with him without Lawrence suspecting anything. She looked at the mobile in her hand and decided against it. *Play it cool, let him call you.* As if by telepathic communication, his name appeared on the screen as it rang. She grinned.

"Hello." She kept her tone casual.

"What are you up to, Gabi?"

"Watching TV, you?"

"Interviewing some dancers for the club."

"You need more dancers?" She felt a stab of jealousy. He had slept with most of them, would he now be sleeping with more?

"We need some fresh faces in here, keep the customers sweet. Plus, I've had a girl leave, so I'm one down."

"Oh right." Would it be strictly business? Gabi opened her mouth to comment, but thought better of it. It wasn't like she was his girlfriend. They weren't official. "Well." She remained calm. "I'm glad business is going well."

"Me too," he agreed.

There was an uncomfortable pause. She wanted to ask him when they could meet again. She hoped he'd bring it up.

"Right." He sighed. "I better get back to these auditions."

Fuck it. If no serious relationship was forthcoming, she didn't need to put on a front, play it safe, play games, try and impress him. She could just take advantage and have fun whilst she could. "Darion?"

"Yeah?"

"I've got two weeks off work, if you fancy doing something sometime?"

Another pause, then, "I'm free on Thursday?"

"Great, I'll come to you?"

"Sure."

"Okay. Well, bye then."

"See ya."

She stuffed her mobile in the pocket of her nightgown and rolled onto her side. She felt stupid getting involved with him. She was already getting jealous. She knew it was a possibility that he could end up hurting her. He had been right to warn her. Yet every time his face popped into her mind, she couldn't stop from smiling. He was gorgeous, and all she wanted to do was see him, kiss him, lay with him, and get to know the real him. Many women were attracted to bad boys that they believed they could tame, enjoyed a challenge, and she was no different. She would have her fun, be the perfect friend-with-benefits, not stress him in any way, and see what happened. She felt ridiculous for willingly allowing a man to use her, yet she trusted herself. Surely she could handle him.

When 9 p.m. came around, Lawrence returned home. Gabi reheated his dinner, and had it on the table for him in minutes. He was in a foul mood, and smelt of alcohol. She hated it when he was like this. She knew better than to question him and make matters worse. Sitting opposite one another whilst Gabi savoured every mouthful of her food, Lawrence wolfed his down quickly, eager to leave the table. Afterwards, Gabi gathered the plates to wash. She hated feeling like she was walking on eggshells. Had he suspected something? She was desperate to pry further, but didn't want to put the thought in his mind.

"I'm going to bed," he growled, exiting the room.

"Are you okay?"

"Yes, Gabi. Nothing I can't handle," he snapped.

"Lawrence, talk to me," she pleaded.

"I'm not in the mood."

"You're never in the mood," she screamed after him.

She watched as he took off for the stairs, and then she began scrubbing the plates furiously. *Asshole*. He never wanted to talk. She could bet money on that they'd be one of those couples in their old age, sitting in a restaurant with nothing to say to one another, their souls dead, plodding along through life. She couldn't wait to get out of the house soon, and relax in the company of a laid back

Darion.

Chapter Fourteen

Gabi raced to the bathroom and frantically searched for her red Chanel lipstick. Rummaging through cosmetic bags, she eventually found it, and returned to the stool at her dressing table. Lawrence was still criticising her here and there, and trying to dictate how she lived her life: the way she dressed, the so-called 'unsuitable friends' she had, such as Mallory, and how she indulged in a glass of wine a few evenings a week to de-stress. *Hypocritical, much?* He was still returning home at stupid o'clock, and taking his bad moods out on her. Lawrence promising to change had obviously all been lies. Well, she'd thought as much until he'd sent her a text message, promising to make it up to her, and take her to a fancy restaurant that night.

She checked the time on her mobile. He'd be parked outside in a matter of minutes. Regardless of everything that had happened between them, Gabi was willing to give Lawrence the benefit of the doubt, to properly discuss the relationship with him. How could she not, after seven years together? She wasn't entirely optimistic that talking would change much, but she felt that she owed it to him.

Raking her fingers through her silky waves, Gabi decided she was happy with the way she looked. Her red bodycon dress revealed her slim waist, slightly curvaceous hips, and tanned legs. She hooked her Louboutin heels onto her feet, grabbed her handbag, and descended the stairs.

She waited for him by the window, but after five minutes passed, she went and dropped onto the couch. It was another ten minutes before she attempted to call him.

"Hi, you've reached Lawrence Lovell's voicemail. If you leave a message, I will return to you as soon as possible."

Annoyance creeping over her, she tapped a text message with her perfectly manicured fingers.

Gabi: Lawrence, where are you?

When fifteen minutes passed, she poured herself a glass of lemonade, and called him again. His mobile was still switched off. Surely he wouldn't stand her up? When she'd finished her drink, she felt a pain slice through her heart when she saw that the clock now showed Lawrence was half an hour late. He wasn't coming. He made her feel rejected, like always. When he came home late from work drunk and argumentative, or stood her up, usually uncontrollable sobs followed, as she questioned herself, whether she was good enough, pretty enough, smart enough. All that was left was anger building up inside of her. How stupid had she been to think that Lawrence cared more about the relationship than he cared about himself, and his own needs. Throwing her hands up in exasperation, she grabbed her car keys and decided to visit Mallory, the only person who understood her.

***

"Here, sweetie." Mallory handed her a cup of steaming tea. "Now, tell me, what's happened?"

"I'm fucking leaving him, Mal. For good." Gabi sat up and took the cup from her.

"Why?"

"Apart from the fact that I don't enjoy being around him? He's stood me up. He promised to take me for dinner. I'm so stupid. I knew not to trust him."

"He hasn't called to cancel or anything?"

Gabi shook her head. She felt the anger drain out of her, leaving her insides empty and hollow. It was the final straw. She wasn't putting up with his crap and false promises any longer.

Mallory huffed. "What will you do?"

"It's over, Mal. It has to be. Nothing will ever change." She cradled her cup and took a sip.

"Perhaps you should move out."

"Me, move out? Why me? It's *our* house. We both pay the mortgage."

"I know, Gab, but you can't leave him *and* take away his home." Mallory sat next to her. "I know he's been an asshole, but you want to do this as amicably as possible."

"Maybe."

"Are you sure that this is what you want?"

"Yes, Mal. I'm more certain now than ever."

"It's not because of that Darion guy, is it?"

Gabi had filled Mallory in briefly on the way to her friend's house, regarding her and Darion's liaison.

"No," she said, and meant it.

"So, how serious is it with you and Darion? Is it just a rebound?"

She shrugged a shoulder. "I've seen him a few times."

"Please tell me you're not falling for him, Gabi, it's a dangerous game."

"I'm not," she exclaimed. "He's just a bit of fun." Gabi knew she sounded uncertain.

"Can you have 'just fun'?" Mallory eyed her curiously.

Gabi nodded.

"Gab, I know you. You're gonna end up falling for this guy."

"I won't."

"You will. I'm worried about you. I don't know what his intentions are."

"I'll be fine. He makes me feel alive, Mal. My confidence has rockcted. Hc makcs mc do things that I wouldn't usually do."

"Like what?"

"I don't know." She shrugged. "I lose all of my inhibitions. I'm happy, excited, daring around him. He brings out this craziness in me." Her face lit up, the remnants of her anger diminishing. "As soon as I leave him, I miss him. It's strange. I can't seem to keep away from him, even though I know he may be bad for me."

"Just finish things with Lawrence first, then have as much fun as you like."

"I need to. I can't go on like this." Gabi crossed her legs, making herself more comfortable on the sofa. "So, how's Steve?"

"He's great." Mallory gave her a lopsided grin. "I love him just that bit more each day."

"I always wanted that with Lawrence. I did try, Mal, for so long." She wiped away a tear that rolled down her cheek.

"I know, honey." Mallory pulled her into an embrace, causing Gabi to crumple into sobs. "You weren't compatible, Gab." Her friend stroked her back gently. "If you married Lawrence, you'd probably end up feeling lonely and trapped. You want to live a little, have fun. You're still young, for fuck's sake."

Gabi pulled away and dabbed at her face with her sleeve.

"Just make sure you don't get attached to Darion." Mallory squeezed her hand. "I don't want to see you upset, crying over another man."

She nodded vehemently.

"If you need to crash here for a month or two, the guest room is yours."

"Thanks, Mal. I might need to take you up on that offer."

***

Gabi knew that she had to break it off with Lawrence. He'd have to accept that it was over.

132

When she returned home at 11 p.m. and there was still no sign of him, the compassion she once had for him vanished. Where was he, especially this late? She refused to believe that he was stuck in the office, slaving away at work. No chance. She had that sickening feeling in her stomach again that something wasn't right, although she was no angel. She didn't have a leg to stand on, as she'd betrayed him with Darion. There was only so much poor treatment a woman could take before she searched for love and attention elsewhere. Lawrence had practically shoved her into Darion's arms.

She'd made up her mind to take Mallory's offer and crash in her friend's spare room until she found an apartment. Gabi grabbed her Louis Vuitton suitcase before she lost her courage, and began packing her favourite clothes and the essentials she'd need. She would collect the rest of her stuff another time.

As she was shoving her shoes into it, she glanced at the clock. 11:30 p.m. She stilled when she heard the front door slam. She sighed heavily and zipped up the case. *Here goes.*

"Gabi?"

"What?" she said through gritted teeth.

"What are you doing?" he asked as he stood in the doorway.

"I'm sorry, Lawrence." She stood up. "I can't drag this out any longer. I'm leaving."

"What?" he yelled. "It's because I didn't take you out?"

"Nope." She shook her head. "That's just the icing on the cake." She crossed her arms across her chest, her lips in a thin line.

"I'll take you out tomorrow. Something came up."

"What came up, Lawrence?" she screamed, charging toward him, not considering the ramifications of her actions. "Where were you this time?" Her voice was pure steel.

"At work…"

She laughed coldly. "Get a new excuse. I can smell the alcohol on your breath!" She returned to her suitcase and picked it up. "You know, I didn't want it to end this way. I cared for you, Lawrence. I wanted to be civil about it, perhaps even remain friends afterwards, but why bother?"

"So, this is it then?"

She nodded.

"I can't believe you're really doing this." Hurt and anger flashed on his face, and he tilted his head back, looking up at the ceiling. "Don't go."

"I have to." She tried to nudge past him.

"Gabi," he bellowed, frightening her. Yanking the suitcase from her, he threw it across the room. "Let's talk about this."

"Nothing you can say will change my mind." She strode toward the suitcase and picked it up. "I'm not living this life anymore. Nothing will ever change, and we both know it," she screamed.

"You can't just walk out of here." His face flushed red.

"Lawrence, I can, and I am."

He pushed her forcefully, causing her to drop the case and land on the bed with a thud. "You can't do this, Gabi. You can't leave me."

"Lawrence." She sat up. "*Move* out of the way."

He towered over her. "Was I so bad?" he cried out. "Did I treat you that bad, Gabi?"

"No, but you didn't treat me that good either," she spat. She scrambled to her feet. "You pushed me away, and now it's too late." Tears stung her lower lids, making her feel weak and pathetic.

"You'll regret this, Gabi."

"Is that a threat?" Anger warmed her cheeks.

"No. But you're making the wrong decision."

"It's a risk I'm willing to take." She couldn't possibly be any less happy. She took hold of her case again. "I'm doing what I think is right. We both deserve better. You'll thank me in the future." She hoped.

She made her way down the stairs, but he followed her.

Gabi opened the front door and headed for her car. Unlocking the boot, she placed the suitcase inside, and glanced at Lawrence one final time. She heard the sound of his voice echoing her name. When she got into the car, his voice was blocked out. She only made it around the corner when she had to pull over and kill the engine.

She buried her face in her hands, crying hysterically. Even though she partly hated him, she still felt *something* for him. She hoped he would be okay. She hoped that he would find someone that was perfect for him, someone who could be the woman he wanted. *He'll be fine.* But would she be okay?

She looked up at the rain that was now hitting the windscreen and wiped her damp cheeks. With a heartfelt sigh, she started the engine and drove away from Lawrence and her old life. It was time to finally and properly move forward.

Chapter Fifteen

Gabi woke up, luxuriating in the soft silk sheets wrapped around her body. She stretched her limbs, and slowly sat up. Although she hadn't expected to, she'd slept like a baby. She couldn't remember the last time that she had slept so well. The room was bright from the sun's rays shining through the windows. Rather than feeling upset, wanting to mope around and eat junk food, she felt fine. She was unsure whether she was in shock. Maybe the breakup hadn't hit her yet. She was certain of one thing, though—the guilty feelings would never go away. She knew she'd find herself worrying about Lawrence from time to time.

She got out of bed and pulled the curtain aside. Gabi stared out at the blue sky, and noticed that the snow was starting to melt. She wondered what to do with her day. Checking her mobile, she noticed she had several missed calls from Lawrence. Her lips thinned. No way was she calling him back, allowing him to kill her mood. Communication would just make it harder for them both. She believed the motto that said sometimes, in life, you had to be cruel to be kind.

Her mobile bleeped in her hand as a message came through. It was Darion asking if she was still on for meeting later. She hesitated for a moment, and then agreed. In all honesty, she couldn't wait to see him. A hug seemed extremely appealing. She hoped Darion would assure her that everything would be okay.

She was relieved that they didn't have to sneak around anymore, hiding what they had, making up lies, and feeling bad about the whole dalliance. Perhaps now she could properly enjoy it for what it was.

After she'd dressed, Gabi drove into town, and headed straight for the dance studio. She wanted to enrol before she ended up changing her mind. She used to rehearse at The Royal Dance Academy when she was a teenager. She knew that they also had adult programmes.

Once inside, she headed for the reception area, where she scanned the different types of classes—ballet, jazz, hip-hop. The classes were for the duration of one hour, once a week.

"Can I help you?" the receptionist asked, beaming.

"I'd like to enrol for the hip-hop dance classes, please."

"Sure. You have the option to pay per lesson, monthly, or annually."

"Erm…" She paused for a moment to think. "I think I'll pay per lesson."

"Great. Can you fill in this form, please?"

Gabi took the form from her. Chatter and laughter behind her caused her to look around. A few men and women about her age were leaving the studio, brimming with excitement, dressed in appropriate dance attire. Gabi felt her spirits lift. She couldn't wait to start dancing again.

After she'd completed the forms, she drove to her old house to collect some more belongings. Lawrence was at work, as usual. As she stuffed her suitcase full of clothes, a pink, shiny bag caught her attention. She took it out and sat cross-legged on the floor. It was the Valentine's Day treat that had never been put to use. She pulled the black ribbon open and emptied the contents. She examined the back of a DVD. It was erotica for couples, just a little bit of nudity, nothing too full on. She tossed it back into the wardrobe.

She picked up the vibrator that was still in its plastic packaging, and placed it into her case along with the massage oils, and flavoured lubes. She was left with the sexy underwear. She picked up the silk black bra, and ran her fingers across the smooth material. She then picked up the miniscule thong and decided to try them on.

When she was dressed in the underwear, she stared at her reflection in the mirror. Mallory had been shopping with her that day and suggested that she try it on. It made her feel sexy. She had thought that Lawrence would've felt the same, but he'd said that it looked cheap. *Oh well, let's see what Darion makes of it.* She slipped into a plain, black dress.

After she'd straightened her hair to perfection, she applied seductive make-up consisting of grey, smoky eyes, and peach coloured lips. The ringing of her mobile startled her. Her phone screen displayed a call from a private number.

"Hello." She held it against her ear.

"Gabi," she heard a husky drawl.

"Hi, Darion." She felt a rush of excitement.

"Where are you?"

"I'm coming now. I just joined a dance class," she said brightly.

"That's great, Gabi," he praised. "I bet you'll look unreal in those tight dance leggings."

She laughed. Darion's enthusiasm for her decision cheered her up, another reason why he was so different from Lawrence. He always spurred her on, supported her, and wanted her to be the best she could be.

"Okay…well, I'll be there soon."

"Good. I'm taking you out somewhere."

"Really?" Her brows shot up. "Where?"

"You'll have to wait and see."

She laughed softly. "Okay."

She loaded her case with a few more things, and carried it to the car. She locked it away in the boot, and set off toward The Black Door.

When she was at the club an hour later, there was no sign of Darion. There were a few regulars at the bar occupying some of the tables, but it was still early, not even midday. She was relieved to see a new barmaid serving the customers. She couldn't face seeing Lexi, Marnie, or Gina. She didn't want anybody knowing about her and Darion. For now.

Gabi sat on a stool and waited for the glass of wine that she had ordered. As she handed a ten pound note to the barmaid, she shook her head, and stated that Darion had been expecting her, that the drink was free of charge. Gabi took a large swig. Where was he? As she uncrossed her legs, she felt a cold breeze up her skirt, and rather than feeling uncomfortable, she felt excited. She couldn't wait until Darion got his hands on her.

"Gabi." The barmaid placed a phone back onto the base. "Darion wants you in his office."

"Okay." Gabi stood up, taking her glass of wine, and walked through the door behind the bar.

She slowly sauntered down the corridor, the sound of her heels on the tiles reverberating. She felt nervous again. *Pull yourself together, this is just a casual relationship that will probably last no longer than a couple of weeks.* She knocked gently on the door. No response. Gabi pushed the door open slightly, and walked in. It was empty. She sighed heavily, and sat on the sofa, downing more of her wine. The nervousness had now evaporated as she was overcome with annoyance. She *hated* waiting around for people.

"Well, don't just sit there," she heard him say softly.

She looked at the leather chair, the back of it facing her. She saw cigarette smoke swirl around the top of it. She shook her head, smiling, and stood up. Darion spun around in the chair slowly. He was completely naked. He stared at her devilishly, a small smile etched across his face.

She threw her head back and laughed, her gaze sweeping over him, her pupils dilating. Gabi was impressed. "You certainly do love to surprise a girl."

He stood up and slowly walked toward her. Picking her up in one swift movement, he began kissing her hungrily. Gabi's fingers found her way through his hair, her body responding eagerly to his mouth. With her dress bunched up her thighs a little, she could feel the nakedness of his warm body against her achingly tender clit. Her heart slammed against her chest frantically. As his tongue slipped into her mouth, the tip of it circling hers, she longed to feel it between her legs. After a few moments of kissing frantically and soft moaning, he pushed her onto the sofa with force.

"Darion," the barmaid's voice came from the other side of the door. "Your clothes are dry now."

Darion unenthusiastically peeled himself away from Gabi and walked toward the door, poking his head around. He returned with a pile of neatly folded clothes. He had obviously slept in the club again. Gabi wondered why he didn't go home. She couldn't understand why he would want to sleep at the club. Then again, maybe he wasn't alone; maybe he didn't want to take the dancers to his apartment. Gabi ignored the niggling feeling that made her want to ask.

"Come here," she pleaded, as he started to dress.

"Patience, Gabi."

"I broke up with my fiancé," she blurted out.

He pinned her with a look. "I wasn't linked to your decision, was I?" Worry flickered across his face.

She shook her head. "I couldn't do it anymore. I haven't been happy for a long time."

Once fully clothed, he stepped toward her. Kneeling down, he grabbed her face. "If a man can't keep his woman satisfied, then another man will," his tone was firm.

"I guess that's where you come in."

"You're not wrong."

Gabi averted her gaze.

"Don't feel bad for doing what you had to do for you, Gabi."

She pursed her lips.

"C'mon, let's go."

Before he could stand, Gabi pulled him toward her again, kissing him, her tongue meeting his. She had waited for this, she didn't know if she could wait much longer. He pulled back with a groan as if doing so required effort.

"Where are we going?" She followed him out of the office.

"You'll see."

He grabbed a pair of black Armani sunglasses from the bar and put them on, followed by a knitted black hat, which covered his hair. *Can he get any sexier?* His naughty eyes were hidden, and only his full, sensuous lips, cheeky grin, and chiselled jaw, complete with stubble, were on show. Gabi tried to keep her face straight, to stop the smug smile that was threatening to show.

The sun shone brightly through the clouds that had gathered, even though rain was predicted. Gabi shielded her face from the light, and climbed into the car, the door of which Darion held open. She wondered where they were going.

After twenty minutes of driving, he parked into a

shopping mall. He assisted her out of the car, and snaked his arm around her waist, guiding her past several stores.

Puzzled, Gabi asked, "Why are we here?"

He turned to look at her, suddenly stopping in his tracks. His gaze lingered on her lips, as he smiled slowly and wickedly. "I'm putting some excitement in your life. How do you like the risk of getting caught?" There was a dangerous purr to his voice, which sent a shiver up her spine.

"What?" Embarrassed giggles choked her.

He grabbed her hand and led her through a department store. Gabi had to practically run to keep up with his hurried pace, which was headed toward the fitting rooms. He paused for a brief moment whilst the shop assistant vanished into the storeroom. As he shoved Gabi into a mirrored cubicle, anxiety and anticipation charged through her. She glanced up at Darion; his face was alight with excitement and mischief.

She could hear the sound of women gossiping, talking about clothes, celebrities, and other general chitchat whilst trying garments on. "What d'ya think of this?" she heard a girl ask, and the sound of a curtain being pulled back.

"Oh, I love that," another voice replied.

Undeterred by the sound of other people, Darion pushed Gabi against the mirror and began kissing her fiercely. Not wasting any time, he yanked her dress over her head, exposing her sexy underwear. Darion let out a soft groan, the appreciation apparent on his face. "Looks like you had a surprise for me."

He spun her around so that she was facing the mirror, his hand diving between her legs. Gabi parted them, instantly feeling moist and heated. She watched him in the mirror as he inserted a finger.

"You're soaking wet, Gabi," he whispered, opening her further with another finger. He thrust upwards gently, tortuously, in and out. Her head fell back, her body tingling, her breaths shallow. As his pace became faster, and another finger pushed inside her, she bit her thumb to stifle the cries as he pleasured her.

The voice of the shop assistant and the sound of hangers being collected terrified her. She couldn't bear to imagine how humiliating it'd be to get caught, like a pair of horny teenagers. She had never had sex in a public place before. Perhaps Darion would make her try *everything* she hadn't experienced before.

She felt a hot flush rise up her chest, and could feel the heat in her face. As he prodded deeply, it sent waves of delightful shivers through her body. Slowly easing his fingers out, he peeled her underwear off. Turning her to face him, Darion crouched down, and hooked her leg over his shoulder. His mouth then sealed over her clit, sucking on it, lashing it with his skilled tongue. Her core clenched, her body aching for more. His hands caressed her behind, gripping her cheeks with his nails roughly, pulling her into his face, onto his rough stubble. She glanced at the mirror, at her naked bottom half, at the stunning man on his knees feasting on her. Burying her fingers into his hair, she rocked her hips backwards and forwards, gasping at every lash of his tongue.

Guttural groans rose from his throat. She loved the sounds of appreciation that he made, that he enjoyed every bit of it, as did she.

He pulled back to put a finger in his mouth, and drenched it with dripping saliva. Resuming licking between her legs, Gabi tensed when she felt his wet finger enter her again. Her heart thudded. She caught her lip with her teeth, her face contorting in pleasure and pain as his pace got faster. As he drove in further, she found herself widening her legs. His tongue was still working her clit, dipping in and out. She grimaced, placing her palms on the wall for support, feeling slightly light-headed, her senses reeling.

"Relax," he said in a sultry tone, before silencing himself between her legs again.

They heard movement outside, but they continued what they were doing. Adrenaline pumped through her veins, and she realised that the risk of getting caught did, in fact, turn her on. She closed her eyes as Darion's finger moved in and out, curving slightly. She rocked her hips, meeting his powerful thrusts. As it went in all the way, she felt she would explode with pleasure.

"You like this, don't you?" Darion chuckled.

She glanced down to see that he had released his hard cock with his free hand. He began to tug on it, rough grunts escaping his lips. He matched the rhythm of his stroking hand to the thrusting and twisting of his finger. Gabi felt the hot moisture between her legs, extremely aroused at the sight of him masturbating.

"Darion, I want you…" she said in between pants.

"Not yet," he whispered. "Come in my mouth, Gabi."

She wriggled, her muscles gripping onto his finger, her body trembling, on the verge of an orgasm. She rode his face, her sex burning and aching with desire, wanting more.

Darion tugged her swollen clit between his teeth, flicking over it with his tongue. "Fuck, Gabi…" He jerked himself faster, his breathing heavy. "I'm so close."

His fingers pounding into her, his tongue lapping up her wetness, and the sound of his pleasured moans sent a violent shiver of arousal through her. Feeling her body tremble and spasm, Gabi pressed her lips together, knowing she was on the brink of an orgasm. His tongue circling her flesh, and with one last deep thrust of his fingers, Gabi felt a rippling eruption of pleasure tear into her.

With her face screwed up, she silently climaxed into Darion's mouth, her insides clenching and throbbing. Her body shuddered in ecstasy. She was too choked with lust to even attempt speaking. She took several deep breaths to calm her thudding heart and heaving chest, and slid to the floor, fearing her suddenly shaky legs would give way.

When she focused on Darion, she saw the satisfied expression on his face. He ran his tongue slowly across his top lip, and gripped his fingers around his cock again. He pulled her in for a kiss. As he continued to pump himself, sliding his hand up and down the shaft, his mouth pressed onto hers, kissing her savagely, firmly, as he moaned into her mouth. Pulling back for air, she watched as torment twisted his face, knowing he was close.

He guided her head downwards. Gabi knew what he wanted. Where else was there to come? She wrapped her mouth around him, sucking his length as far as she could go. She gently massaged his balls in her hand. Her tongue flicked against the groove under the head, making his groaning become louder, his breathing heavier. He was soaking with her saliva, shuddering as her lips made their way down his shaft.

"Fuck." He squirmed.

She bobbed her head, licking and sucking him, circling the tip of his cock with her tongue, moaning in satisfaction simultaneously. It didn't take long until he pushed her head down, shaking violently as he climaxed. He thrust a few times, filling her mouth with his warm, salty cum. Gabi quickly swallowed.

"Gabi…" His chest rose and fell with his ragged breathing as he slouched against the wall. "That was fucking amazing."

"Excuse me, is somebody there?"

They stilled at the stern female voice.

Gabi looked at Darion. She could feel the flush of humiliation sweep up her chest and into her face, fear knotting her stomach. Both remained completely silent, until they were certain she had gone. Gabi reached for her clothes, and yanked them on quickly. When they left the cubicle, and realised that the coast was clear, they dissolved into hysterics. Darion pulled Gabi into an embrace, placing tender kisses over her cheek.

"Next stop." He grinned, and grabbed hold of her hand tightly. "I promised I'd take you somewhere."

Darion took Gabi to a lively bar-restaurant overlooking the canal. With wooden tables, stools, comfy couches, and pictures hanging from every wall, Gabi noticed the majority of the crowd were students. They were laughing and talking, swaying to the music, or downing beers, seemingly celebrating some special occasion. She instantly felt herself relax. She liked it there.

They watched as a narrow, red boat drifted past, a couple of children waving from the window. As they tucked into burger and fries, there was nonstop talking, and laughing, and the evening soon crept upon them.

"Thank you for today." Gabi pressed her lips against Darion's once they were back outside the club. "I had an unusual day." She laughed.

Darion wrapped his arms around her, pressing his lips to her forehead. "You're welcome. And there will be plenty more unusual days." He stroked her cheek. "Drive safe, darlin'."

***

Darion

As Darion climbed the stairs to his apartment, he couldn't stop the grin that played on his face. He'd had a fun day with Gabi, especially in the store changing rooms. He loved the adrenaline rush, the buzz that he got from almost getting caught doing something forbidden. He played every last detail back in his mind, which aroused him. He didn't get people that took themselves too seriously. Life was too short.

He unlocked the door to his apartment, and entered the living room. He took in the bare space and wondered what to do with himself. Switching on the stereo, he allowed "Waiting For The End" by Linkin Park to play. The sofa looked inviting. Perhaps he'd relax for a bit, maybe even doze off.

Retrieving a cigarette from his pocket and lighting it, he dropped onto the sofa. As he lay there, he watched the smoke circling above him, and concentrated on the song lyrics. The words were extremely fitting. His spirits plummeted. He remained there for fifteen minutes, hoping his lids would feel heavy, and tiredness would overtake him. No such luck.

Sitting up abruptly, he felt an urge to visit the club. Perhaps he could get stupidly drunk and have a lock-in with the girls. Or maybe he should do the sensible thing, and shut himself away in the office to sort out the books and the membership applications. *Stay put, Darion.* In the apartment, he couldn't get up to any mischief.

He decided to watch a movie in bed. After he'd undressed, and showered, he got comfortable under the covers. Flicking through the channels, he settled on an action film. He was eager to see explosives, blood, gore, and mind-blowing fights, but it was on a wedding scene. As the bride walked down the aisle, her face merged into Eva's, as his ex-wife once again haunted his mind. His head fell back against the pillow. He tried his hardest to focus on the images before him. But, persistent as the woman herself, the flashback presented itself before him.

He could hear the orchestra, clear as day. He could feel the sun warming his cheeks. He could smell the pretty flower arrangements that surrounded him. He could feel the twist of his stomach, and the thundering of his heart, as he'd felt on that exact day. He remembered his shaking fingers as he'd adjusted his tie, nervous as hell.

It was like he was miraculously back there, standing in the churchyard, on his wedding day. He wiped the beads of sweat from his forehead, and lifted his gaze. He sucked in air, fearing that the happiness he was feeling would stream down his face. He didn't do crying, and he certainly wasn't going to start there.

Eva's black curls hung beautifully over her shoulders. A white veil had been delicately placed on her head. Her petite shoulders were bare, her bosom exposed. The white dress clung to her hips, and expanded at her legs, the long train trailing behind her. She looked stunning, and still as seductive as ever, with her full lips, and green, cat-like eyes. His heart swelled with how much he loved her.

He'd already accidentally seen her dress the night before, when he'd snuck into her room for a kiss goodnight. He should have known it wouldn't have ended at a kiss. They were obsessed with one another.

"Daz." She'd pushed him onto the bed,

straddling him. Wearing just her knickers and a vest, the tattoos that spiralled down one leg were visible. She flung her arms around his neck, and giggled when his stare dropped to her cleavage. "I can't believe we're getting married in the morning."

A lazy smile had teased his lips. "You're gonna look amazing in that dress."

"Shit." She'd grabbed his face, turning his attention to her. "It's bad luck for you to see that."

He'd leant forward and brushed his lips against hers. She responded eagerly, grabbing fistfuls of his hair, and smashing her mouth against his.

"Mrs. Milano." She chuckled. "Has quite a ring to it, don't it?"

"It sure does." He stroked her hair out of her face. "Why are you marrying me, Eva?"

"You know why."

He remained silent, wanting to hear the reasons, needing clarification, reassurance.

"I'm marrying you because you're everything I want in a man." She kissed his forehead. "You're smart." She kissed his cheek. "You love and protect me." She kissed his jaw. "You're amazing in bed." She pecked him on the mouth. "And you're the sexiest man I've ever seen."

He chewed his lip. "Do you mean all that?"

She nodded. "Every fucking word." She yanked his top from over his head, and massaged his shoulders firmly. "Why are you marrying me?"

"You've got all of those qualities, and more." He unclasped her bra, freeing her breasts. "I love every single thing about you. And I'll love every

single thing about you forever."

"Good. Because you've got me forever." She trailed kisses along his collarbone. "This is it, Daz. Me and you against the world."

As she unzipped his jeans, he felt himself falling back onto the bed. Eva Milano. It sounded like music to his ears—the best song he'd ever heard. She was his. Forever. He'd found his girl. He knew that as long as he had her, he'd die a happy man.

Turning his head, he was dragged back to reality. The black sheets came into focus, and then the wardrobe, and the television. Eva's voice was replaced with Angelina Jolie's, and he remembered where he was—his room. His throat tightened, a heavy ache lingering in his chest. He looked up, inhaling deeply, holding in the sadness, heartbreak, humiliation, and anger that wanted to trickle down his face in the form of tears, and never stop. *Don't be a pussy, Darion.* His features hardened, the cords of his neck became taut as he fought to stay in control. It was just another stupid memory.

Grabbing his mobile, he logged onto a gambling website. He needed a distraction. He decided to play poker. It wasn't a good idea. Darion never knew when enough was enough. At that moment, he didn't care one bit.

Chapter Sixteen

Gabi

Gabi stretched one leg in the air before stretching the other. She raised her arms above her head, ensuring that she really worked her muscles. Her hair was tied into a knot, and she was casually dressed in tight black sports leggings, a vest, and trainers. Surrounding her were women and men around the same age, all of whom stood before a huge wall mirror and a dance instructor.

"First thing's first..." The teacher clapped her hands together. "There are different styles of hip-hop, such as old school, street dance, jazz. Today, we'll be doing a variation of them all." She strode toward a stereo. "You've now all warmed up, so, let's get started." She grinned, pressing a button, causing music to boom from the speakers.

The teacher began stepping from left to right, slightly bending her knees as she did so. "Okay, so mirror my feet, and bend your knees with each step like so. Ready? One, Two, Three, Four, Five, Six," she said in between each step.

Gabi copied the instructor, moving her feet from left to right, whilst crouching slightly.

"Great. Now, let's do that again, but this time, move our arms at the same time, like this." As the teacher repeated her steps, she lifted her arms, pushing them forward, and bending them at the elbows. "Ready? One, Two, Three, Four, Five, Six," she said in between moving her feet and arms.

An hour later, after the session had finished, feeling pleased with herself for picking up the moves quite quickly, Gabi grabbed her bag and waved to the teacher and her fellow learners. She almost skipped through reception, as the music still sounded loud in her ears. She was already looking forward to the next lesson.

Stopping at the vending machine, she purchased a bottle of water and drained half of it in one swig. Her skin glistened with sweat, and her face was hotly flushed. She wove her way through bodies, and entered the ladies' room. She checked her mobile before she got in the shower.

She had asked herself for the hundredth time why Darion hadn't called, or responded to her text message. It had been a few days. Maybe the relationship was more hassle than it was worth. She didn't want to feel like some silly little girl waiting by the phone, willing it to ring. She hated being let down. They had previously planned to meet up as much as possible, to make the most of her time off work.

She contemplated calling him, but decided against it, assuming that he was probably busy.

After the hot shower, she dressed in a black, long-sleeved top, white mini skirt, and black ankle boots. She scraped her wavy hair off her face, and fastened it with a clip.

At that moment, her mobile rang. Darion's name lit up the screen. She allowed it to ring three times before answering it, not wanting to come across eager. "Hello."

"Gabi. How's it going?" His voice was croaky, as if he'd just woken up.

"All good, thanks."

"What are you doing?'

"I've just had a dance class."

"Great. You wanna meet me at the club?"

"Ermmm…" She paused. "I'll give it a miss today. Have a few things I need to sort out."

"Well, take care of business, and meet me afterwards."

"I'll see you another time," she said stubbornly. He really did think that she was his play toy, at his beck and call.

"Gabi, I wanna see you today."

She remained silent.

"Come and see me after you're done. Please."

She found herself losing the battle. "Okay." She drummed her fingers on the counter. "I'll see you in a few hours."

"I look forward to it." His soft, seductive tone returned.

Gabi craved a strong coffee and some fresh air. As she was already in town, she stopped at Starbucks and ordered a latte and a muffin. She sat near the window, reading the day's newspaper, taking her time. Darion annoyed her. He had a way of getting under her skin like no one else could. What the fuck was she doing? He had a hold over her that she couldn't shake off. He was like a drug that she couldn't go a day without, she was utterly addicted to him—his sultry voice, his possessive touch, his sweet smell, everything about him. Just thinking about him made her all excited.

In the car on the way to the club, she turned the volume high on the radio, singing along to the music.

An hour later, when she was eventually inside The Black Door, she noticed Gina working behind the bar, a cat-that-got-the-cream smile plastered on her face. Did they still have an ongoing thing? Gabi felt a surge of jealousy pierce her heart, as thoughts of Gina and Darion together invaded her mind. But then again, he had called *her*. Gina was obviously not enough. Darion appeared from a door, his hands full with a pile of letters. "Gina, can you read all this? My head's fuckin' killing me."

"Sure." She took the stack from him.

"It's probably nothin' important, but just to be sure."

With both elbows propped on the bar, Darion casually leant against it. Gabi watched as Gina threw him a provocative look, before pinching his ass. Gabi saw Darion's lips curl, a low, dirty laugh escaping. Gabi's heart beat wildly. She tried to remain calm. *We're not exclusive. He's not my boyfriend,* she told herself over and over. *Accept it.* She knew what she was getting herself into.

Gina sauntered off, not even realising that Gabi

was present. Darion must have felt her eyes burning holes into him, because he looked up. His grin instantly vanished, although his expression was unreadable. "Gabi." She couldn't make out if he was shocked or sorry that she had witnessed the little flirtation that had occurred. "Come to the office."

She hesitated before following him through the back door. *He's such an asshole.*

"So." Darion collapsed on the chair, and ran a hand through his hair, which was swept back neatly. "What do you fancy doing tonight?"

"I don't know." Gabi sat on the sofa, ensuring her gaze didn't meet his. "What do you suggest?"

"You know what I want." He gave her a ghost of a wink. "You."

Right. She was only there for one thing. What did she expect? It was nothing but sex. She stood up, and slowly walked over to him, sitting on the edge of his desk. She stroked the wood, then pulled her hand back, wondering how many women he had had sprawled over it.

"I wanna have fun with you, drink, and party the night away." He licked his lips. "What do you say?"

"Hmmm," she mumbled, unable to hide the petulance in her tone.

His expression turned serious, as he regarded her intently. "Are you pissed off with me?"

"No," she lied, knowing she had no right to slap restrictions on him, but the Gina issue was niggling away at her.

He straightened his posture. "I hope you'd tell me if something was on your mind."

What, like you tell me anything?

Darion pushed himself to his feet, and leant into her, meeting her mouth. With gentle lingering kisses, his tongue explored hers, his hands cupping her face. "Looks like we're both in need of a drink." He slowly pulled back, leaving a few last tender pecks on her lips.

He poured them both a glass of whisky, which they wasted no time in finishing. He then grabbed hold of her hand, giving it a quick squeeze, and led her to the bar. They downed a shot of absinthe each, and sat in a private booth, him closing the curtains behind them. Gabi watched as he made himself comfortable on the red sofa, his gaze boring into her, sparkling with interest.

"Dance for me, Gabi."

The music was playing loud enough to dance to, yet quiet enough to hear one another speak. Gabi contemplated giving him a private dance. She was so into Darion that she found herself trying to please not only him, but herself. Plus, if she could keep Darion's attention on her, and *only* her, maybe they had a better chance of lasting.

She grabbed the bottle of wine that he had taken from the bar, swigged some of it back, and decided she would put on a little show for him. She could see if he was impressed with the new dance moves she'd learnt that day.

Drunkenly giggling, she stepped onto the podium, one hand holding the pole. "She Rides" by Danzig was playing. She swayed her hips, her stare fixed on his. Spreading her legs, she raised her arms above her head, winding her waist in circles, slowly, repeatedly, before turning her back on him, and bending down to touch her toes. She wiggled her ass slowly from side to side, teasing him.

His gaze swept over her appreciatively. Running her hands up her legs, she stood straight again. She slowly twirled around to face him, and peeled her dress off. Her black silk bra and underwear shimmered under the lights. Her fingers travelled down her body, at a leisurely pace. She stepped between his legs, and rotating her hips, she leant forward and whipped off her bra. Her breasts hung teasingly in front of his face.

It didn't take long until the alcohol properly hit her, and when it did, she was completely naked and stumbling on her heels. She was in a fit of giggles, along with Darion. Falling onto the sofa, her blonde head fell in her arms as she took a deep breath. Darion ran tender kisses along her spine.

"You wanna watch the girls dance?"

She shrugged indifferently.

"Spin Spin Sugar" by Sneaker Pimps was now blasting from the speakers, and the club was starting to get busy. Gabi quickly dressed, and she and Darion sat amongst the crowd. Gina was on the pole, with Marnie behind the bar. Gabi fidgeted in her seat, fighting the urge to get up and dance.

Half an hour later, the room was spinning. The music thudded in her ears, loud and clear. The smell of alcohol, and Darion's natural masculine aroma, filled her nostrils. She felt the blood in her veins rush to her heart, causing it to pump in her chest at a rapid pace. Her body felt alive, full of energy.

"Let's go to a nightclub." She took hold of

Darion's hand. "Please."

"Okay." He nodded. "Let's get out of here."

They got a taxi to the nearest nightclub. Treading slowly down the steps, they entered a massive room, which was packed from wall to wall with people dancing. Laser lights filled the room, and podium dancers moved fast to house beats. The atmosphere was lively, and Gabi wanted nothing more than to join in the crowd, and shake off some of her pent-up energy.

"C'mon," she yelled at Darion excitedly, beckoning him over.

"I think I'm too old for this." He laughed.

"Nonsense."

Gabi pulled him toward her, dancing with him, her body pressed against his. They began kissing frantically, like two teenagers who couldn't get enough of one another. Gabi started laughing again, unable to control the urge.

He ran his hands up her dress, kissing her even harder. When his fingertips traced the material of her underwear, her eyes darted around the room, taking in the crowd. Although everyone was dancing, and not paying attention, Gabi felt it was too risky allowing Darion to touch her in such a crowded place.

"I want you now," he moaned into her ear, his hot breath making her tingle, his teeth grazing her skin.

"Not here." She shook her head.

"Well then let's find somewhere."

Gabi looked at him. He was so handsome, so sexy, rough, and rugged. How could she refuse? He was just too irresistible. He hooked his fingers through hers, and led her through the dancing crowd. Surveying the club, he spotted some stairs, which led to another dance floor, with balconies overlooking the room in which they were in. The area was closed off, sealed by a velvet rope.

"Come on."

She hurried after him, feeling nervous, but rebellious at the same time. Once on the secluded dark floor, she expected him to settle in the seating area, but instead he forcefully backed her against the wall.

"How about I fuck you right here?" His hungry gaze burned into hers, awaiting permission to ravage her.

"Addicted to Love" by Serge Devant thudded through her ears. One thing Gabi and Darion particularly loved was music, and there was nothing quite like fucking to it—fast and hard to dubstep or rock 'n' roll, slow and sensual to R&B or soul, or both for house music.

"You never cease to surprise me," she told him.

Her body strained toward his as he lowered his head and began nuzzling her neck. His lips were smooth, whereas his stubble was sharp, grazing her delicate skin. Her nipples hardened against the fabric of her dress, in need of being freed and fondled. She gripped his buttocks tightly, urging for him to take her. He slid his hands under her dress, pulling her underwear to the side. He teasingly stroked her folds, before circling the pad of his thumb on her clit. It elicited a strangled cry from her.

She closed her lids, and completely gave into him, allowing his finger to discreetly plunge in and out of her wetness, kissing her simultaneously. When he inserted another finger, filling her, she bit into his shoulder in a bid to muffle her moans. He penetrated her for a few minutes, and then withdrew his hand. Using his foot, he nudged her legs wider apart. Her mouth dropped open when she felt his erection nudge teasingly against her. The tip slowly slid in, parting her. She glanced down, not having seen him unzip his jeans. He slammed into her a few times, filling her with his length. Gasping, Gabi clawed at his buttocks, pulling him into her.

"You have to stop, Darion," she panted, when she noticed a girl look up to the balcony. "People can see us."

"Gabi, they can't see us from all the way down there," he said smoothly. "Relax."

He continued to gyrate his hips. Gabi felt the pressure start to build with every thrust. His teeth tugged and teased her earlobe, before he flicked his tongue inside. Gabi felt herself go weak at the knees. She was completely lost in the moment.

"You…want…me…to…stop?" he asked breathlessly, sliding out.

Gabi felt a cold chill up her dress, even though her insides were flamed and aching for him. She noticed the tantalising smile on his face, as he knew that by leaving her hanging, he tortured her.

"Get here." She pulled him close, so that his firm chest was pushing her up against the wall. She gasped as he impatiently drove into her again with a violent force. He plunged in and out of her endlessly, making her legs shake. His hands roamed over her back, caressed her buttocks, and then he was kissing her, and she was kissing him back. As their tongues wrestled, Gabi forgot everything around her but the feel and taste of him. She entangled her fingers in his hair, crying out in delight. When she got close to the point of release, he changed the rhythm, slowing down, wanting to prolong their sweet fucking.

"Faster, harder..." she commanded through gritted teeth.

"Gabi..." he growled, hammering into her.

His heavy panting mirrored hers. She watched his face strain as the intensity engulfed him, low grunts escaping his mouth. His irises were raw, almost glowing, his red lips engorged and so tempting, so kissable. He sighed softly against her ear, telling her how wet she was, how he loved the feel of her, and the things that he wanted to do to her, amongst other obscenities. They were so engrossed in one another that the surroundings weren't an issue.

Gabi tiptoed, tilting her pelvis up to meet his, grinding, taking more of him. Sharp, intense waves flooded through her as he pummelled into her repeatedly. She tightened her grip on him, holding him hard against her. He seized her face roughly, and kissed her firmly, devouring her mouth with his. With a few more powerful slams that pinned her against the wall, she felt the tension building, her stomach tightened, their bodies pulsing close to one another. With a sharp intake of breath, their bodies stiffened, until they released, surrendering to the delicious spasms that tore through them, making them cry out in unison, as they climaxed.

Trembling, and aching, their legs weak, they clung onto one another until their bodies cooled, and their breathing evened.

***

Gabi woke up with a groan. Urgh, where was she? Her head was sore, her body aching, and her mouth was dry. She rolled onto her side, and scanned the room. She was in a double bed, which she didn't recognise. She kicked the black cover off, her hot body drenched in sweat. She shakily climbed to her feet. The night before flashed in her mind—the club, them getting thrown out by the bouncers. *Oh no.* She ran her fingers through her hair, her cheeks burning in shame. They had been caught having sex.

"Morning, baby." Darion padded into the room, completely naked. "I'd make you a drink, but I don't have any tea or coffee."

"It's okay," she replied, not wanting to put him out, although she was in desperate need of caffeine.

"I can go and fetch some?" he offered, pulling on some black jeans.

"Don't worry about it."

"No, I'll go. The shop is literally around the corner." He yanked on a blue t-shirt.

"If you really don't mind."

"Have a shower, whatever. Make yourself at home."

As soon as she heard the front door slam, she

took in her surroundings. It was a modern apartment. Everything was brand new: built in mirrored wardrobes, a black leather bed, plasma TV on the wall, and black carpets throughout. She guessed that the kitchen and bathroom were just as modern. Her focus moved to the balcony, where she appreciated the view of the tidy grass area outside, footpath, and benches. It seemed like a nice enough complex.

She dropped back on the bed, yawning. As she turned her head to the side, she stared at the bedside table before her, and had a sudden urge to snoop. She wanted to know more about Darion than what he had revealed. Shuffling over to the small table, she pulled open the top drawer. It was full of mail, lighters, and condoms. She opened the next drawer and found several watches, bracelets, rings, and necklaces. In the last drawer, she found a stack of photographs.

Gabi couldn't help but flip through them. A picture of a tall, slim woman stared up at her. She had jet black hair, mesmerising green eyes, and a full pout. She was wearing a red bikini, posing confidently on the sand. Tattoos ran down the side of her waist, most of which were spiralling black flowers. On one leg, she had even more tattoos that ended at her ankle. The next photograph showed her and Darion kissing, another was of her lying on the bed in just her underwear, and then she found a wedding photo.

Gabi dropped the photos as if they'd burnt her, watching as they scattered on the carpet. She felt sick with jealousy. Darion had been married to *her.*

So this was the ex-wife that had broken his heart. She inhaled deeply, and picked up the photos. She didn't know why, but it pained her to look at the wedding shot. She examined it again. Darion was dressed in a black suit, and looked like he'd burst with happiness. His ex-wife wore a white wedding dress with a tight bodice, revealing some cleavage, and a flowing skirt. She looked naturally pretty. Not the type of woman that you would think was covered in tattoos and whatnot under her dress.

Gabi reminded herself again to not get attached to Darion. Judging by his ex-wife, and Gina, he was into women who were the complete opposite of Gabi—wild, fun, outrageous. She wondered how long they had been married, and then decided that it didn't even matter. She stuffed the photos back in the drawer.

Lying back on the bed, she grabbed her handbag, and rummaged around in it for her mobile. She glanced at the screen. She had three missed calls from Lawrence. It made a change from the twenty missed calls. Maybe he was starting to accept the breakup. She hoped so. It pained her to ignore him, regardless of how he had treated her. A small part of her wanted to ring him, to ensure that he was okay. However, her sensible side told her not to, that it wouldn't help matters. He could see the call as a glimmer of hope that they'd reunite. She certainly didn't want that.

"Gabi?" Darion's voice startled her. She hadn't even heard him return. He appeared in the doorway. "Tea or coffee?"

"Coffee, please. Milky. No sugar."

"Take a shower. It'll be done when you are."

After she'd showered and dressed, she joined him on the balcony, sipping her drink whilst he smoked a cigarette. They sat in a comfortable silence, watching the world below go by. Wanting to be close to him, Gabi placed her cup on the table, and slid onto his lap. She rested her head on his shoulder. As his fingers raked through her hair gently, she sighed in contentment. Darion Milano. What the hell was she going to do with him?

Chapter Seventeen

Gabi searched for Darion amongst the crowd; however he was nowhere to be seen. It was the following night and they had agreed to meet at the club, although she was twenty minutes early. She took up residency on a stool at the bar.

"Gabi." Lexi approached her. "How are you, pretty lady?" The dancer pulled her into a tight embrace.

"I'm good. How are you?"

"Same old, same old." She filled two shot glasses, handing one to her. "What brings you here, *again*? Lover boy?" She winked.

Gabi smiled sheepishly.

"Oh come on, Gabi. I knew Darion would get his dirty paws onto you the minute you walked into the club." She laughed.

Gabi raised the glass to her lips. "Cheers." She downed it quickly. "So, where is he?"

Lexi shrugged. "I haven't been here long." She glanced at her watch. "He should be here by now."

"Oh."

"Head on back to the office."

"Okay."

Gabi rose to her feet, and made her way toward Darion's office. She noticed that the door was slightly ajar. She contemplated whether or not to knock first, or walk in. When she heard a loud groan, she froze to the spot. Surely Darion wasn't having sex with someone minutes before meeting her. Her stomach felt like it was doing somersaults; a sickening feeling engulfed her. She peered in through the small gap. She had to know if he had that little respect for her.

She made out a pair of woman's legs, complete with stockings on the desk. She then saw a pair of hands run along them. Her body trembled with rage. She didn't know who it was in there with Darion. She felt physically sick, and grabbed the wall for support, fearing her legs would give way. She really must have liked him more than she thought she did. She couldn't continue seeing him, no chance. The open relationship probably would hurt her. She slipped off her heels so she wouldn't make a noise as she walked down the corridor. Gabi slowly made her way back into the club.

She sat at the bar, her head in her hands, contemplating what to do. She was just about to stand up when she noticed Darion sitting at a table with a group of men. He was laughing, a pile of cards and money displayed before him. Cigar smoke swirled around them. So it wasn't him in the office. She scolded herself for feeling so relieved about it. She shook her head, grinning. She decided to order a glass of wine, and not interrupt his game.

"Yes," she heard him shout cheerfully, as if he'd won.

She glanced over her shoulder, and watched as he gathered notes of money from the table, then head to the bar. He stilled when he saw Gabi, looking pleasantly surprised. He approached her. "You're early." He leant down to settle his lips over hers, his tongue darting into her mouth.

"No traffic."

"You look fuckin' amazing, Gabi." His predatory stare swept over her.

She had worn a long black dress with a slit exposing her right leg, and a low neckline, which displayed her cleavage. Her hair was tied into a high ponytail, the curls falling down her back, and her make-up was flawless. "Thanks."

"I want you now." He planted gentle kisses along her collarbone, making her skin tingle.

"Sit down, have a drink."

"Don't you think you drank too much the other night?" he teased, winking at her, reminding her of their time at the nightclub.

"Yes." She pushed him playfully. "I'm trying to wipe those antics from my memory."

"Gabi, we both know they'll be embedded there forever." His hand fell into her lap, caressing her leg. Then it moved higher, his thumb gently stroking her inner thigh. Shifting in her seat, she wondered how his slight contact could so thoroughly arouse her.

"I had a good time that night. Did you?"
She nodded.
Gina sauntered over and took their drink orders.

When a Jack Daniels and Coke was placed before Darion, he drained the drink instantly, and ordered another.

"So…why do you drink so much?" Gabi asked him outright, but hoping her voice sounded casual.

He shrugged. "Why not?"

"Are you still upset about your ex-wife?" she asked softly, touching his hand.

"How do you know about that?" He looked at her, his face hardening, pulling his hand away.

"The girls mentioned it to Mallory before," she said quickly. "I'm sorry, I just wanted to help."

Darion stood up. He looked her up and down, a look of disgust appearing that she had never seen before. It cut her like a knife. He stormed through the door behind the bar, leaving her watching after him. Gabi quickly chased after Darion, having to run to keep up with his hurried strides.

"Darion," she yelled. "I didn't mean to hurt your feelings. I just wanted to hear you out, you know, see if you needed someone to talk to. I'm sorry."

She was behind him when he burst into the office. She could immediately sense that he was livid when he saw Marnie bent over his desk, a man pounding into her. Darion gritted his teeth, his fists clenched. Gabi tried to grab his arm, to stop him from doing something drastic. He yanked his arm away as if she had burnt him, his menacing eyes warning her to back off. Gabi took a step back.

"What the fuck are you doing in here, Marnie?"

She looked up, quickly rising to her feet, grabbing her clothes, her face bright red with shame. The man zipped his trousers, and scanned the room, obviously looking for his shirt.

"I'm sorry, Darion," she mumbled. "Usually you don't mind."

"Yes, when it's *me* you're fucking," he said through gritted teeth, taking deep breaths to regain his cool. "Get. Out. Now." His tone was icy, sending a chill up Gabi's spine.

"Hey, don't talk to her like that," the man snapped as he found his shirt and put it on, buttoning it up.

"You what?" Darion stepped closer to him, his nose only inches away from his. "What did you say?"

"I said, don't talk to her like that."

"Nick, don't," Marnie shouted, taking hold of his hand to pull him out of the room.

Darion grabbed the man around the throat, slamming him against the wall. Gabi couldn't make out what Darion was saying, although she was pretty certain he was threatening Nick. Once released, and when Nick regained his composure, he looked Darion squarely in the eye. Darion stood tall, his stare focused on Nick, daring him to say something more.

"C'mon, Nick," Marnie cried out, dragging him to the door by the arm. She shook her head at Darion and left.

Gabi stood there, in silence, her mouth agape. Darion shot a fierce look at her, his chest rising and falling, his breathing heavy. He clenched his teeth. Gabi hated herself for finding him so sexy, even when his aggressive side confused her. She tightened her grasp on the strap of her handbag and fled out of the office. Sexy or not, she couldn't be involved with Darion. He clearly had issues, and was still hung up on his ex-wife. She didn't need that drama in her life.

"Gabi!" she heard him yell.

She ignored him, striding toward the bathroom. She needed to splash her face with water. Her cheeks were burning up, and she was pissed off. Gabi was surprised when she heard his footsteps behind her. Inside the bathroom, she pushed open a cubicle door and stepped inside. Just as she was about to lock the door, Darion pushed it open with force.

"Gabi, why did you run off like that?" He cupped her face in his hands, whilst his body slammed her against the cubicle wall.

"Get off me," she shrieked.

His gaze was fixed on hers, both of them now silent. Before she could scream, he pressed his lips forcefully against hers. His tongue drove itself into her mouth, hungrily, angrily, possessively. Gabi hated herself for responding, but she couldn't stop herself, her body overruling her mind. *What the fuck am I doing?*

His hands moved from her neck to her breasts, where he cupped each one. He pulled them out from her bra and began kissing and licking each of her nipples, making them harden. Gabi groaned. She really couldn't get enough of him. He fiddled with the zip on his trousers, and bunched her dress up over her hips. The head of his penis prodded against her entrance, the tip sliding in. His length eased in and out, opening her. As he pushed in all the way, she gripped his hair, her teeth sinking into his neck, which made him thrust even harder and angrier. *That's it, take your anger out on me.* She looked up into his huge, blazing eyes.

She dug her nails into his back and clawed at his flesh, certain from his gritted teeth that she had drew blood. His face was still red from rage, an angry vein throbbing near his temple, his lips curled into a menacing snarl. It was like a demon had possessed him; she didn't recognise him.

He clutched her hair, yanking her head back, exposing her neck. He leant his face in close, so she could feel the heat of his breath, which tickled her skin. "You sexy bitch…" his voice took on a mean and vicious tone as he glared at her.

Gabi couldn't help but let out a giggle. It was exciting! She loved being dominated. She could feel the moisture of arousal between her legs as he slammed into her violently.

"You think this is funny?" he asked. He levelled his steely gaze directly at hers. "Don't you know that it's rude to run off like that?"

"Fuck you," Gabi spat courageously, not considering the ramifications of such a response.

He shook his head disapprovingly, although his mouth was curling upwards ever so slightly at the sides. "Naughty girl."

He withdrew, and spun her around, so that her back was facing him. He rubbed himself between her legs slowly, before entering her. He pummelled in and out fast, deep, and hard. The intensity shot through her, making her whimper. It was too much. The width, length, and speed of his rhythm made her legs buckle. Darion's hand clamped on her mouth tightly to muffle her sounds. Her face was pressed against the cubicle door. She felt a little drool in the corner of her mouth, and desperately wanted to wipe at it, but her arms were pressed to either side of her. She was helpless.

"How do you like this?" he grunted. "You want more?"

He slammed into her again, making her whole body jerk forward. She winced at the slight pain of the depth of him. He rocked his hips, every forward motion making her build toward climax, almost sending her over the edge. Gabi squeezed her lids tightly shut.

His mouth sucked on her neck hard, making blood rush to that area. She shook her head, trying to protest. He was trying to mark her. She cried out, but he covered her mouth again, and continued to suck on her neck. A part of her wanted him to stop, and a part of her didn't. The sharpness of his mouth on her tender skin sent waves of arousal through her.

He continued to slam into her, just as the tension was building, the pressure became almost unbearable, and she was close to coming. And then he pulled out. Gabi stilled, waiting for his next move. But nothing.

"What are you doing?" she asked incredulously, desperate for release, her insides throbbing and aching.

"You want more?" he teased.

She turned around. "Get here, Darion," she ordered, grabbing hold of his top and pulling him toward her.

"Impatient, are we?" He chuckled.

"Don't keep me hanging," she pleaded, as he took a step backwards. "Darion."

He lifted her in his strong arms, and carried her toward the sink, where he set her down. He parted her legs and thrust into her again. Gabi groaned. She began stroking her clit simultaneously, massaging soft circles. Her mouth fell open with her heavy breathing. She knew it wouldn't take long. She felt the desire in the pit of her stomach, and leant her head back against the mirror.

"Darion…" she said breathlessly.

He grimaced as he pounded away, hitting her sensitive spot. Her breathing grew heavier, her heartbeat raced wildly. She writhed in pleasure at the tingle and vibrations of her fingertips on her engorged clit. She circled it faster, moaning softly as Darion continued to pleasure her. Full of pent-up tension, it didn't take long until they came together violently, shaking, with strangled sobs. When the shivering subsided, and their limp bodies returned to normal, they disentangled themselves.

Darion kissed her gently on the mouth. "Sorry for taunting you, darlin'." He grinned. "I love seeing you mad."

"Don't do that again," she warned, smiling.

He stroked her hair out of her face. "And I'm sorry I can't talk about Eva," he said softly. "Not now."

Eva? Gabi tensed at the sound of her name. *He must still love her.* She readjusted her breasts in her bra, and smoothed her dress down.

"It's okay," she told him. "I shouldn't have intruded."

He took hold of her hand, and pressed his face into her hair. "You're so fuckin' sexy," he mumbled. "What are you doing to me, Gabi?"

She ignored him. *What are you doing to me, more like?*

"Don't hate me for losing it in there with Nick. He was Marnie's ex, up until recently. He knocked her about a lot, broke her wrist before. He had it coming." His gaze met hers. "I'm not a bad person, Gabi." The sincerity was apparent in his eyes. "I only hurt people that deserve it."

Do I deserve it? Gabi kept her mouth tightly closed.

Chapter Eighteen

Gabi and Darion were sat in the VIP section of the club, a small section in the corner near the stage, separated by two red ropes. It held several black tables and chairs, and buckets holding bottles of champagne. There was also a small, private bar, which was occupied by a few regular rich clients. Gina was on the main stage, impressing the audience as always. Darion appeared mesmerised by her. Gabi tried her hardest to push the feelings of jealousy aside. Although he looked at her the same way, for some reason she wanted him to look at *only* her that way. What did she want? Did she want him to be hers? Or was it because she couldn't have him exclusively that these things bothered her? She shook her head as if to erase the thoughts.

She grabbed the bottle of champagne and filled two glasses.

Darion clinked his glass with hers. "To living life." He beamed, as if he didn't have a care in the world.

His mobile rang, causing him to stand up, and

answer it a few feet away. "Gabi, I need to do something. Wait here, I won't be long," he said when the call had ended.

Gabi saw him head toward the main entrance. Maybe he was meeting clients. She took a sip of the refreshing champagne and watched Gina strut her stuff. Sometimes she felt out of her depth in the club, with Darion, and the girls, but it still exhilarated her.

"Hi, babe, you cool?" Marnie approached her, sitting down and filling a glass with champagne. "Darion pisses me off so much sometimes," she said, anger showing itself on her face.

"Does he usually react like that?" Gabi pried.

"Not unless me or the girls are in some sort of danger."

"He must really care about you all." It was out of Gabi's mouth before she could stop it.

"Too much." She rolled her eyes.

Gabi twisted her mouth in annoyance. What was that supposed to mean?

Marnie gulped back her drink. "I'm up next. See you later." With that, she disappeared behind the curtain.

Gabi felt the frustration building inside. *I can't compete with all of these girls.*

***

Darion

Darion met his old work colleague at the door. He hadn't seen Carl Johnson in years. Carl had contacted him online last week, and they had been speaking since. He gave the tall, blond man a pat on the shoulder, pleased as punch to see his friend. They had always gotten on well. He looked at the petite brunette that was with Carl. She was pretty, slim, with pert breasts. Darion kissed her on the cheek, greeting her.

"So." He clapped his hands together. "I told you all about the club, wanna see it in action?"

"I want to be in the *middle* of the action." Carl laughed loudly.

"Good. It's busy tonight, loads of women, and I mean *loads*." Darion grimaced, remembering the girl. "Sorry, darlin'. Forgot you were there for a second."

She giggled nervously.

He led them both up the stairs and into the more glamorous club. Carl handed the brunette a fifty-pound note, and sent her to the bar to order drinks. Darion grinned at Tiana, his employee who was sitting at a desk observing the door, dealing with membership identification and whatnot. "You okay, T?" he asked her.

"Yeah," she chirped. "I'm great, Daz."

Tiana managed the upstairs of the club, so he could concentrate on downstairs. He led Carl to the VIP section, and both of them sat at a round table. One of his scantily clad employees quickly joined them, pouring champagne into the glasses that were on the perfectly made up table.

"So." Carl looked around the club, impressed. "You've done well, Daz. Always knew you would. It was only the strip joint the last time I was in town."

"I know." Darion licked his lips. "Come a long way since then."

"I'm in town on business."

"Who's the brunette?"

"I forgot her name." Carl sighed, waving a hand in the air dismissively. "Carrie or something. Only seen her three times. You're welcome to have a piece." He roared with laughter.

"I'll bear it in mind." Darion shot her a look. She was beautiful. Nowhere near as sexy as Gabi though. No one was as hot as Gabi, not even Eva. She was naturally pretty, and her heart was pure. He thought it rare to find a woman like that.

"How's the wife?" He returned his attention to Carl.

"Same old." Carl groaned. "Moaning, bitching, boring."

"Ha." Darion tilted his head back with a laugh. "Dirty weekend, huh?"

"Something like that. So, tell me, what you got back there?" He nodded toward the black door at the back of the club, which was guarded by a bouncer. "Do you need all this security?"

"You'd be surprised at how many drunks try and force the women into things they don't wanna do, or cause trouble, or trash my fuckin' place. So, yeah, it's necessary."

Carl nodded.

"And I have *everything* back there to suit your needs, Carl. Me, of all people, don't leave nothing out." He winked. "Come on, I'll show you."

***

Gabi

Gabi glanced at her watch and sighed. Darion had been gone for half an hour. She stood up, anger consuming her. She wasn't waiting around for a man, let alone him. *How dare he invite me here, and then leave me sitting on my own?* She swigged the last of her champagne, picked up her bag, and made her way across the room. She'd dealt with enough bullshit from Lawrence. She wouldn't go there again.

When she found that he wasn't in his office, Gabi exited the club. Making her way across the street, she pulled her coat on. The air was cold and bitter in her lungs. She looked back toward the club. The lights were on upstairs. The windows were tinted black, except for one, which had the red, glowing light. She could make out the bar, bottles lined near the window, and one of the barmaids pouring drinks. Gabi contemplated going upstairs, finding out for herself what was up there. *It's probably just another strip club, or a brothel.* She felt uneasy.

Gabi climbed into her car, started the engine, and waited for it to warm up so that she could switch the heaters on. She could see her breath in the air, it was that cold. She was glad she'd only had less than half a glass of champagne, so she was still capable of driving. She needed to get out of there.

Her mobile rang, making her jump. She felt through her bag and took it out. Darion. She pressed

183

the reject button and threw it back into her bag. She wasn't about to go running back to him.

When she was finally lying in the single bed in Mallory's guest room, she felt sad. She had been so used to sleeping and waking up next to Lawrence. Now it was all over. She wondered if she ever would regret it, whether she had made the wrong decision. She hoped not. She yawned and pulled the covers up to her chin. Closing her eyes, it didn't take long until she drifted into a deep sleep.

An hour later, Gabi sat up quickly. Beads of sweat covered her forehead, her breathing heavy. She had had a bad dream. She tried to replay it back in her head, but couldn't remember what it was about. She got out of bed, stepped onto the fluffy carpet, and made her way quietly and slowly to the bathroom. Upon passing Mallory's door, she heard soft moans. She was jealous, but pleased for Mallory at the same time. Why couldn't she have an exclusive relationship that she was happy in?

In the bathroom, she splashed her face with cold water. Gabi looked at her reflection in the mirror. She was wearing a flimsy peach nightie. She felt attractive, she felt pretty. She didn't feel sexy, though. *I don't have that aura about me.* She needed to get sexy again. When she was in her teens, she had felt sexy. Had she let herself go since she had been with Lawrence? Dressed older than she was, become plain? She made up her mind to go shopping tomorrow. Retail therapy always cheered her up. She could buy whatever she wanted without a fiancé to whine at everything she picked up, telling her that it was too revealing.

Back in the bedroom, she picked up her phone, staring at the screen. No more missed calls from Darion. No texts, nothing.

Chapter Nineteen

Gabi scanned through the racks of clothing. She felt the material of several dresses, liking the soft feel of the silk. She wondered which clothes to go for. She picked up a backless, short, red dress, a navy bodycon dress, a blue silk, wrap-over dress, and a gold, sparkly dress that shimmered under the lights. She quickly tried them on, loving the way that they clung to her body, so she purchased them. Gabi then headed to a shoe shop and bought some high black stilettos—the bigger the heel, the better.

Next, she needed some sexy underwear. The sets she usually wore were more for comfort than for how they looked. She purchased several sets in all different colours, and bras to boost her cleavage. Feeling exhausted, and in need of a drink, she made her way to a coffee shop.

She still hadn't heard from Darion. There was no way that she would text or call him. If he wanted her, he knew where she was. She'd be a fool to chase him after he had left her alone last night.

"Gabi?"

She looked up. Suzie. "Hi!" She grinned, standing up to hug her blonde friend. "I haven't seen you in so long."

"Can I sit?" Suzie asked, looking around to see if Gabi had company.

"Sure."

Suzie pulled the chair out and sat down. "Gabi, you look amazing."

"Thank you. So do you."

"What have you been up to?"

"I just had a dance lesson. And I've done a bit of shopping." She glanced down at the shopping bags at her feet.

"Oooh. Nice. So, tell me..." She crossed her arms across her chest. "Where have you been hiding? I sent you a few messages online, didn't hear a thing back."

"I'm sorry. I haven't been online much lately. How have you been?"

"Marvellous." She ordered a hot chocolate from the waiter who had approached them. Gabi ordered a cappuccino. "I've been working so much." A hint of a smile played on her lips. "And," she lowered her voice, "me and Marcus are trying for a baby."

"Wow." Gabi beamed, but she was a little envious that everyone was in happy loving relationships that seemed to be going somewhere. "That's great."

"I know," she said in a low, sing-song voice. "So, no going out to Sasha's anymore."

Sasha's was a bar that she, Mallory, Steve, Lawrence, Suzie, and Marcus used to go socialising. It was always busy in there, great music, a bit pretentious, but a good place to dance and gossip over wine.

"I haven't been in a while," Gabi admitted.

"Why not?"

"Well." She fiddled with her hair. "Me and Lawrence aren't together anymore."

"Oh no." Suzie held a manicured hand to her mouth. "I hope you work things out. You pair were so well suited."

"Really?" Bewilderment showed itself on her face.

"Yes. You brought out the relaxed, fun side in him. He needed a crazy, chirpy girl like you."

"Me, crazy? Lawrence, fun?" She laughed.

"Oh come on, Gabi. You were always rebellious as a teenager."

"I was not," she exclaimed. "I was good as gold. I was the girl stuck with her nose in a book whilst everyone else was out partying."

"Oh, that's right." Suzie paused and thought for a moment. "I was thinking of Dianne." She giggled. "That's right, you were always so well behaved. Perhaps you weren't suited, then."

Gabi shook her head. "Oh, Suzie." She chuckled. "I've missed you."

"Well, come and see me more often." She thanked the waiter who placed their drinks on the table.

"I will, I've just been busy."

"Sleeping with another man already?" She tutted.

Gabi's mouth was agape.

"Relax, I'm kidding. Although I wouldn't blame you, with that gorgeous hair, I bet you certainly break some hearts."

I wish.

She spent the afternoon catching up with Suzie. Everything about her friend's life made Gabi's own life now feel crappy. Suzie rattled on about how they were having so much fun trying for a baby, how very much in love they were, how their house had been completely redecorated. Gabi remembered that she could have had that life with Lawrence, minus the fun, though.

When she received a text from Darion inviting her over, she found herself perking up. Perhaps she was the one having all the fun. She could bet money that *none* of her friends had as much fun as she and Darion did.

***

Darion

Darion put his phone on the side and headed back into the living room. Carl was sleeping on the sofa with Charlie, not Carrie, as he had called her. There were beer bottles, cans, rizlas, and cigarette butts strewn over the tabletop. The apartment needed a serious clean. It had been a good night though.

He had been so occupied with Carl in the club that he had completely forgotten Gabi had been downstairs. When he had returned, she had gone. He had been surprised by her departure. He wasn't used to women leaving him, and Gabi was making quite a habit of it. He wasn't sure whether he hated it, or whether he liked that she kept him on his toes. He had tried to call her, but she had cut him off, so he'd decided to give her time to calm down. He knew what women could be like. He had remained in the club upstairs, got stupidly drunk, and then continued the party at his place.

He still hadn't heard from Gabi. *She's playing hard to get*. He had met several women like her, pretending that they didn't care when they did. He couldn't wait to see her again, though. For some crazy reason, he missed her.

He made his way back to the bedroom. Gina was sprawled stark naked across his bed. Her body was smooth, tanned, inviting. She softly murmured as she opened her eyes. She caught sight of him, unable to refrain from grinning.

"Morning." He stretched. "Sleep well?"

"Sure did." She rolled over and sat up. "I can't remember much about last night." She rubbed her forehead. "What did I do?"

"Maybe him." Darion jerked his head to the left for Gina to look beside her.

She averted her gaze and took in the naked man sleeping. "Oh, shit." She groaned.

Darion put a cigarette in his mouth and lit it. "I was out cold." He blew out smoke. "I'm gonna take a shower. I'll leave you pair to it." He winked.

He dodged the pillow that Gina threw at him.

***

Gabi

Gabi was lying in the bath, enjoying the feel of the bubbles and warmth surrounding her. It was bliss. Mallory was out grocery shopping, and she had the house to herself. Submerging her head, she swilled out the conditioner, massaging her scalp with her fingers. She breathed in the scent of the vanilla bath oils, and closed her lids. She hadn't bothered sending Darion a text back. *Make him stew. Men like him need to be put in their place.*

After the bath, she climbed into bed and switched the television on. An old black and white romance film was showing. She wondered why some men weren't gentlemen these days; the majority of them were players, wanting to sleep with anything and everything. It wasn't fair. Perhaps they needed to get it out of their system before they finally settled down and got married. Then again, even some married men still slept with anything and everything. Did some men ever grow out of their wild ways? She tucked into a bag of popcorn. She was getting used to her own company each day, slowly adapting to life without Lawrence.

Her mobile bleeped. Darion. He asked if she wanted to meet at the club that night. Gabi switched her mobile off. *When he has learnt his lesson, then I will call him.* He definitely didn't have the upper hand in their relationship.

Chapter Twenty

Darion

Darion stood before his spotless apartment. Gina had helped him clean up. She had also bought some groceries and made him a sandwich. Darion loved the way that she sometimes took care of him, reciprocating the help he'd given her over the years. He slouched on the sofa, picking up the half-eaten ham sandwich, and took another bite. He devoured it hungrily.

"I worry about you sometimes." Gina appeared from the kitchen and sat next to him.

He felt himself tense. Not another lecture.

"Daz, don't you ever get lonely?" she asked.

Yeah, all the fucking time. "How can I get lonely when I'm always seeing someone?"

"It's not the same." She shook her head. "Don't you want someone that you can chill with, someone to love, someone to wake up with, come home to?"

"No," he said it sharply, hoping that she would drop it.

"You've been like this for two years now. Are you not ready to start a committed relationship yet? You're how old now?"

"G, please," he moaned. "Don't start. You do this every time." It just ended up making him feel like crap.

"You need to stop all this, Darion. You can't go on like this forever."

"Gina, stop," he said calmly.

"You still love her, don't you?" she asked softly.

Darion looked at her, knowing that she was referring to Eva. His face was expressionless. "Quite the opposite, actually."

"There's a fine line between love and hate, you know." She smirked.

"Whatever," he muttered. Of course he still loved her. But he hated her at the same time. Eva had been everything for him—fun, wild, crazy, daring, and sexy. He hadn't met anyone close, except for Gina. She was all those things and she knew it, so she pushed him all the time. She wanted a relationship with him, but he wasn't giving in. He wasn't sure that he was after that type of woman again. Perhaps he needed the opposite of Gina, and Eva, someone a little shy, intelligent, who had more about them than just the excitement factor.

"You still have photographs of her," Gina gently reminded him. She wasn't afraid of Darion; she was just as likely to hit him if he ever lost his temper with her.

"Quit snooping through my things," he told her. "I'm not inviting you here again." He was irritated.

"Shut it," she snapped.

Silence loomed in the air for a moment. Darion was pissed off that Gina had made him think about Eva again. She must have noticed the flash of distress on his face, because she shuffled down the sofa, motioning for him to lie down. Darion did so, resting his head on Gina's lap. As she massaged her fingers into his hair softly, he felt his body relax. A few seconds later, he closed his eyes.

***

A day later Gabi still hadn't contacted Darion, which had confused the hell out of him. He had tried to call her, yet her mobile was switched off. Maybe he had really taken the piss with her. Perhaps he had lost her interest for good.

He paced the living room. Or perhaps she had gotten back with her fiancé, sorted things out. Jealousy pierced his heart. He scolded himself, wondering why he even cared. He picked up his mobile again, and attempted to ring her. He waited with bated breath, hoping that he didn't get her voicemail. It rang. Relieved, he sat down, and willed her to pick up.

***

Gabi

"Hello." Gabi held her mobile to her ear. *Let's hope he's learnt not to mess me around again.* Girlfriend or not, she wasn't allowing another man to walk all over her.

"Gabi." A blowing sound filled the line as if he was smoking. "I've been trying to reach you."

"I've been busy."

"Okay." She was surprised that he didn't pry.

"So…what happened to you that night?" she asked outright.

"I was sorting some things out with a client. I lost track of time." She heard him clear his throat with a cough. "I'm sorry, Gabi."

"Yeah, well, I don't appreciate sitting around on my own."

"It won't happen again." His tone was serious, sincere. Gabi decided she would accept his apology. "You wanna meet me at the club later?"

"Ummm…" She paused for a second.

"Come on. Don't be like this."

"Okay," she finally agreed.

"In that case, we're going to a party tonight," he told her. "Dress nice."

Gabi ended the call. She needed to see Darion. She missed him. She just hoped that he went by his word, and didn't take the piss again.

She headed upstairs, removing her clothes as she did so, and dumped them in the basket in the bathroom. She'd had a long busy day at work. Mallory and Steve were having a date night, and she had the place to herself. As she showered, she wondered which of her new dresses she should wear. Catching sight of her red polished nails, she decided to go for the red, backless dress.

Later, at the club, she found Darion in his office, sitting at his computer. He appeared to be copying from the screen, scribbling down what she noticed was an address. The sound of her heels broke his concentration. When she was stood before him, he slowly sat back. She watched him swallow before he snagged his lower lip between his teeth. "Nice to see you again."

Gabi sat on the edge of his desk. "So, we're going to a party?"

"That's if you wanna?"

"I suppose it'll be fun."

"Oh, it will."

He stood up, stuffing the paper into his back pocket. He was dressed all in black: jeans and a shirt. His hair was gelled back tidily, and his cologne smelt stronger than usual.

"You look hot, as always."

She felt her pride swell at his compliment. "Thank you. You don't look too bad yourself."

"I would suggest we have a quickie right now." He slapped his desk. "But we need to be on time."

"Who said romance was dead?" She arched a brow.

He opened his mouth to speak, as if to defend himself, but must have decided against it, as he clamped his lips shut.

They drove to the party in silence. Darion had taken his black Audi, rather than the Jeep. Gabi interlaced her fingers to stop herself from fidgeting, worrying thoughts consuming her. She didn't know whose party it was, Darion wasn't giving much away. Did she introduce herself as his girlfriend, his friend? She had no idea.

After half an hour of driving, he parked the car

outside a tall, white building with gigantic windows. It was extravagant looking. Darion led her to the main doors where he pressed a buzzer. "Can I help?" a sultry voice answered.

"Darion, here by invite. Franchesca Doorly."

"See you soon."

The door opened. Gabi anxiously followed him, desperate to take hold of his hand. She entered the elevator closely behind. Stealing a glance at Darion, she saw that he was confident as always, his eyes were shining with excitement. He pressed the button to the top floor. "I just wanna let you know…" He grabbed her hand. "If you're not comfortable here, tell me, and we'll go back to the club."

He took a step back to admire and examine the length of her body. Gabi's tanned back was fully exposed, the dress just skimming above her behind. Darion ran his fingers tenderly up the length of her spine to her neck, and down again. Gabi's stomach fluttered. He moved her hair aside, and planted a trail of soft kisses on the back of her neck, his stubble grazing her skin. Pulling her into him, she could feel the hard bulge in his trousers. His hands reached around and cupped her breasts, his kisses becoming firmer, hungrier. Gabi couldn't stop the soft moan from escaping her lips as she parted them, her head falling back slightly. His fingers tweaking her nipples sent a fire of arousal between her legs. She turned to face him.

"I don't think I can wait much longer," he said, in a low husky tone, pulling her into him.

As he sealed his lips over hers, and began kissing her frantically, Gabi felt herself wedged against the wall. He pulled her dress up, his fingers grabbing the sides of her underwear to yank them down. Gabi's skin was warm and tingling. Her clit pained for his touch, her nipples hard, wanting nothing but his tongue. He stroked tantalisingly between her legs, exploring her with gentle, circular movements. Parting her with his fingers, he slid in and out torturously slowly, his gaze on hers, studying her intently, as always. She knew that he loved to know what pleased her. She whimpered as he drove into her sensitive spot, filling her with ripples of pleasure.

"Shouldn't…we…wait?"

"I can't."

Gabi parted her legs, taking more of his fingers. Her muscles clenched, tightening around him. Her hands searched for his zipper hurriedly, desperate to feel him inside her. She freed him, stroking his erection, sliding her hand up and down the rigid shaft. As she circled the wet tip with her thumb, Darion's features screwed up. He grunted as she tugged at him, her hand gliding over him at a faster speed.

"Come here." His voice was husky, urgent. "Bend over."

Before Gabi had time to position herself, Darion twisted her around, lifted her dress up over her waist, and bent her over, so that her hands were flat on the wall.

"Your ass is perfect, Gabi." He slapped it hard with his hand, hurting but exciting her at the same time. His fingers grabbed a cheek roughly, a satisfied groan seeping from his lips.

Fumbling between her legs for a brief moment, he entered her forcefully, causing her to cry out, her body shooting forward. She bit her thumb, waiting for the discomfort of his length to subside. As he slid in and out, she felt a ripple of desire tear through her. He gripped her by the waist, bending her over further, giving him deeper access.

"Gabi...fuck, this feels good."

He yanked his hips backwards and forwards, groaning. His fingers buried into her hair, roughly. Just as she was getting into it, the dinging sound of the elevator startled her. The doors opened causing her to stiffen. Cheeks heated, she glanced up, expecting the worse. She felt herself relax at the empty corridor, relieved.

"Shall we go?"

"Not yet."

When the doors closed them in again, Darion continued to buck his hips into her. His hand reached around, his fingers playing with her clit. The tingling sensation caused her to twist and writhe fervently, her legs weakening. She felt herself building up to an orgasm with his teasing, gentle fingers, and the tip of his cock hitting into her relentlessly. He pulled out swiftly, causing her to look over her shoulder questioningly. The emptiness was agonising.

"Don't stop." She panted.

With an inscrutable smile, Darion plunged into her again deeply. He glided in and out, his pace quickening.

"Come with me, darlin'..." She heard him grind his teeth.

The pleasure built, spreading through every part of Gabi's body. With a final slam, she felt Darion throb inside her, jerking, until he flooded her, gripping her into him.

Gabi's muscles tensed, clenching him tightly. She felt herself go dizzy, all of her senses heightened. Her heart hammered hard in her chest, a warm wash of lust spreading through her pelvis as an orgasm exploded through her. She shivered and trembled in ecstasy.

When the spasms started to ebb, and her heartbeat calmed, she pulled up her underwear, adjusted her dress, and turned around. Darion was leant against the wall, his breaths short and shallow. His beautiful face appeared tired, but his green eyes were dark and needy. His full lips enticed her. She felt a desperate urge to shower him with kisses. A look passed between them, neither of their gazes wavering. It was as if time froze, and the world had stopped spinning. Gabi felt her heart tighten, and reality hit her with such force that she almost fell. Her feelings for Darion Milano were frighteningly strong—stronger than she had anticipated. As if reading her mind, he straightened, his face etched with worry and fear. Taking a deep breath, he briskly looked away, pressing the elevator button.

When the doors pinged open, Darion stepped out. Gabi couldn't help but notice his firm, sexy bum as he strode in front of her. Once outside a door, he pressed the doorbell. They hadn't had to wait long before a man answered, pleased to see them. He invited them inside, to which they briefly introduced themselves.

In the main living room area, music was playing softly, and the lighting was dim, creating an intimate glow. The white marble floor sparkled, and matching furniture and plush leather sofas surrounded the room, gigantic floor cushions taking up a corner of it. There was a small table holding party nibbles and alcohol.

Gabi noticed, on estimation, that there were twenty other guests. They appeared to be couples in their mid-twenties to late forties. They were reasonably attractive and dressed immaculately. The women mainly wore elegant gowns revealing some leg, or cleavage, and the men were in black trousers and a shirt, or t-shirt. They were generally seated, talking, eating, drinking, and some were even dancing in the corner. The atmosphere was pleasant. Gabi immediately grew comfortable. Maybe it wouldn't be so bad after all.

"You hungry?" Darion asked her, pouring them both a glass of wine.

"No." She had eaten before she came.

"Well." He passed her the glass. "Relax, and have fun tonight." He grinned, taking out a cigarette, setting it between his lips, and lighting it.

Gabi took in her surroundings. She noticed that the guests were focusing on them, examining them like they were circus freaks. She felt paranoia and insecurity soar through her. Her flushed face cooled when they turned back to what they had been doing. Perhaps they knew Darion, and were wondering who she was.

"Darion?" A blonde woman sauntered over. "How nice of you to come. I'm Franchesca." She held out her manicured hand, which Darion took. "Do make yourself comfortable." Her gaze dragged over his body, openly admiring him, her pupils dilating, her mouth curling at the sides. Gabi scowled. She could see Franchesca was impressed with what she saw. She then examined Gabi carefully. "So pretty." She took a piece of her hair in her fingers, stroking it for a moment. "I have a few guests to greet, but I'll be back with you shortly." She gave them a little wave before sauntering off.

"You heard what she said." Darion caressed her behind. "Make yourself comfy." He stubbed his cigarette out in the nearest ashtray.

Gabi followed Darion to the middle of the room. He settled on the sofa next to a couple, leaving no room for her. Patting his knee, he indicated for her to sit. She smoothed down her dress before perching on his knee. A friendly looking blonde woman flashed them a smile. Gabi mirrored her expression, politely.

"I'm Paula. This is my husband, Elliot."

"Darion," he replied, a slow grin surfacing. "And Gabi," he answered for her.

"Nice to meet you." Paula gave Darion a provocative glance, her hand squeezing Elliot's. "I don't think I've seen you here before." Her brows shot up as she tried to remember if she had or not.

"You haven't," Darion said lightly. "Franchesca holds a party twice a month," he informed Gabi.

Oh. She scanned the room. She didn't know why someone would hold so many parties. Franchesca seemed well off, the apartment was exquisite, perhaps she preferred to socialise indoors rather than go out. She noticed as Franchesca and presumably her partner flitted past each couple, pausing for a few moments to talk with each one. *She's certainly popular.*

Darion ran his hand up Gabi's leg, his smile as devilish and delicious as ever, his gaze intense. His lips pressed firmly against her temple, finding their way to her ear, which he nibbled gently. The warmness and tickling of his breath made the hairs on her neck stand up. With leisurely licks of his tongue, Gabi's senses whirled, her body straining for his. Catching a delighted glance from another guest, Gabi tensed, pushing his hand away, a hot flush creeping up her neck.

Darion chuckled, unfazed. "I'm going to the bathroom." He stood up, leaning down to quickly peck her on the cheek. "Don't drink too much." He winked, looking down at her almost empty glass. "Unless you want a repeat performance of the club scenario?"

She watched as he wandered down a corridor. Turning back to the table, she took in the nibbles. She desperately wanted to take a crisp, however nobody really seemed to be eating. She decided to settle on mints that were in a bowl. Sucking one, she focused on the couple again. The man was stroking his wife's inner thigh with his fingers. Gabi assumed they were newlyweds.

"So, this is your first time too?" Paula licked her lips, leaning forward to take a mint, her cleavage on full show. She popped the mint in her mouth. "I do love your dress." She stroked the material, her hand skimming Gabi's knee.

"Thanks." Gabi shifted an inch away, hoping that Paula didn't notice.

"And your boyfriend, he's quite something." She giggled.

Gabi didn't understand how Paula's husband, in earshot, wasn't annoyed with her confession to obviously fancying Darion.

"He's not my boyfriend."

"Oh, it's like that, is it?" Paula nodded vehemently, as if she totally understood what Gabi meant. "So, what are you into?"

"Erm, you mean like, hobbies?"

"Well…" Paula twirled a strand of hair around her finger. "If you can call them hobbies." She threw her head back with a soft laugh.

"Honey, Carol's over there," Elliot interrupted, nodding toward a tall, slim brunette, who was locked in a passionate kiss with a man. "The woman you've been messaging."

"Oh, right." Paula lifted her head to get a better view. "What do you think of her?"

"She's very attractive," he answered, looking at the brunette as his finger rubbed his chin.

Gabi glanced behind her, wondering where Darion was. She scanned the room once more, and noticed two women sitting on the cushions on the floor, kissing. The men that they were with were sitting there watching, appearing to be enjoying the show. Gabi's nose wrinkled in confusion as they all vanished into another room.

When Darion returned, she felt herself relax a little. He resumed his position next to Paula, Gabi once again sitting on his lap.

"So, Darion," Paula purred seductively, "have you ever had a foursome?" She flirted openly.

Gabi rubbed her rigid neck, outraged at such a personal question. She clamped her lips together, unsure of how long she'd be able to bite her tongue.

"There isn't much I haven't done," he confessed. "How about you?"

"Oh, not yet, but I'm easy." She grinned. "I was saying to your beautiful companion how attractive you were. So…" She sat up straighter. "Have you both discussed what level you're willing to go to? Me and Elliot…" she paused, letting out a small groan as his hand was now up her skirt, "we have no objections to anything, except Elliot. His boundaries are women only."

"Same," Darion said. "And I'm sure Gabi has no objections." He glanced at her questioningly.

Gabi ignored him. She didn't know what was going on. She noticed a nearby couple petting heavily. Her forehead creased in confusion as she noticed another man openly caressing a woman's breasts, whilst she kissed another woman. Eagerly, they vanished through another door.

Oh my god! Gabi's palms grew sweaty. Her heart banged against her chest. Her stomach churned, as a sick feeling of anxiety spread through her. Darion bent down to kiss her shoulder gently, a soft trail making its way up her neck. Usually, she wouldn't have minded his touch. Yet here, it felt dirty. She recoiled, noticing Paula's hand sliding up Darion's leg, and then begin to stroke his visible erection. Elliot was hungrily kissing Paula's neck.

"I need the toilet." Gabi jumped to her feet.

"You okay?" Darion asked, his tone soft and concerned. "If you feel uncomfortable, I told you, we can leave."

"No, stay here." *You look like you're having fun.* She silently fumed.

She quickly paced past couples who were getting intimate with one another. She felt like she would vomit. She didn't understand it. It was a swinger's party! She had never met a swinger in her life. She didn't understand how these people were about to willingly have sex with other people, whilst their partners watched, or joined in. Darion had taken her there without even advising her it was a fucking orgy. She felt her blood pressure rise. She had to get out of there.

She yanked the door open and raced toward the elevator, pressing the button several times, willing it to open before Darion caught up with her. As soon as the doors opened, she fled inside. She made out Darion's worried face just as the doors closed. Gabi threw her head back, resting it on the wall. She hastily wiped the tears away that trickled down her cheeks. Wasn't she enough for him? He wanted several women. Was she terrible in bed? Her mind clouded with sickening thoughts. He couldn't care about her, if he could easily have sex with another woman in front of her, or allow her to do so with another man. He had definitely crossed the line this time. There was no way in hell that she would *ever* see the pervert again.

Chapter Twenty-One

Darion

Darion raced down the stairs as fast as he could. His heart pounded in his chest, he had a painful stitch in his side, and he desperately needed to catch his breath. Yet it was imperative that he caught up with Gabi. He needed to explain himself. He should have informed her that it was a swinger's party, but he thought he would surprise her. He stupidly thought that she would be cool with it. She had been so fun lately, opening up to him, exploring new things, having sex in public places. Plus, she hadn't complained about their 'open relationship.'

He'd assumed that she would've been aroused at watching other couples. He hadn't wanted to have sex with another woman, nor she to do so with another man. Just them. Together. Being watched. Losing their inhibitions.

He couldn't understand why she had run off.

Perhaps it was the fact that Paula had started to touch him. Maybe she had become jealous, unable to handle it. He should have discussed rules and boundaries beforehand. He scolded himself for forgetting.

Darion wasn't unfamiliar with swinging. Experiencing it had lit a spark in his past marriage, which kept them feeling alive. He and Eva had even visited a luxurious swinger's resort abroad, fulfilling every fantasy. It had aroused him to see his wife getting pleasured by someone else.

They had met couples who had been swinging for ten years or more, and had never endured problems—couples who truly loved one another, who believed that life was short, that you only lived once. They treated it as a normal night out. Some even had children who were none the wiser. It was a little kinky secret between them. Darion and Eva had had a solid relationship at the time, and had strongly loved one another. He would have died for her. She was his everything. They had been two consenting adults willing to participate in swinging. What could have gone wrong?

They only had *one* rule: he and Eva were only to enjoy the company of another person whilst the other was present, purely to fulfil each ones fantasies and to satisfy. If one was absent, then it was classified as cheating. The rule had been broken.

He only had casual relationships since then. He allowed women to do as they pleased, as could he. If he allowed a woman such as Gabi to be with other men, then he couldn't get hurt. If he never made her his girlfriend, he wouldn't care what she got up to. At least in an open relationship there wasn't a risk of being lied to, or deceived, or made a fool of.

He punched a wall, the concrete digging into his flesh. He fell to the steps, his head between his knees, trying to regain his composure. He had really loved Eva. He had ached for her for a long time. Meaningless flings didn't fill the void, yet they took his mind off her for a night or so.

He hadn't spoken to the bitch since they'd split. He had spoken to her lawyers, though. She wanted half of what was hers—The Black Door. Darion had ran the gentleman's club for years, long before he had met her, yet she had talked him into renovating the upstairs and making more money. She had put in the same costs he had, including payments toward the mortgage, giving her joint ownership. He had been like a lapdog, so into her that he would have done almost anything.

When they'd divorced, she had agreed with him that as long as he kept the club open and gave her half of what money it brought in, that they didn't need to sell the place, and the arrangement had suited them both fine, until now. She had since gone back on her word and wanted the club sold, and was apparently having financial problems. Not that he believed her. She wanted to spite him. Eva wanted to take away all of his hopes and dreams, everything he had worked so hard for. And the worst part was that he couldn't afford to buy out her share. The partying, drinking, and gambling over the years hadn't been kind to his pocket. He even had payments outstanding on his vehicles.

He pushed Eva out of his mind, and rubbed his hands up and down his face. He had hoped to have a fun night with Gabi, but his plan had failed. He wouldn't be surprised if she never wanted to see him again.

***

Gabi

Gabi strode down the road, her shoes pinching her feet. Although she felt the beginning of a blister, she hurried her pace regardless. She wanted to get away from Darion, and quickly. The streets were pitch black, except for the glow of the street lamps. The rain lashed down fast and heavy, drenching her clothes and hair. She didn't have a clue where she was. She had never been to this town before. She surveyed the roads, hoping a taxi would drive by.

Everything was her fault, she decided. Gabi had wanted excitement and adventure. She was the one who had been feeling sorry for herself, stuck with Lawrence, daydreaming of something more. She had gotten more than she'd bargained for tonight. How Darion thought that she would be relaxed with him fucking another girl was beyond her. She hated the fact that he flirted and had done god knows what with Gina, not to mention anyone else, however he wasn't her boyfriend; she could hardly tell him what to do. Why had she walked into the club that night? Why had she set her sights on someone like him?

She saw the beam of car headlights nearby, and

turned her head to see a black Audi. *Shit!* It was Darion. She quickened her pace. She heard the engine stop, and the sound of a car door being opened and closed.

"Gabi," he yelled. "Please, hear me out." The desperation was apparent from his trembling voice, and the sound of his footsteps grew closer.

"Fuck off," she screamed back angrily. "Don't come near me, you fucking pervert."

"I'm sorry," he cried. "I didn't expect you to sleep with anybody else, nor for me to. I just wanted you to get a feel for it. Open your eyes to something new."

Gabi began to sprint. Stealing a quick glance over her shoulder, she saw that he was near. She ran faster. She didn't want his sleazy hands on her. She raced past several buildings, and crossed the road, making her way to what appeared to be a park. She quickly slipped off her heels, her feet sinking in the wet grass. The rain showed no sign of stopping. She shivered; her exposed back was especially cold.

"Gabi. Don't run from me. I want five minutes, that's all."

She tripped over as he caught one of her legs. Her face hit the grass, her nose sinking straight into the dirt. She quickly rolled over and sat up, wiping it away. She was unable to control the sobs that exploded from her, the hot tears pouring down her face.

"Leave me alone. You humiliated me tonight." She drew in a breath, and then another, feeling a little faint and sick to her stomach. "I don't even know who you are."

"Let me explain. I went about it the wrong way, I'm sorry."

She wiped the tears with the back of her hand, and brought her head up to meet his. His wet hair stuck to his forehead, his drenched shirt clung to his body, the outlines of his ripped muscles beneath it visible through the damp fabric. His knuckles were covered in deep cuts, the blood of which was also smeared on his face. The light from the moon flickered in his wide, worried eyes. She had never met anyone so extremely sexy before. Gabi hated herself for being so attracted to him, especially now.

"Gabi." He sank to the ground next to her. "Will you listen, please?"

"Whatever," she snapped. "Say what you will, but you will never see me again."

"I'm sorry." His shoulders drooped, his arms hanging limp by his sides. Usually so confident, all she saw now was a vulnerability that surprised her. "I should have told you what sort of party it was." He ran a hand through his hair, shaking his head. "For some reason I thought you'd enjoy it. I told you I'd bring excitement to your life. I told you when I met you that you wouldn't be the same woman if you kept seeing me." He didn't look at her. "You were starting to open up, doing some crazy things. I thought you liked it when I took control. I really thought that you'd have fun."

"What? Enjoy watching you fuck another woman, right before my very eyes?" she asked, a note of disgust in her voice. She wiped her dress down, which was covered in dirt, ruined.

"I should have discussed the steps and levels of

activity with you first, and whether you'd be comfortable with it." He paused. "I didn't want another woman. I just wanted you to get an experience of swinging. See if you liked it enough to try it sometime."

"Have you done this before?" The question was out of her mouth before she could stop it. She wished she'd never asked when his expression hardened.

"A few times," he confessed.

Gabi swallowed the lump in her throat, and wrapped her arms around herself defensively. Her features were tight with disapproval. She was utterly gobsmacked. Darion, the man she had adored only a short while ago, had enjoyed swinging, and orgies.

He touched her chin, turning her face until she had no choice but to look at him. "I found it fun, liberating. I'm not ashamed of it, Gabi." He fixed her with a look, his face dark and possessed. "Everyone has different fantasies. I just happen to be open-minded, and willing to explore it all. *Everything*."

She looked away from him, bringing her face up to the sky. She was relieved to see that it had stopped raining. A heavy sigh escaped her lips as she took in the scenario. There they were, sitting in the muddy grass, her with dirt over her face, him with blood on his, both of them freezing cold in wet clothes, discussing swinging at 4 a.m. *What a crazy world.* It wasn't so long ago when she was lying in bed with Lawrence, staring at their neatly prepared work clothes, listening to the alarm clock tick, and hating her life.

"What does swinging involve?" she asked carefully, avoiding eye contact, not even sure if she wanted to know.

"Well..." He reached for her hand, but she withdrew. "For starters, you need to be open with one another, especially when it comes to communication. Me and..." He paused. "Me and one of my ex-girlfriends were comfortable with it."

He took the cigarette box from his pocket, pulled out a cigarette, and lit it after it was in his mouth. "We followed rules, no separating, no sex unless we *both* agreed, and safe sex always." He blew out smoke. "We would always ask the other before we did anything. Who could play with who, how far we could take it, where we could do it, you know like the same bed, same room, whatever. We frequently communicated, so it was never a problem." He thudded the ground with his fist. "Well, almost," he corrected himself, focusing on the ground.

"What happened?"

"Why does it matter?" he asked. "You weren't open to trying it, you said you wouldn't enjoy it, and you don't wanna see me again. So, none of this matters, Gabi." He climbed to his feet.

"You didn't warn me," she yelled. "A swinger's party isn't something you just fucking spring on someone." She stood up, anger flooding her.

"I said I'm sorry." He headed for the street. "I don't know why I expected you to enjoy it."

"What's that supposed to mean?" she snapped. "You think I'm boring? Close-minded? Vanilla?"

"I didn't say that." He shook his head, dropping

the cigarette butt to the ground. "Come. I'll take you home."

She followed him in silence toward the car, her heels in her hands. Her feet were now black from the mud. She wondered whether Darion minded her ruining his immaculate car. Oh well. She no longer gave a damn.

She noticed as he wiped his face hastily. Gabi's brow furrowed in confusion. *What happened with his ex-wife?* She knew that he had been talking about her. His expression had been so pained, like he'd break down. If she wasn't so angry with Darion, she may have felt sorry for him.

Back in the car, the silence continued. She had so many unanswered questions and thoughts whirling around in her head. Did she want to see him again? She had heard that threesomes were more common than people tended to think, but orgies, swinging parties? Was it normal? Were people doing that now? Had the 'free love' of the sixties returned?

Darion's bloody fingers gripped the steering wheel. The pressure caused the cuts to reopen and bleed. His chest rose and fell with his loud and heavy breathing. He gritted his teeth like he always did when he was agitated. He didn't look at Gabi once.

He drove faster than ever, like a maniac. The car skidded past corners on the wet roads. Gabi grabbed the handle of the door, hoping that they wouldn't crash. He was scaring her. She tried to look out of the window, but it was complete blackness, plus he was driving so fast that she doubted she would have caught sight of anything. Her heart felt as if it

S. Valentine

would burst out of her chest as fear pulsed through her. She willed for him to slow down.

Did he want to get her home so fast? For some reason, even after everything, she realised that she didn't want to go home.

Chapter Twenty-Two

"Darion, slow down," she screamed as they swerved around another corner, and she slid in her seat.

She could see nothing but fields and trees for miles. She had no idea where they were. She kept picturing them crashing, and being stuck in a ditch. Maybe she was overreacting. *He's a good driver,* she tried to reassure herself.

"Darion," she repeated. "You're scaring me."

He showed no signs of slowing down, keeping his foot firmly on the accelerator. Gabi looked at him, her mouth agape. He seemed to be in some sort of daze, his unblinking eyes staring through the windscreen, as if he wasn't actually seeing the roads.

"Darion." She slapped him on the arm as hard as she could.

"What the fuck," he exclaimed, coming out of his possessed state. He veered off the road, until he

217

came to a deserted spot near some trees. He slammed on the brakes, and pulled up the handbrake forcefully. "Gabi, what are you playing at?"

"I'm not staying in this car with you." She opened the door and climbed out.

It was raining again, pouring down heavily. *Great,* she thought, wishing she hadn't exited the car. She observed the quiet lanes. There were no other cars or people in sight. She huffed, annoyed that they were in the bloody countryside. She'd never find a taxi rank. Darion got out of the car, slamming his door hard. He raced toward her.

"Where are you going? Get back in the car."

"I can't. You're scaring me."

He grabbed her by her arm, and pulled her roughly around to look at him. Her face was only inches away from his. She could feel the warmth of his breath on her skin. Gabi tried to free herself, yet his grip remained tight on her arm, his fingers digging into her.

"Is this over between us?" he asked.

She really didn't know. Was he too much for her? Could she handle him sexually? Were they compatible? What did he want from her? Could she really handle the hurt that he might cause?

Darion's pupils flashed dangerously. It sent shivers up Gabi's spine, and made the hairs on her neck stand on end. His grip tightened as if he didn't want to let her go, not ever. Gabi's stomach knotted as she held her breath, waiting for his next move. She knew what was coming. She wanted it to.

The rain continued to thrash down and soak

them. With one quick movement, he picked her up. She clamped her legs tightly around his waist as his mouth crashed hard against hers. They began kissing with such force that Gabi's jaw ached. Their tongues eagerly massaged one another's, their kiss becoming deeper. Groaning into her mouth, he carried her toward the car, where he lifted her onto the bonnet.

She writhed on the cold metal as he began to kiss and nibble up her legs, paying special attention to her inner thighs, making her ache for him. *Why can't I get away from him?* She was helpless under his touch.

Even though the rain continued to drench them, it didn't deter them from wanting one another immediately. Darion frantically pulled her dress up, and tore off her underwear. She inhaled sharply when he thrust into her. He was clearly too frustrated for foreplay. Gabi's fingers tangled in his wet hair, as she rocked her hips into his, greedily wanting every inch of him. The rain dripped down her skin, causing his chest to slide against hers, back and forth, as he continued to pleasure her. Each slam almost sent her over the edge, as her entrance burned and throbbed with desire.

A low cry eased out of her throat.

Darion grabbed her wrists and banged them against the bonnet, holding her captive. She tried to struggle free, desperately wanting to run her fingers over his bloodied face, over his full, sensuous lips. But, his grip was tight. He stared at her wildly.

With his free hand, he yanked down the top of her dress, freeing her breast from her bra. He hungrily took it in his mouth, sucking it roughly, the soreness exciting her. His tongue met her nipple, flicking over it, making it a hard peak. Gabi arched her back, relishing the feel of his warm, wet strokes. His teeth then clamped down, tugging the nipple. Gabi screamed out in pain, sinking her sharp teeth into the arm that held her down.

His top lip curled back over his teeth wickedly. He leant closer to bite her lip, but she turned her head to the side. His mouth followed hers, to which she quickly snagged his lip with her teeth. She tasted the salty blood instantly. Darion let out a low laugh, shaking his head. He dug his teeth into her neck hard, puncturing her delicate skin. *Owww!* She ground her teeth. It hurt. She wriggled and managed to free one hand, and so she slapped him sharply across the face. Amused, Darion pounded into her even harder and faster.

"You like that?" He tongue lapped at the blood on his lip. "You love it rough, don't you, darlin'?"

What's this man doing to me? She couldn't stop the grin creeping across her face.

She kept sliding up the wet bonnet each time Darion pounded into her. Water droplets fell from their faces, goosebumps covered their freezing and shivering bodies. They were too absorbed in one another, too in the moment, to care. Gabi had never been so turned on in all her life.

As he thrust one last time with force, as if punishing her, he sent her over the edge. Gabi drew a breath, tension coiling in her stomach, her inner muscles contracting around him. Her body stiffened for a moment, until she orgasmed loudly, his name spilling from her throat. Darion followed moments later, bursting into her, his whole body shuddering. Exhausted, he fell on top of her, panting. Gabi didn't move. She was a quivering wreck.

They looked at one another, and burst into hysterics. She stroked his hair as he cuddled her tightly for a moment. She knew that she wouldn't experience this kind of pleasure and chemistry with anyone else, ever.

As he stood up, she pushed her dress down, and followed him to the car. She was shivering from the bitter air. Climbing onto the passenger seat, she strapped herself in. She caught sight of herself in the mirror. Her face was still smeared with dirt, her lip was grazed, and she had a bite mark on her shoulder. She was soaking and wearing a filthy dress. What an eventful night.

"You're crazy," she told him, giggling.

"That's why you like me." He winked at her.

"Darion…" she began. Even though, at times, he infuriated the hell out of her, she felt overwhelmed, excited, and completely in awe of him. Everything he did surprised her.

"Yeah?"

She looked down at her lap. She felt so close, yet so far away from him. "Nothing."

How she wished things were different.

Chapter Twenty-Three

Darion

Darion kissed the slim blonde longingly. Her name was Thelma, or something like that. He couldn't remember. Not that he needed to. She lay on her back, wearing nothing but pink underwear and sexy black fishnet stockings. Her heavily made-up come-to-bed eyes stared up at him, and a slow, seductive smile spread across her face. She sat up, pushing Darion onto his back, taking the lead. He was completely naked. He drew his breath as she placed firm kisses on his chest, softly nibbling him, the kisses going lower, settling below his belly button. He arched his back and closed his eyes for a brief moment, biting his lip, trying not to get so worked up. He didn't want to finish too soon.

He turned his head and looked at another sexy woman, who was on the other side of the room on another rounded bed. She was naked, her breast implants perfectly round, her long, tanned legs open, inviting her male companion, Thelma's boyfriend, Vinnie, to do as he pleased. When his head ducked between her legs, Darion heard her let out a soft moan. She threw Darion a look. Her eyes were wild, full of passion and hungry for him. Eva. His Eva.

He loved seeing her being pleasured. He loved being able to completely focus on her reactions, taking in every inch of her body, how she moved, hearing the noises that she made, and most importantly, how she would be going home with him, engaging in the best sex they ever had, whilst fantasising about the night's events. She kept her curious stare on Darion, as the blonde kept bringing him to the brink of climax with her mouth.

The room was dimly lit with only a gentle glow from the overhead chandelier. The walls and carpet were black. There was a rounded bed in each corner of the room where several people were engaging in foreplay, or full-on intercourse, busy receiving or giving pleasure, yet managing to steal a look at those around them.

Eva stood up, taking her lover Vinnie by the hand, and settling down on the bed next to Darion. As the man continued to feast on her, and the blonde wrapped her lips around Darion's length, he and Eva kissed passionately. Both Thelma and Vinnie knew how to tick their boxes. They were a good-looking wealthy couple, and had been swinging for years.

Thelma sat up straight and looked at him, her eyebrows raised suggestively. Darion knew that she wanted him. He looked at Eva, who slowly nodded. They asked one another first, regardless of how many times they had been swinging. It was something that kept them close, a mutual respect that they had. He was hers, and she was his.

Darion and Eva had been married for five years when they decided to try swinging. They had been fully satisfied with one another, experiencing new things all the time, both of them sexually adventurous, and open-minded. Eva then wanted to try to a new high, to do something that they never had before, to lose their inhibitions completely. They had sat together for several nights on the laptop, a glass of wine in hand, flirting with other couples online. It had been fun.

She had casually mentioned swinging, and had never pressured him. He couldn't see the harm in giving it a go. The first time that they had visited a couple they had met online at their house, they had simply watched and only touched each other, light foreplay, then him and Eva had put on a show. It had been daring, arousing. The next event, a small swingers' party, they had experienced foreplay with other couples, and penetration hadn't been allowed. When they decided to move on from soft swinging, and intercourse was permissible, he and Eva shared partners. She enjoyed men and women, whilst he watched, and he enjoyed women only. However, they had agreed always to be together, never to separate.

Shortly after, Darion had converted the upstairs of the gentleman's club into a sex club, which had been a massive success. They had designed the layout together, the rooms, the bar, the décor. They had spent so much money and time on it. And it had been worth it. Some of the best nights of Darion's life had been in that club, whether it was indulging in swinging, or him and Eva having fun when the club was closed, alone.

Darion shut his lids and allowed himself to fully relax as the blonde straddled him, and brought him to an intense climax. He groaned out loudly, his chest rapidly rising, adrenaline pumping through his veins, his face and body soaked in sweat.

He thought that Eva would have orgasmed by now. He opened his eyes and slowly turned his head. She was gone. Selfishly, he sat up and pushed Thelma off him, not caring that she was almost close to climaxing herself. He wondered where the fuck she was. Rage soared through every cell in his body. They discussed the rules every time they attended an event. No separating, no sex unless they both agreed, and safe sex always.

Neediness and desperation came over him as he looked around the room and the people in it. None of them were Eva, or Vinnie. He felt a stab of pain shoot through his heart. Darion took a deep breath, and rubbed his chest. He had a bad feeling in his gut. He stood up, his mind racing. He frantically scanned the floor, found his boxers, and dressed quickly. Perhaps Eva had gone to the bondage room—she liked to dominate, take control. Still, she should have asked him first.

He peered through the windows of each room, not spotting Eva. He then hurriedly passed the open rooms, witnessing several men and women having sex, whipping one another, enjoying foreplay, threesomes, and orgies.

He strode to the last door, which had no window. It was the room that provided complete privacy, a room that, whatever happened, was kept between those walls. It wasn't uncommon to want privacy. Some people feared being recognised by people that they knew, especially colleagues.

Darion's hand gripped the door handle, willing it to be open. He twisted it. It was locked. He tried it again and again. He banged on the door. No response. He pressed his ear against the thick wood, and heard loud groans. He shouted out her name, and the moaning stopped. He was sure that it was Eva that he could hear. He banged on the door again and shouted her name.

He had no idea what to do. He slid to the floor, quietly waiting. He needed to know whether it was Eva in there. After a few moments of silence, he heard the groans again. It was definitely Eva. It was definitely his wife locked in that room with that man. Had he forced her? Was he holding her captive against her will? The thoughts whirled around in his head.

"Vin, don't stop," she gasped.

No, she wasn't captive. His stomach knotted. He felt physically sick. He took several deep breaths, trying to stay in control, and not vomit. He clenched and unclenched his fists in anger. What was she doing in there? Why had she separated from him? Why was the room locked? Darion had so many unanswered questions in his head. He looked up to the ceiling as he felt tears prick his eyes. He didn't want to cry in public. He didn't want to cry at all. But, he loved that woman in there, and she was hiding something. Why couldn't she stick to the fucking rules? Why, why, why?

Despite banging the door again, there was still no response. Half an hour passed until the door creaked open an inch. Darion stood back up and kicked it open as Vinnie tried to slam it shut again. The door hit Vinnie straight in the jaw.

"What the fuck is going on?" he screamed, heat flooding his face.

"It's not what it looks like," Eva mumbled, standing up, now wearing her underwear.

"We wanted somewhere to relax, Daz."

"Why didn't you tell me? And don't fucking lie to me. I've been out there for half an hour."

Eva's face dropped. She opened her mouth as if to say something, but remained silent. Darion grabbed hold of the door handle, fighting to stand up. He couldn't stop the tears from dripping down his face. He couldn't look at Eva in the same way again. Standing there, guilt spread over her face, she appeared dirty, damaged. As for Vinnie, Darion was moments away from slamming his knuckles into the other man's face, and when he started, he probably wouldn't be able to stop.

He fled from the club, not wanting him or her near him. As far as he was concerned, Eva had cheated. A week later, she had tried to explain herself. Each time he spoke to her, she changed her story. She stated that they had gone somewhere private to relax, that Vinnie had given her a massage, which explained the groans. Darion didn't believe a word that she had said.

And he was right not to. Another week later, Eva had begun a relationship with Vinnie. She had even fallen in love with him. Darion hated her for it. He had willingly allowed her to sleep with other men; he couldn't comprehend why she then wanted only one man? A man that wasn't him. Had she not truly loved him?

His heart had been torn to pieces. He was incapable of ever trusting, or loving, another woman again.

***

Darion sat up, panting. His face and body were soaked in sweat. His heart was pounding against his chest. He let out a soft cry and looked around the room. His room. He wiped his forehead with the back of his hand. A bad dream. Again. *Vin, don't stop.* He heard Eva's voice as if it were only yesterday.

"Darion, are you okay?" He felt a hand touch his back softly.

He stiffened. "I'm fine," he lied, remembering that Gabi was in his bed. He leant over and grabbed his cigarettes from the bedside table. He lit one.

"Did you have a bad dream?" Gabi sat up.

"Something like that," he muttered.

He stood up and made his way to the bathroom. Confronting his reflection in the mirror, he realised he looked like shit. Balancing the cigarette on the edge of the sink, he turned the cold tap on, cupped water into his hands, and splashed his face. *I*

haven't had this dream for months. Why now?
Perhaps almost losing Gabi, or it being her first
swinging experience, had brought it all back. *Pull
yourself together.* Eva was nothing but a bitch who
had broken his heart.

Putting on a brave face, he put the fag in his
mouth, and entered the bedroom. Gabi was still in a
seated position, the sheets covering her naked body.
His mouth curved upwards as he sat down on the
bed, blowing out smoke, allowing it to travel
through the air. He didn't want a long conversation
about his bad dream; he couldn't be arsed. Holding
the cigarette between his fingers, he pulled Gabi's
head toward him and kissed her on the forehead.
His mouth then met her lips. It didn't take long until
he was on top of her, riding her, the cigarette back
in his mouth, remaining there the whole time.

Chapter Twenty-Four

Gabi

"Two more toast, coming up."

Gabi dug her fork into the tomatoes and bacon, and hungrily stuffed them into her mouth. It was 7 a.m. on a Monday morning. Mallory greeting her with a full English breakfast was just what she needed.

"So, how did your night go with Darion?" she asked, taking a sip of her steaming coffee.

"It was great."

"What did you get up to?"

Gabi wondered whether she should tell her friend about the swinger's party. Would she judge Darion poorly? "We just had a few drinks in the club." She avoided eye contact.

"So, things are going good?"

"For now."

Mallory handed her two pieces of toast. "How is

the sexy Darion?"

"He's okay. He had a nightmare last night. It jolted him awake."

"Poor thing." Mallory threw her a look of sympathy. "How's dance class going?"

"I love it, Mal."

"I knew you would."

"Where's Steve?"

"He's working out of town this week, so he set off early."

"Well." Gabi pushed the empty plate aside. "That was delicious, thanks."

"Anytime."

"I suppose we'd better get ready for work."

"Have you heard from Lawrence?"

"He sent me a message this morning asking to meet. I don't think I can face him."

"Just leave him to it. He'll get used to it all soon enough."

"Speak of the devil," she said when her mobile rang. She decided to answer it, and hear him out.

"Hello." She headed for the living room.

"Gabi, how are you?"

"I'm fine, I guess. You?"

"As good as I can be." She heard him sigh. "So, this is definitely it, then? You haven't had any second thoughts?"

She blinked back the tears that stung her lower lids. She felt dreadful. "No, Lawrence. I'm sorry."

"I'll ensure the majority of your stuff is sent to Mallory's."

"Thanks."

"And, Gabi…" he said quickly before she ended

the call, "I knew there was someone else."

"Lawrence," she attempted to deny it.

"Don't even try to insult my intelligence. I just hope he doesn't do to you what you did to me," he said sourly.

Before Gabi could respond, the line went dead. Running a hand through her hair, his words echoed in her mind. She was a true believer in karma. Maybe she did have it coming. So did Lawrence, for that matter. Maybe he'd meet someone who would make him feel worthless and lonely. She screwed up her face bitterly and turned to the window, gazing out at the grey sky. Mallory walked in, and sensing her sadness, put her arm gently around her shoulder.

"I'm gonna have a shower."

"Sure. We've got plenty of time."

Gabi slowly mounted the stairs. She needed a lukewarm, refreshing shower. She gathered her pink towel from the bedroom, and then settled in the bathroom. She felt completely exhausted. Darion had kept her awake most of the night, not that she was complaining. She still got butterflies every time she thought of him. However, she wasn't sure how to take his confession. If swinging was just something he'd experienced a few times, as he'd said, to experiment, kill his curiosities, have a bit of fun with a girlfriend, then she could handle that. Couldn't she?

She tried not to think about it. She needed to scrub herself clean. She turned the shower on, waiting for it to warm up. When hot steam filled the bathroom, she undressed and climbed in. Closing her eyes, she allowed the water to pour through her hair, down her face, and over her body. If only it could wash away her problems, Lawrence's spiteful words, Darion's dark desires, and the confusion which curdled inside her.

***

Darion

Darion sat in his office, his laptop settled on his lap. He clicked on the swingers' forum and scrolled down. Eva hadn't been on it for months. He liked to check now and then to see if she'd returned, selfishly wishing and hoping her and Vinnie's relationship hadn't lasted. He clicked on a few thumbnail pictures that resembled Eva, browsing the profiles. No sign of her. His mobile vibrated in his pocket. Pulling it out, he glanced at the screen before answering.

"Hello," a sultry voice purred down the line.

"Franchesca?"

"Yes. How are you, Darion?"

"I'm good." He lit a cigar.

"Shame you left the party early. I was looking for you."

"Maybe some other time," he said out of politeness.

"We discussed me holding a party at your club?" she reminded him.

"We certainly did."

"Let me pull together some people, and I'll email you a date."

"Sounds great. You'll be more than happy, I can assure you."

"I don't doubt it," she said flirtatiously.

He informed her of the name of the website. "You can fill in your application, upload your photograph, and your membership ID will be ready for you when you get here. I suggest you get your friends to do the same."

"Will do. I'll see you soon, Mr. Milano."

"Can't wait."

He put the phone back in the cradle, and poured himself a shot of vodka. Franchesca was hot. Usually, he'd be excited at spending time with a new woman, especially one that shared the same interests. Why wasn't he excited? Gabi's face appeared in his mind, and he shook his head, annoyed with himself. He needed to get a grip, and quick. Should he distance himself? He realised that he didn't want to. Last night in his bed, with her arms wrapped around him, had made him feel content—until the bad dream.

Gabi was a nice woman, the type of woman who he'd definitely feel secure with, settle down with one day. So why was he trying to change her, introduce her to swinging? Darion believed that you could have it all. Regardless of what Eva had done, you could have love and chemistry and excitement and polygamy. It could work. Couldn't it?

The tap at the door disturbed him. He looked up as Gina walked into the room, wearing a black corset, skirt, and platforms. Her hair and make-up were over the top, as usual.

"Hey, baby." She planted a firm kiss on his

mouth abruptly, causing him to edge away. "You okay?"

"I'm good, G. You?" He slid his chair back a little, creating some distance between them.

"Hmm. I was seeing this guy called Johnny for a while, but he turned out to be a prick." She shrugged. "Anyway, you haven't watched me dance in a while. I've missed you."

"I've been busy." He usually sat at the bar and watched her dance, at least four times a week. She got him so worked up. They'd then go straight to his office to make out. "Maybe you should give Johnny a chance."

"Darion." She stepped forward, placing her hand on his arm, caressing it. "Don't you want me anymore?"

"Gina." He let out a small laugh. "Don't be fuckin' crazy. I've been busy, that's all." He stood up, running a hand through his hair. He didn't want to reject her, or hurt her.

"Oh yeah. I checked your mail this morning," she said drily. "You need to pay off those car bills before they're towed away."

"Shit." He rubbed at the stubble on his chin.

"I take it you're still gambling."

He remained silent as he poured himself a whisky, and Gina a shot.

"I can't believe you blew all your savings, Daz."

"G, please." He pushed the glass toward her. "The club's doing well. I'll get it all back."

"Eva's lawyers are still chasing you. You can't avoid them forever."

"Drink up." He pointed to the shot.

"Alcohol is your solution to everything," she muttered.

"Not a solution…a distraction."

She snaked her arms around his waist, pressing her lips to his chiselled jawline repeatedly.

He pulled her in for a hug, to take her mind off wanting to kiss him.

Gina took a step back, her mouth agape. "That's why you haven't seen me dance…you're under the thumb by that girl, aren't you?"

"Who?" He sighed.

"The pretty blonde, Gabi. You know who I'm talking about, Daz," she said, raising her voice.

He huffed in exasperation. He wasn't in the mood for a heated discussion. "Gina, it's just sex." Was it?

"Come here." She reached out for him again. "I've missed this."

Darion raised the glass to his mouth, swigging the whisky back. He grimaced at the taste.

"I'll catch you later," she grumbled, refusing the drink he offered, pushing the glass away. She headed for the door.

"Gina," he yelled. He didn't want to give her any hope that they'd ever become an item. Together, they'd be trouble. All hell would break loose. It was too risky. Their friendship would suffer. He couldn't lose her that way. "Me and you are never gonna happen." His face hardened. "You knew that from day one."

"Oh yeah." She spun around. "Have you shown little miss upstairs yet?" she asked sharply, narrowing her gaze.

"No, why?"

"It won't last." She smirked. "As soon as she finds out that swinging is your way of life, that you *own* a swingers' club, she'll be gone. Not many people can handle that sort of stuff. I'm everything you want, Daz. You just can't admit it."

He swallowed the lump that had formed in his throat, his fingers gripping the edge of the desk. He said nothing as she walked off. He tapped his foot on the floor repeatedly, lost in thought. Seconds later, he poured another drink and tossed it back. He needed to get out of the club; he felt suffocated. He hoped a ride on his bike would clear his head.

Chapter Twenty-Five

Gabi

After a fairly quick day in the office, Gabi had had another dance class, which had gone well. The more she went, the more she enjoyed it. She'd even made a few new friends, which she was pleased about. As usual, she'd taken a fresh set of clothes with her, showered, and dressed.

When she exited The Royal Dance Academy, she was hit with rushing bodies, either shopping, on their way to work, or on their way to meeting family, friends, or a lover. Instead of the discontented expressions that she usually noticed, everyone appeared to be deliriously happy. Or perhaps that was her positive side, seeing the good in everyone and everything.

As the indoor shopping centre was open until ten that evening, she decided to do a bit of browsing, not particularly needing anything, but curious about new stock. It didn't take her long to be tempted by a new pair of shoes, and a CD for the car. She was about to set off, laden with shopping bags, when she passed a woman's lingerie store, which she knew also sold adult toys for women and men. Perhaps she could try some new things with Darion. She entered the cool, air-conditioned space, and scanned the racks of lingerie, sexy outfits, and shelves of toys, X-rated DVDs, books, and novelty gifts. A few items caught her attention, and after she'd paid for them, she left with a pink bag, giddy with anticipation.

Gabi had only been predictable sexually with Lawrence because he hadn't been experimental. She hadn't been able to introduce new things into the bedroom and be wild and daring, which she knew that she could be. As usual, she was looking forward to seeing Darion. She never knew what to expect with him.

When she was outside Darion's apartment, she wondered why he hadn't invited her to the club. With clammy palms, she tapped on the door, growing anxious. He yanked the door open. He welcomed her with a slow grin, and stepped aside to allow her to enter. He was shirtless and barefoot, wearing only black jeans that hung low on his hips, the Calvin Klein waistband of his boxers visible. Gabi ignored the somersaults that her stomach was doing, and sat down.

She scanned over the place. It smelt of incense sticks, and he had cleaned up.

"You hungry?" he asked, leaning down and kissing her hair.

"Not really."

"Well, I've been shopping and spent a fortune, so you better get hungry." He stroked her cheek gently. "What do you fancy?"

"Anything." She wasn't particularly fussed.

"I'm glad you're open when it comes to trying different foods." He headed into the kitchen.

I'll show you who's open. She turned to look at the plasma TV that was switched on. *Goodfellas* was showing. She sat further back in her chair. She liked this film. Just as she was getting into it, Darion returned with a tray of a variety of foods: meat nibbles, sushi, pizza sticks, and more.

"Thanks." She took a cheese and ham dipper.

"You want a drink?"

"Wine, if you have some."

He beamed. "Wine, it is."

Gabi needed a glass at least to calm her nerves. "Darion." She gulped back the wine as soon as it touched her fingers. "Are you okay after the other night?" she asked.

"What d'ya mean?"

"Getting so worked up. And the dream."

"I'm good." His expression said otherwise.

"You can talk to me, you know." She placed a hand on his arm. "I know this isn't serious between us, but I'm here if you ever want to talk."

He took a deep breath and looked up at the ceiling, obviously trying to remain calm. "I'm a mess, Gabi, what can I say?" He looked at her and shrugged.

"We're all a little messed up, if you think about it." It was true. Everybody had some sort of baggage, issues, past drama, insecurities, or whatever.

"Oh yeah. You're fucked up?" He raised a brow. "How?" he challenged her, his mouth curling ever so slightly at the sides.

"Okay." Gabi refilled her glass. "I've not had many serious relationships. The longest one I had was my ex-fiancé. I thought I was happy with him. I thought I wanted the house, the marriage, and the kids." She rubbed her nose nervously. "But I didn't. I didn't want all that."

"Why?" Darion's forehead crinkled with confusion. "What woman wouldn't want that?"

"Well, I do want that, I think," she corrected herself. "Just not with him."

"Why not? Surely something was right, if you were engaged to him." Darion lit a cigarette.

"I wanted it at first. Then I grew bored, unhappy, scared of the future. I don't know." She toyed with the stem of her glass.

"Bored?" Darion's mouth was a straight line. "So you cheated on him out of boredom. Nice."

Gabi looked at him. He was judging her, making her feel small, and low. He was the one that had instigated it, called her. It took two to tango.

"You weren't innocent in it all," she snapped. "I was also unhappy and scared of the future," she repeated. "I was lonely. I didn't feel loved. Something was missing. Something wasn't right."

"So, why didn't you try and work on it? Why didn't you tell him this?"

"I did. I tried my hardest to make it work. We weren't compatible."

"You should have realised that before you got engaged," he grumbled, puffing on his cigarette.

"Well I didn't know then. We grew apart. He changed. That happens, Darion."

"Oh, don't I know it."

"Just because you had some fucked up marriage doesn't give you the right to judge my life." Her tone was sharp as heat flooded her face. "I used to lie in bed, crying myself to sleep, nights I spent neglected, alone, wondering where he was. Then there were the days he came back moody, the times we spent together, bored shitless. God forbid we have any fun. I hated myself for feeling like I did. But I realised I wanted more." She wiped a few tears away. "Life's too short to never smile, to never laugh."

He shot her a look.

"At times I was a bit afraid of him too," she confessed, her head dropping.

"Why? Did he hurt you, Gabi?" Darion scrutinised her intently, his expression hardening. "Answer me."

"He was drunk, I got in the way," she attempted to make excuses.

Darion jumped to his feet, grinding his teeth, his fists curled, as rage obviously consumed him. He grabbed his t-shirt. "Where is he? I'll kill him." His chilling voice was menacing. He yanked the t-shirt on.

"Darion, stop," she pleaded. "It's over with now."

"No man should ever fucking put his hands on a woman," he spat. "I know we get rough during sex, but I'd never hurt you." He crouched down, grabbing her hands. "You know that, right?"

She nodded.

"Do you want me to go and pay him a visit?" She was touched by the concern that was apparent on his face that he wanted to protect her from harm.

"No. It's in the past."

"You're not miserable now. Are you?" he asked.

"I don't know," she mumbled. She had nothing.

"Hey." He shifted closer to her, his arm snaking around her waist. "What's wrong, Gabi?"

"I don't know," she repeated sternly. "I'm an idiot, that's what."

"Why?"

"You don't want to know."

"Try me."

Although Gabi could tell that he wanted to help, his face was a picture of worry.

Her heart beat rapidly, her fingers trembling. She didn't know whether to be upfront, or keep things to herself. What if the truth scared him? She inhaled deeply. "I think I like you too much, Darion." She focused on the carpet, not daring to look at him. "I've tried not to. Even you taking me to a swinger's party didn't put me off. You excite me. I'm happy when I'm around you." She shrugged. "I don't know what to say."

After a moment of silence, he sighed heavily. "I've told you I'm no good for you, Gabi."

"Why aren't you?"

He turned his head away.

"I think I know what I'm getting myself into, Darion." She stroked his fingers, and slowly leant toward him. Her lips met his. She liked him too much. She believed that if she were patient, Darion would eventually see sense, and properly commit to her.

"Don't." He pulled back, rubbing the stubble on his chin. "Don't get attached to me, Gabi. Don't be stupid."

"It's too late," she said irritably. "If you don't feel happy being with me, or you feel nothing at all for me, then I'll leave. I thought I could handle casual, but I can't."

"You mean, you wanna be exclusive?" His mouth dropped.

Yes. "No," she lied instead, shaking her head, not wanting to push him away. "Do whatever you want, I don't want to control you. I just don't want to waste my time on you if you feel nothing at all for me. If I know that you like me back, just even a little bit, that's enough. I can work with that." *Just a little bit of hope that it might lead somewhere.*

He bit his lip. His fingers tapped anxiously on his leg. "Of course I like you, Gabi."

"Yes, but is this just sex for you? You can be honest with me."

"I hoped it would be. I really did." So, he did feel *something* for her. "I can't do this though." He inhaled deeply. "I just can't." His head fell in his hands. "You need to go."

"What?" she spluttered. "Go? But why?"

"I can't do this anymore. Just go. Now." His voice was shaky.

"Darion." She knelt down before him, taking hold of his hands. "Why are you pushing me away?"

"Gabi, please just go."

"I'm not going anywhere until you speak to me," she yelled. "If I leave this apartment now, I assure you, I will never come back. You don't play with my feelings like this. Not when I've had the guts to admit I feel something for you."

"I can't give you what you want." He stood up, blowing out an exasperated puff of air.

"So you want me to leave, and that be it? Is this what you want?" She stood up. "Tell me now, and I'll go. You never have to hear from me again."

He let out a laugh. "Neither of us know what we want, do we? We're just gonna drag each other down until we're done with one another."

"You don't know that," she said softly.

"Relationships are fucked up. Someone always gets hurt in the end."

"That's bullshit. There are successful relationships and marriages."

"Yeah, and I wonder how many cheat behind their partners' back."

Gabi hooked her handbag over her shoulder and headed for the door. "If that's how you feel, Darion, then I guess I'm wasting my time." She stared at him for a moment, before turning on her heel, tears burning her lower lids. Maybe he couldn't give her what she wanted.

Chapter Twenty-Six

Darion

Darion intertwined his fingers. What the fuck was wrong with him? He didn't know whether it was anger or sadness, but he felt like he'd explode any minute. He felt like he needed to let his emotions out. He never lost his cool in front of women, ever. Except for Gina. But Gina couldn't be the one. She couldn't be. She wasn't fun when she was sober, she was quiet and withdrawn, and they didn't share many interests outside of the bedroom. At least Gabi was a laugh when sober *and* drunk, and they seemed to have things in common. He lit another cigarette and took a long drag.

"Gabi?" He called her back, his tone a plea. "Sit back down, please."

She was reluctant at first, but then she sat back on the sofa.

"Why don't we just roll with it, see what

happens? No rules, no restrictions."

She chewed her nail.

"Let's give it a chance. But I can't give you promises, and I can't give you my word that I won't ever be tempted by other women again." He shrugged. "I'll try. I don't trust women to commit fully, Gabi. Not even you." He paused. "Not yet."

"You're scared of getting your heart broke?"

He stilled, as if she saw right through his fears and insecurities. "Isn't everybody?" he replied.

"I suppose."

He changed the subject quickly. "We make each other laugh, we have fun, don't we? Let's keep it at that. You feel a little something for me." He swigged his wine. "And..." he paused, as if struggling to find or say the words. "I feel a little something for you. That's a good start, right?"

Gabi nodded. He stroked the hair out of her pretty face. He did feel something for her. He couldn't control it. He hadn't planned it. He could never stop thinking about her. Denying Gina in the office was the first time that he had ever done that. Before now, he never refused sex, ever. Gabi must have some sort of hold on him. He hated it. He did fear that she would hurt him. He couldn't give his all to another woman and be left heartbroken again. He could start off slow, sure. He could get to know Gabi properly and see whether there was a slight chance that it could work out. He couldn't keep up the game forever. He couldn't sleep with different women every week for the rest of his life. Gina had been right about that.

"Would you rather me be the man that promised

you the world and let you down? Or be honest and tell you that I'm not sure where this will lead?" His eyes were wide, serious. "It would never be my intention to hurt you, but I know for certain that it's hard for me to commit at the moment, Gabi."

"I understand." She nodded. She was obviously disappointed. Maybe she had wanted to hear all the right words—that he cared for her, wanted only her, and would change his ways. But he was right. If he said all those things then he would be lying. But wasn't it better to be hurt by the truth, than protected with a lie?

"So." He pulled her toward him, kissing her. "What's with the bag?" He nodded toward the pink bag in the corner of the room.

"Oh." She sat back casually. "Take a look."

He leant over and picked up the bag. He loved surprises. He emptied the contents: silver handcuffs, whip, blindfold, lubricants, toys, and massage oils. He looked at Gabi, instantly feeling himself getting hard. They could definitely have fun with this lot. He stood over her, staring down into her face, a devilish glint in his eye. She didn't look away this time.

"Submissive or dominant?" he asked out of curiosity, a note of amusement in his voice.

"Dominant." She stood up.

She slipped off the thin material of her dress to reveal a dark blue corset, and minuscule underwear. In her black platforms, she slowly sashayed toward the bedroom. Darion's heartbeat quickened. Shoving the items back in the bag, he followed her.

He became excited. He tore his t-shirt off, and

wriggled out of his jeans. His cock was straining against the fabric of his boxers, desperate for release. She thought that she could dominate him. *Ha!* She had another thing coming. She would be begging for him, never mind him begging for her. Women could never resist him.

***

Darion panted breathlessly. He wriggled his arms, but it was no use. The metal handcuffs dug into his wrists. He was still hooked to the bedposts. He couldn't see a thing. He couldn't even remove the blindfold. He didn't mind being dominated, however he didn't like being teased, brought to the brink of climax, and being left there. One of his own tricks being reversed on him. The room was silent. Had she gone into the other room?

He had been happily enjoying her performing oral on him, licking and teasing his whole body, lathering scented oil all over him with her soft hands. He had begged for her for a while. His body was beginning to ache, and he desperately needed her, but she wasn't giving in to him. He was surprised when he felt something wet touch his lips, and he realised it was her tongue. Darion stuck his out, but hers was gone. He felt it again as it licked his, then stopped, and then licked again. He moved his head forward, trying to find it. It was no use. He felt it again, this time she allowed him to suck on it hungrily for a few moments, his tongue shooting right inside her mouth, circling her tongue, groaning at the same time. Then she was gone again.

"Gabi, I want you now."

Silence. He felt her lips touch his neck. He hadn't even heard her lay beside him. The hairs on his body stood on end. Shivers ran down his spine as she planted soft, slow kisses down his chest. Then he felt the sharp pain of leather bite into his skin, and he screamed out in pain. He hadn't expected that.

"Fuck," he roared. "Gabi, you bitch."

"What did you call me?" He felt the warmness of her whisper in his ear, which turned him on even more. "Did you just call me a bitch?"

"Maybe…" He felt the leather again on his tender skin, sharp and painful, cutting into him. "You just wait until you unlock me."

"I hope that's not a threat, Mr. Milano."

"It is. I'm gonna make you wish you were never born." He laughed sadistically.

"You're making this worse for yourself."

He felt her pleasuring his cock with her mouth. He groaned loudly. He was going to come. He knew it. He curled up his fingers and toes, grinding his teeth. Then she stopped, and the whip was back, this time hitting his stomach. He grimaced. Then silence.

"Gabi?"

No answer. He shouted her name again. She couldn't leave him hanging like that. He listened for noise. He heard the sound of the handcuffs being unlocked. Then he heard footsteps as if she had run into the living room. He pulled his arms free. Yanking the blindfold off, he wiped the sweat from his brow, and slowly climbed to his feet. He noticed the whip on the floor. A grin crept across his face as he picked it up, along with the handcuffs. Still naked and erect, he stepped into the living room.

Gabi was sitting on the far corner of the sofa, an anxious look on her face, as if she didn't know what to expect. He was in control now. It was his turn to dominate. *Payback time.* Darkness clouded his eyes. He drew a deep breath.

"As I said." His voice was husky. "I'm gonna make you wish you were never born…darlin'."

He switched the stereo on. Rock 'n' roll blasted at a loud volume. He didn't want the neighbours to hear. There would certainly be a lot of noise coming from his apartment. He stepped toward her, his fingers tightening around the whip, the handcuffs clanging together.

"Come here," he instructed, his voice low and authoritative.

Reluctantly, Gabi obeyed. *Not so confident now.* His gaze locked with hers. They stared at one another intently for what felt like the longest time.

"Give me your wrists. Now."

Chapter Twenty-Seven

Gabi

"How was your night, sweetie?" Mallory asked Gabi in the car on the way to work. They hadn't had chance to properly catch up.

"It was fun. What about yours?"

"Suzie and Marcus came around. We ordered Chinese and watched a movie."

"How are they?"

"I've never seen them happier." Mallory swerved into the car park opposite Miller & Co. Publishers, and peered through the windscreen, searching for an available parking space.

"I'm pleased for them." Gabi reapplied her lipstick. "There's a space." She pointed to a spot.

Mallory reversed into the space, and turned off the engine.

"I hope today doesn't drag." Gabi grabbed her handbag.

"Me too. I'm so not cut out for work today."

Gabi placed her hand over her mouth as she yawned.

"Have you heard anything more from Lawrence?"

She shook her head. "I haven't, actually."

"Well, that's a good thing."

"Yeah." Gabi nodded in agreement as she followed Mallory toward work. "I hope he's okay."

"Lawrence knows how to take care of number one, Gabi. He's been doing it for long enough."

"Hmmm."

The girls headed straight for their workplace kitchen, where they made coffee, and chatted with colleagues that worked on the same floor. Gabi caught sight of her reflection in the window. She was wearing a white, knee-length dress and black stilettos. Her hair was scraped back into a high ponytail. She'd dressed partly for meeting Darion later, who had agreed to collect her from work.

Taking her coffee, she scurried to her office before she got caught up in work gossip, which could sometimes go on for far too long. She had a backlog that needed taking care of.

She managed to edit quarter of a manuscript by the time 5 p.m. rolled by. Ensuring her desk was tidy, and everything was prepared for the following day, she headed to the elevator. Mallory had already set off for home.

She found Darion parked nearby, in the Jeep. As soon as she climbed in the car, he leant over and gave her a soft, lingering kiss. Her breath caught in her throat as pleasure jolted through her. He didn't stop there, as his hands cupped her face, pulling her as close to him as she could possibly be. His tongue sliding across her own, filling her mouth, was divine. Her stomach tightened. Finally tearing away, she felt giddy as a salacious grin teased his face. Would she ever get enough of him?

"How was your day?" he asked, the tyres screeching on the tarmac as he sped off.

"Productive." She fastened her belt. "How was yours?"

"Not too bad." He grabbed hold of her hand, and squeezed it. "If you fancy having a drink at the club, I can take you home later?"

"Sounds tempting."

Darion switched the stereo on, and they sat comfortably, listening to "Uprising" by Muse. Gabi rested her head on the headrest. After half an hour of driving, the busy streets and high-rise buildings were replaced with the green countryside.

When they got inside the club, they were immediately greeted by Lexi. "What can I get ya, Gabi?" she asked, chewing gum simultaneously.

"Um…a red wine, please."

Darion's mobile rang just as he perched on a stool. He stepped aside to answer it. "Gabi." He shoved the phone into his pocket a few seconds later. "I need to meet someone for fifteen minutes, they've got a few questions about the place. You'll be okay here, right?"

"Sure."

He planted a tender kiss on her forehead, before dashing out of the room. Gabi drained half of her wine as soon as it was placed before her. Marnie approached, and made general chitchat. She informed Gabi that she had a new boyfriend, and the relationship was currently going well. It was like music to Gabi's ears—one girl down, another one to go. She glanced over her shoulder to see that Gina was twirling around the pole. She was left with a sour taste in her mouth at how sensational the dancer looked. But if Gina was enough, why hadn't she and Darion ever had anything serious?

Over the next fifteen minutes, Marnie supplied her with more wine. Gabi hadn't realised how many she'd actually consumed until she felt a dizzy rush go to her head.

Giggling, she shakily made her way toward the ladies' bathroom. She lowered herself onto the toilet lid, appreciating a short break from the thumping music. She was unable to stop the dreamy expression that took over her face. Darion hadn't been gone that long, and she was thinking about him already. She was falling for him. She knew it. She hated that it was happening so fast. She never usually got attached this quickly.

Gabi was glad that he had decided to give the relationship a go. She hoped that he wouldn't see other women. It would devastate her if he did, but what could she do? She would have to leave him. For now, she'd sit back and wait and see if she alone was enough for him. She was happy that he had admitted to feeling something for her.

She made her way toward the mirror, leaning closer to it to inspect her make-up. Her pupils were bigger than usual. She quietly laughed to herself. She was certainly making a habit of all of the nights out. She couldn't help it, though. Whenever she was at The Black Door, she wanted to join in all the fun. Perhaps she was making up for years of lost time.

She turned the tap on and leant under it, swigging the cold water, swallowing mouthfuls. The cold liquid oozing down her throat was just what she needed. She stood back up slowly and jumped at the reflection in the mirror, startled.

Darion stood near one of the cubicles, smoking a cigarette, watching her. The black jeans and matching shirt he was wearing hugged his frame perfectly. Three buttons were open, displaying his cutting collarbones and some of his muscular lean chest. His hair had now been smoothed back with gel, the length just skimming his collar. He looked sophisticated, smart.

A smile surfaced on his face, as if he knew the effect he was having on her. He took two steps toward her and held out his hand. Gabi took hold of it. He pulled her toward him, his tongue darting into her mouth as their lips met. She pressed her body against his, sinking her fingers into his hair.

"Let's go relax at the bar before I take you home."

They walked back to the bar, hand in hand. Several customers greeted Darion with nods of appreciation. He was a largely respected businessman, without the attitude to go with it. And he certainly knew how to enjoy himself, and have fun with the customers.

Caressing Gabi's behind, he led her toward one of the booths, where they lounged on a comfortable, velvet sofa. Knowing their drink orders by heart,

Marnie was soon placing a glass of whisky and a glass of wine on the table before them. Darion instructed her to shut the curtain after her, which she did.

He lifted Gabi onto his lap, so that she was straddling him. His gaze on her was intense. Gabi took in his features—his strong jawline, his plump lips, perfect teeth, and secretive, captivating eyes. She wanted him desperately, and knew the feelings were mutual. But first, she decided to tease him, to make him wait, to make him beg, like he'd made her do many times before. Now that she knew him better, she felt confident around him.

Gracefully climbing to her feet, she stepped onto the platform, where the pole was. "Addicted to Love" by Robert Palmer blasted from the speakers. Darion sat forward in interest, his hand rubbing over his rough stubble.

Gabi took hold of the pole with one hand, and circled it. Then, with her back pressed against it, she moved her hips slowly to the music, running her hands through her hair that she freed from the band. She bent down to touch her toes, wiggling her bum slowly, copying what she'd seen the girls do. Darion's tongue skimmed across his top lip, and she noticed him adjusting himself in his trousers.

As she unzipped her dress, Gabi allowed it to drop to the floor, and stepped out of it. She could see her reflection in the huge wall mirror before her, her legs long and tanned, her chest voluptuous in a pink bra, and her hair in wild waves framing her shoulders. She felt sexy.

She twisted her waist slowly from side to side,

teasing her body with her fingers. When she unhooked a bra strap, she caught the blazing longing on Darion's face. Unhooking her bra, the silk skimmed against her arms, as she removed it. She tossed it at him. He chuckled softly, leaning back, clearly eager to see more, devouring every inch of her with his stare.

Crouching down, she crawled leisurely across the platform toward him. On her knees, she ran her hands up her thighs, and between her legs, before hooking her fingers through the top of her underwear. Darion was tapping his fingers in an impatient manner, as if self-restraint was proving difficult. She gave him a sultry, playful wink.

"Come here," he commanded, his voice low.

She shook her head, and rose on her heels again, pushing out her chest, and arching her back, so that her breasts were more prominently displayed. She returned to winding her hips, giving him a glimpse of her pert behind.

Darion was standing now. His teeth snagged his bottom lip, and he began unbuttoning his shirt. As he stepped onto the platform, Gabi could feel his dangerous, seductive aura. He loosened the final buttons, and in a swift movement, he shed his top. Gabi's stomach tightened with desire. Her palms stroked over his firm chest, and rock hard muscles, which caused an appreciative moan to escape her lips. He slipped his arms loosely around her waist, and pressed his erection against her pelvic region. Grinding his hips, she ached for contact, her body becoming warm with delight.

"Are you going to dance for me?" she asked,

mesmerised by his arse that she could see in the mirror, swaying from side to side. "I didn't know you could dance."

Looking down at her under his dark lashes, she could see the fire in his irises. "I can't dance...but I can strip." His low, sultry voice was close to her ear, making her skin tingle. He took a step back, and slowly unzipped his jeans, his brows raised suggestively.

Gabi threw her head back with laughter. She studied him closely, desperate to see his fit, firm arse, and strong, muscular thighs, not to mention the hardness in his trousers that was straining for release. She had never seen a man strip before. Judging by his cocky, arrogant attitude, and smug expression, she already knew that he'd put on a good show. And she already knew that he'd done it before. She was turned on, and he wasn't even naked yet.

Chapter Twenty-Eight

Darion

Darion woke with a loud groan. His body ached. He could still hear the music pumping in his head. He needed a few days out, to relax, that was for certain. As much as he loved the party lifestyle, he did appreciate a cosy night, chilling on the sofa, watching movies, eating junk, and talking about weird topics, usually with whatever woman he was sleeping with at the time. He could have that with Gabi, if he didn't worry so much about falling for her, and possibly hurting her, and himself.

Sometimes, he wished he weren't so messed up and didn't overanalyse everything. Kicking back the covers, he sat up. After he'd dropped Gabi home last night, he'd returned to the club, spent a couple of hours with the girls, and retired to his office.

His vision could only take so much of the strong glare of his laptop screen. He'd put in more orders for personalised matches, flyers, and membership cards for The Black Door. He'd then stupidly gambled online, and decided enough was enough when he'd blown two hundred pounds in less than ten minutes. It had helped him sleep, though. He'd managed to doze off on the sofa, and actually slept peacefully, without needing the comforting disturbance of Gina, Lexi, or Marnie to check in. Perhaps his sleepless nights were slowly starting to become a thing of the past. He hoped so.

Darion pulled on some black jeans, a white t-shirt, and slung his jacket over his shoulder. Helmet in hand, he realised he hadn't taken the beast out in a while. The weather had been dire, but now that the roads were clear it was the perfect opportunity. Darion was a man who loved his boy toys: cars, bikes, electrical gadgets, the lot. He made his way toward his Yamaha R1, just as his mobile rang.

"Yeah?"

"Daz?"

"Gina." He sighed loudly. Lately all she'd done was bust his balls over not giving her enough attention.

"Nice welcome," she snapped.

"Gina, I'm real busy today—"

"With Gabi, huh? You're wasting your time. Stop trying to be somebody you're not, Daz." She laughed lightly. "You can put on an act for a few months, perhaps. But you *know* who you are."

He tensed. "Stop interfering, Gina." He groaned. "You don't know what you're talking about. Why are you being like this?" He rubbed his throbbing head with his free hand. "I thought we were good with what we had?"

"We were. But we don't even have *that* anymore," she spat.

"I'm sure you can survive without my once-a-week fuck."

"It was more than once a week," she said sulkily. "And it will be tough." She giggled.

"I know it will." He found himself smiling.

"What if I don't find someone like you?"

"That's the whole point. I'm no good for you, Gina. You're too fragile. I'll end up hurting you, and you know it." She'd had quite a difficult past when it came to men, and he wasn't about to be added to her list of disappointments.

"Well what about Gabi? Do you think she can handle you?"

"We'll soon find out." He ran a hand through his hair. "Look, you know how fucked up I am about Eva. Gabi's good for me at the moment."

She was silent for a moment before finally saying, "You're right. I'm sorry."

"Are we gonna be okay or not?"

"I guess so."

"Look, you know I'm *always* here for you, G. *Always.*"

"K." She huffed into the phone. "I should probably give Johnny a call. I suppose he wasn't all that bad."

"Yeah," he agreed. "I think you should."

"I'll see ya later."

"Bye, babe."

Now he definitely needed the drive to clear his head. There was nothing quite like the adrenaline rush he got from speeding down countryside lanes, the freedom his motorbike gave him. He put his jacket and helmet on, and climbed on the bike.

He gripped the handlebars when the engine roared to life. Setting off, he drove down the main roads, ignoring looks of admiration from groups of young girls. *Don't even look this way, ladies—I'd fuck you all into next week. At the same time.* They definitely wouldn't be able to handle him.

Twenty minutes later, he was racing down the quiet lanes. There was nothing or no one in sight, just the way he liked it. The breeze hitting him in the face, the air filling his lungs, was refreshing.

Picking up speed, he allowed the roads to take him wherever. He didn't know where he was going. He didn't care.

Gina had pissed him off. Didn't he deserve to be happy? It was all he wanted, but sometimes it frightened him. But who was Gina to suggest that he wasn't capable of ever having a normal, loving relationship? Just because he lived life on the edge didn't mean that he wasn't suited to someone like Gabi.

He would show Gabi his true self. Reveal the club to her. He would let her know exactly what she was getting herself into by being with him. If she couldn't accept him for who he was, he supposed he had no choice but to end it.

***

Gabi

It had been a tiresome day at work, but Gabi had still managed to drag herself to a dance class. Her moves were getting better, her confidence soared, and her abs, ass, and thighs were becoming firmer with each lesson. Exercise really did release feel-good endorphins, and she doubted anything could spoil her cloud-nine mood.

She popped in her local supermarket to stock up on some groceries. She wanted to cook up a thank you dinner for Mallory and Steve for allowing her to temporarily live at their house. Mallory had given her some telephone numbers for apartments to rent. She had called them throughout the day, and was pleased that one sounded ideal, not too far from work, or from Westhaven. Bang in the middle of both, it was the perfect location. She was feeling a little excited at moving on, having her own independence, and being able to decorate according to her own taste.

She filled the trolley with lettuce, tomatoes, and cucumbers, and wheeled it to the alcohol aisle. She scanned the bottles of wine on the shelves and picked up red wine. She carefully placed the bottle in the trolley. She would be sad to leave Mallory, as she'd gotten used to waking up with her, and starting every morning with having breakfast and a good gossip. Then again, they could always catch up at work.

She spun around when she heard a familiar laugh. She came face to face with Lawrence. She froze for a moment, unsure of what to do. She felt overdressed in her tight black jeans, a low-cut white blouse, and Louboutin heels. Lawrence and his female companion were both wearing long coats. Gabi immediately looked her over, noticing her long, flowing brown hair and minimal make-up.

"L-Lawrence," she stuttered.

"Gabi," he said, his lips tightening into a thin line.

She didn't know how he'd react to seeing her for the first time in so long. Was he still mad at her? She waited with bated breath for his next move. She prayed he didn't hate her. Although she should technically hate him for everything he had put her through, she had no ill feelings toward him at all.

"How are you?" He shifted uncomfortably. His focus then landed on her clothes. His mouth parted, as if he didn't recognise her anymore.

Yeah, I'm twenty-seven, Lawrence, and aren't I just dressing like it? she thought, relieved that she no longer had to dress to his standards.

"I'm getting there," she responded, not wanting to shout from the hills that she was actually in a happy place. She didn't want to rub his nose in it. "You?"

"I'm…fine." He glanced at her cleavage once more, and then turned to his companion. "Oh, this is um, this is Lorna."

"Nice to meet you." Lorna waved.

"Likewise," Gabi said, wondering who the new woman was. Why did she even care?

An awkward silence filled the air.

"Well, nice to see you," Lawrence said, breaking the tension.

"You look well," Gabi blurted out. It was true. His dark blonde hair was gelled, and underneath his coat he was wearing a black suit. Armani.

"You too." Admiration was visible on his face.

What? "Um…well." She inhaled. "I'll um…leave you to it."

"Bye, Gabi."

Gabi slowly walked off, the stupid trolley wobbling from side to side, making a squeaking noise. Before she turned the corner of the aisle, she sneaked a look back. Lawrence had his arm around the woman's waist. She felt a pang of jealousy. Then he peered over his shoulder. He smiled softy, which Gabi mirrored before vanishing out of his line of sight. She needed to get out of the shop and quickly. She felt hot, claustrophobic, and emotional.

Although Lawrence had a temper, neglected her, bored her to tears at times, he had offered her things Darion didn't—emotional stability, security. She knew that he had loved her. She knew deep down in her heart that he never would have left her.

Could a woman ever have it all? Perhaps it was one or the other, stability and commitment, or exciting and risky. Maybe even heartbreak.

Was she playing with fire?

***

Gabi carried the plates to the table and set them down. She then filled each of the three glasses with wine and turned the stereo on, where the radio started playing pop music. She lit the candles and stood back, smiling. It looked intimate, and nice.

Was it too intimate? She blew the candles out. It was a dinner for three, not for two. She heard the key in the lock, and waved at Mallory, who immediately took off her heels and hung her coat in the hallway.

"Something smells nice."

"I wanted to say thank you for helping me out. I'm viewing an apartment next week."

"That's great. You know you can stay as long as you like." She entered the kitchen and looked around, grinning. "Wow. You really made an effort, Gab."

"It's no problem."

Mallory lit a cigarette and collapsed onto a chair. "Long day." She sighed heavily. "This is just what I needed." She took a sip of her wine.

"How did your meeting go?" Mallory had had her annual review meeting with their team leader.

"It went well. How's your day been?"

Gabi sat down opposite her. "Dance class went well. Then I bumped into Lawrence."

"Shit. How is he?"

"He seemed okay." Gabi tucked a strand of hair behind her ear.

"Are you having second thoughts about him?"

"I don't think so," she said, although there was a slight tremor of uncertainty in her tone.

"Well, how are things going with Darion?"

"I know he likes me, but I'm not sure how much. I don't know if I'm wasting my time, Mal. I know I said I didn't want a serious relationship, but I'm into him more than I thought."

"I knew this would happen." Mallory shook her

head. "What's not to like?"

"I've never met a man so challenging before." A dreamy expression covered her face. "He knows how to press *all* of my buttons, and it's like I'm addicted to him or something, it's crazy. It's stupid."

"It's not stupid. You're smitten with him. And who doesn't want to tame the bad boy?" Mallory laughed. "I haven't seen you this happy, this glowing, in a while. He might hurt you, he might not." Her friend chewed her bottom lip. "But if you're happy now, then enjoy the moment."

They heard the jingle of keys in the lock. Shortly afterwards, Steve walked in carrying a soaked umbrella. He closed the door, and the umbrella, and hung up his coat. Mallory stood up and kissed him lightly when he reached the kitchen.

"Good day, handsome?" She beamed.

"Busy. What's all this?"

"Gabi cooked for us. She's moving out soon."

"Yes," he joked, punching the air.

"Hey. You'll miss me." Gabi giggled.

"Like a hole in the head."

"Shut it, you." Mallory slapped his bum. "Of course we'll miss having you here, Gab."

"We will." Steve sat down.

Gabi set out dinner, and they ate hungrily, talking nonstop. It wasn't long until Mallory popped open a bottle of champagne that had been sitting in the cabinet for months. Gabi watched as Mallory and Steve kept holding hands, him nuzzling her neck and making her giggle. She had that with Darion. The affection. The closeness.

Her mobile bleeped. She clicked the inbox and opened the text message.

Darion: Hey, baby. I want to take you somewhere tomorrow night. X

She felt nervous, her stomach tightened. She hoped that it wasn't anything to do with seedy swinging again. She looked up at Mallory's concerned expression.

"Everything okay?"

"Yeah." She manufactured a grin.

She looked down as a picture message then came through.

Darion: You're beautiful. Always. Xx

She peered closer at the picture of the woman sleeping, her blonde hair fanned out across the pillow, her eyes shut and a small smile on her face as if she were having a nice dream. It was her. Darion had taken a photograph of her when she was asleep. She was touched. He watched her sleep. She felt warm and giddy inside.

Chapter Twenty-Nine

Gabi looked in the mirror for the final time. She was wearing a tight fitting, khaki shirt dress, teamed with black heeled ankle boots, and her hair hung straight down her back. She grabbed her Chanel clutch bag and made her way outside. Darion had texted her a postcode where to meet him. She climbed into her car, entered the postcode into her satellite navigation system, and set off driving.

She switched the radio on to hear a house song playing. She nodded her head along to the tune, belting out the words when the chorus kicked in. It wasn't long until darkness fell. When the sat-nav read that she was five minutes away from her destination, she peered through the window, wondering where the hell she was. She could see nothing but trees and fields for miles. Had Darion gotten the postcode wrong? She turned several corners, driving up the winding roads of a hill, until she saw his Jeep parked on the grass.

Gabi parked and climbed out, walking around the back of his vehicle. She stepped forward and looked over the hill, her mouth falling open. There was a spectacular view of the city, its lights dotted around under the full moon and twinkling stars of the night sky. It was beautiful. She could make out Darion's silhouette sitting a few yards away.

"Hey," she called out.

He eased himself off the ground, and slowly made his way toward her. His hair was product-free, tucked behind his ears. His jawline was unshaved, and his emerald eyes shone beneath dark, long lashes. He was dressed casually in navy jeans, and a matching hooded coat. He brushed his lips lightly against hers.

"You're not planning on killing and burying me up here, are you?" she joked, again surveying the deserted area.

"I'm not ready to kill you just yet." He smiled playfully and lazily. "There's a nice restaurant back here," he informed her, interlacing his fingers with hers. "Not many people know about it."

They walked for a few minutes, until they came to a little secluded restaurant, tucked away in the trees. With its wooden decked terrace, populated with tables and chairs, it had a perfect view of the city. Darion led her inside, where it was warm and modern. The white tiled floor glittered under the dim spotlights, creating a romantic and intimate vibe. Black tables and chairs filled the room, facing the floor-to-ceiling windows, which didn't restrict the stunning view of the nature surrounding them. The restaurant was empty, bar two couples in both

271

corners of the room, who were eating and talking. A few waitresses and bar-staff also stood, observant, waiting to tend to their customers' needs.

"Right this way, please." A waitress led them to a table by the window, overlooking the terrace. "I'll give you a moment." She sauntered off.

Darion didn't sit opposite Gabi, as most people would have. As always, he sat on the same side as her, as close as possible. She loved Darion's affectionate side.

"What's this about?" she asked, picking up the menu, trying to ignore the leaping sensation in her stomach. Her mind was whirling with the mixed signals he was giving her. She thought he'd given up on romance a long time ago.

"I've been thinking…" He reached out and stroked her hand. "If we're gonna be seeing each other, we may as well make the most of it." He paused for a moment. "Like you said, who knows how long this will last?"

Her heat sank, but she hid her disappointment with a tight smile.

"May as well make some good memories."

They were silent for a moment as they both scanned the menu. "I already ate before I came, so I'll just have a drink." She closed the menu.

"Yeah." He nodded. "Me too."

The waitress appeared again, and took their drink orders. They didn't speak until she had returned with a bottle of wine and two glasses.

"If you need anything, let me know." She beamed.

Darion reached for the bottle, and filled two

glasses. "To meeting you, Gabi." He passed her one.

She clinked her glass against his. "To meeting you, Darion." Her mouth curled at the corners, before she took a sip, and set the glass down.

"C'mere." He pulled her toward him, unzipping his coat and pulling her to his chest to share it with her. She snuggled close to him, and inhaled the masculine scent of his cologne. "You like it here?"

"It's lovely."

"I come here sometimes, to take time out." He reached for his drink. Gabi saw the faraway look in his eyes, a hint of sadness and uncertainty entering them. There was more to him than he let on—a lot more. Gabi wanted nothing more than to knock down the walls he had put up to protect himself. He may look after everyone else around him, but she could bet that he needed rescuing too. He needed someone to be there for him, just as much. As he plastered on a smile, and looked up, the sadness and uncertainty had gone, and as usual, he was playing it safe, pretending that he was okay, when Gabi knew that that was far from the truth.

He leant forward, and cupped her face in his hands. Gabi stared back at him unblinkingly. She felt her heart tighten in her chest. He pressed his lips firmly against hers, his lids closing. His tongue greedily explored her mouth, wrestling with her tongue savagely. Gabi felt herself melt under his touch, desire coursing through her body. She ached for him.

He entangled his fingers through her hair, gripping it roughly, his teeth nibbling at her lips.

273

With soft moans, their mouths crashing together, they groped one another's bodies desperately. As Darion's hand slid up her dress, under the table, Gabi squirmed in excitement. *I fucking love you, Darion Milano!* She was dying inside, desperate to tell him. But she couldn't. She didn't want to risk sending him running for the hills.

"Let's go," he murmured in between pleasure filled grunts.

Her thighs trembled. Fire heated her loins, as she craved to be touched. "But we just got here."

"We'll come again." He grabbed his glass, draining the wine back.

Gabi did the same. "You know that we're that annoying couple that people roll their eyes at because we can't get enough of each other." She giggled. "The couple that people hate?"

"I can live with that." He grinned. "Come on."

Darion settled the bill with the waitress, and led Gabi to his car. Once inside, he started the engine, informing her that he needed to park somewhere a little more out of sight. As the car swerved through trees and bushes, when the footpath could no longer be seen, Darion killed the engine, but left the ignition on. "Angel" by Massive Attack came softly from the speakers, making the moment all the more sexy. His chest was rising and falling rapidly, his expression fierce, raw, and hungry.

Attacking her lips again, he climbed over the centre console and onto the back seat. Gabi joined him, glad that the Jeep was spacious. She felt herself being lowered onto the seat, her arms pinned to her sides. As Darion ripped her buttons open, one by one, allowing a cold breeze to send a shiver down her spine, Gabi's excitement heightened.

His smouldering stare travelled down her body, taking in her lacy, violet underwear. Gabi saw the bulge in his trousers, his cock thick and straining for contact. As his fingers trailed gently up her leg, Gabi writhed slightly, feeling herself moisten. Her lips parted, and she took a small breath. His index finger met her clit, circling it, all while he gauged her reactions. Gabi felt it throb as heat rushed through her groin.

"You're so fucking beautiful, Gabi." He snagged her bottom lip between his teeth.

She wriggled in anticipation. Peeling off her dress, he slowly massaged her shoulders, his strong hands rubbing them firmly. She moaned in lust with the feelings he was awakening. He massaged her for a good few minutes, and then his hands stroked their way down her body, as he kissed her lightly. He stopped to quickly pull off his coat and unzip his jeans. He lay on top of her, kissing her neck desperately, burying his hands in her hair. Before she could catch her breath, he thrust inside her, holding her by the waist and pulling her into him.

He continued to slam in and out of her quickly, whilst his fingers pulled her breasts out of her bra, tantalising her nipples until they stood at attention. Gabi felt the heat rising in her chest as her heartbeat quickened, and her breathing turned to panting. It felt so good, she never wanted it to end. The groaning sounds that he was making in her ear were turning her on even more. He banged against her faster and faster until she clenched her teeth, feeling her muscles contract. He fit perfectly. She savoured every single pleasurable second. It was heavenly.

And then she could no longer take it. As the pleasure built inside her, she felt the fluttering of an orgasm. As his fingers dug into her hips, squeezing, pulling her into him, deeper, harder, faster, Gabi took a deep breath. A climax ripped through her whole body, making her cry out.

He quickly crouched down, his tongue buried between her legs. The tip of it met each delicious spasm. He lapped at her hungrily, licking, sucking, and swallowing the result of her arousal. The fact that he loved it made her enjoy it even more.

When she relaxed, desperate for his own release, Darion plunged into her again a few times, until he stilled, crying out, his moans loud in her ear. His face strained, the cords tightening in his neck. She felt him shudder and spasm inside her. Eventually he collapsed onto her, inhaling and exhaling deeply.

"Fuck," he panted. "It feels so good with you."

They lay staring up at the stars in the black sky through the window. She felt him link his fingers with hers. They remained still and silent for a while.

"You okay to drive?" he asked eventually, pulling himself up.

"I've only had a drop of wine, I'm fine."

He squeezed her hand, and then kissed her knuckles. "You following me back to my place?"

"Sure."

Back in his apartment, they lay naked on his king-size bed, their limbs entwined as they watched *Pretty Woman,* which was showing on the TV. Gabi felt content. She couldn't refrain from grinning like the Cheshire cat. She felt like she was finally getting somewhere with Darion, their bond was getting stronger. She rested her head on his chest, his rapid heartbeat pounding against her ear. She placed a tender kiss on his chest before closing her eyes, and shortly afterwards, she drifted into a deep sleep.

Chapter Thirty

Darion

"I love you more than life itself." Darion nibbled on Eva's earlobe. "Promise me you'll never fuck me over." He grabbed her roughly by the face, turning her to look at him. "Promise?" he repeated sternly.

"Never," she said, unzipping his jeans and sliding to her knees. "I'm yours, Daz. Forever."

***

Darion jolted upright in his bed. *Fuck!* He punched the mattress in anger. Another nightmare. What was happening to him? He wiped the beads of sweat from his forehead. He felt a stabbing pain in his chest and cried out. He needed air. He pulled open the window, and holding onto the ledge, he inhaled a deep breath. Her face. He couldn't get her face out of his head. He cared about Gabi now, so why was Eva appearing in his dreams? Why was he

278

still hurting? Why couldn't he forget about his ex-wife? Perhaps he needed closure. Where were Gina's comforting words when he needed them? He stopped to think for a moment, deciding what to do. Shakily, he grabbed for the phone and pressed the buttons. It rang. *Please pick up.*

After five rings, she answered.

"Come over now. I need to see you," his voice was low, shaky.

Putting the phone on the bed, he turned the stereo on. Music made him feel a tiny bit better. "Do I Wanna Know" by Arctic Monkeys came from the speakers. He collapsed on the floor, his head between his legs. He couldn't sit still. Angrily, he stood up, and with force whacked the ornaments from the shelf, causing them to fall and break.

"Eva," he roared loudly. "Why did you do this to me?" he cried out. "I let you fuck anyone. ANYONE. Why did you leave me for someone else?" The veins in his neck were protruding, his jaw clenched and his fists curled into tight balls. He was seething. His chest rose up and down rapidly. *Why, why, why?*

He straightened his posture, trying to compose himself. Running a hand through his hair, he sighed heavily. Perhaps he shouldn't have invited her around. He would take his anger out on her, with dirty, filthy sex. He was an animal when he was angry.

He decided to have a cool shower to calm down. He stripped and walked toward the bathroom. He leant on the bathroom mirror and looked up at his bloodshot eyes. He looked possessed. He needed closure when it came to Eva, that was all. He needed to know why she had done it. He'd never had the guts to ask before, to hear the truth.

After he showered, he heard the doorbell. He wrapped the towel around his waist, not bothering to properly dry himself. His heart was still banging against his chest, and he was still overwhelmed with emotions. He needed to de-stress, and quick. He pulled open the door to find her worried, beautiful face. He sighed in contentment, Eva leaving his mind.

"Gabi." He pulled her toward him, holding her tightly. "I fancied some company." He didn't want to tell her that he had lost it over his past, and his ex-wife, again.

"I bought pizza." She held a box in the air.

Perhaps he could count on Gabi. Perhaps he really could open up to her. He just hoped and prayed that the upstairs of The Black Door didn't scare her away.

Chapter Thirty-One

Gabi

Present Day

The next week passed in a blur. Work and dance class had however been going well for Gabi. At work, she didn't have a backlog for once, and in dance class she'd been having a blast getting to know everyone, and jumping and dancing around for an hour made her feel energised, upbeat.

She had also chosen and moved into a small apartment, and loved it. Adorned with books, photographs, candles, and some clutter, it was everything her old home wasn't—cosy.

She and Darion had been spending more time together, eating out at restaurants, partying, and getting merry in his club. They were starting to draw a lot of attention to themselves. Their feelings for one another had intensified. Gina wasn't fond of their public displays of affection. Lexi, on the other hand, was happy for them. She thought Gabi was perfect for Darion.

It was a Friday night at The Black Door, and they were seated at the bar. Darion lit and took a drag on a cigar. After he'd smoked it, and eventually stubbed it out, Gabi felt his fingers caress her leg. She shivered in delight. His smouldering eyes held an alluring mix of lust and desperation. A slow, lewd grin covered his face as he pulled her toward him. He brought his mouth down hard on hers, opening her lips with his tongue. As the kiss deepened, he let out a low moan. Gabi's tongue crashed against his. She sucked on Darion's tongue, wanting it deeper in her mouth, over her body, between her legs. Her heart thundered as heat flooded through her. She squeezed her eyes shut to savour the sensation, gasping when Darion's fingers crept up her skirt.

Her legs fell apart, and he burrowed under her skirt with determined fingers. Her inner muscles tightened with arousal. She flexed her hips toward him. The kiss was powerful, now urgent, heated. With his index finger, Darion tantalisingly stroked her throbbing clit. Her thighs trembled, a needy ache lingered in her body.

"Let's go to the office," he said softly.

She didn't hesitate, but said, "All we seem to do is have sex."

His brow arched. "Are you complaining?"

She shook her head, giggling.

They headed to Darion's office, and once there,

they made themselves comfortable on the sofa. Darion wasted no time in parting her legs, his fingers tracing up them. With his thumb, he stroked the fine cotton of her underwear, slowly caressing her clit.

Gabi felt her knees go weak, an excited shiver running up her spine, as her legs widened further. Darion licked his lips slowly. She let out a gasp when he moved her underwear aside, and carefully slipped a finger in. She squirmed in the seat in pleasure, a warm sensation blossoming between her shaking thighs. Darion inserted another finger, gently thrusting in and out, torturously slowly, all the while scrutinising her.

When the pace got faster, Gabi moaned softly. Darion leant forward, so his forehead pressed against hers, and she knew that he was about to kiss her. Taking a breath, he slipped his tongue into her mouth, caressing hers with a fast, firm urgency.

"Oh, Darion…" She sighed breathlessly.

"You like this?" he asked. Yanking down her corset top, he freed her breasts. His thumb and fingers closed hard on her nipples, tweaking them. Gabi arched her back, desperate for his tongue to caress them. His breath was hot on her skin as he nuzzled her neck, gently kissing his way to her chest. He slowly and lasciviously licked her nipple, then took it between his teeth and tugged on it hard, eliciting a gasp from her. Gabi reached down to stroke the erection through his trousers.

He sucked her breast, his tongue flicking repeatedly over it, making it tingle. Rough, satisfied groans escaped his lips. His mouth met her other breast, where her gently nibbled the nipple, finally taking it in his wet mouth. His fingers were inside her again, thrusting away powerfully, sending waves of pleasure so high that he had to silence her with a kiss.

"Ahhh…" she murmured breathlessly, writhing in ecstasy.

His fingers continued to work their way to bringing her to an orgasm, plunging in and out.

"Don't stop," she panted.

He slid to his knees, parting her legs further, hitching her skirt up to her waist. As he buried his head between her thighs, his tongue found her clit, and the tip of it teased her. Gabi's nails clawed the sofa. His warm saliva added to her wetness, and she cried out as his tongue probed her entrance. Gabi's head dropped back. She wished he would never stop.

As three fingers slid in deeper, pounding into her, his tongue lapping at her clit, Gabi knew she was close. Her inner muscles throbbed and quivered. A cry eased out of her throat. He withdrew his hand, sliding it under her buttocks to lift her closer to his hungry mouth, tantalising and teasing her with his tongue. Gabi grabbed fistfuls of his hair as he feasted on her, in between muffled moans. She wriggled at the intensity.

"Darion, please…" she begged, panting, trying to reach for his zipper. "Come here."

He shook his head, and continued to flick with his tongue. Gabi rocked her hips forwards and backwards onto his mouth, every lick sending her over the edge. She bit her thumb to stifle her cries.

She heard a low chuckle from Darion. When she looked down, she noticed he was intently gauging her reaction, a raw, animalistic lust in his eyes. His tongue lapped at her, his lips sucking her, urging her toward climax.

"I'm close," she mumbled.

Darion licked her faster, circling his tongue. He spread her legs wider, the tip of his tongue flicking her sensitive spot. His fingers burrowed in again. She threw her head back, grinding her teeth. Her breathing grew heavy. A hot flush spread up her chest and into her face, spasms of pleasure shooting through her body.

"Look at me," he commanded. Her hands clutched his hair again, and she did as he told her to. As he continued to pummel in and out, she felt pressure build inside of her. She drew in a breath, and then another. With one final, deep thrust of his hand, her body tensed. Her inner muscles gripped his fingers, burning and throbbing. She shook as a rippling orgasm tore through her body, making her shudder and scream out in pleasure.

"You're fucking sexy, Gabriella Woods." He grinned slowly and wickedly.

She allowed her body to sink into the sofa. She felt disoriented for a moment. Her chest rose and fell with her panting. When her body finally relaxed, and her breathing subsided, Darion sat next to her. He placed his engorged lips over hers.

Eventually, he pulled back. "I haven't shown you the club properly, have I? The upstairs?"

Gabi felt a wash of anticipation spread though her gut. With a small intake of breath, she said in a low tone, "No, you haven't."

Darion held out his hand for her to take. That same devilish glint sparkled in his irises. His expression showed that he was brimming with excitement and urgency to show her what was upstairs. Instead of his casual attire, he was smartly dressed in navy jeans, and a navy shirt, the top buttons open. His hair was gelled back, rather than hanging loose. The musky aftershave he was wearing smelt stronger than usual. He was obviously trying to make a good impression, but for her, or for other women?

Gabi felt her hands shaking. Why had it taken him until now to show her the rest of the club? She hoped whatever was upstairs wouldn't change her feelings for him. She hooked her fingers through his and allowed him to lead her up the stairs. She couldn't deny that she had been curious about that place for a long time.

She could feel the loud vibrations on the stairs coming from the enormous speakers. When they made it to the second floor, she saw a beautiful brunette, who sat at a desk piled with papers. She stood up as if to ask for ID or something, and when she realised it was Darion, she sat back down. Gabi noticed a sign that read **'*Members Only.*'**

She looked around the large room to take in her surroundings. It looked like a normal bar, but more glamorous. The dim lighting came from many overhead red spotlights, which created an intimate vibe. It held several red velvet sofas, and chairs surrounded by black marble tables. There were red curtains to many private booths along the right hand side of the bar. There was a strip of red carpet that led to another door at the back of the room—a black door.

She turned to look at the rounded bar in the centre of the room. There were cocktails lined on it with lit sparklers in each of the glasses. Around a hundred bottles of alcohol lined the shelf above. The bar staff was comprised of stunning women, and a couple of men, all with flawless bodies. They were slowly gyrating to the music whilst they served the many customers who were sitting on the stools. There were poles on either side of the bar, which two brunette dancers occupied, dancing provocatively. Gabi recognised one of them as being Wendy.

She stepped forward and instantly felt all eyes burning into her like she was a piece of meat. The men and women took in her every feature, slowly looking her up and down hungrily, like a pack of wolves on the hunt for their prey. A long time ago she would have felt shy at the attention. Things were different now. She had more confidence. But there was only one man's attention she wanted—Darion's. The old her, being a little shy and inexperienced, would not have gotten Darion. She had had to let go of all her inhibitions and try wild things that she never thought she'd do.

Her long, blonde waves hung loosely down her back. Her lids were enhanced by smoky grey eye make-up and the darkest eyeliner she could find. Her full lips were stained in red lip gloss. She wore a tight gold corset, her boobs uplifted, with a black skirt, teamed with black platforms.

She stood tall and strode behind Darion toward the bar. He glanced back at her, a massive grin spread on his face in admiration. He informed her that it was in fact a swingers' club, and that he wanted Gabi to experience the playrooms with him. She ordered a strong cocktail, flabbergasted, unsure of what to respond with.

"Good choice, darlin'." He squeezed her hand. "You'll need it for what I'm about to show you."

They both swallowed a shot of alcohol. Gabi welcomed the burning sensation, knowing she'd need the effect of alcohol to calm her unbearable nerves. Darion led her toward a booth, and promised to tell her *everything* about the club. As she followed him, drink in hand, her legs shook. Her stomach was doing somersaults, and she suddenly felt nauseated. She swallowed the lump in her throat and hooked her hands together nervously.

In the booth, Gabi's glass was half-full when Darion proceeded to explain what was behind *the* door. He'd smoked a cigar, and offered it to her, which she found herself uncharacteristically accepting. She probably would have gladly consumed anything in that moment to calm her pounding heart.

He also drained his whiskey throughout the duration of his perfectly practised speech, that he'd no doubt given a hundred times, his voice thick with pride. Before Gabi could properly digest the information, Darion ran his fingers up her leg, sending a shiver of excitement up her spine, and when he kissed her, he made her forget everything and everyone for a moment.

"I can't wait to fuck you." His voice was a hot whisper, his lips curled into a sinister smile.

Gabi was plagued with confusion, although a tiny bit of her was curious about the tempting playrooms.

Darion then told her that he needed to tell her something more, that he hadn't been entirely truthful about himself. Inviting her to see the playrooms, he climbed to his feet, towering over her. She stared at his outstretched hand for what felt like an eternity.

Chapter Thirty-Two

"You ready?" Darion asked.

"What else do you have to tell me?" She shot him a questioning look.

Darion ran a hand through his hair, and slowly sat back down. As he poured another drink, and gulped the last of it back, she shifted awkwardly in her seat. She could tell that Darion was tense, she waited patiently for him to continue, whilst trying to ignore the dizzying rush of her pulse.

"Remember when I said I'd only tried swinging a few times?" He set the glass down, and faced her.

She nodded.

"It's not true." She could see that his fists were clenched on either side of him. She didn't think she'd ever seen him so nervous.

"What do you mean?" Her forehead creased, as confusion formed on her face.

"I've been swinging for years, Gabi."

Years? Her mouth fell open. She was speechless,

bewildered. That meant that he probably participated in the playrooms a lot.

"I've experienced it probably hundreds of times," he said, as if he'd read her mind.

She felt a sick, acidic feeling rising in her stomach. Is this why he'd tried to warn her away so many times, and told her that he was no good for her?

"I don't understand it," she mumbled, unable to see his fascination with it.

"It's fun. I enjoy it."

Gabi sensed there was more to it, irrespective of whether he enjoyed it. His ex-wife cheating on him flashed into her mind; the reason why he feared women getting close to him. "You think swinging protects you from getting hurt, don't you? You can't be cheated on if you're allowing it to happen, if you're both doing what you want."

Darion's features softened, and Gabi knew that she had hit the nail on the head. She placed her hand over his, but he withdrew.

"I bet it wasn't your idea. I bet that deep down a part of you wondered why your ex wanted to try swinging, why she wanted to sleep with other men. A part of you must have felt like you weren't enough for her?"

"You don't know anything."

"I'm right, Darion. I know I am." Gabi didn't know what to think about the whole situation, although she did respect him for his honesty. Surely he had to give up swinging one day. She just hoped that it was sooner rather than later.

"Gabi, the hows, buts, and whys don't matter,"

he said with a tilt of his head. "This is me." He waved his arms in the air, indicating the club and the playrooms. "It's down to you whether you can accept that."

"You'll never change?" she asked. *Ever?*

"Will you change?" he fired back.

Gabi was silent.

"Let me show you the playrooms, Gabi. You'll understand more then."

Ignoring the nervousness that overcame her, she took hold of his outstretched hand. Tightening her grasp around his fingers, she allowed him to lead her toward the back of the club. She was relieved that the lighting was dim, because her cheeks were already burning in embarrassment.

After passing a red velvet rope, Gabi noticed a security guard stood at the door; several black lockers lined the wall behind him. Catching sight of the rules pinned to the wall, Gabi leant forward, reading the content.

No mobile phones. No cameras. No recording devices. No weapons of any kind. No smoking. No use of drugs or prostitution. You may bring your own toys. Lockers and use of showers are at no charge. Rules will be strictly enforced. Any violation of the rules will result in ejection from the club.

The guard gave Darion a welcoming nod, and moved aside to allow them to enter, although it wasn't open for another hour. Gabi stepped inside. The only illumination came from the ceiling spotlights, which cast a red, gentle glow. Gabi noticed that the left side of the room held many rooms separated by walls, but had no doors, so people could get a clear view inside. On the right hand side were more rooms, but were made slightly private with round glass windows to peep in through the doors. She noticed several nude portraits hung on the walls. Upon closer inspection Gabi realised Gina, Marnie, and Lexi were on some. She also spotted small condom machines outside every room.

While still holding her hand, he led her on a tour. They passed the first room, where Darion pushed open the door. Gabi peered inside to see every wall was mirrored. There was a hot tub in the middle, full of steaming water, surrounded by black glittery specked tiles throughout. There were four black loungers to lie on. Gabi noticed her crimson reflection in the mirror, but felt herself relax. *This room isn't so bad.*

They stepped back out. To her left hand side she noticed that the first room held nothing but a huge, king-sized bed with red silk sheets and a ceiling mirror. She stared incredulously, realising that it was a bed where you could be watched by other people, and the mirror could be used to watch yourself. She let go of his hand and wrapped her arms tightly around herself, feeling exposed. She couldn't think why anybody would want to writhe around naked in full view of others. Had Darion been on that bed? She willed her heart to slow its frenetic pounding.

"You wanna see more?" he asked concernedly.

"Gabi, this is *normal*. Some people want to improve their marriages, their sex lives, seek adventure, variety, and experiment with the same sex. Others just want an escape. Singles and couples can lose their inhibitions, totally let go, nothing is off limits." He reached for her hand again, which Gabi didn't give.

She was disgusted. She couldn't see herself changing her opinion on the matter. Couples couldn't love one another to allow their other half to engage in intercourse with a stranger, in front of them whilst they watched. She felt sick, but curiosity got the better of her. She had never seen anything like it before, except that party he had taken her to. Even then, she had only seen the living room. She *had* to know more.

The next room on the right contained huge, red cushions. The floor felt like one big mattress, and once again the walls and ceilings were mirrored. Back outside, the room to her left resembled a dungeon, as it had black walls with one large mirror. Leather cuffs on straps hung from the ceiling near the opposite wall, and several handcuffs, paddles, and whips were on a nearby table. There was a leather sex-swing hanging in a corner, and a king-sized leather bed in the other, next to a rail of garments. She could make out several black PVC catsuits, leather corsets, masks, and shoes of many sizes—black shiny stilettos, thigh-high boots, and platforms. It was obviously a room for roleplay, BDSM fantasies. Darion threw her a provocative glance. *It must be a favourite of his.*

"Mmmm, Gabi." He nuzzled her neck, wrapping his arms around her. "I'd love to get you on that swing."

Gabi didn't speak.

They made their way into the next room. It was a simple room with a bed in the corner, a mirror on one wall near a stripper pole, and a rack of outfits. She caught sight of several kinds of uniforms for men in different sizes: fire brigade, police officer, military soldier, blue mechanic overalls, and for women there were: schoolgirl, maid, army, and nurse outfits. There was a black basket with a lid on it near the door with a sign above stating:

Please put outfits in here for washing once worn. Thank you.

"Which one would you wanna see me in?" he asked, arching a brow.

"Police officer," she said without hesitating. Her body ached just at the thought of it. She could imagine Darion, a corrupt officer dangling handcuffs, barking orders at her, and taking control, punishing her for misbehaving.

"I wouldn't mind seeing you in a PVC catsuit," he purred in her ear, his warm breath making the hairs on her neck stand up. "You could tie me up." He winked. "And anything else you had in mind." His brow shot up, challenging her.

"Do you like women who take control, Darion?"

"I love it. I love it all, Gabi."

She examined a glass cabinet. It contained several different coloured toys and objects for purchase. Gabi leant in closer to look at them. Some she had never seen in her life. Double ended vibrators, butt plugs, anal beads, strap-ons, whips, paddles and more. It must have been a room to fulfil any fantasy that one might have. As she turned her head, she caught sight of Darion's amused expression. She remained tight-lipped, and followed him into another room.

A huge television screen hung from the wall, showing an erotic movie. There was a large, king-sized bed, and mirror. There were lit candles throughout, and fake red roses. It looked as romantic as could be in that sort of club.

The last room had no peephole. There was a sign above the door stating *'Couples Only.'* Gabi realised that this was obviously where most of the couple swapping took place. Inside, there were round, gigantic beds in each of the four corners, which automatically spun slowly round. G*reat viewing*. There were two stripper poles in the centre of the room.

At the back of the club, there was another room, again with no peephole, but this time a key lock on the door for maximum privacy. As they neared it, Gabi noticed Darion become unbearably tense, his jaw twitched; his fists clenched on either side of him. As his hand gripped the handle, he inhaled a deep breath and pushed open the door. He hovered for a moment in the doorway.

"Um…" He turned to Gabi, avoiding eye contact. "This used to be a room offering complete privacy. But, not anymore. It's, um, it's a dressing room for the girls, and the dancers."

What's got into him? Gabi thought, puzzled. Why had he changed it into a dressing room? Did it bring back bad memories or something? Before she could drive herself crazy with unanswered questions, he held his hand out, indicating for her to enter.

Gabi was surprised to see six beautiful women applying make-up, or brushing their hair at a large dressing table mirror. Each of them wore miniscule fantasy outfits: dominatrix, school uniform, nurse, army gear, and more. They were unbelievably sexy. Gabi could have stood and gawped at them all day. She noticed the sign above the door.

For assistance in roleplay, please request a price list and choose a member of staff in this area.

She couldn't believe it. Darion really had gone all out. She wondered if these women just aroused the men, gave them their fantasy, or actually slept with them.

"These girls help to create a scene for the customers, play along. They're not prostitutes. They don't offer *anything* else," Darion's voice was firm. "No other club puts in this much effort, Gabi. I've ensured it has everything to appeal to the customers."

"Hey, boss." One of them grinned, twiddling one of her pigtails round her fingers.

"Hey, Clara."

"Hi, Darion," another employee greeted him smoothly, giving him a little wave, and adjusting her nurse's hat.

He beamed at them.

"You love the attention," Gabi said when they'd backed out of the room.

He let out a laugh. "What man wouldn't, Gabi?"

"So, where are the men?" She arched a brow. "I don't see the army guys, officers, or firemen anywhere."

"I don't like competition," he told her, smacking her ass, which made her yelp. "Besides, I'm the only army guy, officer, or fireman that you need. And trust me…" He nailed her against the wall, bringing her face up to his. "I look more than good in uniform."

He tugged her lip gently with his teeth, igniting a spark in the pit of her belly. His tongue slowly slid in her mouth, invading it. Helpless to his touch, Gabi gripped his bottom, pulling him closer, devouring him. Grinding his hips, she felt the prod of his erection against her pelvis, and a throb of desire pulsed between her legs. His kiss became aggressive, possessive, as he let out an agonising cry of ecstasy. She forgot everything but the feel and taste of him.

"I cannot wait to see you in one," she said breathlessly.

"You will." He slowly pulled back, a playful twinkle in his eye. "Come on." He grabbed her hand. "There's more to show you."

He opened the double doors to his left. Inside, a large room had an open shower area, private shower area, and two hot tubs. As the steaming water bubbled, Gabi felt extremely tempted to strip off her clothes, and climb into one with Darion.

She looked over her shoulder, surveying the corridor again. Overall the club looked glamorous, expensive, and inviting. *Darion must earn a fortune.*

"What do you say, me and you put one of the rooms to good use?" He picked her up, causing her to wrap her legs tightly around his waist. His tongue traced along her bottom lip.

She felt fear rise inside her, and asked, "Just me and you?"

"Just me and you, darlin'." He winked. "We have this place all to ourselves. Which room are you in the mood for?"

Gabi thought for a moment. The dungeon suite had looked scarily sexy. And something about a tight PVC catsuit and thigh-high boots appealed to her. Or perhaps Darion could bend her over and really show her who was boss. As if reading her mind, Darion's lips curled at the sides.

"Mmm. You wanna be punished, don't you?"

"What makes you say that?"

"It's the most popular room."

Gabi wrapped her arms around his neck as he carried her to the dungeon. She'd never experienced proper pain with pleasure before.

Chapter Thirty-Three

After they'd spent a good forty minutes in the dungeon suite, both of them reaching a satisfying climax, Darion led her out of the playrooms and back into the main bar.

"Let's go have a drink, and wait for the playrooms to open. I really want you to try it, Gabi, with other people." Darion studied her. "Just see if you enjoy it."

In the bar, she found it much busier, as more people had arrived. Looking around her, Gabi noticed lots of displays of public affection, couples kissing, men kissing women, men kissing men, women kissing women. The doors opened to the playrooms, and Gabi watched as a few people passed the red velvet rope and entered.

"So, what do you think of the club overall?" Darion asked as he took up residence on a sofa. A bartender instantly came and brought a tray of alcoholic drinks. Another one put a bottle of champagne in a standing bucket of ice. Gabi caught one of them flashing Darion a smirk, before sexily sauntering off.

Gabi bit her lip, feeling anger and jealousy boil up inside her. Sure, the rooms had looked impressive—when empty. She wondered whether Darion had fucked that girl in one of the rooms, whipped her, used toys on her, had an orgy. She wondered how many times he had used the rooms, how many people he had slept with. She felt her stomach tighten, suddenly afraid that she would vomit. Just the thought of sharing him made tears prick her eyes.

Darion took a bottle of champagne and poured them each a glass. "Go and check out the place in action," he told her.

"Um…I'm going to the ladies', I'll be right back," she excused herself, standing up.

When she turned the corner, out of Darion's sight, she caught her breath. It was all too much for her. She was overwhelmed with emotions. She realised she couldn't do it. She didn't want to see other people writhing about naked, having sex. She didn't want to see Darion watching other women, touching her, and desiring other women. What went on in those rooms was perverted. She needed to get out of the club, and quick. She had originally thought that he owned only a gentleman's club, but he owned a swingers' club too. He also engaged in swinging frequently. It wasn't just a now and then hobby. How could she ever trust him when he owned this type of place? Her head was throbbing. It was way too much to digest.

Did she really want to join the world of swinging?

Chapter Thirty-Four

Gabi took a sip of her hot chocolate and placed it on the table. She was sitting inside a quiet café, not far from her apartment. Her mobile had been switched off since she had left the club last night, and she didn't want Darion to come looking for her at her place. She needed peace. She needed time to herself to think.

She pulled out the iPad from her oversized Mulberry handbag and switched it on. *Research time.* She needed to know more about Darion. Needed to know more about swingers and swingers' clubs.

She looked around her to make sure that nobody would be peering over her shoulder. She typed in the word 'swingers.' Several websites appeared on the screen before her. She took a deep breath and clicked onto the first one. She scanned the paragraphs, reading sections.

`'Swinging    is    a    non-monogamous`
`behaviour,   in   which   singles,   or`
`partners in a committed relationship,`
`engage   in   sexual   activities   with`
`others,  as  a  recreational  or  social`
`activity.    It    can    range    from`
`spontaneous     sexual     activity     at`
`informal  gatherings  of  friends,  to`
`like-minded  people  at  a  swingers'`
`club.'`

Gabi took another sip of her drink. She felt heat flooding her chest and face. She took her jacket off and hung it on the back of her chair. She continued to read. As Darion stated, the reasons for swinging were to increase quality and frequency of sex, to add something to their sex life, or due to curiosity. Some couples saw it as a healthy outlet to strengthen their relationship. It took place in clubs, hotels, resorts, cruise ships, and in private homes.

Gabi clicked onto a swingers' website and gasped when she saw that it had thousands of members. She couldn't believe it. She scrolled through the members profiles' and photographs; there were pretty girls as young as twenty. There were several handsome men and stunning women. There were couples with children, people of all professions and ages.

They all stated that they were adventurous, open-minded, curious, and liked to make the most of life, and one couple stated that they had been married for thirty years and simply wanted to spice up their marriage. They stated that everything happened in the same room, that they weren't betraying one another. They were very much in love, and their relationship was strong enough to handle some fun. They were consenting adults and weren't hurting anyone, and swinging was better than all the secret affairs that went on.

Gabi looked at swingers' resorts. Some were held abroad in luxury hotels, where freedom and broad-mindedness was guaranteed. They didn't look any different from relaxing spa hotels. Except the packages were different, consisting of in-night clubs, nudist beach visits, and private parties with swimming pools for skinny-dipping.

Gabi read through tips on beginner swingers, on how to set boundaries, communicate regularly, and how to be comfortable with it. She tapped her fingers on the table. Did she want to try it? The Internet made it sound more common than she had thought.

Swinging had never ever crossed Gabi's mind before. A small part of her had always wondered what it would feel like to kiss a girl, but that was it. The thought of group sex or threesomes didn't appeal to her at all. She wasn't sure whether she could handle Darion being with someone else. Would it upset her? Outrage her? Make her insanely jealous?

She scanned the images online, and to her surprise she found plenty of photos of men who were just her type, that she really fancied the look of, and women who she was drawn to. Was there any harm in giving it one try with Darion? If she didn't like it, she never had to do it again. She switched the iPad off and sighed heavily. She reached for her mobile and switched it on. She had several missed calls, voice mails, and text messages from Darion.

She finished the last of her drink, paid for it, and slowly walked back to her apartment. Once inside the warmth of her living room, she called Darion.

"Gabi?" His voice was shaky, panicked. "What's going on?"

"I'm sorry," she said. "It was all too much for me last night, so I had to leave. I should have told you."

"Is this over?"

"No, Darion. I just don't know what to make of it all, I'm so confused. I can't make my mind up about this whole thing. One minute it makes me feel sick, and the next it makes me feel slightly curious."

"I understand. It took a while until I got used to it. I secretly hated Eva for suggesting it at first...shit." He groaned. Gabi knew that he was annoyed with himself for indulging the fact that he'd starting swinging with his ex-wife, as she'd suspected.

"So, you didn't like it at first?' she asked.

She heard him drinking something. "I couldn't understand why she wanted other men, why she wanted to involve other people in our marriage. Then we tried it and never looked back."

"Oh."

"Gabi, I showed you the club, I wanted to be open with you about my business, and what I'm into." He sighed. "I took you to that party, and you made it clear how you felt about it. Of course I'd love you to be open to trying swinging, but I'll never push it on you."

But you'll keep asking until I give it a go. It's how you live. How could she ever take that away from him? She took a deep breath. "I've made up my mind...I will try it."

"You don't have to," Darion said quickly. "Don't feel that you have to do this to satisfy my needs."

"Please, Darion. I've made up my mind. It can't hurt to try it out once. I'll just get drunk beforehand." She let out a nervous laugh.

"Well," he began. "You never know. You might enjoy it. You might become addicted to the way that it makes you feel."

"Doubtful."

"What are you considering? Soft or full swinging?"

"I can't sleep with another man." She chewed her nails worriedly.

"It's okay. Don't do anything you're not comfortable with. Anything is possible, nothing is mandatory. If you wanna get a feel of the place, watch other people, indulge in foreplay, or just stick with me, it's not a problem."

"I'll see you later, then." She walked into the bathroom and began filling the bath. "I'm sorry I took off like that."

"I was worried sick," he confessed. "When your mobile was off, I thought it was over."

"I'm not that cruel."

"You really do surprise me, Gabriella Woods."

"Hmmm. I know the feeling."

"Hey," he said sharply. "You've gotta stop all of

this running away when you're out of your comfort zone, or when things get tough. Talk to me about it," he urged.

"Okay." She released a heartfelt sigh. "I'll try. Bye, Darion."

She hung up and placed her mobile on the side table. She decided that she would stick to Darion, and perhaps kiss a woman, or whatever, depending on how the night went. No way could she have another man's hands on her though. No way. It felt wrong. It felt like she would be betraying Darion, even though he'd be agreeing to it happening. She hoped that she could show Darion that she'd given it a try, get it out of her system, and let that be it.

Chapter Thirty-Five

Darion

Darion sat on his couch, half-naked, with the TV on, but he wasn't really concentrating on it. He was glad that he had spoken to Gabi. He really thought that he had scared her off. He had been angry with himself for showing her the club and revealing his true self, but he couldn't live a lie, pretend to be someone he wasn't.

He was pleased that she hadn't been put off by him, that she didn't find him repulsive. He was relieved that she wasn't judgemental like some of the women that he had met. How could people mock something that they had never tried, or didn't understand? At least Gabi was willing to give it a try. He respected her for it.

He shifted down on the couch and decided he'd have a power nap before he saw her later. It would be a busy night. He wanted to feel fresh and full of energy. He yawned and grabbed a cushion, propping it behind his head. He lay down and closed his eyes. He was soon snoring away.

***

Gabi

It was party time at The Black Door, and not just any ordinary party, but Franchesca Doorly's private party. The swingers' club was packed, and the atmosphere was relaxed, with talking and laughter all around.

"Right, first thing's first." Darion took a drag of his cigarette. "And don't break the rules, Gabi. I've had enough heartache before." He drew in a breath, and then recited the rules that they had to stick to when in the playrooms.

He was dressed in black jeans, and a white t-shirt that hugged his body. His hair, again, was gelled back, hanging down the nape of his neck. Gabi knew that the women in the party would be queuing up to get their hands on him. Especially Franchesca. *She can keep her hands off,* Gabi thought, a sour taste appearing in her mouth.

"Remember, Gabi, *always* ask each other first before we do anything." He grabbed her by the chin, turning her face to look at him. "Do you hear me?"

She nodded. "What happened with you, Darion?" she asked him bravely.

"I don't wanna talk about it," he replied quickly, pouring himself a drink. "Another time," he added when he saw her disappointed expression.

"I'm nervous," she admitted.

"Hey." He stroked her hair. "If you don't wanna do this, don't. I'll never force you, Gabi."

Yes, but it's something you're into. If I don't, this relationship won't last. You'll get bored and move onto someone more exciting.

"I think you'll enjoy it," he said confidently. "I really do. I'm gonna pop down to the office quickly, get freshened up. Finish your drink, and come get me."

Gabi made a trip to the bathroom. She fixed her make-up, ensuring that it was immaculate. She then smoothed down the dark blue silk wrap-over dress that she was wearing. Her cleavage and long slim legs were on show. She wore her hair down perfectly straight. *I can do this. I just have to try it.* She swallowed the lump that formed in her throat and took a deep breath. She soaked her trembling hands under the cold water and rubbed them together, cleaning them.

Darion could be right. She might enjoy it. She made her way to his office. He sat comfortably on his chair, his legs on the table, crossed at the ankles.

"Come here." He waved Gabi over with his hand. "Did I tell you how good you look tonight?" He stared at her with obvious admiration.

She felt a surge of happiness. "No, you didn't, but thank you." She walked over to him.

"So, soft swinging tonight?" He pulled her onto his lap.

She nodded.

He looked at her searchingly. She feigned

nonchalance. His lips firmly caught hers. As Gabi moved her mouth in sync with his, she could taste and smell the alcohol on him. She had downed a few shots herself. Dutch courage.

"If you wanna be watched, we go in the open rooms, okay? If you want a little more privacy, we go in the peephole rooms. Whatever you're comfortable with, right?"

Gabi looked down at the papers on his desk, anything to keep herself from meeting his gaze. She could feel the heated blush rising from her chest to her face. She made out some membership forms. She scanned the price list. Single women had the lowest fee, couples were slightly higher, and single men were charged the highest price. She picked up one of the glossy leaflets and turned the pages curiously. There were photographs of the rooms and a main photograph of the bar with several people, standing around grinning. It looked inviting, it looked glamorous, and it looked fun. One caption read that the club was **'relaxing and comfortable.'** She had actually found the atmosphere relaxed, and with another drink, she was sure that she would feel more at ease.

"You're beautiful, Gabi. Be prepared to have a lot of attention." He ran the tips of his fingers up and down her leg. Gabi felt a shiver run up her spine. "Let's go."

She took hold of his hand and allowed him to lead her upstairs. He had told her to do whatever she felt comfortable with. She had decided that she'd stick with Darion in one of the more private rooms. She wasn't ready to allow people to watch her, if ever.

Once seated on the red sofas, Gabi took in the people around her. There was definitely a variety in terms of appearance and age. Several men had already caught her eye, and gave her a little wave. She grinned back out of politeness, desperately trying to hide her nerves.

A tall blonde sat down on the sofa opposite them. The black, low-cut dress that she wore exposed a lot of cleavage. Her surgically enhanced lips grinned at Gabi, her long, red nails tapping on her wine glass. She was wearing a lot of diamonds, and the shoes she was wearing were Jimmy Choo. She looked wealthy. She undressed Gabi with a sweeping look, taking in every feature, every detail, and then she turned to look at Darion. Her eyes widened, a flicker of interest in them. She licked her lips. Clearly the newcomer wanted him. The blonde woman looked at Darion the way that Gabi looked at him. Darion's head tilted a little higher as he took her in. Slowly, he flashed her his killer smile. Gabi felt jealous already.

How am I meant to do this? she thought, panicking. She poured herself a glass of champagne.

"I'm Audrina."

Darion took hold of the woman's outstretched hand and shook it. Gabi did the same, introducing herself.

"Is this your first time?"

"Not for me. But it's Gabi's first time," Darion informed her.

"Oh." She beamed at Gabi. "It's only my third

time," she confessed, letting out a giggle. Her mobile bleeped, so she pulled it out of her bag, pressing the buttons.

"I'm sorry, ma'am, no mobiles or cameras in here," the security guard said as he walked over. "There are lockers over there where you can store it."

"Oh. I forgot, I'm sorry. I'll be back in a tic," she told Darion, walking off.

"We get doctors, judges, actors, and other people in here who wouldn't want their reputation damaged in any way," Darion informed Gabi. "People come here to express their sexuality. Some people are ashamed of it, so rather than go local, they drive miles out here, where no one will know them."

At that moment, a couple in their mid-thirties sat down opposite them. Darion shook both their hands, grinning at them. He clearly knew them. They must have been regulars. The woman waved at Gabi and began making small talk, throwing a few compliments her way. She asked if Gabi minded her sitting next to her. Gabi knew that people expected her to be game; she was, after all, in a swingers' club. Darion and the man began chatting, seemingly both eager for their girlfriends to get it on.

"So, we hire a babysitter once every three months, and just come here, let loose, get wild." The woman laughed loudly. "Me and my husband were always a bit daring anyways," she confided in Gabi, taking a swig from her martini.

"How did you get into coming here?"

"We used to chat online to other couples and

meet up with them. Then, they recommended this club, and we have been visiting this place for three years now. Darion's a great guy."

Gabi bit her lip, wondering whether she had slept with him.

"You know." She paused. "There were all these fantasies that I had, but I had no idea that I'd be fulfilling them. Honestly…" She put her hand on Gabi's knee. "Just relax and have fun. Enjoy it."

Audrina returned and asked Gabi if she wanted to get a drink or have a dance. Gabi sighed in relief; she had wanted rescuing from the older woman. She wasn't attracted to her or her husband in the slightest. At least Audrina was definitely more her type. She agreed and headed toward the bar with her.

"Don't be nervous, honey. You don't have to do anything you don't want to. You can do as much or as little as you like."

"What got you into swinging?" Gabi couldn't help but ask.

"I came with my ex-boyfriend in the past. I really enjoyed it. I've never had a threesome before, so I'm hoping to meet a man and a woman who are up for it," she hinted at Gabi. "What about you? What are you looking for?"

"I'm not sure." Gabi surveyed the room, catching Franchesca talking to Darion. *What am I curious about?* The question rang in her ears.

"Threesome with two men? Another woman? S&M?" She shot Gabi a questioning look.

"Um…" Gabi laughed shyly. "I don't know." She ordered three shots of Sambuca and necked two back immediately, then handed one to Audrina, who did the same.

"I was like that the first time too. We couple swapped though. The first time was okay. I really fancied the guy, but Shane didn't click with the woman, at all. But he took one for the team, and we swapped partners. Then, the night after, I didn't take to the man, but I just went along with it. He didn't have a clue what he was doing."

Gabi giggled. Audrina was certainly an open book.

"Shane was in his element. Another woman joined him, and there he was, getting off on these two women, and I was getting screwed by some clueless man. It was awful. So, that night, we swapped again, and fortunately we met another couple that we both fancied."

"Did you ever just stick to Shane?" Gabi asked, hoping that it was common to not swap partners.

"Oh yeah. For the first hour, me and Shane had sex, but it felt ordinary, so we allowed people to watch us. Really turned me on. It feels like you're a pornstar or something, putting on a show." She giggled. "Trying to impress people, you know? Then I saw like, so many hot guys, and women, and just decided I was up for swapping."

"Are you here alone?" Gabi asked, wondering if a man was meeting her.

"Yeah. Well, I'm meant to be meeting a girl from the Internet, but I think she'll chicken out. I'm horny as hell tonight."

Gabi spotted Gina entering the room. She paused near the door and scanned the area as if looking for someone.

"She's hot." Audrina checked Gina out. "I definitely wouldn't mind getting to know her a bit better."

Audrina turned to order a drink for she and Gabi, and they returned to the table. The sofas were now empty. Gabi noticed that Darion was at Gina's side, and they appeared to be arguing about something. Gabi felt her blood boil. Gina knew that they were together. She was almost certain that Gina wanted something serious with Darion. She gulped back her wine quickly until it was only half full.

"So." Audrina took hold of her hand. "Can I show you the rooms?"

Gabi stood up. "Let me get Darion. We agreed on no separating."

"Sure."

Gabi slowly made her way toward Darion. She sensed people watching her every move. She fought back a blush. Gently placing her hand on Darion's arm, she asked if he wanted to head to the playrooms. Gina glared at him, obviously hoping that he'd decline. He agreed and told Gina to return to dancing downstairs. Annoyed, she turned on her heel.

"You wanna go together, or have you met someone?" he asked her, snaking his arm around her waist.

"I met someone."

Darion looked at her. "Great." His voice was thick with pride.

She could do this. She could get intimate with Audrina, couldn't she? When the blonde woman joined them again, they headed toward the playrooms. Gabi clenched her fists so that her long nails dug into the palms of her hands as nervousness swept over her. She desperately wanted the alcohol to kick in. She shot Darion one last glance before their relationship reached a new level. His expression was full of admiration, and most of all, longing.

Chapter Thirty-Six

Gabi hesitated at the black door before her. She couldn't believe that she was about to enter the depth of Darion's lifestyle, that she was going to try swinging for the first time ever. It would be the scariest and most daring thing that she had ever done in her entire life. She caught the gaze of many couples and singles, watching them as they slowly walked past. She noticed many of the couples were locked in passionate kisses, their hands roaming, eager to hit the playrooms also. There was a difference, though. They were extremely turned on, whereas Gabi was unbearably tense. Did she really love Darion enough to give it a shot? She couldn't imagine being without him. But was their relationship strong enough to survive it? She didn't know.

"Gabi, we can ditch Audrina if you're feeling uncomfortable," he whispered in her ear. "We can stop this whole thing if you're not ready."

"I'll be fine," she reassured him. She was beginning to feel the effect of the alcohol. Her head felt light and slightly dizzy.

At the other side of the door, she decided to check out each room before picking one to enter. In the first room on the left, she noticed a man lying on the king size bed receiving oral sex from a blonde who was being pleasured by a brunette woman. There was another couple lying down on the floor, fornicating, the man on his back, the woman straddling him. Gabi could hear several moans of pleasure from each person. Three of them glanced up, not stopping what they were doing. One of the women waved at Darion, making Gabi's stomach turn. She must have been one of his lovers at some stage, not that it surprised her.

They continued walking until they reached the next room on the left—the dungeon suite. She could make out gimps and dominatrices, surrounded by leather, PVC, chains, collars, masks, and whatnot. A man was pinned against the wall, attached by leather cuffs. A woman with long, black hair wearing a black PVC outfit was whipping his naked skin. Another woman was bent over, handcuffed and blindfolded, being spanked with a leather paddle. A man in a corner pleasured himself whilst he watched, and two women were positioned in the sixty-nine position, performing oral on one another whilst stealing glances at the people around them. Gabi wasn't sure how she felt.

The next room, was full of people having intercourse, or enjoying oral sex. They didn't bother checking out the shower or hot tub area. Darion advised her that it was always busy, probably too busy for Gabi's liking. They turned around and continued walking to view the rooms on the opposite side. They passed a room where a foursome was happening on one bed, a threesome on another, and two woman were simultaneously going down on a man on another bed.

They peered in another room, which was full of red cushions, Gabi could make out around twenty naked bodies writhing in pleasure. One woman was being pleasured by two men at the same time. There were men kissing, foursomes, threesomes, and men and women pleasuring themselves solo whilst watching others.

Gabi turned to look at Darion to gauge his reaction. His face told her that he was getting a thrill. He stroked Gabi's cheek gently, tracing his finger along her lower lip.

"The lights go off in this room after a while," he said, his voice husky, needy. "Hands are everywhere; you just feel about and get on with it. If you're shy, and don't wanna be watched, this is ideal." He arched a brow, as if suggesting it.

"No." Gabi shook her head. "I don't like the look of that room, Darion." She wrapped her arms around herself protectively, feeling exposed.

"Hey, it's not a problem," he soothed, pulling her closer to him. "I think the last room is more your type. C'mon, Audrina."

Patiently, Audrina followed them. Darion was breathing heavily, clearly becoming aroused from the tour and what he had witnessed. He squeezed Gabi's behind firmly, his mouth kissing the back of her neck. He led her into the last room with the hot tub and black lounge chairs. To Gabi's surprise, it was empty. She was relieved. Darion asked her if she wanted the door locked. He stated that he couldn't hide the peephole in the door though, as people did like to see what was happening. Gabi declined. She didn't want him shutting off rooms just for her. It wasn't fair to other people.

"Just relax, honey. Get in the hot tub and go with the flow, see how you feel." Audrina pulled off her dress so that she was in only her underwear. She placed her dress and heels on a shelf. Darion shot Audrina a grateful smile, obviously glad that she was there. Another woman made Gabi feel more at ease.

Gabi rubbed her temples. She was beginning to feel hot and flustered. Perhaps the water would do her good. She watched Audrina as she slowly stepped into the hot tub. Her body was slim, tanned, and perfect; she had curves in all the right places. Darion's head was bowed to the floor. Gabi knew that he was probably avoiding looking, out of respect for her.

Gabi pulled her dress over her head, slipped off her heels, and placed them on the shelf. She looked down at her body. She felt attractive in the scarlet coloured bra and underwear she was wearing. She had never been particularly body conscious, but at that moment she felt vulnerable.

Audrina, on the other hand, giggled excitedly. She checked Gabi out as she slowly lowered herself into the bubbling water. It was warm and soothing. She slid next to Audrina, and focused on Darion. He was now naked except for his black boxer shorts, the outline of his hard dick visible. He grinned at her wickedly.

She clenched her knuckles under the water. Her thighs were trembling slightly. Darion appeared from the shadows and stepped into the water. This was most men's fantasy—two women at the same time. Although she knew that it definitely wasn't a new thing for him; it was probably the same old for Darion.

Gabi lay back against the side of the hot tub. The bubbling water shot between her legs, sending a thrill through her body. The room appeared blurry. All she could see was the outline of Darion and Audrina. She splashed her face with water. *Much better.*

Darion gingerly glided toward her and parted her legs, so he could sit between them. She sat up straighter, tightening her legs around his waist. His hair and skin glistened with droplets of water. His body looked sensational and tempting as ever, but she couldn't feel smug, for he wasn't only hers.

He caressed the insides of her thighs with both hands with firm, massaging movements. Gabi's chest rapidly rose as she breathed quickly, her skin tingling in anticipation. His lips met her neck as he planted soft wet kisses down it and across her collarbone. Each lingering kiss made Gabi arch her body backwards as she released a small moan.

He pulled back to kiss her, his firm, hungry kisses and nibbles driving her wild.

She could feel how hard he was through his shorts, as he pushed against her clit, rubbing himself up and down. Gabi felt her legs tense, wanting him. She pulled him into her, rocking her hips.

Darion tugged her hair gently, pulling her head slightly back as his tongue traced along her bottom lip. She sealed her mouth over his, moaning into it. Audrina sat watching them, and wasting no time, her hand travelled down, and settled between her legs as she pleasured herself.

"You pair look so hot…" Audrina murmured breathlessly.

Gabi was taken aback when Audrina's lips crashed against hers. Unlike Darion's, her lips were smooth, her kisses slow, the stroking of her tongue gentle. As Gabi responded, moving her mouth in sync, she heard Darion sigh loudly in contentment, his fingers gripping her leg, as if the scene displayed before him was threatening his self-restraint.

"Fuck…girls, you're driving me crazy," he groaned, his voice needy.

What am I doing? She kept her lips firmly in contact with Audrina's, more for the blonde woman's and Darion's pleasure than for her own. She willed herself to stay calm. It was only a kiss. Regardless, if it hadn't been for the alcohol, she'd be as stiff as a board. It was all well having fantasies and desires, but when they become a reality, and you were actually acting them out, the reality was somewhat different. It was nerve-wracking. Her inner voice told her that there was nothing wrong with experimenting with another girl, trying something new, and pushing boundaries to see if she enjoyed it. *Just roll with it, Gabi.* She allowed her body to overrule her mind, before her courage failed her.

Eventually tearing herself away, she found Darion stroking the bulge in his shorts, a dark expression possessed his face, and she knew that the alcohol had also hit him hard, not to mention his lust-filled gaze at witnessing Gabi participating in his wild fantasies.

Audrina edged closer to him, and Darion fixed Gabi with a look that asked, *can I?* She inhaled deeply, and found herself nodding, giving him permission to kiss another woman right before her very eyes.

Darion's mouth met Audrina's, and they kissed savagely, their tongues entwined. Audrina's hand vanished into her underwear again. Gabi wasn't sure how she felt seeing him kissing the other woman, but part of her was impressed at how such a kiss from her man was turning Audrina on. Their tongues were darting in and out of one another's mouths, desperate to explore, both of them groaning. Gabi wondered for a second whether he fancied Audrina more than he fancied her. She swallowed, suddenly feeling like a third wheel, like this wasn't her territory. After all, she was the inexperienced newbie.

"Hey." Darion grabbed her chin, forcing her to look at him. "Are you okay?" Genuine concern etched his face.

She nodded.

"If you want me to stop, tell me. We can leave anytime you want."

"It's fine." She manufactured a grin.

She didn't know if she'd be able to go further than a kiss with Audrina, or whether she could allow Darion to. She silently prayed to God that there was a way out of it. She wasn't ready just yet. She needed more time. As if answering her prayers, an attractive couple entered the room. In a bid to give Audrina the hint to back off, Gabi slid onto Darion's lap, hooking her arms around his neck. She kissed him fiercely, her hands grabbing fistfuls of his hair, willing him to stay focused on her and only her.

When she glanced over her shoulder a few minutes later, she could see that Audrina was talking to the other couple. Gabi felt her body relax.

"Darion..." she whispered into his ear silkily. "How about we watch some of the couples in the other rooms?"

"Now?" His mouth fell.

She nodded. She'd do anything to get out of that room, and get rid of her anxious feelings.

"Whatever you want, baby," he responded. "Come on, let's dry ourselves off."

Once they had towel dried themselves down and dressed, she noticed that Audrina was locked in a passionate embrace with the new woman from the couple who had just come in, whilst the man was fondling her body. Gabi flashed her a small smile before leaving the room.

She and Darion wandered around the playrooms. Gabi was surprised at how much it did actually turn her on watching others writhing about in pleasure, hearing couples moaning, groaning, seeing them thrusting, licking, biting, kissing, and touching one another. Darion's fingers slid underneath her dress as he caressed between her legs, whilst fixated on the nakedness in front of him. When Gabi could take no more, they fled from the club and only made it to his lounge floor, visions from the night blazing through her mind.

Chapter Thirty-Seven

"I can't believe it." Gabi sat up rubbing her sore head, then reached over to grab a glass of water and down it. "Last night was…different."

"Didn't you enjoy it?" He was lying on the bed next to her, completely naked, a cigarette in his mouth, having woken before her.

"I don't know what to think," she replied honestly. "Kissing Audrina wasn't so bad, and watching others wasn't so bad either." It had been arousing. The sex between her and Darion after spending a while viewing each playroom had been intense, mind-blowing. "God, but what would my friends think?" *Wasn't it perverted?* A worried expression etched her face.

"It's none of their business, Gabi." His tone was stern. "Besides, you don't know what they get up to behind closed doors."

"True," she mumbled.

"Gabi." He sat up, his fingers caressing her back

tenderly. "You've done nothing wrong. We had a good night. Don't feel guilty for enjoying yourself and experiencing something new. We're not hurting anybody."

"I suppose." She pulled the covers over her exposed body. "I just hope this doesn't change anything between us."

He placed his cigarette in the nearest ashtray and cradled her face. "Nothing will ever change," he said, his soft words soothing her fears. "I will never leave you for any girls that we get intimate with. Swinging is just sex, just fun, right?"

She nodded.

"If you decide to experience it again, I will *never* fuck you over when we're swinging and go against what we've agreed. Do you understand?"

"Yes."

"I mean it, Gabi. Trust me, please."

"Darion," she whispered, eyeing him cautiously. "What happened with your ex-wife?"

He looked away. "Why do you need to know?" His voice was low.

"So I never hurt you like she did," she confessed.

He turned back to look at her, his scrunched up features softening. His fingers shook as they stroked her face. "She broke the rules when we were swinging."

Before Gabi could console him, he climbed out of bed and made his way into the bathroom, shutting the door behind him. She heard the sound of the water from the shower and thought it best not to question him further. It was obviously still a sore subject, and she didn't want to push it. She thought of the rules: no separating, no sex unless *both* agreed, and safe sex always. So when his ex-wife had cheated on Darion, it had been when they were swinging. She must have separated from him. Sadness rose inside her, on his behalf. If Darion had left the room last night with another woman, she would have been devastated. There would be no going back.

Pulling the covers off, Gabi rose to her feet. She paused near the bathroom door, wondering if she should go and comfort him. She felt awful for bringing Eva up. Then she felt insanely jealous and upset; Gabi was unsure if he still loved his ex-wife.

***

"He what?" Mallory's jaw hit the floor before she screwed her face up in disgust. "Gabi, he leads a swinging lifestyle. You have to leave him." She crossed her arms over her chest. "That's disgusting. He fucks a load of different people. Oh god." She rubbed her forehead. "Sexual diseases. Have you been checked out?"

"Mallory!" Gabi said sharply. "Please, keep it down." She didn't want the whole office hearing. She wished that she hadn't confided in her friend now. Perhaps Mallory wasn't as open-minded as she thought. "He *used* to sleep with different women, but not anymore. Not since he's been with me. Plus, condoms are mandatory with swinging."

"How do you know he doesn't still sleep with other people?" She snorted.

"Mallory, please. I thought I could talk to you."

Gabi rose from her chair, standing over her friend.

"You can." Mallory shook her head vehemently. "But this is crazy. I'm starting to wish you'd stayed with Lawrence now."

"Mal, his ex-wife introduced him to it. It seemed to work for them for years," Gabi told her, sitting back down. "He was honest about it with me. He didn't have to tell me."

Mallory took a swig of the steaming coffee. "Gabi, what have you got yourself into? Can you really trust him?"

Gabi nodded. "I think I can. He was hurt by his ex-wife. I don't think he'd put someone else that he cares about through that."

"Well, what if he asks you to try swinging?" Mallory shot her a serious look.

"Mal." Gabi's face reddened.

"You've done it?" She raised her voice, her mouth agape.

"Mal, please. Listen to me." Gabi felt her heart hammering against her chest, and tears threatened to flow. The last thing she wanted was for her best friend to judge her. She swallowed the lump in her throat, and regained her composure. "I didn't actually take part. I just kissed another woman briefly, and we watched others couples for a short while."

"Oh." Mallory shrugged. "So, what else happened?" She leant forward, clearly intrigued and eager for gossip.

"Not much."

"A swingers' club, though." Bewilderment showed on her face. "This is a lot to take in."

"Mal, I told you because we share practically everything. You'd be surprised, but a lot of people do it," Gabi informed her.

"Just be careful, Gabi." She reached over, taking her hand and squeezing it. "You're my friend, and I won't judge you if you like to have fun this way."

"I'm not sure if I like it." Gabi withdrew her hand. "I'm not sure how I feel about the whole thing."

"Well, only time will tell."

"I really love Daz, Mal. I really, really do."

"Well does he love you? Because, if so, you alone should be enough for him, Gabi."

Gabi remained silent. She took a deep breath. She had thought the exact same thing, but she didn't want to admit it. "But people that have been married for like over twenty years are swingers. They're happy and love one another. They're just sharing their sexual fantasies, bringing more excitement into their lives. It seems to work for them."

"I think it will end in tears," Mallory said. "Jealousy, wondering if he'll leave you for another swinging partner. I know you, you'll feel pressured to continue it for his sake, even if you go off the idea. There are too many emotional challenges, Gabi. I can't see how relationships survive this."

"They must do, Mal. They must have this strong bond or something. It depends on the couple, I suppose. Obviously some don't survive it." Gabi sipped her tea. "Recreational sex isn't for everybody, but there's a bit of exhibitionist and voyeurism in all of us, Mal, though some of us don't like to admit it. Some hide it. Some act upon it."

"Well." Mallory hesitated. "Suzie admitted to having some girl-on-girl-action at uni. And Steve's had threesomes in the past." She pursed her lips. "I've slept with a lot of men in my time, Gabi, but never at the same time, or with an audience. I just can't get my head around it."

"I don't need you to understand, Mal. I just thought I'd tell you about it. He owns a sex club, he's into swinging, and I hope I'm doing the right thing in being with him." She chewed her nail anxiously.

"Gabi, as long as you're okay with it, and he treats you right, what you do in the privacy of your own bedroom..." She paused, correcting herself, "Swinging rooms, it's not my business. Perhaps it is fun. It is the twenty-first century, pretty much anything goes now. There are so many open relationships these days. Free love." She laughed. "I've heard about the clubs, watched documentaries on TV. As long as you're happy, I'm happy. But just ask yourself this, are you doing it to please him, or to please yourself?"

Gabi didn't answer. She felt relieved when the ringing telephone on her desk interrupted them. Mallory left the office. Gabi was more confused than ever. Why couldn't she just enjoy swinging and push away all the thoughts in her head? Darion would want to do it again. She knew he would.

Chapter Thirty-Eight

Gabi was unable to stop tossing and turning in bed. She kicked the covers off, wondering if it had anything to do with the heat in the room. She positioned herself on her side, and concentrated on a sleeping Darion. He was snoring ever so lightly, his mouth parted, his bare chest rising and falling. One of his legs dangled off the edge of the bed, and a muscular arm clutched his pillow tightly. He looked handsome. She really did love him. It was strange how sometimes she felt like she knew so much about Darion, and other times she felt she knew nothing about him at all. She wondered whether he would ever properly let her in. She couldn't resist, so she stroked his cheek softly. He grunted, rubbing his face.

Gabi didn't want to wake him. She didn't want to lie in bed for the rest of the day either. It was bad enough that she had slept until late afternoon. It definitely wasn't like her. Yet, when she was with

Darion she seemed to sleep in longer. It must have been his comforting arms around her, which made her feel warm and relaxed.

She was glad that the working week had flown by, and she'd gotten dance class out of the way, and was able to spend the entire weekend with him again.

She slowly climbed out of bed, making her way into the kitchen. Her stomach rumbled, so she made a cheese sandwich, carrying it to the living room, and settling on the sofa. Taking a bite, she took in the room. It was a decent sized apartment, clean and stylish, but definitely a bachelor's pad. There wasn't a touch of femininity. She wondered whether it had been the apartment that he shared with his ex-wife, or whether he had moved there alone after the break-up.

She asked herself whether the relationship between them would ever get serious, whether she could see them living together, having a solid future. She couldn't ever see herself getting tired of him. If only he could have a different fantasy, a different desire that didn't involve other women. How could she ever get used to it?

"Babe," he croaked, appearing from the bedroom in just his boxers, stretching his fit, firm body.

"Morning," she welcomed him brightly, wiping her hands together to rid the crumbs. "Sleep well?"

"Actually, I did." He sat down, grinning at her. "You fancy doing anything today?" He turned his head to glance out the window. It was cloudy, but there was no sign of rain.

"Sure. What do you have in mind?"

He leant forward so his body was over her, holding up his weight with his arms, and planted a kiss on her lips. "Whatever you fancy." A glint appeared in his eye.

"How about we go for a meal?"

He pecked her lips. "Sure." He sat up. "If you're hungry."

"I will be again in the next hour."

"I'm gonna go shower. You wanna join me?" he asked, raising an eyebrow.

"Why not?" She grinned.

He took hold of her hand and pulled her to her feet. It didn't take long for the bathroom to steam up from the hot water. Darion slowly undressed Gabi, leaving a trail of kisses on the back of her neck, and down her spine. He placed his fingers around her hips, guiding her underneath the water. Squirting shampoo, he lathered it in his hands before massaging it into her hair with gentle, circular motions. As his fingers really worked her scalp, she sighed in contentment. The warmth of the water trickled down her wet, smooth body, and the feel of his touch was relaxing.

Lifting her chin up with his fingers, he tilted her head back to enable the water to wash the shampoo away. Then, rubbing a soap bar between his palms, he massaged it into her shoulders tenderly, and the tension in her muscles subsided. When his fingers met her breasts, rubbing in the bubbles and caressing them lightly, she drew in a breath, her nipples stiffening.

Her stomach tightened in anticipation when she felt the tingle of his touch. His hand travelled lower, where it settled between her legs. A low groan eased out of Darion's throat as he met her moist entrance, sliding a finger in carefully. He pushed in and out in a slow rhythm, whilst circling her clit with his thumb. She saw that he watched the reaction each touch elicited from her, his stare intense.

Gabi's gaze flicked down to his arousal, his cock twitching ever so slightly, desperate to be fondled. Gabi snaked her fingers around it, tugging it gently, causing him to grunt softly. He clamped his teeth together when she moved faster up and down his shaft.

Her head dropped back as he took a pink nipple in his mouth. As his tongue licked and sucked, she felt the early pulse of an orgasm, as she was on the verge of losing control.

Darion withdrew his finger, and in a swift movement he probed between the lips of her labia with his cock, teasing her with the tip. Gabi followed the line of his spine with her hands, all the way down to his buttocks, where she pulled him into her, the deepness of his thrust making her cry out. Her sex twitched as he plunged in out and out. She rocked in rhythm with him, her pelvis crashing against his.

"Gabi…" There was an aching need in his voice.

"I know…" she responded, her breathing ragged. She knew exactly how he felt. The sex was incredible, as always.

His tongue skimmed her lips, so they naturally parted. A moan rose in his throat with his deep, devouring kisses. Their tongues wrestled with one another greedily. Darion cupped the curve of her bottom roughly, anchoring her to him. Panting and groaning, he yanked her hips to meet his, whilst ravishing her with his mouth.

Gabi felt herself building higher and higher, the convulsing, throbbing and pulsing of her inner muscles around him driving her further. She whimpered incoherently as he moved in and out of her endlessly. With a final, deep plunge, she screamed out loudly, gripping onto his shoulders as delightful waves flooded her body, setting her groin on fire. And then she went limp, her knees buckling as she fell into his protective arms.

"Ahhhh…I'm close," he growled.

Darion continued to pummel in and out, fast and hard, making rough sounds of appreciation. His features hardened, and his body went rigid as he clutched her tightly. His head fell back as he came. He grunted and panted as he filled her.

Seizing her face in his hands, he kissed her tenderly.

Gabi had never felt so in love. She wondered if he loved her. Or, if not yet, whether he ever would.

***

Darion

In the restaurant, Darion ordered food and drinks for them both. He had taken her to a small restaurant in the area that he had been to several times. It was cosy with lit candles on each table, and soft music was playing.

Gabi looked as stunning as ever. She wore a low-cut, grey blouse, black pencil skirt, and high, black stilettos. As soon as he had seen her ready, he wanted to pull her back indoors and cancel the reservation. With her cleavage on show, and her full, sensuous lips, he was turned on just looking at her. He didn't want to break promises, though. He couldn't just keep her shacked up in his apartment or the club like some booty call. He had to treat her now and then. Plus, he wanted to, regardless of whether or not he was allowing her to get too close.

The waiter brought over their starters of garlic bread and chicken wings with different flavoured sauces. Just as he was tucking in, his mobile bleeped. He glanced down at the screen, grinding his teeth in annoyance.

Gina: Daz, the office phone is going crazy. You need to call Eva's lawyers pronto. This shit needs sorting.

He stuffed the mobile back into his pocket. He wasn't in the mood to discuss the club with Eva's lawyer. They were really pushing it. Eva was desperate to spite him. Rumour had it that she had split up with her boyfriend, Vinnie.

"Who was that?" Gabi asked, sensing his changed mood.

"Gina."

Gabi's features hardened, and he knew she sensed it was something else, something going on between them. He decided to be straight up with her. "It's about my ex-wife's lawyer," he told her,

339

taking a bite of the garlic bread and chewing it fast.

"Is everything okay?"

"She wants the club sold. Wants her half of the money."

"Oh." He was sure he saw a hint of glee in her expression. "What will you do?"

"I don't wanna sell it." He swigged his beer. "Why should I? I put a lot of money and effort into that place. It's doing really well. She can't just change her mind and…" He paused, taking a breath, realising that he was getting himself worked up. "Fuck it. Never mind."

"Can't you buy her half?"

"I can't afford it, Gabi." He shook his head, not wanting to reveal the money he'd blown on partying, drinking, and gambling over the years. He was relying on the club now to pay off his two cars and motorbike. He would have sold them, but he was certain he'd soon start earning a decent profit soon, so it wasn't necessary. "Apparently she's having money problems, but I don't believe a word of it. She's trying to piss me off. Things have gone wrong for her and now she wants to cause shit for me."

"I'm sure you'll sort something out," Gabi reassured him.

"Let's not ruin our meal." He squeezed her hand.

Silence descended over them for a moment.

"What?" Gabi asked, raking her hand through her hair awkwardly.

Darion blinked. He hadn't realised that he'd been staring at her, grinning in a smitten state, and there was nothing sexual about it either. *Shit.* He tensed his fingers around hers, before leaning back in his chair and letting go.

"Nothing." He shrugged, guarding his expression.

He felt relieved when the waitress interrupted them with their main meal. The delicious smell instantly of barbecue chicken filled their nostrils. They ate it and really got talking. Darion realised that he was enjoying himself with Gabi. She was sweet *and* intelligent. They could have fun outside the bedroom too. A part of him hated himself for getting so close to her, yet the other part was pleased that she was slowly restoring his faith in women.

He couldn't deny it, though; Eva still found a way of getting under his skin. He didn't want to give the club up. Why should he? After everything she'd done, after all the shit that she'd caused him, she was breaking agreements again. He needed to face her, to discuss it properly. But first, he had to find her. He couldn't keep avoiding the situation.

Chapter Thirty-Nine

Gabi

Gabi turned the key in the front door, pushed it open, and stepped inside. *Home sweet home.* It was Sunday afternoon, and she was glad to be back in her apartment. She had piles of ironing that needed doing, and hadn't tidied in a while. Darion had certainly been a distraction from her normal routine.

She hung her coat and handbag on the rack in the hallway, and slipped off her shoes, sighing. She was exhausted. Darion was definitely hard work. The freshness of the relationship meant that he couldn't keep his hands off her. Not that she could see that changing in the future. He'd probably have a high libido his whole life, no matter who he was with. He found no better pleasure than sex. Although drinking and smoking were close seconds.

Two hours later, she had ironed the clothes and put them away in the wardrobes. Gabi sat on the sofa with a glass of red wine, and switched through the channels on the television. She stopped on the series *Sons Of Anarchy*. Lifting her feet up, she lay across the sofa, getting comfortable.

She tried her hardest to concentrate on the screen, but even Jax Teller couldn't keep her focused this time. Darion's ex-wife entered her head again. She felt jealous, and had a bad feeling in the pit of her stomach that she couldn't get rid of. For some reason she sensed that there would be a confrontation, and soon. Just as things were going well with them, just as Darion was starting to forget about Eva—even his bad dreams had stopped—his ex-wife cropped up. Maybe she wanted him back. Gabi tried to stop her feelings of paranoia, but she'd be lying to herself if she said she didn't feel threatened.

She wanted Darion to sell the swingers' club; of course she did. It may have turned some women on, seeing their men get off with other women, but it didn't float her boat. She knew that Darion didn't want to sell, and would most definitely put up a fight. His heart and soul had gone into the club. He would miss it too much. He'd probably attend swingers' parties elsewhere if he did sell.

Gabi rubbed her aching temples. Why did she always do it to herself? Why did she always overthink everything? She loved him, that's why. She was worried about the situation. All she could do was sit back and see what happened. Hopefully, Darion cared about her enough not to let his ex-wife come into the picture and spoil what they had.

***

The next day at work, Gabi had just finished reading the pile of papers on her desk, when Mallory walked in with two cups of coffee in hand. She was relieved to have had a productive morning, managing to keep her mind clear of Darion and the issues that came with him.

"Gab, how was your weekend?" She placed the cups on the table, sat on a chair, and propped her legs up.

"It was good." Gabi took a sip of the steaming liquid.

"You get up to much?" She raised an eyebrow, clearly after the gossip.

"I spent the weekend with Darion. He took me for a nice meal."

"How are things with you both?"

"Not bad," she replied vaguely.

"Gabi." Mallory's voice was stern. "What's up?" Mallory eyed her suspiciously.

Gabi hesitated heavily. Why did Mallory have the ability to read her like a book? "His ex is back on the scene."

"Ouch. The one that broke his heart? As in, the *ex-wife?*"

She nodded.

"Why?"

"She wants the club sold that they jointly own."

"Well, that's good news, isn't it? Gab, this swinging lark isn't good for your relationship..." she said, clearly starting on the path of giving Gabi a lecture.

"Mal. He doesn't want to sell it. Plus, he hasn't seen her in years. What if his feelings come flooding back?" She knotted her fingers together nervously. "I don't know why I feel like this. I just like him so much."

"If he still loves her, then you don't want to be with a man who's in love with somebody else when he's with you. Do you?" Her expression was sympathetic.

"Suppose not."

"Besides, surely lawyers will be sorting all this. Who says he will see her?"

"I just have a weird gut feeling."

"Gabi, don't stress yourself out. You're probably getting yourself all worked up over nothing."

"I hope so."

"Oh, I saw Lawrence yesterday," she blurted out.

"Where?"

"The salon up the road. He was getting his hair cut. Got mine trimmed." She stroked the ends of her smooth hair.

"Did he speak to you?" Curiosity swept over her.

"He said hello, and introduced me to some chick called Lorna."

The same woman Gabi had seen him with at the store. "Did he seem happy?"

"He did." Mallory grabbed her hand tightly. "I have some bad news. I don't know if I should tell you."

"What is it, Mal?" Gabi let out a nervous laugh.

"Lawrence proposed to her. They're engaged."

Gabi swallowed. She should feel happy for him. Yet, a part of her was jealous. Upset, even. He was in a happy, normal, loving relationship, whilst she was out gallivanting with a man into swinging, with issues, and a wild ex-wife that threatened their relationship. She sighed heavily. All she wanted was the stability, normality, and predictability of a mature relationship.

"I'm happy for him," she lied. "I thought he would have told me."

"I think he moved on as best as he could, Gabi. You know he's always wanted to get married, be properly settled in life."

"That could have been me." She inwardly scolded herself for saying it out loud.

"Yes, it could have. But that life wouldn't have made you happy. You were bored senseless. You wanted out for many reasons. Don't be so hard on yourself, Gab. You did the right thing."

"I really hope so." Her head fell onto the back of the chair. "A part of me is a bit worried about Darion, Mal. I just need to know that it will definitely go somewhere, that we have a future. I know we're in a relationship, but I feel like something is holding us back."

"Gab, just enjoy yourself, okay? It's still only early days. Don't ruin the moment. What's meant to be will be." She stood up and drained the last of her coffee. "Don't have second thoughts now. You love Darion. You're just a bit insecure at the moment; we all go through these phases in relationships."

"True."

"Let me just finish these edits and I'll come back in a few hours."

"Thanks, Mal." She beamed, and then

remembered how rude she'd been. "I'm sorry I've been so self-involved, I haven't even asked how things are with you." She felt riddled with guilt.

"Oh, don't worry about it." Mallory laughed. Gabi was glad that her friend wasn't the sensitive type. "I'm fine. Me and Steve are always fine. Same old."

"And your hair looks beautiful, as ever."

"Thanks, Gab."

Mallory gently shut the office door after her. Gabi stared at the telephone on her desk contemplating whether she should call Lawrence and congratulate him. She wondered to herself, if she had the chance, would she have ever returned to Lawrence, if things had been different, had he treated her better?

She glanced down at the mobile phone on her desk. The screensaver was a photograph of Darion; his mischievous face stared back up at her, his mouth curled dangerously, his big, green eyes holding their usual glint. He wore all black and was sitting on his motorbike.

Many times she had wondered whether it was a wild phase that she was going through with Darion Milano. Her heart skipped a beat. *No chance.* She loved him more than anything. Her heart thumped frantically, and her body became heated just thinking about him. Mallory was right. She didn't need to bring the relationship down by worrying. She needed to continue with it as it was. It was fine at the moment. Wasn't it?

Chapter Forty

Darion

"Can you give me her number so I can speak with her?" Darion's voice was icy. "What do you mean you can't give out confidential information? I *need* to speak with her."

Darion paced the room, holding the mobile against his ear, puffing on a cigarette. He shook his head and mumbled something before throwing the mobile on the sofa.

"Fucking idiot," he snapped.

"Daz, calm down." Gina stood up and stroked his back.

"I can't calm down, G! She wants the club sold. I'm gonna lose it, I know it." He sat down, his head falling into his hands. He was stressed out. He hated Eva. She was trying to hurt him. But why? If he could just talk to her, perhaps he could persuade her to stick to the arrangement. Eva wasn't stupid though, she knew his intentions, which was why she was avoiding him. The only place she wanted to see him was in court, where he'd be served with an order to sell the club. He thought of ways to buy her share. Perhaps he could try and lend the money from somewhere, although he had no idea who to ask. Requesting a loan at the bank wasn't an option; not only would they likely refuse, but he didn't want further debts.

"Can't you just sell it, Daz? Buy a new club?"

"No, Gina. It was convenient for me with the strip club downstairs. I've worked my ass off on building the reputation of the swingers' club, paid hundreds on promotion. Everybody knows where it is now. Everybody associates me with the place. You know how many clients I have now. I can't start again from scratch. Besides, I don't have that kind of cash." He stood back up, his breathing heavy. He ran his hands through his hair. "I don't know what to do."

"I know you love that place," Gina said softly. "And you have worked so hard on it. Hopefully Eva will come around," she said soothingly.

"I doubt it. Don't you know anybody that knows her?" he asked her. "Or Vinnie? I need to find her."

"No." Gina shook her head. "Haven't heard a word about them since you split and she moved outta town."

"I didn't even know where she moved to." Darion clenched his fists. "I wanted nothing to do with her after that. Fucking hell, I've avoided all this. I knew she'd come back to haunt me one day."

"She's always been big on revenge."

"Oh yeah." Darion nodded furiously. "She always was a bitch."

"Come here." Gina patted the sofa, blinking up at him with her false black lashes.

Darion sat down. Gina moved to sit behind him and began massaging his shoulders. Gina always knew how to de-stress him. He'd actually missed her shoulder and back massages. They had always led to sex, though. He let out a soft moan as her fingers worked into the muscles of his broad shoulders. He allowed his body to fully relax. He hoped that he didn't get turned on. Like Eva, Gina was a part of his past. She was his employee, and now *only* his employee.

He felt her legs snake around his waist as she really went for it, her firm fingers massaging circles on his shoulder blades. Without asking, she stripped him of his top and threw it to the floor. Before he could whine at her, her hands brought him to another moan. His head fell back, his lids closing. It felt good. Really good. Her fingers began massaging his lower back, digging into his flesh. One of her sharp, manicured nails accidentally scratched him. He had a flashback of when he used to love her long nails scratching into his skin during sex, the times when it was rough, animalistic, and passionate, the times when they fought after a drunken row. Scratching, biting, hitting. He moaned again. *Fuck!* He felt Gina's warm breath on his neck as she leant her head closer to him. His chest rose slowly up and down, his fists were no longer clenched, but relaxed, and his body was falling back into Gina.

Then he remembered the time on the car bonnet. In the rain. With Gabi. Both of them soaking wet.

Naked, drenched, hot, frustrated. The time when he was so aroused he'd almost ripped her dress off. Her loud moans. He could hear them. He wanted her. Now.

He shot up when he realised that he was stiff. Not because of Gina, but because of his thoughts of Gabi. And when Gina pressed her lips against his back, he stood up quickly. He hoped she didn't notice the bulge in his trousers.

"G, I'm gonna take a shower, hit the sack."

"Why? Weren't you enjoying it?"

"Yeah." He nodded. "I'm just tired."

"Daz." Gina stood up, her body close to his. "I wish you loved me."

He pulled her close and wrapped his arms around her tightly, in a bid to end the conversation.

"What's wrong with me?"

"Nothing's wrong with you." He pulled back, cupping her face with his hands, his eyes blazing. "Don't you ever fucking think that." His voice was loud, sharp. He stroked her hair. "Gina, I never wanna hurt you. And because it was always a physical thing with us, it never really reached an emotional level. I'll always be here for you. No matter what." He tilted her face up. "You know that, right?"

"Yeah." She sighed. "You're a good guy, Daz. You've just got a lot of baggage, like me. Even though I'm pissed off beyond belief and it kills me to say this." She paused. "I do think Gabi's right for you."

"You do?" he asked, bewildered.

"Yep. I haven't seen you this happy, even with

Eva. I really think that you can have something special with her."

"Thanks, G." He pulled her into an embrace again. "You mean a lot to me."

"Go and relieve your sexual tension, before I can't trust myself not to pounce on you." She winked, indicating his erection, amusement on her face.

Darion let out a laugh.

She pressed her lips against his, lingering for a second longer than necessary. Darion led her out of the apartment before making his way into his bedroom. He needed a shower. But first, he needed to replay the memory with Gabi. He picked up his mobile and scanned through the naked photos that she had sent him. *Mmm. All mine.* He was frustrated and needed to do something about it. And quick. How he had denied Gina's advances again, he didn't know. She was there, willing, available, and up for it. He really was a changed man. Well, a little changed.

Chapter Forty-One

Gabi

Gabi confronted her wild mane in the mirror. She had back combed her dark blonde hair, creating volume. It made her look sexier. Her lids were lined with black pencil, making them seductively stand out. Not that she really needed to do them; she would be wearing an eye mask. She slipped into red, six-inch platforms, and scrutinised her whole look. The short, black silk dress clung in all the right places, showing off her curves. The dress was beautiful. Not much material to it though; the gown looked like a sexy nightie she'd wear to bed. She had glammed it up with silver accessories. Gabi wanted to look perfect. She knew that she had tough competition. She wanted to stand out from all the women who would be at the club. She wanted Darion's eyes on *her*.

She was going to a themed fancy dress party at

The Black Door. Regular members had hired the upstairs for a party of around forty people. Gabi was excited, yet nervous at the same time. Excited that she and Darion always had a fun night at the club in general, never knowing what would quite happen, but nervous that it was her second time in the playrooms. When she arrived at the club, she headed to his office.

"So, Darion, what am I to expect tonight?" she asked him when she was perched on his desk.

He grinned. "Themed masked night, fancy dress costumes, and a night for couples into roleplay. It's exciting," he reassured her. Smoke escaped his mouth from the cigar he was smoking, finding its way toward Gabi.

"What will you wear?" she asked him, swallowing the shot of vodka that he had prepared for her.

With a tilt of his head, he said, "You'll have to wait and see."

"Come here." She pulled him toward her, desperate for a kiss.

He took a step away from her. "Wait until later," he teased, dousing the cigar in an ashtray.

"Not even a kiss?" she asked, open-mouthed.

He leant over her, planting soft kisses down her neck. She moaned softly and tilted her head, allowing him more access. His kisses got firmer, his stubble sharp on her skin. She felt a needy ache between her legs, in desperate need of release. She didn't think she could wait until later. His gentle fingertips traced up her trembling legs and parted them. She could feel his rigid length standing between them, skimming her heated pelvis. She grabbed hold of his ass with both hands, pulling him in closer. He groaned in pleasure as he rubbed himself against her, up and down. Cradling her face, he brushed his mouth softly against her lips. Gabi parted them, inviting his kiss, but it never came. He tilted his head out of the way.

"Later," he said huskily. "Now, get out. I need to get changed."

"Charming." She shook her head. "You are cruel, Mr. Milano."

"I'll meet you upstairs. Get yourself a drink, darlin'."

Gabi stood up and shakily made her way toward the door. Her hands began to get clammy. She inhaled deeply, wishing that her nerves would go away. *Tonight will be good,* she told herself.

"Hey," he called out.

She swivelled around.

"Remember the rules. And if you ever feel uncomfortable," he said, pausing momentarily, "you let me know, okay?"

"Sure."

Gabi was soon upstairs, sitting on one of the velvet couches, glass of white wine in hand. She wondered what Darion would be wearing, and excitement overcame her. She could bet that he'd look as sexy as ever. She couldn't wait to get her hands on him. Could she have sex with him in the playrooms in front of several people? Would wearing a mask make her feel less intimidated? More confident?

She turned her head and noticed a poster on the

wall; it read, **'*Young, Free, and Swinging.*'** She scanned the room and noticed a few tall, slender women wearing long ball gowns and glittery, black masks, which covered the top part of their faces with only two eyeholes present. There were also women wearing just their underwear and stockings with similar masks. Very Moulin Rouge. One woman in particular caught Gabi's attention: her underwear was sparkly gold, her eye mask matching, with lots of accessories, and her lips were painted a shade of bright red. She looked glamorous, almost like an Egyptian princess.

Others were dressed as French maids, nurses, dominatrices, or schoolgirls, and the men wore plain black eye masks, or gladiator, fire fighter, army, or police officer uniforms. Gabi could see that everybody had made an effort.

She adjusted her glittery silver eye mask before draining the last of her drink eagerly, awaiting Darion's return. After twenty minutes had passed, and she had witnessed enough touchy-feely kissing couples, and engaged in small talk with two other couples, she headed to the bar for another drink. The playrooms were now open, and people were slowly vanishing inside each room. Gabi ordered another wine; she needed to get tipsy. She wanted to unwind and hopefully try to relax and have some fun with Darion, to be the woman he craved.

She turned around when she sensed someone watching her. It was a couple seated on some stools at the bar. She couldn't make out their faces, as they were both in costume. He was wearing a black, lycra gimp mask, which covered his whole face except for his eyes and full lips. Gabi blushed, and felt herself shudder, both with excitement at the mystery of the man behind the mask, and fear at the weirdness of it. She craned her neck, only catching sight of the long-sleeved black top he was wearing, the tightness of it revealing muscular arms.

The woman was wearing a black PVC eye mask and a black PVC catsuit. She had faint whiskers drawn on her face. Her blonde hair was pulled back into a ponytail.

Gabi turned her head away and concentrated on the dancers on the pole. A few moments passed, and then she felt a hand run up her thigh. It sent shivers up her spine, and her heartbeat quickened. She shot a quick glance behind her, noticing that it was the man in the mask. Feeling a little shy and uncomfortable, she didn't look anywhere other than the bar ahead of her. She didn't want to attract attention until Darion was there. They agreed not to do anything until either one of them gave their consent, and there was no separating. She felt his body brush up against her back, his hot breath tickled her neck as his strong hands continued to caress her bare legs. Before she could speak, his moist lips pressed onto her neck. The softness of the mask brushed against her skin.

"Excuse me." She edged away. "I'm waiting for someone."

"His name wouldn't happen to be Darion, would it?" He flashed a set of perfect white teeth. He held her chin, turning her face around to look at him, and caught her mouth in a rough kiss. Gabi felt butterflies in her stomach. She silently scolded herself, and kissed him back hungrily, pulling him into her. It felt odd not being able to see his face, his expression, but the kinkiness of the mask heightened her excitement.

She eventually pulled back and giggled. "You look freaky."

"I know." There was a wicked, dark, and wild gleam in his eye. "Do you want me to fuck you wearing it?"

She bit her lip. "It looks a little scary."

"I found it in the back room. I've never particularly been one for dress-up." He removed the mask, and grinned.

"Who's that?" She nodded toward cat-woman.

"Gina." He ordered a drink. "She's waiting for her boyfriend, Johnny."

"Oh."

"So." He took hold of her hand, licking his lips slowly. "You ready?"

She nodded and headed with him toward the playrooms. Darion's hand dropped to stroke her buttocks. Gabi looked around at the faces that were staring longingly at them—Darion, with his muscular broad frame, hypnotic, seductive eyes, and naughty grin, and Gabi, with her never-ending legs, slim body, curves in all the right places, and beautiful face. They made a hot couple. Practically everyone in the room wanted a piece of them, wanted to share the intimacy and passion they had.

"See how many men wanna fuck you?" he whispered into her ear, grazing it with his teeth, nibbling it.

"And how many women want you," she replied

flatly, jealous.

Darion didn't let her choose a room this time. He chose the room. The large room was filled with nothing but cushions, and it was dimly lit. Gabi could make out silhouettes of people having sex and engaging in foreplay. She could hear loud moans and groans. The whole room smelt of sex. She was relieved that it wasn't easy to make out what others were doing, unless you were sitting before them, really focusing on them. Perhaps she wouldn't feel so nervous. If she just closed her eyes and reminded herself that nobody could really see one another, then surely she'd be fine. She could even enjoy it. As Darion shut the door behind them, a few faces looked up, curiosity obviously getting the better of them. They probably wanted to see who was joining the orgy, to see if they were attracted to the newcomers.

Gabi shifted awkwardly from one foot to the other, wondering where to place herself. Trepidation ran through her veins, thick and heavy. She drew in a short, shallow breath to compose herself. The little voice in her head told her that she was in control of the situation; she could do as little, or as much as she wanted. If she wasn't enjoying it, she could stop at any time.

Taking a few tentative steps forward, she dropped onto some cushions in the middle of the room, where there was a space. Darion joined her. He regarded her with uncertainty at first. She manufactured a small grin, which he obviously mistook as her being comfortable and giving him the green light.

He didn't waste any time, and began kissing her passionately, his hands running through her hair. The wine was starting to take hold and Gabi allowed herself to give in to Darion, to indulge in pleasure. As he kissed her neck, she stole a look around the writhing bodies near her. She had to really strain her eyes to make out the activities taking place in the shadows. She noticed what appeared to be two men kissing, a woman straddling a man, a man feasting on a woman, and more entwined limbs. She looked at the woman lying next to her, who had completely succumbed to temptation. Gabi wondered whether she had partner swapped, and if she was getting intimate with a stranger.

She gasped as Darion pulled the neckline of her dress down and began kissing her nipple, gently biting it, teasing her. *Enjoy yourself, Gabi.* She curled her fingers around his neck and wriggled in ecstasy. His wet, warm tongue flicked over her nipple. He went in circles as he licked it slowly, sucking it. Her nipple stood to attention as his lips hungrily sucked harder, and then he moved onto her other breast.

Gabi sighed in contentment as she felt his hand go under her dress as he massaged between her legs, his fingers stroking her. She parted her legs. Now, as her body overruled her mind, she no longer cared who was in the room, as all that mattered was his touch that she had awaited for hours. He unzipped her dress and peeled it off, leaving her exposed in her underwear. He ensured that her heels remained on.

She groaned when he pulled her underwear aside in a swift movement, and entered her. He was impatient, not even bothering with foreplay. *Relax, relax, relax,* she repeated in her head. *Nobody can see you. Besides, they're all too busy doing their own thing.*

Darion thrust into her, and then pulled out for a moment, teasing her, making her inner muscles throb. Her heart beat frantically in her chest. He thrust into her again, his full length hammering into her repeatedly. She bit into his shoulder trying to stifle her moans, digging her nails into his ass as she pulled him closer into her, deeper.

"Are you okay?" He stilled for a moment.

"Yes, don't stop," she found herself pleading.

He slammed into her with force, almost sending her over the edge. Both of his hands fondled her breasts as he thrust into her deeply, back and forth. Gabi felt some lips press against hers. She realised that it was the attractive woman next to her. Gabi reciprocated. Her soft lips, soft skin, and tender kisses were a change from Darion's firm kisses. She felt Darion quicken his pace, making low grunts of pleasure.

She gasped when she felt an intense vibration on her clit, and quickly looked down to see that Darion had produced a small sex toy—a bullet vibrator. Gabi squirmed, unsure of whether she could handle how powerful it was, she tried to close her legs, but since Darion was still inside her, he prohibited her from doing so. He pounded in and out, matching the speed and circling motion of the toy.

She felt him twitch inside her, knowing that he

was on the brink of climaxing. He pulled out and penetrated her with his fingers, fast and deep, making her shiver with delight.

"Ah…" She panted, squirming.

Darion entered her again, jerking his hips, tweaking her nipple with one hand. The tingling of her nipples, the buzzing toy on her clit, and Darion's full length diving in and out of her was intense to the point of almost being unbearable. She felt her inner muscles clenching and contracting around him.

He flashed her a wicked smile, not breaking his gaze from hers. Now, with one free hand he squeezed Gabi's fingers tightly, and whispered that he loved her.

Gabi froze. It was so quiet, so soft, she wasn't sure whether she had imagined it.

He shrugged, as if the feelings had been out of his control, as if he'd tried to fight it, but failed miserably.

Gabi licked her lips, her throat dry, her heart hammering frantically. *He loves me!* She felt like she'd burst with happiness; she could probably even come on the spot. Never had those words sounded so good. With an audible intake of air, she replied, "I love you too."

"It doesn't mean I trust you, though." He shot her a look.

"Well, I hope you will one day," she said, and meant it.

In one swift movement, he lifted her legs over his shoulders, and resumed pleasuring her. Gabi bit her lip at the depth of him hitting her sensitive spot.

Darion groaned deep in his throat, running his fingers along her smooth legs, planting several kisses on her shins and ankles, running his tongue up them seductively, eyeing her intently.

As a woman wearing a gold eye mask moved closer to Darion, he dropped Gabi's legs so they were back at his waist. Sitting behind Darion, the woman began kissing his neck tenderly. Darion's brow rose in a questioning gesture, checking if it was okay. She nodded. The woman's partner leant toward Gabi. She hesitated at first, but decided to go for it. What was a little kiss? She allowed him to attach his lips to hers. His kisses were quick, desperate, his tongue invading her mouth. He made low, appreciative grunts as his fingers roamed her body simultaneously. Gabi edged away, feeling slightly uncomfortable at his touch whilst having sex with Darion. The couple then reunited, starting to pleasure one another.

"Are you okay, darlin'?" Darion asked breathlessly into her ear.

She nodded, clawing the floor. She was close to falling apart, to surrendering to the orgasm that was building inside.

Darion flexed his hips, moving slowly. She watched his expression as his features screwed up in agonised pleasure. He clenched his teeth, his fingers digging into her hips, trying his hardest not to come.

She arched her back, sighing loudly. Rocking her hips, she matched him thrust for thrust. She felt herself building. Her body stiffened as he continued to fill her, pounding harder and faster, in and out. He ran his tongue slowly across his top lip making

Gabi's insides throb.

Her chest rose up and down as her breathing was short and quick in between groans. This was what she wanted, *just* him. And it felt so much better now he'd told her he loved her. She zoned out as she tightly closed her lids. She felt her pelvic muscles spasm, her heart racing wildly. A hot flush travelled down from her face, over her chest and body.

"Ah...Darion." She gasped.

Darion changed his pace, moving torturously slowly. The toy was still buzzing against her sensitive clit, tingling her nerve endings, making it swell with heat. She clenched her fists, tensed her legs—the vibrations were unbearable. Gabi felt a ball of fire in the pit of her stomach at the feel of his hard length sliding out, then thrust back in with force. Burning. Aching. *Fuck!* She threw her head back, crying out. Her panting was heavy, her body damp with sweat.

She whimpered incoherently, before inhaling a deep breath.

He rotated his hips, plunging in deeper. A delightful chill ran up her spine, tension coiling in her stomach. Her clit throbbed, her muscles quivered, and her legs shook.

"Ahhhhh," she screamed out as he hammered into her deeply, gripping her buttocks. Darion flexed his hips and pounded away until she reached a shuddering orgasm, rippling spasms engulfing her. She screamed out. *Oh my god!* She then laughed quietly, fully satisfied. Darion always ensured he gave her a mind-blowing fuck. Her body stilled for a minute, her panting becoming soft breaths. She allowed herself to relax. When she finally caught her breath, she glanced at Darion. His face broke into a proud smile. She had done it. She had managed to totally let go of her inhibitions and enjoy the playrooms.

Not wanting to keep Darion hanging, she bucked up and down, spreading her legs, taking all of his cock, willing him to climax. As she groaned at his hard length gliding in and out, she noticed that he'd stopped moving. She glanced at him and noticed his attention was on the door behind her. He pushed into her fast, viciously, making her whimper. Gabi clenched her fists, squirming in discomfort. He was hurting her. His face was red with rage, a storm brewing in his eyes. With a few more thrusts, she felt him explode powerfully inside her, filling her, loud grunts escaping his lips.

"Fuuuuuuck…" he cried.

He went rigid, and then collapsed on top of her, his whole body weight crushing her. She could feel the slamming of his heartbeat against her chest. He was gasping for air, sucking it in.

She looked up at him again and noticed that he was still focused on the door. Coldly, he lifted his body up and moved away from her. Gabi followed his angry stare and gasped. A woman stood tall, wearing tight black leather trousers, black platforms, and a white vest top, her obvious false breasts protruding over the top. Her petite arms were covered in black, swirly tattoos, her long black hair cascaded down her back, and her red lips were set in a thin line. Her piercing emerald eyes could be seen a mile off. She oozed sex. As she stood in the doorway, obviously looking for Darion, Gabi realized it was his ex-wife.

It was Eva.

Chapter Forty-Two

"What the fuck?" Darion inhaled deeply, sharply.

Gabi quickly sat up and searched for her dress. By the time she struggled to put it on, Darion and Eva were gone. She felt a stab of anger inside her, pissed off that he had left her like that. What happened to no separating? What happened to being in love with her? Where had they gone? Why had his ex-wife shown up like that, with no warning? Eva did seem like the type of woman who enjoyed making an entrance. Gabi had started to fully enjoy herself with Darion, but now she felt dirty and humiliated. She wondered how long Eva had been in the doorway, watching them. She had looked the same as her photograph, only with more tattoos. Gabi's mind went into overdrive. Darion hadn't been able to take his eyes off her, and had jumped up as soon as he saw his ex-wife. Had his feelings returned? Did he still love her? Gabi stood up shakily and stepped over the mass of writhing bodies. She had no idea what to do. Had Eva come regarding the club?

Gabi quietly shut the door behind her and was soon facing all of the other playrooms. She peered inside each one that she passed, and then spotted Gina. She was sprawled out on a king-sized bed, giggling as a woman kissed her neck whilst others had sex around them. Gabi beckoned her over. Gina immediately stopped what she was doing and made her way over to Gabi, genuine concern on her face.

"Gabi, what's up? You not having fun?" Gina stroked Gabi's face, and then pulled her forward for a kiss. "Fancy joining me?"

"G-Gina," she stuttered, a tear escaping down her cheek. "Eva's here."

The colour drained from Gina's face as her mouth dropped open. Gabi wasn't sure if it was out of jealousy of Eva, or compassion for her. Gina pulled Gabi by her elbow, hurriedly leading her out of the rooms and into the bar area. She found a private booth and pulled the curtain shut to give them some privacy. Gabi was glad for the relative solitude, she felt like she was about to cry at any moment.

"Where are they?" she yelled.

"I don't know," Gabi cried.

"He won't take her to the office, he's always been strict about her going in there if she ever turned up unannounced. Don't like her seeing the paperwork and his future plans and renovations for the club, or some shit. They've gotta be in the bar somewhere." She paused, in thought for a moment.

Panic crossed her face. "Or still in the playrooms."

Gabi was silent.

"You want me to go look?"

Gabi nodded. She didn't want to. She was afraid of what she might see. What if they were having explosive make-up sex, releasing years of pent-up sexual frustration? She couldn't bear to witness it. Gina vanished, leaving Gabi and her thoughts alone. She didn't want him to be taken from her. The thought of losing him made her feel physically sick. She was addicted to Darion. She couldn't understand the hold he had over her. She had never felt a love so strong. She loved the feeling, but hated feeling weak when it came to him.

It felt like a decade until Gina returned, none the wiser. Gabi sighed heavily, fiddling with her nails nervously. "Gina," she said, daring to ask, "should I expect the worse?"

Gina shrugged. "Darion, I think you can trust." She pouted her lips, "Eva, on the other hand, you can't. Usually what she wants, she gets."

Gabi felt all the air leave her body. Her face contorted in anguish as her heart twisted in her chest. She breathed deeply, determined to stop crying. Eva was back. It was the ultimate test.

"He hasn't seen her in years." Gabi rubbed her aching temples. "Do you think she's here for him?" Her voice was shaky.

"Could be. Or could be the club. He had a massive argument with her lawyer on the phone about it. Told him to tell Eva to go fuck herself, and to see him if she wanted to discuss things." Gina peered through the gap in the curtain, then back to face Gabi. "Perhaps he pissed her off."

"What am I doing?" Gabi looked up at the ceiling. "I can't do this anymore." She shook her head furiously. "This isn't for me, Gina. I need to get the hell out of here."

"What's not for you, Gabi?" Gina's tone was sharp. "The club? Or Darion?"

"The club, I suppose," she mumbled. "All this." She waved her arms in the air to indicate her surroundings. "It's a part of Darion. It comes with him. I just can't do this anymore."

Gabi had had enough. She was done fighting for him. He was right from the start, she would end up hurt. If you play with fire, you get burnt. She felt foolish. She had tried to be someone she wasn't. As much as she had started to take to swinging, she just couldn't actually imagine swapping partners. She had to accept it, she was far too jealous. She had to accept that it could work for some people, but not for her.

"And if he gives up the club, the swinging?" Gina challenged her.

"Then I'll never let him go." Gabi looked at her. "I love him, Gina, so, so much."

Gina looked glum, as if she were feeling the exact same. "I know you do."

Gabi looked down, feeling deflated. "Where's your boyfriend?" she eventually asked, suddenly remembering.

"Probably fucking someone in those rooms," she said, lighting a cigarette.

"I'm sorry. Did I ruin your experience? You can go back, I'll be fine."

"Nah," she spat. "Johnny looked like he was having fun without me."

"I'm sorry, Gina."

"Don't worry about it. He just liked the idea of dating a stripper. I'll keep on having my fun, do what I'm good at, not get my heart broke." She sighed.

Gabi looked down at the carpet as Darion's face invaded her mind.

"Gabi, Darion's a good guy, ya know. A little fucked up, insecure, has baggage and whatnot, but he has his reasons for being the way he is. And it goes *way* beyond his ex-wife." Gina's face was sympathetic. "He'd never hurt you intentionally." She blew out smoke. "He could have had me whenever he wanted, we've got quite a past." She let out a laugh. "Since you and him became exclusive, he's never crossed the line, never gave in to temptation. And that, for Darion, is a world record."

"Yeah, well," Gabi said softly, "where is he now, Gina? He's not here, that's for sure." She stood up. "I'm getting a taxi home. I guess this is it. I can't handle all this heartbreak, I can't handle not properly knowing *him*, how he feels about his ex-wife, and I can't handle his love for swinging."

He'd never give up the club, his wild lifestyle, or Eva. It was all over. It had to be.

"Gabi, don't go." Gina took a step closer, her hand stroking Gabi's hair, her face, her lips, staring at her intently, mirroring her miserable expression.

"I'll see ya, Gina." She hugged her tightly. "Tell Lexi goodbye, and you take care of her?"

371

"I will. Take care of you, Gabi."

Gabi pulled the curtain back and walked toward the door. She searched the bar one last time. No sign of Darion. She slowly descended the stairs. Curiosity getting the better of her caused her to quickly peep in the gentleman's club to see if she could see him. She couldn't.

Gabi exited The Black Door, shivering against the cold bitter air. She groaned inwardly as it began to rain. She contemplated going back in the club until the rain subsided, but thought better of it. She needed to get away from the smoke, from the loud music, from the club, from Eva, and from Darion.

She needed to go home, where she belonged.

Chapter Forty-Three

The rain lashed down powerfully, drenching everything, especially Gabi's clothes and hair. She stood on the pavement, her arms wrapped around herself for warmth. She didn't care that it was freezing cold and that she didn't know where she was going. She felt sick to the stomach, although the fresh air should do her good, even though it was sharp in her lungs. She felt a stabbing pain, and emptiness in her heart. She had lost Darion. She couldn't compete with the wild, sexually adventurous Eva. Nobody could. All she could be was herself. And that obviously hadn't been enough.

She looked at the club for the final time, the red glow from the window illuminating the street. She wondered whether he had already given in to the temptations of Eva, whether he was in the playrooms with her right that moment. The thought depressed her. At least the relationship had taught her something—swinging definitely wasn't for her.

Gabi wiped her wet hair from off her forehead and slowly continued down the road staring at the blackness of the night before her. How had he looked at Eva? With anger, or with lust? She scolded herself for replaying the moment in her head. What was it they said about swinging? It could light a fire, but it could also burn the house down. The house had definitely burnt down, leaving nothing but ash to be swept away in the wind, gone, like it never even existed, probably like her relationship with Darion, to become a distant memory. She crumpled into breathless sobs. There was no point hiding it; she was devastated. Gabi walked on, wiping her sniffling nose and tear-stained face. When she noticed a taxi drive past, she lifted her arm to hail it down. It stopped. Gabi made her way toward it, taking a deep breath, and regaining her composure. She didn't want the driver to see her in such a humiliating state.

"Gabi!"

She turned around swiftly. Darion. He was drenched. The rain dripped from his hair, his face, and his clothes. She was unable to read his expression until he was before her. His eyes were red and puffy. He looked worn out, tired, like he had the weight of the world on his shoulders.

"Gabi." He stepped toward her, leaving a small gap between them, concern etched on his face. "I've been looking everywhere for you. Why did you leave?"

"Why did you?" Her tone was thick with rage and jealousy.

"I don't know if you know, but that was my *bitch* of an ex-wife in there," he said through clenched teeth. "We were discussing the club. I didn't want her anywhere near you." He ran his hand through his hair, clearly frustrated, and then he took in a shaky breath. "I have some bad news."

Could it get any worse? She was silent, willing him to continue.

"She's back in town," his voice shook with emotion. "For good."

Gabi felt her heart twist. Definite deal breaker. "I can't do this anymore, Darion." She shook her head vehemently. "I can't handle any of it, I'm sorry…it's over."

Darion looked up, clamping his jaw shut, as if willing himself not to break down. "I love you, Gabi. Isn't that enough?"

Before she knew it, Darion pulled her into a tight embrace, crushing her body against his, as if he never wanted to let her go. His fingers gripped the material of her dress. She stumbled back a step as he balanced his weight on her, like he no longer had the energy to stand. He was openly showing his vulnerable side, his weaknesses, his obvious fears of being alone, but he also demonstrated his fears of being attached.

In a sense, he'd opened up to Gabi, slowly learning how to love again, and she was taking it away from him. Feeling her throat tighten, and sadness sweep over her, Gabi hesitantly hooked her arms around him. They remained entwined for a moment in silence.

Darion eventually pulled back, cupping her face

in his hands. "Don't do this, Gabi. I can't be without you," he said sternly. "I'll do *anything*." Gabi studied his face for any signs that he was being insincere. He wasn't. *Anything?* She wondered if that meant giving up swinging and selling The Black Door.

When his soft lips met hers, kissing her tenderly, she reciprocated. His kisses grew firmer, holding so much passion and so much love.

He squeezed her tightly again, his fingers gently stroking her hair. Gabi screwed her eyes shut. She breathed in his delicious, intoxicating cologne, cherished the feel of his soft face pressed against hers, relaxed in his protective arms, and listened to the sound of his pounding heart against her own. And she realised there was nowhere else she'd rather be.

Although Gabi had no idea what the future held, and it frightened her, she knew one thing—she loved Darion more than anything in the world. At times, even though she contemplated leaving him, she knew she couldn't go through with it. The feelings of lust, love, addiction, and passion wouldn't go away.

For a moment, she almost felt like they could get through it all—one day at a time.

And then she felt someone's presence. Slowly blinking her eyes open, she saw Eva. Gabi felt a jolt of fear run through her body, all the air leaving her. Leant against the wall, her arms folded across her chest, Eva's eyes examined her carefully, the kind of inspection that was meant to unnerve. Her lips curled into a small, secret smile, a look that told

Gabi she was in for a big surprise.

She was back to claim what was hers—The Black Door, and Darion.

Book Playlist

Nine Inch Nails–"Physical"
Bruce Springsteen–"I'm on Fire"
Nine Inch Nails–"Closer"
Steppenwolf–"Born to be Wild"
Robert Palmer–"Addicted to Love"
Whitesnake–"Still of the Night"
Muse–"Supermassive Black Hole"
Rolling Stones–"Satisfaction"
Kid Rock–"So Hott"
Five Finger Death Punch–"The Bleeding"
In This Moment–"Adrenalize"
Danzig–"She Rides"
Linkin Park–"Crawling"
Linkin Park–"Waiting for the End"
Three Days Grace–"Animal I Have Become"
Arctic Monkeys–"Do I Wanna Know"
Interpol–"Turn On the Bright Lights"
Evanescence–"Going Under"
Evanescence–"Bring Me to Life"
Massive Attack–"Angel"
Muse–"Uprising"
Nirvana–"Smells Like Teen Spirit"
Cranberries–"Zombie"
Sneaker Pimps–"Spin Spin Sugar"
Serge Devant–"Addicted To Love"

Acknowledgements

To the readers, thank you for reading the first book of *The Black Door* trilogy. I hope you enjoyed it, and will continue to follow Gabi and Darion's journey because it definitely isn't over. There are a few surprises in store!

A big thank you to all of my family, especially my mom and dad; my sisters, Annastasia and Angelique; and my brother, Michael. You all support me in whatever I do! Not to mention my friends.

To the wonderful authors, bloggers, and readers who I connect with daily online, you make the journey that more enjoyable. To those who reviewed my book, I made it the best it could be with your help. You're the best! And, of course, my gratitude goes to the wonderful Limitless team!

About the Author

S. Valentine grew up in England. Studying English language and literature, as well as law, she worked in a solicitors' for many years before moving to Spain. She does however still visit the UK, which, in a way, will always be home.

Returning to her lifelong passion of writing books, she's also a weekly columnist for *The Ibizan* newspaper for their lifestyle and fashion section. Her other interests include reading, shopping, enjoying a nice glass of wine, and watching shows such as *Sons Of Anarchy*, *Dexter, Gossip Girl*, and *SATC*. She's a social media addict, and loves connecting with new people.

For more information, please visit: www.s-valentine.wix.com/books. If you join her newsletter, you will be the first to receive sneak peeks of chapters, teasers, news, giveaway prizes, and more!

Facebook:
http://www.facebook.com/SophiaValentineAuthor

Twitter:
http://www.twitter.com/SophiaVAuthor

Goodreads:
http://www.goodreads.com/SophiaValentine

Instagram:
http://www.instagram.com/sophiavalentinauthor

Pinterest:
http://www.pinterest.com/sophiavwrites

Author's Note

If you liked this book, it would absolutely make my day if you could please leave a review on Amazon. If you send me the link to your review, I will enter you into my monthly prize draws to win other eBooks and prizes! My author page is: www.facebook.com/SophiaValentineAuthor

I'd also be thrilled if you'd recommend my book to your friends.

To receive updates on my upcoming material, free chapters, and teasers before anyone else, including prize draws and competitions, join my newsletter by entering your email at my website: www.s-valentine.wix.com/books.

I love connecting with you readers and hearing your thoughts.